HAUNTED

Joyce Carol Oates

HAUNTED

TALES OF THE
GROTESQUE

A WILLIAM ABRAHAMS BOOK

DUTTON

DUTTON
Published by the Penguin Group
Penguin Books USA Inc., 375 Hudson Street,
New York, New York 10014, U.S.A.
Penguin Books Ltd, 27 Wrights Lane, London W8 5TZ, England
Penguin Books Australia Ltd, Ringwood, Victoria, Australia
Penguin Books Canada Ltd, 10 Alcorn Avenue,
Toronto, Ontario, Canada M4V 3B2
Penguin Books (N.Z.) Ltd, 182–190 Wairau Road, Auckland 10, New Zealand

Penguin Books Ltd, Registered Offices: Harmondsworth, Middlesex, England

First published by Dutton, an imprint of Dutton Signet,
a division of Penguin Books USA Inc.
Distributed in Canada by McClelland & Stewart Inc.

First Printing, February, 1994
10 9 8 7 6 5 4 3 2 1

For acknowledgments, please see page 309.

 REGISTERED TRADEMARK—MARCA REGISTRADA

LIBRARY OF CONGRESS CATALOGING IN PUBLICATION DATA:
Oates, Joyce Carol, 1938–
    Haunted : tales of the grotesque   Joyce Carol Oates.
        p.   cm.
    A William Abrahams book.
    ISBN 0-525-93655-6
    1. Horror tales, American.   2. Grotesque—Fiction.   I. Title.
PS3565.A8H38   1994
813'.54—dc20   93-25223
                                                        CIP

Printed in the United States of America
Set in Garamond no. 3
Designed by Eve L. Kirch

PUBLISHER'S NOTE
These stories are works of fiction. Names, characters, places, and incidents either are the products of the author's imagination or are used fictitiously, and any resemblance to actual persons, living or dead, events, or locales is entirely coincidental.

To Ellen Datlow

CONTENTS

PART I.

Haunted	3
The Doll	26
The Bingo Master	49
The White Cat	72

PART II.

The Model	99

PART III.

Extenuating Circumstances	147
Don't You Trust Me?	154
The Guilty Party	158
The Premonition	172
Phase Change	188

PART IV.

Poor Bibi	211
Thanksgiving	219

CONTENTS

Blind   232

The Radio Astronomer   247

Accursed Inhabitants of the House of Bly   254

Martyrdom   284

An Afterword by the Author   303

PART

I

Haunted

Haunted houses, forbidden houses. The old Medlock farm. The Erlich farm. The Minton farm on Elk Creek. NO TRESPASSING the signs said but we trespassed at will. NO TRESPASSING NO HUNTING NO FISHING UNDER PENALTY OF LAW but we did what we pleased because who was there to stop us?

Our parents warned us against exploring these abandoned properties: the old houses and barns were dangerous, they said. We could get hurt, they said. I asked my mother if the houses were haunted and she said, Of course not, there aren't such things as ghosts, you know that. She was irritated with me; she guessed how I pretended to believe things I didn't believe, things I'd grown out of years before. It was a habit of childhood—pretending I was younger, more childish, than in fact I was. Opening my eyes wide and looking puzzled, worried. Girls are prone to such trickery, it's a form of camouflage, when every other thought you think is a forbidden thought and with your eyes open staring sightless you can sink into dreams that leave your skin clammy and your heart pounding— dreams that don't seem to belong to you that must have come to you from somewhere else from someone you don't know who knows *you*.

There weren't such things as ghosts, they told us. That was just superstition. But we could injure ourselves tramping around where we weren't wanted—the floorboards and the staircases in old houses were likely to be rotted, the roofs ready to collapse, we could cut ourselves on nails and broken glass, we could fall into uncovered wells—and you never knew who you might meet up with, in an old house or barn that's supposed to be empty. "You mean a bum?—like somebody hitch-hiking along the road?" I asked. "It could be a bum, or it could be somebody you know," Mother told me evasively. "A man, or a boy—somebody you know . . ." Her voice trailed off in embarrassment and I knew enough not to ask another question.

There were things you didn't talk about, back then. I never talked about them with my own children, there weren't the words to say them.

We listened to what our parents said, we nearly always agreed with what they said, but we went off on the sly and did what we wanted to do. When we were little girls: my neighbor Mary Lou Siskin and me. And when we were older, ten, eleven years old, tomboys, roughhouses our mothers called us. We liked to hike in the woods and along the creek for miles, we'd cut through farmers' fields, spy on their houses—on people we knew, kids we knew from school—most of all we liked to explore abandoned houses, boarded-up houses if we could break in, we'd scare ourselves thinking the houses might be haunted though really we knew they weren't haunted, there weren't such things as ghosts. Except—

I am writing in a dime-store notebook with lined pages and a speckled cover, a notebook of the sort we used in grade school. *Once upon a time* as I used to tell my children when they were tucked safely into bed and drifting off to sleep. *Once upon a time* I'd begin, reading from a book because it was safest so: the several times I told them my own stories they were frightened by my voice and couldn't sleep and afterward I couldn't sleep either and my husband would ask what was wrong and I'd say, Nothing, hiding my face from him so he wouldn't see my look of contempt.

I write in pencil, so that I can erase easily, and I find that I am constantly erasing, wearing holes in the paper. Mrs. Harding, our fifth grade teacher, disciplined us for handing in messy notebooks: she was a heavy, toad-faced woman, her voice was deep and husky and gleeful when she said, "You, Melissa, what have you to say for yourself?" and I stood there mute, my knees trembling. My friend Mary Lou laughed behind her hand, wriggled in her seat she thought I was so funny. Tell the old witch to go to hell, she'd say, she'll respect you then, but of course no one would ever say such a thing to Mrs. Harding. Not even Mary Lou. "What have you to say for yourself, Melissa? Handing in a notebook with a ripped page?" My grade for the homework assignment was lowered from A to B, Mrs. Harding grunted with satisfaction as she made the mark, a big swooping B in red ink, creasing the page. "More is expected of you, Melissa, so you disappoint me more," Mrs. Harding always said. So many years ago and I remember those words more clearly than words I heard the other day.

One morning there was a pretty substitute teacher in Mrs. Harding's classroom. "Mrs. Harding is unwell, I'll be taking her place today," she said, and we saw the nervousness in her face, we guessed there was a secret she wouldn't tell and we waited and a few days later the principal himself came to tell us that Mrs. Harding would not be back, she had died of a stroke. He spoke carefully as if we were much younger children and might be upset and Mary Lou caught my eye and winked and I sat there at my desk feeling the strangest sensation, something flowing into the top of my head, honey-rich and warm making its way down my spine. *Our Father Who art in Heaven* I whispered in the prayer with the others my head bowed and my hands clasped tight together but my thoughts were somewhere else leaping wild and crazy somewhere else and I knew Mary Lou's were too.

On the school bus going home she whispered in my ear, "That was because of us, wasn't it!—what happened to that old bag Harding. But we won't tell anybody."

* * *

Once upon a time there were two sisters, and one was very pretty and one was very ugly. . . . Though Mary Lou Siskin wasn't my sister. And I wasn't ugly, really: just sallow-skinned, with a small pinched ferrety face. With dark almost lashless eyes that were set too close together and a nose that didn't look right. A look of yearning, and disappointment.

But Mary Lou *was* pretty, even rough and clumsy as she sometimes behaved. That long silky blond hair everybody remembered her for afterward, years afterward. . . . How, when she had to be identified, it was the long silky white-blond hair that was unmistakable. . . .

Sleepless nights but I love them. I write during the nighttime hours and sleep during the day; I am of an age when you don't require more than a few hours sleep. My husband has been dead for nearly a year and my children are scattered and busily absorbed in their own selfish lives like all children and there is no one to interrupt me no one to pry into my business no one in the neighborhood who dares come knocking at my door to see if I am all right. Sometimes out of a mirror floats an unexpected face, a strange face, lined, ravaged, with deep-socketed eyes always damp, always blinking in shock or dismay or simple bewilderment—but I adroitly look away. I have no need to stare.

It's true, all you have heard of the vanity of the old. Believing ourselves young, still, behind our aged faces—mere children, and so very innocent!

Once when I was a young bride and almost pretty my color up when I was happy and my eyes shining we drove out into the country for a Sunday's excursion and he wanted to make love I knew, he was shy and fumbling as I but he wanted to make love and I ran into a cornfield in my stockings and high heels, I was playing at being a woman I never could be, Mary Lou Siskin maybe, Mary Lou whom my husband never knew, but I got out of breath and frightened, it was the wind in the cornstalks, that dry rustling sound, that dry terrible rustling sound like whispering like voices you can't quite identify and he caught me and tried to hold me and I pushed him away sobbing and he said, What's wrong? My God what's wrong? as if he really loved me as if his life was focused on me and I knew I could never be equal to it, that love, that importance, I knew I was only Melissa the ugly one the one the boys wouldn't give a second glance, and one day he'd understand and know how he'd been cheated. I pushed him away, I said, Leave me alone! don't touch me! You disgust me! I said.

He backed off and I hid my face, sobbing.

But later on I got pregnant just the same. Only a few weeks later.

Always there were stories behind the abandoned houses and always the stories were sad. Because farmers went bankrupt and had to move away. Because somebody died and the farm couldn't be kept up and nobody wanted to buy it—like the Medlock farm across the creek. Mr. Medlock died aged seventy-nine and Mrs. Medlock refused to sell the farm and lived there alone until someone from the county health agency came to get her. Isn't it a shame, my parents said. The poor woman, they said. They told us never, never to poke around in the Medlocks' barns or house—the buildings were ready to cave in, they'd been in terrible repair even when the Medlocks were living there.

It was said that Mrs. Medlock had gone off her head after she'd found her husband dead in one of the barns, lying flat on his back his eyes open and bulging, his mouth open, tongue protruding, she'd gone to look for him and found him like that and she'd never gotten over it they said, never got over the shock. They had to commit her to the state hospital for her own good (they said) and the house and the barns were boarded up, everywhere tall grass and thistles grew wild, dandelions in the spring, tiger lilies in the summer, and when we drove by I stared and stared narrowing my eyes so I wouldn't see someone looking out one of the windows—a face there, pale and quick—or a dark figure scrambling up the roof to hide behind the chimney—

Mary Lou and I wondered was the house haunted, was the barn haunted where the old man had died, we crept around to spy, we couldn't stay away, coming closer and closer each time until something scared us and we ran away back through the woods clutching and pushing at each other until one day finally we went right up to the house to the back door and peeked in one of the windows. Mary Lou led the way, Mary Lou said not to be afraid, nobody lived there any more and nobody would catch us, it didn't matter that the land was posted, the police didn't arrest kids our ages.

We explored the barns, we dragged the wooden cover off the well and dropped stones inside. We called the cats but they wouldn't come close enough to be petted. They were barn cats, skinny and diseased-looking, they'd said at the county bureau that Mrs. Medlock had let a dozen cats live in the house with her so that the house was filthy from their messes. When the cats wouldn't come we got mad and threw stones at them and they ran away hissing—nasty dirty things, Mary Lou said. Once we crawled up on the tar-paper roof over the Medlocks' kitchen, just for fun, Mary Lou wanted to climb up the big roof too to the very top but I got frightened and said, No, No please don't, no Mary Lou please, and I sounded so strange Mary Lou looked at me and didn't tease or mock as she usually did. The roof was so steep, I'd known she would hurt herself. I could see her losing her footing and slipping, falling, I could see her astonished face and her flying hair as she fell, knowing nothing could save her. You're no fun, Mary Lou said, giving me a hard little pinch. But she didn't go climbing up the big roof.

Later we ran through the barns screaming at the top of our lungs just for fun for the hell of it as Mary Lou said, we tossed things in a heap, broken-off parts of farm implements, leather things from the horses' gear, handfuls of straw. The farm animals had been gone for years but their smell was still strong. Dried horse and cow droppings that looked like mud. Mary Lou said, "You know what—I'd like to burn this place down." And she looked at me and I said, "Okay—go on and do it, burn it down." And Mary Lou said, "You think I wouldn't?—just give me a match." And I said, "You know I don't have any match." And a look passed between us. And I felt something flooding at the top of my head, my throat tickled as if I didn't know would I laugh or cry and I said, "You're crazy—" and Mary Lou said with a sneering little laugh, *"You're* crazy, dumbbell—I was just testing you."

By the time Mary Lou was twelve years old Mother had got to hate her, was always trying to turn me against her so I'd make friends with other girls. Mary Lou had a fresh mouth, she said. Mary Lou didn't respect her elders—not even her own parents. Mother guessed that Mary Lou laughed at her behind her back, said things about all of us. She was mean and snippy and a smart-ass, rough sometimes as her brothers. Why didn't I make other friends? Why did I always go running when she stood out in the yard and called me? The Siskins weren't a whole lot better than white trash, the way Mr. Siskin worked that land of his.

In town, in school, Mary Lou sometimes ignored me when other girls were around, girls who lived in town, whose fathers weren't farmers like ours. But when it was time to ride home on the bus she'd sit with me as if nothing was wrong and I'd help her with her homework if she needed help, I hated her sometimes but then I'd forgive her as soon as she smiled at me, she'd say, "Hey 'Lissa are you mad at me?" and I'd make a face and say no as if it was an insult, being asked. Mary Lou was my sister I sometimes pretended, I told myself a story about us being sisters and looking alike, and Mary Lou said sometimes she'd like to leave her family her god-damned family and come live with me. Then the next day or the next hour she'd get moody and be nasty to me and get me almost crying. All the Siskins had mean streaks, bad tempers, she'd tell people. As if she was proud.

Her hair was a light blond, almost white in the sunshine, and when I first knew her she had to wear it braided tight around her head—her grandmother braided it for her, and she hated it. Like Gretel or Snow White in one of those damn dumb picture books for children, Mary Lou said. When she was older she wore it down and let it grow long so that it fell almost to her hips. It was very beautiful—silky and shimmering. I dreamt of Mary Lou's hair some-times but the dreams were confused and I couldn't remember when I woke up whether I was the one with the long blond silky hair, or someone else. It took me a while to get my thoughts clear lying there in bed and then I'd remember Mary Lou, who was my best friend.

She was ten months older than I was, and an inch or so taller, a bit heavier, not fat but fleshy, solid and fleshy, with hard little muscles in her upper arms like a boy. Her eyes were blue like washed glass, her eyebrows and lashes were almost white, she had a snubbed nose and Slavic cheekbones and a mouth that could be sweet or twisty and smirky depending upon her mood. But she didn't like her face because it was round—a moon-face she called it, staring at herself in the mirror though she knew damned well she was pretty —didn't older boys whistle at her, didn't the bus driver flirt with her?—calling her "Blondie" while he never called me anything at all.

Mother didn't like Mary Lou visiting with me when no one else was home in our house: she didn't trust her, she said. Thought she might steal something, or poke her nose into parts of the house where she wasn't welcome. That girl is a bad influence on you, she said. But it was all the same old crap I heard again and again so I didn't even listen. I'd have told her she was crazy except that would only make things worse.

Mary Lou said, "Don't you just hate them?—your mother, and mine? Sometimes I wish—"

I put my hands over my ears and didn't hear.

The Siskins lived two miles away from us, farther back the road where it got narrower. Those days, it was unpaved, and never got plowed in the winter. I remember their barn with the yellow silo, I remember the muddy pond where the dairy cows came to drink, the muck they churned up in the spring. I remember Mary Lou saying she wished all the cows would die—they were always sick with something—so her father would give up and sell the farm and they could live in town in a nice house. I was hurt, her saying those things as if she'd forgotten about me and would leave me behind. Damn you to hell, I whispered under my breath.

I remember smoke rising from the Siskins' kitchen chimney, from their wood-burning stove, straight up into the winter sky like a breath you draw inside you deeper and deeper until you begin to feel faint.

Later on, that house was empty too. But boarded up only for a few months—the bank sold it at auction. (It turned out the bank owned most of the Siskin farm, even the dairy cows. So Mary Lou had been wrong about that all along and never knew.)

As I write I can hear the sound of glass breaking, I can feel glass underfoot. *Once upon a time there were two little princesses, two sisters, who did forbidden things.* That brittle terrible sensation under my shoes— slippery like water—"Anybody home? Hey—anybody home?" and there's an old calendar tacked to a kitchen wall, a faded picture of Jesus Christ in a long white gown stained with scarlet, thorns fitted to His bowed head. Mary Lou is going to scare me in another minute making me think that someone is in the house and the two of us will scream with laughter and run outside where it's safe. Wild frightened laughter and I never knew afterward what was funny or why we did these things. Smashing what remained of windows, wrenching at stairway railings to break them loose, running with our heads ducked so we wouldn't get cobwebs in our faces.

One of us found a dead bird, a starling, in what had been the parlor of the house. Turned it over with a foot—there's the open eye looking right up calm and matter-of-fact. *Melissa*, that eye tells me, silent and terrible, *I see you.*

That was the old Minton place, the stone house with the caved-in roof and the broken steps, like something in a picture book from long ago. From the road the house looked as if it might be big but when we explored it we were disappointed to see that it wasn't much bigger than my own house, just four narrow rooms downstairs, an-other four upstairs, an attic with a steep ceiling, the roof partly caved in. The barns had collapsed in upon themselves; only their stone foundations remained solid. The land had been sold off over the years to other farmers, nobody had lived in the house for a long time. The old Minton house, people called it. On Elk Creek where Mary Lou's body was eventually found.

In seventh grade Mary Lou had a boy friend she wasn't supposed to have and no one knew about it but me—an older boy who'd dropped out of school and worked as a farmhand. I thought he was a little slow—not in his speech which was fast enough, normal enough, but in his way of thinking. He was sixteen or seventeen years old. His name was Hans; he had crisp blond hair like the bristles of a brush, a coarse blemished face, derisive eyes. Mary Lou was crazy for him she said, aping the older girls in town who said they were "crazy for" certain boys or young men. Hans and Mary Lou kissed when they didn't think I was watching, in an old ruin of a cemetery behind the Minton house, on the creek bank, in the tall marsh grass by the end of the Siskins' driveway. Hans had a car borrowed from one of his brothers, a battered old Ford, the front bumper held up by wire, the running board scraping the ground. We'd be out walking on the road and Hans would come along tapping the horn and stop and Mary Lou would cimb in but I'd hang back knowing they didn't want me and the hell with them: I preferred to be alone.

"You're just jealous of Hans and me," Mary Lou said, unforgivably, and I hadn't any reply. "Hans is sweet. Hans is nice. He isn't like people say," Mary Lou said in a quick bright false voice she'd picked up from one of the older, popular girls in town. "He's—" And she stared at me blinking and smiling not knowing what to say as if in fact she didn't know Hans at all. "He isn't *simple*," she said angrily, "—he just doesn't like to talk a whole lot."

When I try to remember Hans Meunzer after so many decades I can see only a muscular boy with short-trimmed blond hair and protuberant ears, blemished skin, the shadow of a moustache on his upper lip—he's looking at me, eyes narrowed, crinkled, as if he understands how I fear him, how I wish him dead and gone, and he'd hate me too if he took me that seriously. But he doesn't take me that seriously, his gaze just slides right through me as if nobody's standing where I stand.

There were stories about all the abandoned houses but the worst story was about the Minton house over on the Elk Creek Road about three miles from where we lived. For no reason anybody ever discovered Mr. Minton had beaten his wife to death and afterward killed himself with a .12-gauge shotgun. He hadn't even been drinking, people said. And his farm hadn't been doing at all badly, considering how others were doing.

Looking at the ruin from the outside, overgrown with trumpet vine and wild rose, it seemed hard to believe that anything like that had happened. Things in the world even those things built by man are so quiet left to themselves. . . .

The house had been deserted for years, as long as I could remember. Most of the land had been sold off but the heirs didn't want to deal with the house. They didn't want to sell it and they didn't want to raze it and they certainly didn't want to live in it so it stood empty. The property was posted with NO TRESPASSING signs layered one atop another but nobody took them seriously. Vandals had broken into the house and caused damage, the McFarlane boys had tried to burn down the old hay barn one Hallowe'en night. The summer Mary Lou started seeing Hans she and I climbed in the house through a rear window—the boards guarding it had long since been yanked away—and walked through the rooms slow as sleepwalkers our arms around each other's waist our eyes staring waiting to see Mr. Minton's ghost as we turned each corner. The inside smelled of mouse droppings, mildew, rot, old sorrow. Strips of wallpaper torn from the walls, plasterboard exposed, old furniture overturned and smashed, old yellowed sheets of newspaper underfoot, and broken glass, everywhere broken glass. Through the ravaged windows sunlight spilled in tremulous quivering bands. The air was afloat, alive: dancing dust-atoms. "I'm afraid," Mary Lou whispered.

She squeezed my waist and I felt my mouth go dry for hadn't I been hearing something upstairs, a low persistent murmuring like quarreling like one person trying to convince another going on and on and on but when I stood very still to listen the sound vanished and there were only the comforting summer sounds of birds, crickets, cicadas.

I knew how Mr. Minton had died: he'd placed the barrel of the shotgun beneath his chin and pulled the trigger with his big toe. They found him in the bedroom upstairs, most of his head blown off. They found his wife's body in the cistern in the cellar where he'd tried to hide her. "Do you think we should go upstairs?" Mary Lou asked, worried. Her fingers felt cold; but I could see tiny sweat beads on her forehead. Her mother had braided her hair in one thick clumsy braid, the way she wore it most of the summer, but the bands of hair were loosening. "No," I said, frightened. "I don't know." We hesitated at the bottom of the stairs—just stood there for a long time. "Maybe not," Mary Lou said. "Damn stairs'd fall in on us."

In the parlor there were bloodstains on the floor and on the wall—I could see them. Mary Lou said in derision, "They're just waterstains, dummy."

I could hear the voices overhead, or was it a single droning persistent voice. I waited for Mary Lou to hear it but she never did.

Now we were safe, now we were retreating, Mary Lou said as if repentant, "Yeah—this house *is* special."

We looked through the debris in the kitchen hoping to find something of value but there wasn't anything—just smashed chinaware, old battered pots and pans, more old yellowed newspaper. But through the window we saw a garter snake sunning itself on a rusted water tank, stretched out to a length of two feet. It was a lovely coppery color, the scales gleaming like perspiration on a man's arm; it seemed to be asleep. Neither one of us screamed, or wanted to throw something—we just stood there watching it for the longest time.

*   *   *

Mary Lou didn't have a boy friend any longer, Hans had stopped coming around. We saw him driving the old Ford now and then but he didn't seem to see us. Mr. Siskin had found out about him and Mary Lou and he'd been upset—acting like a damn crazy man Mary Lou said, asking her every kind of nasty question then interrupting her and not believing her anyway, then he'd put her to terrible shame by going over to see Hans and carrying on with him. "I hate them all," Mary Lou said, her face darkening with blood. "I wish—"

We rode our bicycles over to the Minton farm, or tramped through the fields to get there. It was the place we liked best. Sometimes we brought things to eat, cookies, bananas, candy bars, sitting on the broken stone steps out front, as if we lived in the house really, we were sisters who lived here having a picnic lunch out front. There were bees, flies, mosquitoes, but we brushed them away. We had to sit in the shade because the sun was so fierce and direct, a whitish heat pouring down from overhead.

"Would you ever like to run away from home?" Mary Lou said. "I don't know," I said uneasily. Mary Lou wiped at her mouth and gave me a mean narrow look. " 'I don't know,' " she said in a falsetto voice, mimicking me. At an upstairs window someone was watching us—was it a man or was it a woman—someone stood there listening hard and I couldn't move feeling so slow and dreamy in the heat like a fly caught on a sticky petal that's going to fold in on itself and swallow him up. Mary Lou crumpled up some wax paper and threw it into the weeds. She was dreamy too, slow and yawning. She said, "Shit—they'd just find me. Then everything would be worse."

I was covered in a thin film of sweat but I'd begun to shiver. Goose bumps were raised on my arms. I could see us sitting on the stone steps the way we'd look from the second floor of the house, Mary Lou sprawled with her legs apart, her braided hair slung over her shoulder, me sitting with my arms hugging my knees my backbone tight and straight knowing I was being watched. Mary Lou said, lowering her voice, "Did you ever touch yourself in a certain place, Melissa?" "No," I said, pretending I didn't know what she meant. "Hans wanted to do that," Mary Lou said. She sounded disgusted. Then she started to giggle. "I wouldn't let him, then he wanted to do something else—started unbuttoning his pants—wanted me to touch *him*. And—"

I wanted to hush her, to clap my hand over her mouth. But she just went on and I never said a word until we both started giggling together and couldn't stop. Afterward I didn't remember most of it or why I'd been so excited my face burning and my eyes seared as if I'd been staring into the sun.

On the way home Mary Lou said, "Some things are so sad you can't say them." But I pretended not to hear.

A few days later I came back by myself. Through the ravaged cornfield: the stalks dried and broken, the tassels burnt, that rustling whispering sound of the wind I can hear now if I listen closely. My head was aching with excitement. I was telling myself a story that we'd made plans to run away and live in the Minton house. I was carrying a willow switch I'd found on the ground, fallen from a tree but still green and springy, slapping at things with it as if it was a whip. Talking to myself. Laughing aloud. Wondering was I being watched.

I climbed in the house through the back window and brushed my hands on my jeans. My hair was sticking to the back of my neck.

At the foot of the stairs I called up, "Who's here?" in a voice meant to show it was all play, I knew I was alone.

My heart was beating hard and quick, like a bird caught in the hand. It was lonely without Mary Lou so I walked heavy to let them know I was there and wasn't afraid. I started singing, I started whistling. Talking to myself and slapping at things with the willow switch. Laughing aloud, a little angry. Why was I angry, well I didn't know, someone was whispering telling me to come upstairs, to walk on the inside of the stairs so the steps wouldn't collapse.

The house was beautiful inside if you had the right eyes to see it. If you didn't mind the smell. Glass underfoot, broken plaster, stained wallpaper hanging in shreds. Tall narrow windows looking out onto wild weedy patches of green. I heard something in one of the rooms but when I looked I saw nothing much more than an easy chair lying on its side. Vandals had ripped stuffing out of it and tried to set it afire. The material was filthy but I could see that it had been pretty once—a floral design—tiny yellow flowers and green ivy. A woman used to sit in the chair, a big woman with sly staring eyes. Knitting in her lap but she wasn't knitting just staring out the window watching to see who might be coming to visit.

Upstairs the rooms were airless and so hot I felt my skin prickle like shivering. I wasn't afraid!—I slapped at the walls with my springy willow switch. In one of the rooms high in a corner wasps buzzed around a fat wasp's nest. In another room I looked out the window leaning out the window to breathe thinking this was my window, I'd come to live here. She was telling me I had better lie down and rest because I was in danger of heatstroke and I pretended not to know what heatstroke was but she knew I knew because hadn't a cousin of mine collapsed haying just last summer, they said his face had gone blotched and red and he'd begun breathing faster and faster not getting enough oxygen until he collapsed. I was look- ing out at the overgrown apple orchard, I could smell the rot, a sweet winey smell, the sky was hazy like something you can't get clear in your vision, pressing in close and warm. A half-mile away Elk Creek glittered through a screen of willow trees moving slow glittering with scales like winking.

Come away from that window, someone told me sternly.

But I took my time obeying.

In the biggest of the rooms was an old mattress pulled off rusty bedsprings and dumped on the floor. They'd torn some of the stuff- ing out of this too, there were scorch marks on it from cigarettes. The fabric was stained with something like rust and I didn't want to look at it but I had to. Once at Mary Lou's when I'd gone home with her after school there was a mattress lying out in the yard in the sun and Mary Lou told me in disgust that it was her youngest brother's mattress—he'd wet his bed again and the mattress had to be aired out. As if the stink would ever go away, Mary Lou said.

Something moved inside the mattress, a black-glittering thing, it was a cockroach but I wasn't allowed to jump back. Suppose you have to lie down on that mattress and sleep, I was told. Suppose you can't go home until you do. My eyelids were heavy, my head was pounding with blood. A mosquito buzzed around me but I was too tired to brush it away. Lie down on that mattress, Melissa, she told me. You know you must be punished.

I knelt down, not on the mattress, but on the floor beside it. The smells in the room were close and rank but I didn't mind, my head was nodding with sleep. Rivulets of sweat ran down my face and sides, under my arms, but I didn't mind. I saw my hand move out slowly like a stranger's hand to touch the mattress and a shiny black cockroach scuttled away in fright, and a second cockroach, and a third—but I couldn't jump up and scream.

Lie down on that mattress and take your punishment.

I looked over my shoulder and there was a woman standing in the doorway—a woman I'd never seen before.

She was staring at me. Her eyes were shiny and dark. She licked her lips and said in a jeering voice, "What are you doing here in this house, miss?"

I was terrified. I tried to answer but I couldn't speak.

"Have you come to see me?" the woman asked.

She was no age I could guess. Older than my mother but not old-seeming. She wore men's clothes and she was tall as any man, with wide shoulders, and long legs, and big sagging breasts like cows' udders loose inside her shirt not harnessed in a brassiere like other women's. Her thick wiry gray hair was cut short as a man's and stuck up in tufts that looked greasy. Her eyes were small, and black, and set back deep in their sockets; the flesh around them looked bruised. I had never seen anyone like her before—her thighs were enormous, big as my body. There was a ring of loose soft flesh at the waistband of her trousers but she wasn't fat.

"I asked you a question, miss. Why are you here?"

I was so frightened I could feel my bladder contract. I stared at her, cowering by the mattress, and couldn't speak.

It seemed to please her that I was so frightened. She approached me, stooping a little to get through the doorway. She said, in a mock-kindly voice, "You've come to visit with me—is that it?"

"No," I said.

"No!" she said, laughing. "Why, of course you have."

"No. I don't know you."

She leaned over me, touched my forehead with her fingers. I shut my eyes waiting to be hurt but her touch was cool. She brushed my hair off my forehead where it was sticky with sweat. "I've seen you here before, you and that other one," she said. "What is her name? The blond one. The two of you, trespassing."

I couldn't move, my legs were paralyzed. Quick and darting and buzzing my thoughts bounded in every which direction but didn't take hold. "Melissa is *your* name, isn't it," the woman said. "And what is your sister's name?"

"She isn't my sister," I whispered.

"What is her name?"

"I don't know."

"You don't know!"

"—don't know," I said, cowering.

The woman drew back half sighing half grunting. She looked at me pityingly. "You'll have to be punished, then."

I could smell ashes about her, something cold. I started to whimper started to say I hadn't done anything wrong, hadn't hurt anything in the house, I had only been exploring—I wouldn't come back again—

She was smiling at me, uncovering her teeth. She could read my thoughts before I could think them.

The skin of her face was in layers like an onion, like she'd been sunburnt, or had a skin disease. There were patches that had begun to peel. Her look was wet and gloating. Don't hurt me, I wanted to say. Please don't hurt me.

I'd begun to cry. My nose was running like a baby's. I thought

I would crawl past the woman I would get to my feet and run past her and escape but the woman stood in my way blocking my way leaning over me breathing damp and warm her breath like a cow's breath in my face. Don't hurt me, I said, and she said, "You know you have to be punished—You and your pretty blond sister."

"She isn't my sister," I said.

"And what is her name?"

The woman was bending over me, quivering with laughter.

"Speak up, miss. What is it?"

"I don't know—" I started to say. But my voice said, "Mary Lou."

The woman's big breasts spilled down onto her belly, I could feel her shaking with laughter. But she spoke sternly saying that Mary Lou and I had been very bad girls and we knew it her house was forbidden territory and we knew it hadn't we known all along that others had come to grief beneath its roof?

"No," I started to say. But my voice said, "Yes."

The woman laughed, crouching above me. "Now, miss, 'Melissa' as they call you—your parents don't know where you are at this very moment, do they?"

"I don't know."

"Do they?"

"No."

"They don't know anything about you, do they?—what you do, and what you think? You and 'Mary Lou.' "

"No."

She regarded me for a long moment, smiling. Her smile was wide and friendly.

"You're a spunky little girl, aren't you, with a mind of your own, aren't you, you and your pretty little sister. I bet your bottoms have been warmed many a time," the woman said, showing her big tobacco-stained teeth in a grin, ". . . your tender little asses."

I began to giggle. My bladder tightened.

"Hand that here, miss," the woman said. She took the willow switch from my fingers—I had forgotten I was holding it. "I will now administer punishment: take down your jeans. Take down your panties. Lie down on that mattress. Hurry." She spoke briskly now, she was all business. "Hurry, Melissa! *And* your panties! Or do you want me to pull them down for you?"

She was slapping the switch impatiently against the palm of her left hand, making a wet scolding noise with her lips. Scolding and teasing. Her skin shone in patches, stretched tight over the big hard bones of her face. Her eyes were small, crinkling smaller, black and damp. She was so big she had to position herself carefully over me to give herself proper balance and leverage so that she wouldn't fall. I could hear her hoarse eager breathing as it came to me from all sides like the wind.

I had done as she told me. It wasn't me doing these things but they were done. Don't hurt me, I whispered, lying on my stomach on the mattress, my arms stretched above me and my fingernails digging into the floor. The coarse wood with splinters pricking my skin. Don't don't hurt me O please but the woman paid no heed her warm wet breath louder now and the floorboards creaking beneath her weight. "Now, miss, now 'Melissa' as they call you—this will be our secret won't it—"

When it was over she wiped at her mouth and said she would let me go today if I promised never to tell anybody if I sent my pretty little sister to her tomorrow.

She isn't my sister, I said, sobbing. When I could get my breath.

I had lost control of my bladder after all, I'd begun to pee even before the first swipe of the willow switch hit me on the buttocks, peeing in helpless spasms, and sobbing, and afterward the woman scolded me saying wasn't it a poor little baby wetting itself like that. But she sounded repentant too, stood well aside to let me pass, Off you go! Home you go! And don't forget!

And I ran out of the room hearing her laughter behind me and down the stairs running running as if I hadn't any weight my legs just blurry beneath me as if the air was water and I was swimming

I ran out of the house and through the cornfield running in the cornfield sobbing as the corn stalks slapped at my face *Off you go! Home you go! And don't forget!*

I told Mary Lou about the Minton house and something that had happened to me there that was a secret and she didn't believe me at first saying with a jeer, "Was it a ghost? Was it Hans?" I said I couldn't tell. Couldn't tell what? she said. Couldn't tell, I said. Why not? she said.

"Because I promised."

"Promised who?" she said. She looked at me with her wide blue eyes like she was trying to hypnotize me. "You're a goddamned liar."

Later she started in again asking me what had happened what was the secret was it something to do with Hans? did he still like her? was he mad at her? and I said it didn't have anything to do with Hans not a thing to do with him. Twisting my mouth to show what I thought of him.

"Then who—?" Mary Lou asked.

"I told you it was a secret."

"Oh shit—what kind of a secret?"

"A secret."

"A secret *really?*"

I turned away from Mary Lou, trembling. My mouth kept twisting in a strange hurting smile. "Yes. A secret *really,*" I said.

The last time I saw Mary Lou she wouldn't sit with me on the bus, walked past me holding her head high giving me a mean snippy look out of the corner of her eye. Then when she left for her stop she made sure she bumped me going by my seat, she leaned over to say, "I'll find out for myself, I hate you anyway," speaking loud enough for everybody on the bus to hear, "—I always have."

*   *   *

Once upon a time the fairy tales begin. But then they end and often you don't know really what has happened, what was meant to happen, you only know what you've been told, what the words suggest. Now that I have completed my story, filled up half my notebook with my handwriting that disappoints me, it is so shaky and childish—now the story is over I don't understand what it means. I know what happened in my life but I don't know what has happened in these pages.

Mary Lou was found murdered ten days after she said those words to me. Her body had been tossed into Elk Creek a quarter mile from the road and from the old Minton place. Where, it said in the paper, nobody had lived for fifteen years.

It said that Mary Lou had been thirteen years old at the time of her death. She'd been missing for seven days, had been the object of a county-wide search.

It said that nobody had lived in the Minton house for years but that derelicts sometimes sheltered there. It said that the body was unclothed and mutilated. There were no details.

This happened a long time ago.

The murderer (or murderers as the newspaper always said) was never found.

Hans Meunzer was arrested of course and kept in the county jail for three days while police questioned him but in the end they had to let him go, insufficient evidence to build a case it was explained in the newspaper though everybody knew he was the one wasn't he the one?—everybody knew. For years afterward they'd be saying that. Long after Hans was gone and the Siskins were gone, moved away nobody knew where.

Hans swore he hadn't done it, hadn't seen Mary Lou for weeks. There were people who testified in his behalf said he couldn't have done it for one thing he didn't have his brother's car any longer and he'd been working all that time. Working hard out in the fields—couldn't have slipped away long enough to do what police were saying he'd done. And Hans said over and over he was innocent. Sure he was innocent. Son of a bitch ought to be hanged my father said, everybody knew Hans was the one unless it was a derelict or a fisherman—fishermen often drove out to Elk Creek to fish for black bass, built fires on the creek bank and left messes behind—sometimes prowled around the Minton house too looking for things to steal. The police had records of automobile license plates belonging to some of these men, they questioned them but nothing came of it. Then there was that crazy man that old hermit living in a tarpaper shanty near the Shaheen dump that everybody'd said ought to have been committed to the state hospital years ago. But everybody knew really it was Hans and Hans got out as quick as he could, just disappeared and not even his family knew where unless they were lying which probably they were though they claimed not.

Mother rocked me in her arms crying, the two of us crying, she told me that Mary Lou was happy now, Mary Lou was in Heaven now, Jesus Christ had taken her to live with Him and I knew that didn't I? I wanted to laugh but I didn't laugh. Mary Lou shouldn't have gone with boys, not a nasty boy like Hans, Mother said, she shouldn't have been sneaking around the way she did—I knew that didn't I? Mother's words filled my head flooding my head so there was no danger of laughing.

Jesus loves you too you know that don't you Melissa? Mother asked hugging me. I told her yes. I didn't laugh because I was crying.

They wouldn't let me go to the funeral, said it would scare me too much. Even though the casket was closed.

It's said that when you're older you remember things that happened a long time ago better than you remember things that have just happened and I have found that to be so.

For instance I can't remember when I bought this notebook at Woolworth's whether it was last week or last month or just a few days ago. I can't remember why I started writing in it, what purpose I told myself. But I remember Mary Lou stooping to say those words in my ear and I remember when Mary Lou's mother came over to ask us at suppertime a few days later if I had seen Mary Lou that day—I remember the very food on my plate, the mashed potatoes in a dry little mound. I remember hearing Mary Lou call my name standing out in the driveway cupping her hands to her mouth the way Mother hated her to do, it was white trash behavior.

"'Lissa!" Mary Lou would call, and I'd call back, "OK I'm coming!" *Once upon a time.*

The Doll

Many years ago a little girl was given, for her fourth birthday, an antique dolls' house of unusual beauty and complexity, and size: for it seemed large enough, almost, for a child to crawl into.

The dolls' house was said to have been built nearly one hundred years before, by a distant relative of the little girl's mother. It had come down through the family and was still in excellent condition: with a steep gabled roof, many tall, narrow windows fitted with real glass, dark green shutters that closed over, three fireplaces made of stone, mock lightning rods, mock shingleboard siding (white), a veranda that nearly circled the house, stained glass at the front door and at the first floor landing, and even a cupola whose tiny roof lifted miraculously away. In the master bedroom there was a canopied bed with white organdy flounces and ruffles; there were tiny window boxes beneath most of the windows; the furniture—all of it Victorian, of course—was uniformly exquisite, having been made with the most fastidious care and affection. The lampshades were adorned with tiny gold fringes, there was a marvelous old tub with claw feet, and nearly every room had a chandelier. When she first saw the dolls' house on the morning of her fourth birthday the little girl was so astonished she could not speak: for the present was unexpected, and uncannily "real." It was to be the great present, and the great memory, of her childhood.

Florence had several dolls which were too large to fit into the house, since they were average-size dolls, but she brought them close to the house, facing its open side, and played with them there. She fussed over them, and whispered to them, and scolded them, and invented little conversations between them. One day, out of nowhere, came the name *Bartholomew*—the name of the family who owned the dolls' house. Where did you get that name from, her parents asked, and Florence replied that those were the people who lived in the house. Yes, but where did the name come from? they asked.

The child, puzzled and a little irritated, pointed mutely at the dolls.

One was a girl-doll with shiny blond ringlets and blue eyes that were thickly lashed, and almost too round; another was a red-haired freckled boy in denim coveralls and a plaid shirt. It was obvious that they were sister and brother. Another was a woman-doll, perhaps a mother, who had bright red lips and who wore a hat cleverly made of soft gray-and-white feathers. There was even a baby-doll, made of the softest rubber, hairless and expressionless, and oversized in relationship to the other dolls; and a spaniel, about nine inches in length, with big brown eyes and a quizzical upturned tail. Sometimes one doll was Florence's favorite, sometimes another. There were days when she preferred the blond girl, whose eyes rolled in her head, and whose complexion was a lovely pale peach. There were days when the mischievous red-haired boy was obviously her favorite. Sometimes she banished all the human dolls and played with the spaniel, who was small enough to fit into most of the rooms of the dolls' house.

Occasionally Florence undressed the human dolls, and washed them with a tiny sponge. How strange they were, without their clothes . . . ! Their bodies were poreless and smooth and blank, there was nothing secret or nasty about them, no crevices for dirt to hide in, no trouble at all. Their faces were unperturbable, as always. Calm wise fearless staring eyes that no harsh words or slaps could disturb. But Florence loved her dolls very much, and rarely felt the need to punish them.

Her treasure was, of course, the dolls' house with its steep Victorian roof and its gingerbread trim and its many windows and that marvelous veranda, upon which little wooden rocking chairs, each equipped with its own tiny cushion, were set. Visitors—friends of her parents or little girls her own age—were always astonished when they first saw it. They said: Oh, isn't it beautiful! They said: Why, it's almost the size of a real house, isn't it?—though of course it wasn't, it was only a dolls' house, a little less than thirty-six inches high.

Nearly four decades later while driving along East Fainlight Avenue in Lancaster, Pennsylvania, a city she had never before visited, and about which she knew nothing, Florence Parr was astonished to see, set back from the avenue, at the top of a stately elm-shaded knoll, her old dolls' house—that is, the replica of it. The house. The house itself.

She was so astonished that for the passage of some seconds she could not think what to do. Her most immediate reaction was to brake her car—for she was a careful, even fastidious driver; at the first sign of confusion or difficulty she always brought her car to a stop.

A broad handsome elm- and plane tree–lined avenue, in a charming city, altogether new to her. Late April: a fragrant, even rather giddy spring, after a bitter and protracted winter. The very air trembled, rich with warmth and color. The estates in this part of the city were as impressive, as stately, as any she had ever seen: the houses were really mansions, boasting of wealth, their sloping, elegant lawns protected from the street by brick walls, or wrought-iron fences, or thick evergreen hedges. Everywhere there were azaleas, that most gorgeous of spring flowers—scarlet and white and yellow and flamey-orange, almost blindingly beautiful. There were newly cultivated beds of tulips, primarily red; and exquisite apple blossoms, and cherry blossoms, and flowering trees Florence recognized but could not identify by name. *Her* house was surrounded by an old-fashioned wrought-iron fence, and in its enormous front yard were red and yellow tulips that had pushed their way through patches of weedy grass.

She found herself on the sidewalk, at the front gate. Like the unwieldy gate that was designed to close over the driveway, this gate was not only open but its bottom spikes had dug into the ground; it had not been closed for some time and could probably not be dislodged. Someone had put up a hand-lettered sign in black, not long ago: 1377 EAST FAINLIGHT. But no name, no family name. Florence stood staring up at the house, her heart beating rapidly. She could not quite believe what she was seeing. Yes, there it was, of course—yet it *could* not be, not in such detail.

The antique dolls' house. *Hers.* After so many years. There was the steep gabled roof, in what appeared to be slate; the old lightning rods; the absurd little cupola that was so charming; the veranda; the white shingleboard siding (which was rather weathered and gray in the bright spring sunshine); most of all, most striking, the eight tall, narrow windows, four to each floor, with their dark shutters. Florence could not determine if the shutters were painted a very dark green, or black. What color had they been on the dolls' house . . . She saw that the gingerbread trim was badly rotted.

The first wave of excitement, almost of vertigo, that had overtaken her in the car had passed; but she felt, still, an unpleasant sense of urgency. Her old doll's house. Here on East Fainlight Avenue in Lancaster, Pennsylvania. Glimpsed so suddenly, on this warm spring morning. And what did it mean . . . ? Obviously there was an explanation. Her distant uncle, who had built the house for his daughter, had simply copied this house, or another just like it; no doubt there were many houses like this one. Florence knew little about Victorian architecture but she supposed that there were many duplications, even in large, costly houses. Unlike contemporary architects, the architects of that era must have been extremely limited, forced to use again and again certain basic structures, and certain basic ornamentation—the cupolas, the gables, the complicated trim.

What struck her as so odd, so mysterious, was really nothing but a coincidence. It would make an interesting story, an amusing anecdote, when she returned home; though perhaps it was not even worth mentioning. Her parents might have been intrigued but they were both dead. And she was always careful about dwelling upon herself, her private life, since she halfway imagined that her friends and acquaintances and colleagues would interpret nearly anything she said of a personal nature according to their vision of her as a public person, and she wanted to avoid that.

There was a movement at one of the upstairs windows that caught her eye. It was then transmitted, fluidly, miraculously, to the other windows, flowing from right to left. . . . But no, it was only the reflection of clouds being blown across the sky, up behind her head.

She stood motionless. It was unlike her, it was quite uncharacteristic of her, yet there she stood. She did not want to walk up to the veranda steps, she did not want to ring the doorbell, such a gesture would be ridiculous, and anyway there was no time: she really should be driving on. They would be expecting her soon. Yet she could not turn away. Because it *was* the house. Incredibly, it was her old dolls' house. (Which she had given away, of course, thirty —thirty-five?—years ago. And had rarely thought about since.) It was ridiculous to stand here, so astonished, so slow-witted, so perversely vulnerable . . . yet what other attitude was appropriate, what other attitude would not violate the queer sense of the sacred, the otherworldly, that the house had evoked?

She would ring the doorbell. And why not? She was a tall, rather wide-shouldered, confident woman, tastefully dressed in a cream-colored spring suit; she was rarely in the habit of apologizing for herself, or feeling embarrassment. Many years ago, perhaps, as a girl, a shy, silly, self-conscious girl: but no longer. Her wavy graying hair had been brushed back smartly from her wide, strong forehead. She wore no makeup, had stopped bothering with it years ago, and with her naturally high-colored, smooth complexion, she was a handsome woman, especially attractive when she smiled and her dark staring eyes relaxed. She *would* ring the doorbell, and see who came to the door, and say whatever flew into her head. She was looking for a family who lived in the neighborhood, she was canvassing for a school millage vote, she was inquiring whether they had any old clothes, old furniture, for . . .

Halfway up the walk she remembered that she had left the keys in the ignition of her car, and the motor running. And her purse on the seat.

She found herself walking unusually slowly. It was unlike her, and the disorienting sense of being unreal, of having stepped into another world, was totally new. A dog began barking somewhere near: the sound seemed to pierce her in the chest and bowels. An attack of panic. An involuntary fluttering of the eyelids. . . . But it was nonsense of course. She would ring the bell, someone would open the door, perhaps a servant, perhaps an elderly woman, they would have a brief conversation, Florence would glance behind her into the foyer to see if the circular staircase looked the same, if the old brass chandelier was still there, if the "marble" floor remained. Do you know the Parr family, Florence would ask, we've lived in Cummington, Massachusetts, for generations, I think it's quite possible that someone from my family visited you in this house, of course it was a very long time ago. I'm sorry to disturb you but I was driving by and I saw your striking house and I couldn't resist stopping for a moment out of curiosity. . . .

There were the panes of stained glass on either side of the oak door! But so large, so boldly colored. In the dolls' house they were hardly visible, just chips of colored glass. But here they were each about a foot square, starkly beautiful: reds, greens, blues. Exactly like the stained glass of a church.

I'm sorry to disturb you, Florence whispered, but I was driving by and . . .

I'm sorry to disturb you but I am looking for a family named Bartholomew, I have reason to think that they live in this neighborhood. . . .

But as she was about to step onto the veranda the sensation of panic deepened. Her breath came shallow and rushed, her thoughts flew wildly in all directions, she was simply terrified and could not move. The dog's barking had become hysterical.

When Florence was angry or distressed or worried she had a habit of murmuring her name to herself, Florence Parr, Florence Parr, it was soothing, it was mollifying, Florence Parr, it was often vaguely reproachful, for after all she *was* Florence Parr and that carried with it responsibility as well as authority. She named herself, identified herself. It was usually enough to bring her undisciplined thoughts under control. But she had not experienced an attack of panic for many years. All the strength of her body seemed to have fled, drained away; it terrified her to think that she might faint here. What a fool she would make of herself. . . .

As a young university instructor she had nearly succumbed to panic one day, mid-way through a lecture on the metaphysical poets. Oddly, the attack had come not at the beginning of the semester but well into the second month, when she had come to believe herself a thoroughly competent teacher. The most extraordinary sensation of fear, unfathomable and groundless fear, which she had never been able to comprehend afterward. . . . One moment she had been speaking of Donne's famous image in "The Relic"—a bracelet of "bright hair about the bone"—and the next moment she was so panicked she could hardly catch her breath. She wanted to run out of the classroom, wanted to run out of the building. It was as if a demon had appeared to her. It breathed into her face, shoved her about, tried to pull her under. She would suffocate: she would be destroyed. The sensation was possibly the most unpleasant she had ever experienced in her life though it carried with it no pain and no specific images. Why she was so frightened she could not grasp. Why she wanted nothing more than to run out of the classroom, to escape her students' curious eyes, she was never to understand.

But she did not flee. She forced herself to remain at the podium. Though her voice faltered she did not stop; she continued with the lecture, speaking into a blinding haze. Surely her students must have noticed her trembling . . . ? But she was stubborn, she was really quite tenacious for a young woman of twenty-four, and by forcing

herself to imitate herself, to imitate her normal tone and manner-
isms, she was able to overcome the attack. As it lifted, gradually,
and her eyesight strengthened, her heartbeat slowed, she seemed to
know that the attack would never come again in a classroom. And
this turned out to be correct.

But now she could not overcome her anxiety. She hadn't a podium to grasp, she hadn't lecture notes to follow, there was no one
to imitate, she was in a position to make a terrible fool of herself.
And surely someone was watching from the house. . . . It struck her
that she had no reason, no excuse, for being here. What on earth
could she say if she rang the doorbell? How would she explain herself
to a skeptical stranger? I simply must see the inside of your house,
she would whisper, I've been led up this walk by a force I can't
explain, please excuse me, please humor me, I'm not well, I'm not
myself this morning, I only want to see the inside of your house to
see if it *is* the house I remember. . . . I had a house like yours. It
was yours. But no one lived in my house except dolls; a family of
dolls. I loved them but I always sensed that they were blocking the
way, standing between me and something else. . . .

The barking dog was answered by another, a neighbor's dog.
Florence retreated. Then turned and hurried back to her car, where
the keys were indeed in the ignition, and her smart leather purse
lay on the seat where she had so imprudently left it.

So she fled the dolls' house, her poor heart thudding. What a
fool you are, Florence Parr, she thought brutally, a deep hot blush
rising into her face.

The rest of the day—the late afternoon reception, the dinner
itself, the after-dinner gathering—passed easily, even routinely, but
did not seem to her very real; it was not very convincing. That she
was Florence Parr, the president of Champlain College, that she was
to be a featured speaker at this conference of administrators of small
private liberal arts colleges: it struck her for some reason as an im-
posture, a counterfeit. The vision of the dolls' house kept rising in
her mind's eye. How odd, how very odd the experience had been,

yet there was no one to whom she might speak about it, even to minimize it, to transform it into an amusing anecdote. . . . The others did not notice her discomfort. In fact they claimed that she was looking well, they were delighted to see her and to shake her hand. Many were old acquaintances, men and women, but primarily men, with whom she had worked in the past at one college or another; a number were strangers, younger administrators who had heard of her heroic effort at Champlain College, and who wanted to be introduced to her. At the noisy cocktail hour, at dinner, Florence heard her somewhat distracted voice speaking of the usual matters: declining enrollments, building fund campaigns, alumni support, endowments, investments, state and federal aid. Her remarks were met with the same respectful attention as always, as though there were nothing wrong with her.

For dinner she changed into a linen dress of pale blue and dark blue stripes which emphasized her tall, graceful figure, and drew the eye away from her wide shoulders and her stolid thighs; she wore her new shoes with the fashionable three-inch heel, though she detested them. Her haircut was becoming, she had manicured and even polished her nails the evening before, and she supposed she looked attractive enough, especially in this context of middle-aged and older people. But her mind kept drifting away from the others, from the handsome though rather dark colonial dining room, even from the spirited, witty after-dinner speech of a popular administrator and writer, a retired president of Williams College, and formerly—a very long time ago, now—a colleague of Florence's at Swarthmore. She smiled with the others, and laughed with the others, but she could not attend to the courtly, white-haired gentleman's astringent witticisms; her mind kept drifting back to the dolls' house, out there on East Fainlight Avenue. It was well for her that she hadn't rung the doorbell, for what if someone who was attending the conference had answered the door; it was, after all, being hosted by Lancaster College. What an utter fool she would have made of herself. . . .

She went to her room in the fieldstone alumni house shortly after ten, though there were people who clearly wished to talk with her, and she knew a night of insomnia awaited. Once in the room with its antique furniture and its self-consciously quaint wallpaper she regretted having left the ebullient atmosphere downstairs. Though small private colleges were in trouble these days, and though most of the administrators at the conference were having serious difficulties with finances, and faculty morale, there was nevertheless a spirit of camaraderie, of heartiness. Of course it was the natural consequence of people in a social gathering. One simply cannot resist, in such a context, the droll remark, the grateful laugh, the sense of cheerful complicity in even an unfortunate fate. How puzzling the human personality is, Florence thought, preparing for bed, moving uncharacteristically slowly, when with others there is a public self, alone there is a private self, and yet both are real. . . . Both are experienced as real. . . .

She lay sleepless in the unfamiliar bed. There were noises in the distance; she turned on the air conditioner, the fan only, to drown them out. Still she could not sleep. The house on East Fainlight Avenue, the dolls' house of her childhood, she lay with her eyes open, thinking of absurd, disjointed things, wondering now why she had *not* pushed her way through that trivial bout of anxiety to the veranda steps, and to the door, after all she was Florence Parr, she had only to imagine people watching her—the faculty senate, students, her fellow administrators—to know how she should behave, with what alacrity and confidence. It was only when she forgot who she was, and imagined herself utterly alone, that she was crippled by uncertainty and susceptible to fear.

The luminous dials of her watch told her it was only 10:35. Not too late, really, to dress and return to the house and ring the doorbell. Of course she would only ring it if the downstairs was lighted, if someone was clearly up. . . . Perhaps an elderly gentleman lived there, alone, someone who had known her grandfather, someone who had visited the Parrs in Cummington. For there *must* be a connection. It was very well to speak of coincidences, but she knew, she knew with a deep, unshakable conviction, that there was a connection between the dolls' house and the house here in town, and a connection between her childhood and the present house. . . . When she explained herself to whoever opened the door, however, she would have to be casual, conversational. Years of administration had taught her diplomacy; one must not appear to be *too* serious. Gravity in leaders is disconcerting, what is demanded is the light, confident touch, the air of private and even secret knowledge. People do not want equality with their leaders: they want, they desperately need, them to be superior. The superiority must be tacitly communicated, however, or it becomes offensive. . . .

Suddenly she was frightened: it seemed to her quite possible that the panic attack might come upon her the next morning, when she gave her address ("The Future of the Humanities in American Education"). She was scheduled to speak at 9:30, she would be the first speaker of the day, and the first real speaker of the conference. And it was quite possible that that disconcerting weakness would return, that sense of utter, almost infantile helplessness. . . .

She sat up, turned on the light, and looked over her notes. They were handwritten, not typed, she had told her secretary not to bother typing them, the address was one she'd given before in different forms, her approach was to be conversational rather than formal though of course she would quote the necessary statistics. . . . But it had been a mistake, perhaps, not to have the notes typed. There were times when she couldn't decipher her own handwriting.

A drink might help. But she couldn't very well go over to the Lancaster Inn, where the conference was to be held, and where there was a bar; and of course she hadn't anything with her in the room. As a rule she rarely drank. She never drank alone. . . . However, if a drink would help her sleep: would calm her wild racing thoughts.

The dolls' house had been a present for her birthday. Many years ago. She could not recall how many. And there were her dolls, her little family of dolls, which she had not thought of for a lifetime. She felt a pang of loss, of tenderness. . . .

Florence Parr who suffered quite frequently from insomnia. But of course no one knew.

Florence Parr who had had a lump in her right breast removed, a cyst really, harmless, absolutely harmless, shortly after her thirty-eighth birthday. But none of her friends at Champlain knew. Not even her secretary knew. And the ugly little thing turned out to be benign: absolutely harmless. So it was well that no one knew.

Florence Parr of whom it was said that she was distant, even guarded, at times. You can't get close to her, someone claimed. And yet it was often said of her that she was wonderfully warm and open and frank and totally without guile. A popular president. Yet she had the support of her faculty. There might be individual jealousies here and there, particularly among the vice presidents and deans, but in general she had everyone's support and she knew it and was grateful for it and intended to keep it.

It was only that her mind worked, late into the night. Raced. Would not stay still.

Should she surrender to her impulse, and get dressed quickly and return to the house? It would take no more than ten minutes. And quite likely the downstairs lights would *not* be on, the inhabitants would be asleep, she could see from the street that the visit was totally out of the question, she would simply drive on past. And be saved from her audacity.

If I do this, the consequence will be. . . .

If I fail to do this. . . .

She was not, of course, an impulsive person. Nor did she admire impulsive "spontaneous" people: she thought them immature, and frequently exhibitionistic. It was often the case that they were very much aware of their own spontaneity. . . .

She would defend herself against the charge of being calculating. Of being overly cautious. Her nature was simply a very pragmatic one. She took up tasks with extreme interest, and absorbed herself deeply in them, one after another, month after month and year after year, and other considerations simply had to be shunted to the side. For instance, she had never married. The surprise would have been not that Florence Parr had married, but that she had had time to cultivate a relationship that would end in marriage. I am not opposed to marriage for myself, she once said, with unintentional naiveté, but it would take so much time to become acquainted with a man, to go out with him, and talk. . . . At Champlain where everyone liked her, and shared anecdotes about her, it was said that she'd been even as a younger woman so oblivious to men, even to attentive men, that she had failed to recognize a few years later a young linguist whose carrel at the Widener Library had been next to hers, though the young man claimed to have said hello to her every day, and to have asked her out for coffee occasionally. (She had always refused, she'd been far too busy.) When he turned up at Champlain, married, the author of a well-received book on linguistic theory, an associate professor in the Humanities division, Florence had not only been unable to recognize him but could not remember him at all, though he remembered her vividly, and even amused the gathering by recounting to Florence the various outfits she had worn that winter, even the colors of her knitted socks. She had been deeply embarrassed, of course, and yet flattered, and amused. It was proof, after all, that Florence Parr was always at all times Florence Parr.

Afterward she was somewhat saddened, for the anecdote meant, did it not, that she really *had* no interest in men. She was not a spinster because no one had chosen her, not even because she had been too fastidious in her own choosing, but simply because she had no interest in men, she did not even "see" them when they presented themselves before her. It was sad, it was irrefutable. She was an ascetic not through an act of will but through temperament.

It was at this point that she pushed aside the notes for her talk, her heart beating wildly as a girl's. She had no choice, she *must* satisfy her curiosity about the house, if she wanted to sleep, if she wanted to remain sane.

As the present of the dolls' house was the great event of her childhood, so the visit to the house on East Fainlight Avenue was to be the great event of her adulthood: though Florence Parr was never to allow herself to think of it, afterward.

It was a mild, quiet night, fragrant with blossoms, not at all intimidating. Florence drove to the avenue, to the house, and was consoled by the numerous lights burning in the neighborhood: of course it wasn't late, of course there was nothing extraordinary about what she was going to do.

Lights were on downstairs. Whoever lived there was up, in the living room. Waiting for her.

Remarkable, her calmness. After so many foolish hours of indecision.

She ascended the veranda steps, which gave slightly beneath her weight. Rang the doorbell. After a minute or so an outside light went on: she felt exposed: began to smile nervously. One smiled, one soon learned how. There was no retreating.

She saw the old wicker furniture on the porch. Two rocking chairs, a settee. Once painted white but now badly weathered. No cushions.

A dog began barking angrily.

Florence Parr, Florence Parr. She knew who she was, but there was no need to tell *him*. Whoever it was, peering out at her through the dark stained glass, an elderly man, someone's left-behind grandfather. Still, owning this house in this part of town meant money and position: you might sneer at such things but they do have significance. Even to pay the property taxes, the school taxes. . . .

The door opened and a man stood staring out at her, half smiling, quizzical. He was not the man she expected, he was not elderly, but of indeterminate age, perhaps younger than she. "Yes? Hello? What can I do for . . . ?" he said.

She heard her voice, full-throated and calm. The rehearsed question. Questions. An air of apology beneath which her confidence held firm. ". . . driving in the neighborhood earlier today, staying with friends. . . . Simply curious about an old connection between our families. . . . Or at any rate between my family and the people who built this. . . ."

Clearly he was startled by her presence, and did not quite grasp her questions. She spoke too rapidly, she would have to repeat herself.

He invited her in. Which was courteous. A courtesy that struck her as unconscious, automatic. He was very well mannered. Puzzled but not suspicious. Not unfriendly. Too young for this house, perhaps—for so old and shabbily elegant a house. Her presence on his doorstep, her bold questions, the bright strained smile that stretched her lips must have baffled him but he did not think her *odd*: he respected her, was not judging her. A kindly, simple person. Which was of course a relief. He might even be a little simple-minded. Slow-thinking. He certainly had nothing to do with . . . with whatever she was involved in, in this part of the world. He would tell no one about her.

". . . a stranger to the city? . . . staying with friends?"

"I only want to ask: does the name Parr mean anything to you?"

A dog was barking, now frantically. But kept its distance.

Florence was being shown into the living room, evidently the only lighted room downstairs. She noted the old staircase, graceful as always. But they had done something awkward with the wainscoting, painted it a queer slate blue. And the floor was no longer of marble but a poor imitation, some sort of linoleum tile. . . .

"The chandelier," she said suddenly.

The man turned to her, smiling his amiable quizzical worn smile.

"Yes . . . ?"

"It's very attractive," she said. "It must be an antique."

In the comfortable orangish light of the living room she saw that he had sandy red hair, thinning at the crown. But boyishly frizzy at the sides. He might have been in his late thirties but his face was prematurely lined and he stood with one shoulder slightly higher than the other, as if he were very tired. She began to apologize again for disturbing him. For taking up his time with her impulsive, probably futile curiosity.

"Not at all," he said. "I usually don't go to bed until well past midnight."

Florence found herself sitting at one end of an overstuffed sofa. Her smile was strained but as wide as ever, her face had begun to grow very warm. Perhaps he would not notice her blushing.

". . . insomnia?"

"Yes. Sometimes."

"I too . . . sometimes."

He was wearing a green-and-blue plaid shirt, with thin red stripes. A flannel shirt. The sleeves rolled up to his elbows. And what looked like work-trousers. Denim. A gardener's outfit perhaps. Her mind cast about desperately for something to say and she heard herself asking about his garden, his lawn. So many lovely tulips. Most of them red. And there were plane trees, and several elms. . . .

He faced her, leaning forward with his elbows on his knees. A faintly sunburned face. A redhead's complexion, somewhat freckled.

The chair he sat in did not look familiar. It was an ugly brown, imitation brushed velvet. Florence wondered who had bought it: a silly young wife perhaps.

". . . Parr family?"

"From Lancaster?"

"Oh no. From Cummington, Massachusetts. We've lived there for many generations."

He appeared to be considering the name, frowning at the carpet.

". . . *does* sound familiar. . . ."

"Oh, does it? I had hoped. . . ."

The dog approached them, no longer barking. Its tail wagged and thumped against the side of the sofa, the leg of an old-fashioned table, nearly upsetting a lamp. The man snapped his fingers at the dog and it came no further; it quivered, and made a half growling, half sighing noise, and lay with its snout on its paws and its skinny tail outstretched, a few feet from Florence. She wanted to placate it, to make friends. But it was such an ugly creature—partly hairless, with scruffy white whiskers, a naked sagging belly.

"If the dog bothers you . . ."

"Oh no, no. Not at all."

"He only means to be friendly."

"I can see that," Florence said, laughing girlishly. ". . . He's very handsome."

"Hear that?" the man said, snapping his fingers again. "The lady says you're very handsome! Can't you at least stop drooling, don't you have any manners at all?"

"I haven't any pets of my own. But I like animals."

She was beginning to feel quite comfortable. The living room was not exactly what she had expected but it was not *too* bad. There was the rather low, overstuffed sofa in which she sat, the cushions made of a silvery-white, silvery-gray material, with a feathery sheen, plump, immense, like bellies or breasts, a monstrous old piece of furniture yet nothing one would want to sell: for certainly it had come down in the family, it must date from the turn of the century. There was the Victorian table with its coy ornate legs, and its tasseled cloth, and its extraordinary oversized lamp: the sort of thing Florence would smile at in an antique shop, but which looked fairly reasonable here. In fact she should comment on it, since she was staring at it so openly.

". . . antique? European?"

"I think so, yes," the man said.

"Is it meant to be fruit, or a tree, or . . ."

Bulbous and flesh-colored, peach-colored. With a tarnished brass stand. A dust-dimmed golden lampshade with embroidered blue trim that must have been very pretty at one time.

They talked of antiques. Of old houses. Families.

A queer odor defined itself. It was not unpleasant, exactly.

"Would you like something to drink?"

"Why yes I—"

"Excuse me just a moment."

Alone she wondered if she might prowl about the room. But it was long and narrow and poorly lighted at one end: in fact, one end dissolved into darkness. A faint suggestion of furniture there, an old spinet piano, a jumble of chairs, a bay window that must look out onto the garden. She wanted very much to examine a portrait above the mantel of the fireplace but perhaps the dog would bark, or grow excited, if she moved.

It had crept closer to her feet, shuddering with pleasure.

The redheaded man, slightly stooped, brought a glass of something dark to her. In one hand was his own drink, in the other hand hers.

"Taste it. Tell me what you think."

"It seems rather strong. . . ."

Chocolate. Black and bitter. And thick.

"It should really be served hot," the man said.

"Is there a liqueur of some kind in it?"

"Is it too strong for you?"

"Oh no. No. Not at all."

Florence had never tasted anything more bitter. She nearly gagged.

But a moment later it was all right: she forced herself to take a second swallow, and a third. And the prickling painful sensation in her mouth faded.

The redheaded man did not return to his chair, but stood before her, smiling. In the other room he had done something hurried with his hair: had tried to brush it back with his hands, perhaps. A slight film of perspiration shone on his high forehead.

"Do you live alone here?"

"The house does seem rather large, doesn't it?—for a person to live in it alone."

"Of course you have your dog. . . ."

"Do *you* live alone now?"

Florence set the glass of chocolate down. Suddenly she remembered what it reminded her of: a business associate of her father's, many years ago, had brought a box of chocolates back from a trip to Russia. The little girl had popped one into her mouth and had been dismayed by their unexpectedly bitter taste.

She had spat the mess out into her hand. While everyone stared.

As if he could read her thoughts the redheaded man twitched, moving his jaw and his right shoulder jerkily. But he continued smiling as before and Florence did not indicate that she was disturbed. In fact she spoke warmly of the living room's furnishings, and repeated her admiration for handsome old houses like this one. The man nodded, as if waiting for her to say more.

". . . a family named Bartholomew? Of course it was many years ago."

"Bartholomew? Did they live in this neighborhood?"

"Why yes I think so. That's the real reason I stopped in. I once knew a little girl who—"

"Bartholomew, Bartholomew," the man said slowly, frowning. His face puckered. One corner of his mouth twitched with the effort of his concentration: and again his right shoulder jerked. Florence was afraid he would spill his chocolate drink.

Evidently he had a nervous ailment of some kind. But she could not inquire.

He murmured the name *Bartholomew* to himself, his expression grave, even querulous. Florence wished she had not asked the question because it was a lie, after all. She rarely told lies. Yet it had slipped from her, it had glided smoothly out of her mouth.

She smiled guiltily, ducking her head. She took another swallow of the chocolate drink.

Without her having noticed, the dog had inched forward. His great head now rested on her feet. His wet brown eyes peered up at her, oddly affectionate. A baby's eyes. It was true that he was drooling, in fact he was drooling on her ankles, but of course he could not help it. . . . Then she noted that he had wet on the carpet. Only a few feet away. A dark stain, a small puddle.

Yet she could not shrink away in revulsion. After all, she was a guest and it was not time for her to leave.

". . . Bartholomew. You say they lived in this neighborhood?"

"Oh yes."

"But when?"

"Why I really don't . . . I was only a child at the. . . ."

"But when was this?"

He was staring oddly at her, almost rudely. The twitch at the corner of his mouth had gotten worse. He moved to set his glass down and the movement was jerky, puppet-like. Yet he stared at her all the while. Florence knew people often felt uneasy because of her dark over-large staring eyes: but she could not help it. She did not *feel* the impetuosity, the reproach, her expression suggested. So she tried to soften it by smiling. But sometimes the smile failed, it did not deceive anyone at all.

Now that her host had stopped smiling she could see that he was really quite mocking. His tangled sandy eyebrows lifted ironically.

"You said you were a stranger to this city, and now you're saying you've been here. . . ."

"But it was so long ago, I was only a . . ."

He drew himself up to his full height. He was not a tall man, nor was he solidly built. In fact his waist was slender, for a man's —and he wore odd trousers, or jeans, tight-fitting across his thighs and without zipper or snaps, crotchless. They fit him tightly in the crotch, which was smooth, seamless. His legs were rather short for his torso and arms.

He began smiling at Florence. A sly accusing smile. His head jerked mechanically, indicating something on the floor. He was trying to point with his chin and the gesture was clumsy.

"You did something nasty on the floor there. On the carpet."

Florence gasped. At once she drew herself away from the dog, at once she began to deny it. "I didn't— It wasn't—"

"Right on the carpet there. For everyone to see. To smell."

"I certainly did not," Florence said, blushing angrily. "You know very well it was the—"

"Somebody's going to have to clean it up and it isn't going to be *me*," the man said, grinning.

But his eyes were still angry.

He did not like her at all: she saw that. The visit was a mistake, but how could she leave, how could she escape, the dog had crawled up to her again and was nuzzling and drooling against her ankles, and the redheaded man who had seemed so friendly was now leaning over her, his hands on his slim hips, grinning rudely.

As if to frighten her, as one might frighten an animal or a child, he clapped his hands smartly together. Florence blinked at the sudden sound. And then he leaned forward and clapped his hands together again, right before her face. She cried out for him to leave her alone, her eyes smarted with tears, she was leaning back against the cushions, her head back as far as it would go, and then he clapped his hands once again, hard, bringing them against her burning cheeks, slapping both her cheeks at once, and a sharp thin white-hot sensation ran through her body, from her face and throat to her belly, to the pit of her belly, and from the pit of her belly up into her chest, into her mouth, and even down into her stiffened legs. She screamed for the redheaded man to stop, and twisted convulsively on the sofa to escape him.

"Liar! Bad girl! Dirty girl!" someone shouted.

She wore her new reading glasses, with their attractive plastic frames. And a spring suit, smartly styled, with a silk blouse in a floral pattern. And the tight but fashionable shoes.

Her audience, respectful and attentive, could not see her trembling hands behind the podium, or her slightly quivering knees. They would have been astonished to learn that she hadn't been able to eat breakfast that morning—that she felt depressed and exhausted though she had managed to fall asleep the night before, probably around two, and had evidently slept her usual dreamless sleep.

She cleared her throat several times in succession, a habit she detested in others.

But gradually her strength flowed back into her. The morning was so sunny, so innocent. These people were, after all, her colleagues and friends: they certainly wished her well, and even appeared to be genuinely interested in what she had to say about the future of the humanities. Perhaps Dr. Parr knew something they did not, perhaps she would share her professional secrets with them. . . .

As the minutes passed Florence could hear her voice grow richer and firmer, easing into its accustomed rhythms. She began to relax. She began to breathe more regularly. She was moving into familiar channels, making points she had made countless times before, at similar meetings, with her deans and faculty chairmen at Champlain, with other educators. A number of people applauded heartily when she spoke of the danger of small private colleges competing unwisely with one another; and again when she made a point, an emphatic point, about the need for the small private school in an era of multiversities. Surely these were remarks anyone might have made, there was really nothing original about them, yet her audience seemed extremely pleased to hear them from her. They *did* admire Florence Parr—that was clear.

She removed her reading glasses. Smiled, spoke without needing to glance at her notes. This part of her speech—an amusing summary of the consequences of certain experimental programs at Champlain, initiated since she'd become president—was more specific, more interesting, and of course she knew it by heart.

The previous night had been one of her difficult nights. At least initially. Her mind racing in that way she couldn't control, those flame-like pangs of fear, insomnia. And no help for it. And no way out. She'd fallen asleep while reading through her notes and awakened suddenly, her heart beating erratically, body drenched in perspiration—and there she was, lying twisted back against the headboard, neck stiff and aching and her left leg numb beneath her. She'd been dreaming she'd given in and driven out to see the dolls' house; but of course she had not, she'd been in her hotel room all the time. *She'd never left her hotel room.*

She'd never left her hotel room but she'd fallen asleep and dreamt she had but she refused to summon back her dream, not that dream nor any others; in fact she rather doubted she did dream, she never remembered afterward. Florence Parr was one of those people who, as soon as they awake, are *awake*. And eager to begin the day.

At the conclusion of Florence's speech everyone applauded enthusiastically. She'd given speeches like this many times before and it had been ridiculous of her to worry.

Congratulations, handshakes. Coffee was being served.

Florence was flushed with relief and pleasure, crowded about by well-wishers. This was her world, these people her colleagues, they knew her, admired her. Why does one worry about anything! Florence thought, smiling into these friendly faces, shaking more hands. These were all good people, serious professional people, and she liked them very much.

At a distance a faint fading jeering cry *Liar! Dirty girl!* but Florence was listening to the really quite astute remarks of a youngish man who was a new dean of arts at Vassar. How good the hot, fresh coffee was. And a thinly layered apricot brioche she'd taken from a proffered silver tray.

The insult and discomfort of the night were fading; the vision

of the doll's house was fading, dying. She refused to summon it
back. She would not give it another thought. Friends—acquaintances—well-wishers were gathering around her, she knew her skin
was glowing like a girl's, her eyes were bright and clear and hopeful;
at such times, buoyed by the presence of others as by waves of
applause, you forget your age, your loneliness—the very perimeters
of your soul.

Day is the only reality. She'd always known.

Though the conference was a success, and colleagues at home
heard that Florence's contribution had been particularly well received, Florence began to forget it within a few weeks. So many
conferences!—so many warmly applauded speeches! Florence was a
professional woman who, by nature more than design, pleased both
women and men; she did not stir up controversy, she "stimulated
discussion." Now she was busily preparing for her first major conference, to be held in London in September: "The Role of the Humanities in the 21st Century." Yes, she was apprehensive, she told
friends—"But it's a true challenge."

When a check arrived in the mail for five hundred dollars, an
honorarium for her speech in Lancaster, Pennsylvania, Florence was
puzzled at first—not recalling the speech, nor the circumstances.
How odd! She'd never been there, had she? Then, to a degree, as
if summoning forth a dream, she remembered: the beautiful Pennsylvania landscape, ablaze with spring flowers; a small crowd of
well-wishers gathered around to shake her hand. Why, Florence
wondered, had she ever worried about her speech?—her public self?
Like an exquisitely precise clockwork mechanism, a living manne-
quin, she would always do well: you'll applaud too, when you hear
her.

The Bingo Master

Suddenly there appears Joe Pye the Bingo Master, dramatically late by some ten or fifteen minutes, and everyone in the bingo hall except Rose Mallow Odom calls out an ecstatic greeting or at least smiles broadly to show how welcome he is, how forgiven he is for being late—"Just look what he's wearing tonight!" the plump young mother seated across from Rose exclaims, her pretty face dimpling like a child's. "*Isn't* he something," the woman murmurs, catching Rose's reluctant eye.

Joe Pye the Bingo Master. Joe Pye the talk of Tophet—or *some parts* of Tophet—who bought the old Harlequin Amusements Arcade down on Purslane Street by the Gayfeather Hotel (which Rose had been thinking of as boarded up or even razed, but there it is, still in operation) and has made such a success with his bingo hall, even Rose's father's staid old friends at church or at the club are talking about him. The Tophet City Council had tried to shut Joe Pye down last spring, first because too many people crowded into the hall and there was a fire hazard, second because he hadn't paid some fine or other (or was it, Rose Mallow wondered maliciously, a bribe) to the Board of Health and Sanitation, whose inspector had professed to be "astonished and sickened" by the conditions of the rest rooms, and the quality of the foot-longs and cheese-and-sausage pizzas sold at the refreshment stand: and two or three of the churches, jealous of Joe Pye's profits, which might very well eat into *theirs* (for Thursday-evening bingo was a main source of revenue for certain Tophet churches, though not, thank God, Saint Matthias Episcopal Church, where the Odoms worshipped), were agitating that Joe Pye be forced to move outside the city limits, at least, just as those "adult" bookstores and X-rated film outfits had been forced to move. There had been editorials in the paper, and letters pro and con, and though Rose Mallow had only contempt for local politics and hardly knew most of what was going on in her own home-town—her mind, as her father and aunt said, being elsewhere—she had followed the "Joe Pye Controversy" with amusement. It had pleased her when the bingo hall was allowed to remain open, mainly because it upset people in her part of town, by the golf course and the park and along Van Dusen Boulevard; if anyone had suggested that she would be visiting the hall, and even sitting, as she is to-night, at one of the dismayingly long oilcloth-covered tables beneath these ugly bright lights, amid noisily cheerful people who all seem to know one another, and who are happily devouring "refreshments" though it is only seven-thirty and surely they've eaten their dinners beforehand, and *why* are they so goggle-eyed about idiotic Joe Pye! —Rose Mallow would have snorted with laughter, waving her hand in that gesture of dismissal her aunt said was "unbecoming."

Well, Rose Mallow Odom *is* at Joe Pye's Bingo Hall, in fact she has arrived early, and is staring, her arms folded beneath her breasts, at the fabled Bingo Master himself. Of course, there are other workers—attendants—high-school-aged girls with piles of bleached hair and pierced earrings and artfully made-up faces, and even one or two older women, dressed in bright-pink smocks with *Joe Pye* in a spidery green arabesque on their collars, and out front there is a courteous milk-chocolate-skinned young man in a three-piece suit whose function, Rose gathered, was simply to welcome the bingo players and maybe to keep out riffraff, white or black, since the hall *is* in a fairly desreputable part of town. But Joe Pye is the center of attention. Joe Pye is everything. His high rapid chummy chatter at the microphone is as silly, and halfway unintelligible, as any local disc jockey's frantic monologue, picked up by chance as Rose spins the dial looking for something to divert her; yet everyone listens eagerly, and begins giggling even before his jokes are entirely completed.

The Bingo Master is a very handsome man. Rose sees that at once, and concedes the point: no matter that his goatee looks as if it were dyed with ink from the five-and-ten, and his stark-black eyebrows as well, and his skin, smooth as stone, somehow unreal as stone, is as darkly tanned as the skin of one of those men pictured on billboards, squinting into the sun with cigarettes smoking in their fingers; no matter that his lips are too rosy, the upper lip so deeply indented that it looks as if he is pouting, and his getup (what kinder expression?—the poor man is wearing a dazzling white turban, and a tunic threaded with silver and salmon pink, and wide-legged pajama-like trousers made of a material almost as clingy as silk, jet black) makes Rose want to roll her eyes heavenward and walk away. He *is* attractive. Even beautiful, if you are in the habit —Rose isn't—of calling men beautiful. His deep-set eyes shine with an enthusiasm that can't be feigned; or at any rate can't be entirely feigned. His outfit, absurd as it is, hangs well on him, emphasizing his well-proportioned shoulders and his lean waist and hips. His teeth, which he bares often, far too often, in smiles clearly meant to be dazzling, are perfectly white and straight and even: just as Rose Mallow's had been promised to be, though she knew, even as a child of twelve or so, that the ugly painful braces and the uglier "bite" that made her gag wouldn't leave her teeth any more attractive than they already were—which wasn't very attractive at all. Teeth impress her, inspire her to envy, make her resentful. And it's all the more exasperating that Joe Pye smiles so often, rubbing his hands zestfully and gazing out at his adoring giggling audience.

Naturally his voice is mellifluous and intimate, when it isn't busy being "enthusiastic," and Rose thinks that if he were speaking another language—if she didn't have to endure his claptrap about "lovely ladies" and "jackpot prizes" and "mystery cards" and "ten-games-for-the-price-of-seven" (under certain complicated conditions she couldn't follow)—she might find it very attractive indeed. Might find, if she tried, *him* attractive. But his drivel interferes with his seductive power, or powers, and Rose finds herself distracted, handing over money to one of the pink-smocked girls in exchange for a shockingly grimy bingo card, her face flushing with irritation. Of course the evening is an experiment, and not an entirely serious experiment: she has come downtown, by bus, unescorted, wearing stockings and fairly high heels, lipsticked, perfumed, less ostentatiously homely than usual, in order to lose, as the expression goes, her virginity. Or perhaps it would be more accurate, less narcissistic, to say that she has come downtown to acquire a lover? . . .

But no. Rose Mallow Odom doesn't want a lover. She doesn't want a man at all, not in any way, but she supposes one is necessary for the ritual she intends to complete.

"And now, ladies, ladies and gentlemen, if you're all ready, if you're all ready to begin." Joe Pye sings out, as a girl with carrot-colored frizzed hair and an enormous magenta smile turns the handle of the wire basket, in which white balls the size and apparent weight of Ping-Pong balls tumble merrily together, "*I* am ready to begin, and I wish you each and all the very, very best of luck from the bottom of my heart, and remember there's more than one winner each game, and dozens of winners each night, and in fact Joe Pye's iron-clad law is that *nobody's* going to go away empty-handed—Ah, now, let's see, now: the first number is—"

Despite herself Rose Mallow is crouched over the filthy cardboard square, a kernel of corn between her fingers, her lower lip caught in her teeth. *The first number is—*

It was on the eve of her thirty-ninth birthday, almost two months ago, that Rose Mallow Odom conceived of the notion of going out and "losing" her virginity.

Perhaps the notion wasn't her own, not entirely. It sprang into her head as she was writing one of her dashed-off swashbuckling letters (for which, she knew, her friends cherished her—*isn't Rose hilarious*, they liked to say, *isn't she brave*), this time to Georgene Wescott, who was back in New York City, her second divorce behind her, some sort of complicated, flattering, but not (Rose suspected) very high-paying job at Columbia just begun, and a new book, a collection of essays on contemporary women artists, just contracted for at a prestigious New York publishing house. *Dear Georgene*, Rose wrote, *Life in Tophet is droll as usual what with Papa's & Aunt Olivia's & my own criss-crossing trips to our high-priced $peciali$t pals at that awful clinic I told you about. & it seems there was a scandal of epic proportions at the Tophet Women's Club on acc't of the fact that some sister club which rents the building (I guess they're leftwingdogooder types, you & Ham & Carolyn wld belong if you were misfortunate enough to dwell hereabout) includes on its membership rolls some two or three or more Black Persons. Which, tho' it doesn't violate the letter of the Club's charter certainly violates its spirit. & then again,* Rose wrote, very late one night after her Aunt Olivia had retired, and even her father, famously insomniac like Rose herself, had gone to bed, *then again did I tell you about the NSWPP convention here . . . at the Holiday Inn . . . (which wasn't built yet I guess when you & Jack visited) . . . by the interstate expressway? . . . Anyway: (& I fear I did tell you, or was it Carolyn, or maybe both of you) the conference was all set, the rooms & banquet hall booked, & some enterprising muckraking young reporter at the Tophet* Globe-Times *(who has since gone "up north" to Norfolk, to a better-paying job) discovered that the NSWPP stood for National Socialist White People's Party which is (& I do not exaggerate, Georgene, tho' I can see you crinkling up your nose at another of Rose Mallow's silly flights of fancy, "Why doesn't she scramble all that into a story or a* Symboliste *poem as she once did, so she'd have something to show for her exile & her silence & cunning as well," I can hear you mumbling & you are 100% correct) none other than the (are you PREPARED???) American Nazi Party! Yes. Indeed. There is such a party & it overlaps Papa says sourly with the Klan & certain civic-minded organizations hereabouts, tho' he declined to be specific, possibly because his spinster daughter was looking too rapt & incredulous. Anyway, the Nazis were denied the use of the Tophet Holiday Inn & you'd have been impressed by the spirit of the newspaper editorials denouncing them roundly. (I hear tell—but maybe it is surreal rumor—that the Nazis not only wear their swastika armbands in secret but have tiny lapel pins on the insides of their lapels, swastikas natcherlly. . . .* And then she'd changed the subject, relaying news of friends, friends' husbands and wives, and former husbands and wives, and acquaintances' latest doings, scandalous and otherwise (for of the lively, gregarious, genius-ridden group that had assembled itself informally in Cambridge, Mass., almost twenty years ago, Rose Mallow Odom was the only really dedicated letter writer—the one who held everyone together through the mails— the one who would continue to write cheerful letter after letter even when she wasn't answered for a year or two), and as a perky little postscript she added that her thirty-ninth birthday was fast approaching and she meant to divest herself of her damned virginity as a kind of present to herself. *As my famous ironing-board figure is flatter than ever, & my breasts the size of Dixie cups after last spring's ritual flu & a rerun of that wretched bronchitis, it will be, as you can imagine, quite a challenge.*

Of course it was nothing more than a joke, one of Rose's whimsical self-mocking jokes, a postscript scribbled when her eyelids had begun to droop with fatigue. And yet . . . And yet when she actually wrote *I intend to divest myself of my damned virginity*, and sealed the letter, she saw that the project was inevitable. She would go through with it. She *would* go through with it, just as in the old days, years ago, when she was the most promising young writer in her circle, and grants and fellowships and prizes had tumbled into her lap, she had forced herself to complete innumerable projects simply because they were challenging, and would give her pain. (Though Rose was scornful of the Odoms' puritanical disdain of pleasure, on intellectual grounds, she nevertheless believed that painful experiences, and even pain itself, had a generally salubrious effect.)

And so she went out, the very next evening, a Thursday, telling her father and her aunt Olivia that she was going to the downtown library. When they asked in alarm, as she knew they would, why on earth she was going at such a time, Rose said with a schoolgirlish scowl that that was her business. But was the library even open at such a strange time, Aunt Olivia wanted to know. Open till nine on Thursdays, Rose said.

That first Thursday Rose had intended to go to a singles bar she had heard about, on the ground floor of a new high-rise office building; but at first she had difficulty finding the place, and circled about the enormous glass-and-concrete tower in her ill-fitting high heels, muttering to herself that no experience would be worth so much effort, even if it was a painful one. (She was of course a chaste young woman, whose general feeling about sex was not much different than it had been in elementary school, when the cruder, more reckless, more knowing children had had the power, by chanting certain words, to make poor Rose Mallow Odom press her hands over her ears.) Then she discovered the bar—discovered, rather, a long line of young people snaking up some dark concrete steps to the sidewalk, and along the sidewalk for hundreds of feet, evidently waiting to get into the Chanticleer. She was appalled not only by the crowd but by the exuberant youth of the crowd: no one older than twenty-five, no one dressed as she was. (*She* looked dressed for church, which she hated. But however else did people dress?) So she retreated, and went to the downtown library after all, where the librarians all knew her, and asked respectfully after her "work" (though she had made it clear years ago that she was no longer "working"—the demands her mother made upon her during the long years of her illness, and then Rose's father's precarious health, and of course her own history of respiratory illnesses and anemia and easily broken bones had made concentration impossible). Once she shook off the solicitous cackling old ladies she spent what remained of her evening quite profitably —she read *The Oresteia* in a translation new to her, and scribbled notes as she always did, excited by stray thoughts for articles or stories or poems, though in the end she always crumpled the notes up and threw them away. But the evening had not been an entire loss.

The second Thursday, she went to the Park Avenue Hotel, Tophet's only good hotel, fully intending to sit in the dim cocktail lounge until something happened—but she had no more than stepped into the lobby when Barbara Pursley called out to her; and she ended by going to dinner with Barbara and her husband, who were visiting Tophet for a few days, and Barbara's parents, whom she had always liked. Though she hadn't seen Barbara for fifteen years, and in truth hadn't thought of her once during those fifteen years (except to remember that a close friend of Barbara's had been the one, in sixth grade, to think up the cruel but probably fairly accurate nickname The Ostrich for Rose), she did have an enjoyable time. Anyone who had observed their table in the vaulted oak-paneled dining room of the Park Avenue, taking note in particular of the tall, lean, nervously eager woman who laughed frequently, showing her gums, and who seemed unable to keep her hand from patting at her hair (which was baby-fine, a pale brown, in no style at all but not unbecoming), and adjusting her collar or earrings, would have been quite astonished to learn that that woman (of indeterminate age: her "gentle" expressive chocolate-brown eyes might have belonged to a gawky girl of sixteen or to a woman in her fifties) had intended to spend the evening prowling about for a man.

And then the third Thursday (for the Thursdays had become, now, a ritual: her aunt protested only feebly, her father gave her a library book to return) she went to the movies, to the very theater where, at thirteen or fourteen, with her friend Janet Brome, she had met . . . or almost met . . . what were thought to be, then, "older boys" of seventeen or eighteen. (Big boys, farm boys, spending the day in Tophet, prowling about for girls. But even in the darkened Rialto neither Rose nor Janet resembled the kind of girls these boys sought.) And nothing at all happened. Nothing. Rose walked out of the theater when the film—a cloying self-conscious comedy about adultery in Manhattan—was only half over, and took a bus back home, in time to join her father and her aunt for ice cream and Peek Freans biscuits. "You look as if you're coming down with a cold," Rose's father said. "Your eyes are watery." Rose denied it; but came down with a cold the very next day.

She skipped a Thursday, but on the following week ventured out again, eyeing herself cynically and without a trace of affection in her bedroom mirror (which looked wispy and washed-out—but do mirrors actually age, Rose wondered), judging that, yes, she might be called pretty, with her big ostrich eyes and her ostrich height and gawky dignity, by a man who squinted in her direction in just the right degree of dimness. By now she knew the project was doomed but it gave her a kind of angry satisfaction to return to the Park Avenue Hotel, just, as she said in a more recent letter (this to the girl, the woman, with whom she had roomed as a graduate student at Radcliffe, then as virginal as Rose, and possibly even more intimidated by men than Rose—and now Pauline was divorced, with two children, living with an Irish poet in a tower north of Sligo, a tower not unlike Yeats's, with *his* several children) for the brute hell of it.

And the evening had been an initially promising one. Quite by accident Rose wandered into the Second Annual Conference of the Friends of Evolution, and sat at the rear of a crowded ballroom, to hear a paper read by a portly, distinguished gentleman with pince-nez and a red carnation in his buttonhole, and to join in the enthusiastic applause afterward. (The paper had been, Rose imperfectly gathered, about the need for extraterrestrial communication—or was such communication already a fact, and the FBI and "university professors" were united in suppressing it?) A second paper by a woman Rose's age who walked with a cane seemed to be arguing that Christ was in space—"out there in space"—as a close reading of the Book of Saint John the Divine would demonstrate. The applause was even more enthusiastic after this paper, though Rose contributed only politely, for she'd had, over the years, many thoughts about Jesus of Nazareth—and thoughts about those thoughts—and in the end, one fine day, she had taken herself in secret to a psychiatrist at the Mount Yarrow Hospital, confessing in tears, in shame, that she knew very well the whole thing—*the whole thing*—was nonsense, and insipid nonsense at that, but—still—she sometimes caught herself wistfully "believing"; and was she clinically insane? Some inflection in her voice, some droll upward motion of her eyes, must have alerted the man to the fact that Rose Mallow Odom was someone like himself—she'd gone to school in the North, hadn't she?—and so he brushed aside her worries, and told her that of course it was nonsense, but one felt a nagging family loyalty, yes one did quarrel with one's family, and say terrible things, but still the loyalty was there, he would give her a prescription for barbiturates if she was suffering from insomnia, and hadn't she better have a physical examination?—because she was looking (he meant to be kindly, he didn't know how he was breaking her heart) worn out. Rose did not tell him that she had just *had* her six months' checkup and that, for her, she was in excellent health: no chest problems, the anemia under control. By the end of the conversation the psychiatrist remembered who Rose was—"Why, you're famous around here, didn't you publish a novel that shocked everyone?"—and Rose had recovered her composure enough to say stiffly that no one was famous in this part of Alabama; and the original topic had been completely forgotten. And now Jesus of Nazareth was floating about in space . . . or orbiting some moon . . . or was He actually in a spacecraft (the term "spacecraft" was used frequently by the conferees), awaiting His first visitors from planet earth? Rose was befriended by a white-haired gentleman in his seventies who slid across two or three folding chairs to sit beside her, and there was even a somewhat younger man, in his fifties perhaps, with greasy quill-like hair and a mild stammer, whose badge proclaimed him as H. Speedwell of Sion, Florida, who offered to buy her a cup of coffee after the session was over. Rose felt a flicker of—of what?—amusement, interest, despair? She had to put her finger to her lips in a schoolmarmish gesture, since the elderly gentleman on her right and H. Speedwell on her left were both talking rather emphatically, as if trying to impress her, about *their* experiences sighting UFO's, and the third speaker was about to begin.

The topic was "The Next and Final Stage of Evolution," given by the Reverend Jake Gromwell of the New Holland Institute of Religious Studies in Stoneseed, Kentucky. Rose sat very straight, her hands folded on her lap, her knees primly together (for, it must have been by accident, Mr. Speedwell's right knee was pressing against her), and pretended to listen. Her mind was all a flurry, like a chicken coop invaded by a dog, and she couldn't even know what she felt until the fluttering thoughts settled down. Somehow she was in the Regency Ballroom of the Park Avenue Hotel on a Thursday evening in September, listening to a paper given by a porkish-looking man in a tight-fitting gray-and-red plaid suit with a bright-red tie. She had been noticing that many of the conferees were disabled—on canes, on crutches, even in wheelchairs (one of the wheelchairs, operated by a hawkfaced youngish man who might have been Rose's age but looked no more than twelve, was a wonderfully classy affair, with a panel of push-buttons that would evidently do nearly anything for him he wished; Rose had rented a wheelchair some years ago, for herself, when a pinched nerve in her back had crippled her, and *hers* had been a very ordinary model)— and most of them were elderly. There *were* men her own age but they were not promising. And Mr. Speedwell, who smelled of something blandly odd, like tapioca, was not promising. Rose sat for a few more minutes, conscious of being polite, being good, allowing herself to be lulled by the Reverend Gromwell's monotonous voice and by the ballroom's decorations (fluorescent-orange and green and violet snakes undulated in the carpet, voluptuous forty-foot velvet drapes stirred in the tepid air from invisible vents, there was even a garishly-inappropriate but mesmerizing mirrored ceiling with "stardust" lighting which gave to the conferees a rakish, faintly lurid air despite their bald heads and trembling necks and crutches) before making her apologetic escape.

Now Rose Mallow Odom sits at one of the long tables in Joe Pye's Bingo Hall, her stomach somewhat uneasy after the Tru-Orange she has just drunk, a promising—a highly promising—card before her. She is wondering if the mounting excitement she feels is legitimate, or whether it has anything to do with the orange soda: or whether it's simple intelligent dread, for of course she doesn't want to win. She can't even imagine herself calling out *Bingo!* in a voice loud enough to be heard. It is after ten-thirty p.m. and there has been a number of winners and runners-up, many shrieking, ecstatic *Bingos* and some bellowing *Bingos* and one or two incredulous gasps, and really she should have gone home by now, Joe Pye is the only halfway attractive man in the place (there are no more than a dozen men there) and it isn't likely that Joe Pye in his dashing costume, with his glaring white turban held together by a gold pin,

and his graceful shoulders, and his syrupy voice, would pay much
attention to *her*. But inertia or curiosity has kept her here. What the
hell, Rose thinks, pushing kernels of corn about on much-used
squares of thick cardboard, becoming acquainted with fellow To-
phetians, surely there are worse ways to spend Thursday night? . . .
She will dash off letters to Hamilton Frye and Carolyn Sears this
weekend, though they owe her letters, describing in detail her newly
made friends of the evening (the plump, perspiring, good-natured
young woman seated across from her is named Lobelia, and it's ironic
that Rose is doing so well this game, because just before it started
Lobelia asked to exchange cards, on an impulse—"You give me
mine and I'll give you yours, Rose!" she said, with charming inac-
curacy and a big smile, and of course Rose had immediately obliged)
and the depressingly bright-lit hall with its disproportionately large
American flag up front by Joe Pye's platform, and all the odd,
strange, sad, eager, *intent* players, some of them extremely old, their
faces wizened, their hands palsied, a few crippled or undersized or
in some dim incontestable way not altogether *right*, a number very
young (in fact it is something of a scandal, the children up this late,
playing bingo beside their mamas, frequently with two or three cards
while their mamas greedily work at four cards, which is the limit),
and the dreadful taped music that uncoils relentlessly behind Joe
Pye's tireless voice, and of course Joe Pye the Bingo Master himself,
who has such a warm, toothed smile for everyone in the hall, and
who had—unless Rose, her weak eyes unfocused by the lighting,
imagined it—actually directed a special smile and a wink in her
direction earlier in the evening, apparently sighting her as a new
customer. She will make one of her droll charming anecdotes out of
the experience. She will be quite characteristically harsh on herself,
and will speculate on the phenomenon of suspense, its psychological
meaning (isn't there a sense in which all suspense, and not just bingo
hall suspense, is asinine?), and life's losers who, even if they win,
remain losers (for what possible difference could a home hair dryer,
or $100 cash, or an outdoor barbecue grill, or an electric train com-
plete with track, or a huge copy of the Bible, illustrated, bound in
simulated white leather, make to any of these people?). She will

record the groans of disappointment and dismay when someone screams *Bingo!* and the mutterings when the winner's numbers, read off by one of the bored-looking girl attendants, prove to be legitimate. The winners' frequent tears, the hearty handshaking and cheek-kissing Joe Pye indulges in, as if each winner were specially dear to him, an old friend hurrying forth to be greeted; and the bright-yellow mustard splashed on the foot-longs and their doughy buns; and the several infants whose diapers were changed on a bench unfortunately close by; and Lobelia's superstitious fingering of a tiny gold cross she wears on a chain around her neck; and the worn-out little girl sleeping on the floor, her head on a pink teddy bear someone in her family must have won hours ago; and—

"You won! Here. Hey! She won! Right here! This card, here! Here! Joe Pye, *right here!*"

The grandmotherly woman to Rose's left, with whom she'd exchanged a few pleasant words earlier in the evening (it turns out her name is Cornelia Teasel; she once cleaned house for the Odoms' neighbors the Filarees), is suddenly screaming, and has seized Rose's hand, in her excitement jarring all the kernels off the cards; but no matter, no matter, Rose *does* have a winning card, she has scored bingo, and there will be no avoiding it.

There are the usual groans, half-sobs, mutterings of angry disappointment, but the game comes to an end, and a gum-chewing girl with a brass helmet of hair reads off Rose's numbers to Joe Pye, who punctuates each number not only with a *Yes, right* but *Keep going, honey* and *You're getting there*, and a dazzling wide smile as if he'd never witnessed anything more wonderful in his life. A $100 winner! A first-time customer (unless his eyes deceive him) and a $100 winner!

Rose, her face burning and pulsing with embarrassment, must go to Joe Pye's raised platform to receive her check, and Joe Pye's heartiest warmest congratulations, and a noisy moist kiss that falls uncomfortably near her mouth (she must resist stepping violently back—the man is so physically vivid, so real, so *there*). "*Now* you're smiling, honey, aren't you?" he says happily. Up close he is just as handsome, but the whites of his eyes are perhaps too white. The gold pin in his turban is a crowing cock. His skin is *very* tanned, and the goatee even blacker than Rose had thought. "I been watching you all night, hon, and you'd be a whole lot prettier if you eased up and smiled more," Joe Pye murmurs in her ear. He smells sweetish, like candied fruit or wine.

Rose steps back, offended, but before she can escape Joe Pye reaches out for her hand again, her cold thin hand, which he rubs briskly between his own. "You *are* new here, aren't you? New tonight?" he asks.

"Yes," Rose says, so softly he has to stoop to hear.

"And are you a Tophet girl? Folks live in town?"

"Yes."

"But you never been to Joe Pye's Bingo Hall before tonight?"

"No."

"And here you're walking away a hundred-dollar cash winner! How does that make you feel?"

"Oh, just fine—"

"What?"

"Just fine—I never expected—"

"Are you a bingo player? I mean, y'know, at these churches in town, or anywheres else."

"No."

"Not a player? Just here for the fun of it? A $100 winner, your first night, ain't that excellent luck!—You know, hon, you *are* a real attractive gal, with the color all up in your face, I wonder if you'd like to hang around, oh say another half hour while I wind things up, there's a cozy bar right next door, I noted you are here tonight alone, eh?—might-be we could have a nightcap, just the two of us?"

"Oh I don't think so, Mr. Pye—"

"Joe Pye! Joe Pye's the name," he says, grinning, leaning toward her, "and what might your name be? Something to do with a flower, isn't it?—some kind of a, a flower—"

Rose, very confused, wants only to escape. But he has her hand tightly in his own.

"Too shy to tell Joe Pye your name?" he says.

"It's—it's Olivia," Rose stammers.

"Oh. Olivia. Olivia, is it," Joe Pye says slowly, his smile arrested. "*Olivia*, is it. . . . Well, sometimes I misread, you know; I get a wire crossed or something and I misread; I never claimed to be 100% accurate. Olivia, then. Okay, fine. Olivia. Why are you so skittish, Olivia? The microphone won't pick up a bit of what we say. Are you free for a nightcap around eleven? Yes? Just next door at the Gayfeather where I'm staying, the lounge is a cozy homey place, nice and private, the two of us, no strings attached or nothing . . ."

"My father is waiting up for me, and—"

"Come *on* now, Olivia, you're a Tophet gal, don't you want to make an out-of-towner feel welcome?"

"It's just that—"

"All right, then? Yes? It's a date? Soon as we close up shop here? Right next door at the Gayfeather?"

Rose stares at the man, at his bright glittering eyes and the glittering heraldic rooster in his turban, and hears herself murmur a weak assent; and only then does Joe Pye release her hand.

And so it has come about, improbably, ludicrously, that Rose Mallow Odom finds herself in the sepulchral Gayfeather Lounge as midnight nears, in the company of Joe Pye the Bingo Master (whose white turban is dazzling even here, in the drifting smoke and the lurid flickering colors from a television set perched high above the bar), and two or three other shadowy figures, derelict and subdued, solitary drinkers who clearly want nothing to do with one another. (One of them, a fairly well-dressed old gentleman with a swollen pug nose, reminds Rose obliquely of her father—except for the alcoholic's nose, of course.) She is sipping nervously at an "orange blossom"—a girlish sweet-acetous concoction she hasn't had since 1962, and has ordered tonight, or has had her escort order for her, only because she could think of nothing else. Joe Pye is telling Rose about his travels to distant lands—Venezuela, Ethiopia, Tibet, Iceland—and Rose makes an effort to appear to believe him, to appear to be naïve enough to believe him, for she has decided to go through with it, to take this outlandish fraud as her lover, for a single night only, or part of a night, however long the transaction will take. "Another drink?" Joe Pye murmurs, laying his hand on her unresisting wrist.

Above the bar the sharply tilted television set crackles with machine-gun fire, and indistinct silhouettes, probably human, race across bright sand, below a bright turquoise sky. Joe Pye, annoyed, turns and signals with a brisk counterclockwise motion of his fingers to the bartender, who lowers the sound almost immediately; the bartender's deference to Joe Pye impresses Rose. But then she is easily impressed. But then she is *not*, ordinarily, easily impressed. But the fizzing stinging orange drink has gone to her head.

"From going north and south on this globe, and east and west, traveling by freighter, by train, sometimes on foot, on foot through the mountains, spending a year here, six months there, two years somewhere else, I made my way finally back home, to the States, and wandered till things, you know, felt right: the way things sometimes feel right about a town or a landscape or another person, and you know it's your destiny," Joe Pye says softly. "If you know what I mean, Olivia."

With two dark fingers he strokes the back of her hand. She shivers, though the sensation is really ticklish.

". . . destiny," Rose says. "Yes. I think I know."

She wants to ask Joe Pye if she won honestly; if, maybe, he hadn't thrown the game her way. Because he'd noticed her earlier. All evening. A stranger, a scowling disbelieving stranger, fixing him with her intelligent skeptical stare, the most conservatively and tastefully dressed player in the hall. But he doesn't seem eager to talk about his business, he wants instead to talk about his life as a "soldier of fortune"—whatever he means by that—and Rose wonders if such a question might be naïve, or insulting, for it would suggest that *he* was dishonest, that the bingo games were rigged. But then perhaps everyone knows they are rigged?—like the horse races?

She wants to ask but cannot. Joe Pye is sitting so close to her in the booth, his skin is so ruddy, his lips so dark, his teeth so white, his goatee Mephistophelian and his manner—now that he is "offstage," now that he can "be himself"—so ingratiatingly intimate that she feels disoriented. She is willing to see her position as comic, even as ludicrous (she, Rose Mallow Odom, disdainful of men and of physical things in general, is going to allow this charlatan to imagine that *he* is seducing *her*—but at the same time she is quite nervous, she isn't even very articulate); she must see it, and interpret it, as *something*. But Joe Pye keeps on talking. As if he were halfway enjoying himself. As if this were a normal conversation. Did she have any hobbies? Pets? Did she grow up in Tophet and go to school here? Were her parents living? What sort of business was her father in?—or was he a professional man? Had *she* traveled much? No? Was she ever married? Did she have a "career"? Had she ever been in love? Did she ever expect to be in love?

Rose blushes, hears herself giggle in embarrassment, her words trip over one another. Joe Pye is leaning close, tickling her forearm, a clown in black silk pajama bottoms and a turban, smelling of something overripe. His dark eyebrows are peaked, the whites of his eyes are luminous, his fleshy lips pout becomingly; he is irresistible. His nostrils even flare with the pretense of passion. . . . Rose begins to giggle and cannot stop.

"You are a highly attractive girl, especially when you let yourself go like right now," Joe Pye says softly. "You know—we could go up to my room where we'd be more private. Would you like that?"

"I am not," Rose says, drawing in a full, shaky breath, to clear her head, "I am not a *girl*. Hardly a girl at the age of thirty-nine."

"We could be more private in my room. No one would interrupt us."

"My father isn't well, he's waiting up for me," Rose says quickly.

"By now he's asleep, most likely!"

"Oh no, no—he suffers from insomnia, like me."

"Like you! Is that so? I suffer from insomnia too," Joe Pye says, squeezing her hand in excitement. "Ever since a bad experience I had in the desert . . . in another part of the world. . . . But I'll tell you about that later, when we're closer acquainted. If we both have insomnia, Olivia, we should keep each other company. The nights in Tophet are so long."

"The nights *are* long," Rose says, blushing.

"But your mother, now; *she* isn't waiting up for you."

"Mother has been dead for years. I won't say what her sickness was but you can guess, it went on forever, and after she died I took all my things—I had this funny career going. I won't bore you with details—all my papers—stories and notes and such—and burnt them in the trash, and I've been at home every day and every night since, and I felt good when I burnt the things and good when I remember it, and—and I feel good right now," Rose says defiantly, finishing her drink. "So I know what I did was a sin."

"Do you believe in sin, a sophisticated girl like yourself?" Joe Pye says, smiling broadly.

The alcohol is a warm golden-glowing breath that fills her lungs and overflows and spreads to every part of her body, to the very tips of her toes, the tips of her ears. Yet her hand is fishlike: let Joe Pye fondle it as he will. So she is being seduced, and it is exactly as silly, as clumsy, as she had imagined it would be, as she imagined such things would be even as a young girl. So. As Descartes saw, I am I, up in my head, and my body is my body, extended in space, *out there*, it will be interesting to observe what happens, Rose thinks calmly. But she is not calm. She has begun to tremble. But she *must* be calm, it is all so absurd.

On their way up to Room 302 (the elevator is out of commission or perhaps there is no elevator, they must take the fire stairs, Rose is fetchingly dizzy and her escort must loop his arm around her) she tells Joe Pye that she didn't deserve to win at bingo and really should give the $100 back or perhaps to Lobelia (but she doesn't know Lobelia's last name!—what a pity) because it was really Lobelia's card that won, not hers. Joe Pye nods though he doesn't appear to understand. As he unlocks his door Rose begins an incoherent story, or is it a confession, about something she did when she was eleven years old and never told anyone about, and Joe Pye leads her into the room, and switches on the lights with a theatrical flourish, and even the television set, though the next moment he switches the set off. Rose is blinking at the complex undulating stripes in the carpet, which are very like snakes, and in a blurry voice she concludes her confession: ". . . she was so popular and so pretty and I hated her, I used to leave for school ahead of her and slow down so she'd catch up, and sometimes that worked, and sometimes it didn't, I just hated her, I bought a valentine, one of those joke valentines, it was about a foot high and glossy and showed some kind of an idiot on the cover, *Mother loved me*, it said, and when you opened it, *but she died*, so I sent it to Sandra, because her mother had died . . . when we were in fifth grade . . . and . . . and . . ."

Joe Pye unclips the golden cock, and undoes his turban, which is impressively long. Rose, her lips grinning, fumbles with the first button of her dress. It is a small button, cloth-covered, and resists her efforts to push it through the hole. But then she gets it through, and stands there panting.

She will think of it, *I must think of it*, as an impersonal event, bodily but not spiritual, *like a gynecological examination*. But then Rose hates those gynecological examinations. Hates and dreads them, and puts them off, canceling appointments at the last minute. *It will serve me right*, she often thinks, *if . . .* But her mother's cancer was elsewhere. Elsewhere in her body, and then everywhere. Perhaps there is no connection.

Joe Pye's skull is covered by mossy, obviously very thick, but close-clipped dark hair; he must have shaved his head a while back and now it is growing unevenly out. The ruddy tan ends at his hairline, where his skin is paste-white as Rose's. He smiles at Rose, fondly and inquisitively and with an abrupt unflinching gesture he rips off the goatee. Rose draws in her breath, shocked.

"But what are *you* doing, Olivia?" he asks.

The floor tilts suddenly so that there is the danger she will fall, stumble into his arms. She takes a step backward. Her weight forces the floor down, keeps it in place. Nervously, angrily, she tears at the prim little ugly buttons on her dress. "I—I'm—I'm hurrying the best I can," she mutters.

Joe Pye rubs at his chin, which is pinkened and somewhat raw-looking, and stares at Rose Mallow Odom. Even without his majestic turban and his goatee he is a striking picture of a man; he holds himself well, his shoulders somewhat raised. He stares at Rose as if he cannot believe what he is seeing.

"Olivia?" he says.

She yanks at the front of her dress and a button pops off, it is hilarious but there's no time to consider it, something is wrong, the dress won't come off, she sees that the belt is still tightly buckled and of course the dress won't come off, if only that idiot wouldn't stare at her, sobbing with frustration she pulls her straps off her skinny shoulders and bares her chest, her tiny breasts, Rose Mallow Odom, who had for years cowered in the girls' locker room at the public school, burning with shame, for the very thought of her body filled her with shame, and now she is contemptuously stripping before a stranger who gapes at her as if he has never seen anything like her before.

"But Olivia what are you *doing?* . . ." he says.

His question is both alarmed and formal. Rose wipes tears out of her eyes and looks at him, baffled.

"But Olivia people don't *do* like this, not this way, not so fast and angry," Joe Pye says. His eyebrows arch, his eyes narrow with disapproval; his stance radiates great dignity. "I think you must have misunderstood the nature of my proposal."

"What do you mean, people don't *do* . . . What people . . ." Rose whimpers. She must blink rapidly to keep him in focus but the tears keep springing into her eyes and running down her cheeks, they will leave rivulets in her matte makeup which she lavishly if contemptuously applied many hours ago, something has gone wrong, something has gone terribly wrong, why is that idiot staring at her with such pity?

"Decent people," Joe Pye says slowly.

"But I—I—"

"*Decent* people," he says, his voice lowered, one corner of his mouth lifted in a tiny ironic dimple.

Rose has begun to shiver despite the golden-glowing burn in her throat. Her breasts are bluish-white, the pale-brown nipples have

gone hard with fear. Fear and cold and clarity. She tries to shield
herself from Joe Pye's glittering gaze with her arms, but she cannot:
he sees everything. The floor is tilting again, with maddening slow-
ness. She will topple forward if it doesn't stop. She will fall into his
arms no matter how she resists, leaning her weight back on her shaky
heels.

"But I thought—Don't you—Don't you want—?" she whispers.

Joe Pye draws himself up to his fullest height. He is really a
giant of a man: the Bingo Master in his silver tunic and black wide-
legged trousers, the rashlike shadow of the goatee framing his small
angry smile, his eyes narrowed with disgust. Rose begins to cry as
he shakes his head No. And again No. No.

She weeps, she pleads with him, she is stumbling dizzily forward. Something has gone wrong and she cannot comprehend it. In
her head things ran their inevitable way, she had already chosen the
cold clever words that would most winningly describe them, but
Joe Pye knows nothing of her plans, knows nothing of her words,
cares nothing for *her*.

"No!" he say sharply, striking out at her.

She must have fallen toward him, her knees must have buckled,
for suddenly he has grasped her by her naked shoulders and, his face
darkened with blood, he is shaking her violently. Her head whips
back and forth. Against the bureau, against the wall, so sudden, so
hard, the back of her head striking the wall, her teeth rattling, her
eyes wide and blind in their sockets.

"No no no no *no*."

Suddenly she is on the floor, something has struck the right side
of her mouth, she is staring up through layers of agitated air to a
bullet-headed man with wet mad eyes whom she has never seen
before. The naked lightbulb screwed into the ceiling socket, so far
far away, burns with the power of a bright blank blinding sun behind his skull.

"But I—I thought—" she whispers.

"Prancing into Joe Pye's Bingo Hall and defiling it, prancing
up *here* and defiling my room, what have you got to say for yourself,
miss!" Joe Pye says, hauling her to her feet. He tugs her dress up

and walks her roughly to the door, grasping her by the shoulders
again and squeezing her hard, hard, without the slightest ounce of
affection or courtesy, why he doesn't care for her at all!—and then
she is out in the corridor, her patent-leather purse tossed after her,
and the door to 302 is slammed shut.

It has all happened so quickly. Rose cannot comprehend; she
stares at the door as if expecting it to be opened. But it remains
closed. Far down the hall someone opens a door and pokes his head
out and, seeing her in her disarray, quickly closes *that* door as well.
So Rose is left completely alone.

She is too numb to feel much pain: only the pin-prickish sensation in her jaw, and the throbbing in her shoulders where Joe
Pye's ghost-fingers still squeeze with such strength. Why, he didn't
care for her at all. . . .

Weaving down the corridor like a drunken woman, one hand
holding her ripped dress shut, one hand pressing the purse clumsily
against her side. Weaving and staggering and muttering to herself
like a drunken woman. She *is* a drunken woman. "What do you
mean, people—*What* people—"

If only he had cradled her in his arms! If only he had loved her!

On the first landing of the fire stairs she grows very dizzy suddenly, and thinks it wisest to sit down. To sit down at once. Her
head is drumming with a pulsebeat she can't control, she believes
it is maybe the Bingo Master's pulsebeat, and his angry voice too
scrambles about in her head, mixed up with her own thoughts. A
puddle grows at the back of her mouth—she spits out blood,
gagging—and discovers that one of her front teeth has come loose:
one of her front teeth has come loose and the adjacent incisor also
rocks back and forth in its socket.

"Oh Joe Pye," she whispers, "oh dear Christ what have you
done—"

Weeping, sniffing, she fumbles with the fake-gold clasp of her
purse and manages to get the purse open and paws inside, whimpering, to see if—but it's gone—she can't find it—ah; but there it
is: there it is after all, folded small and somewhat crumpled (for
she'd felt such embarrassment, she had stuck it quickly into her

purse): the check for $100. A plain check that should have Joe Pye's large, bold, black signature on it, if only her eyes could focus long enough for her to see.

"Joe Pye, *what* people," she whimpers, blinking. "I never heard of—*What* people, where—?"

The White Cat

There was a gentleman of independent means who, at about the age of fifty-six, conceived of a passionate hatred for his much-younger wife's white Persian cat.

His hatred for the cat was all the more ironic, and puzzling, in that he himself had given the cat to his wife as a kitten, years ago, when they were first married. And he himself had named her—Miranda—after his favorite Shakespearean heroine.

It was ironic, too, in that he was hardly a man given to irrational sweeps of emotion. Except for his wife (whom he'd married late—his first marriage, her second) he did not love anyone very much, and would have thought it beneath his dignity to hate anyone. For whom should he take that seriously? Being a gentleman of independent means allowed him that independence of spirit unknown to the majority of men.

Julius Muir was of slender build, with deep-set somber eyes of no distinctive color; thinning, graying, baby-fine hair; and a narrow, lined face to which the adjective *lapidary* had once been applied, with no vulgar intention of mere flattery. Being of old American stock he was susceptible to none of the fashionable tugs and sways of "identity": He knew who he was, who his ancestors were, and thought the subject of no great interest. His studies both in America and abroad had been undertaken with a dilettante's rather than a scholar's pleasure, but he would not have wished to make too much of them. Life, after all, is a man's primary study.

Fluent in several languages, Mr. Muir had a habit of phrasing his words with inordinate care, as if he were translating them into a common vernacular. He carried himself with an air of discreet self-consciousness that had nothing in it of vanity, or pride, yet did not bespeak a pointless humility. He was a collector (primarily of rare books and coins), but he was certainly not an obsessive collector; he looked upon the fanaticism of certain of his fellows with a bemused disdain. So his quickly blossoming hatred for his wife's beautiful white cat surprised him, and for a time amused him. Or did it frighten him? Certainly he didn't know what to make of it!

The animosity began as an innocent sort of domestic irritation, a half-conscious sense that being so respected in public—so recognized as the person of quality and importance he assuredly was—he should warrant that sort of treatment at home. Not that he was naively ignorant of the fact that cats have a way of making their preferences known that lacks the subtlety and tact devised by human beings. But as the cat grew older and more spoiled and ever more choosy it became evident that she did not, for affection, choose *him*. Alissa was her favorite, of course; then one or another of the help; but it was not uncommon for a stranger, visiting the Muirs for the first time, to win or to appear to win Miranda's capricious heart. "Miranda! Come here!" Mr. Muir might call—gently enough, yet forcibly, treating the animal in fact with a silly sort of deference—but at such times Miranda was likely to regard him with indifferent, unblinking eyes and make no move in his direction. What a fool, she seemed to be saying, to court someone who cares so little for you!

If he tried to lift her in his arms—if he tried, with a show of playfulness, to subdue her—in true cat fashion she struggled to get down with as much violence as if a stranger had seized her. Once as she squirmed out of his grasp, she accidentally raked the back of his hand and drew blood that left a faint stain on the sleeve of his dinner jacket. "Julius, dear, are you hurt?" Alissa asked. "Not at all," Mr. Muir said, dabbing at the scratches with a handkerchief. "I think Miranda is excited because of the company," Alissa said. "You know how sensitive she is." "Indeed I do," Mr. Muir said mildly, winking at their guests. But a pulse beat hard in his head and he was thinking he would like to strangle the cat with his bare hands—were he the kind of man who was capable of such an act.

More annoying still was the routine nature of the cat's aversion to him. When he and Alissa sat together in the evening, reading, each at an end of their sofa, Miranda would frequently leap unbidden into Alissa's lap—but shrink fastidiously from Mr. Muir's very touch. He professed to be hurt. He professed to be amused. "I'm afraid Miranda doesn't like me any longer," he said sadly. (Though in truth he could no longer remember if there'd been a time the creature *had* liked him. When she'd been a kitten, perhaps, and utterly indiscriminate in her affections?) Alissa laughed and said apologetically, "Of course she likes you, Julius," as the car purred loudly and sensuously in her lap. "But—you know how cats are."

"Indeed, I am learning," Mr. Muir said with a stiff little smile.

And he felt he *was* learning—something to which he could give no name.

What first gave him the idea—the fancy, really—of killing Miranda, he could not have afterward said. One day, watching her rubbing about the ankles of a director-friend of his wife's, observing how wantonly she presented herself to an admiring little circle of guests (even people with a general aversion to cats could not resist exclaiming over Miranda—petting her, scratching her behind the ears, cooing over her like idiots), Mr. Muir found himself thinking that, as he had brought the cat into his household of his own volition and had paid a fair amount of money for her, she was his to dispose of as he wished. It was true that the full-blooded Persian was one of the prize possessions of the household—a household in which possessions were not acquired casually or cheaply—and it was true that Alissa adored her. But ultimately she belonged to Mr. Muir. And he alone had the power of life or death over her, did he not?

"What a beautiful animal! Is it a male or a female?"

Mr. Muir was being addressed by one of his guests (in truth, one of Alissa's guests; since returning to her theatrical career she had a new, wide, rather promiscuous circle of acquaintances) and for a moment he could not think how to answer. The question lodged deep in him as if it were a riddle: *Is it a male or a female?*

"Female, of course," Mr. Muir said pleasantly. "Its name after all is Miranda."

He wondered: Should he wait until Alissa began rehearsals for her new play—or should he act quickly, before his resolution faded? (Alissa, a minor but well-regarded actress, was to be an understudy for the female lead in a Broadway play opening in September.) And how should he do it? He could not strangle the cat—could not bring himself to act with such direct and unmitigated brutality—nor was it likely that he could run over her, as if accidentally, with the car. (Though *that* would have been fortuitous, indeed.) One midsummer evening when sly, silky Miranda insinuated herself onto the lap of Alissa's new friend Alban (actor, writer, director; his talents were evidently lavish) the conversation turned to notorious murder cases —to poisons—and Mr. Muir thought simply, *Of course. Poison.*

Next morning he poked about in the gardener's shed and found the remains of a ten-pound sack of grainy white "rodent" poison. The previous autumn they'd had a serious problem with mice, and their gardener had set out poison traps in the attic and basement of the house. (With excellent results, Mr. Muir surmised. At any rate, the mice had certainly disappeared.) What was ingenious about the poison was that it induced extreme thirst—so that after having devoured the bait the poisoned creature was driven to seek water, leaving the house and dying outside. Whether the poison was "merciful" or not, Mr. Muir did not know.

He was able to take advantage of the servants' Sunday night off—for as it turned out, though rehearsals for her play had not yet begun, Alissa was spending several days in the city. So Mr. Muir himself fed Miranda in a corner of the kitchen where she customarily ate—having mashed a generous teaspoon of the poison in with her usual food. (How spoiled the creature was! From the very first, when she was a seven-weeks' kitten, Miranda had been fed a special high-protein, high-vitamin cat food, supplemented by raw chopped liver, chicken giblets, and God knows what all else. Though as he ruefully had to admit, Mr. Muir had had a hand in spoiling her, too.)

Miranda ate the food with her usual finicky greed, not at all conscious of, or grateful for, her master's presence. He might have been one of the servants; he might have been no one at all. If she sensed something out of the ordinary—the fact that her water dish was taken away and not returned, for instance—like a true aristocrat she gave no sign. Had there ever been any creature of his acquaintance, human or otherwise, so supremely complacent as this white Persian cat?

Mr. Muir watched Miranda methodically poison herself with an air not of elation as he'd anticipated, not even with a sense of satisfaction in a wrong being righted, in justice being (however ambiguously) exacted—but with an air of profound regret. That the spoiled creature deserved to die he did not doubt; for after all, what incalculable cruelties, over a lifetime, must a cat inflict on birds, mice, rabbits! But it struck him as a melancholy thing, that *he*, Julius Muir—who had paid so much for her, and who in fact had shared in the pride of her—should find himself out of necessity in the role of executioner. But it was something that had to be done, and though he had perhaps forgotten why it had to be done, he knew that he and he alone was destined to do it.

The other evening a number of guests had come to dinner, and as they were seated on the terrace Miranda leapt whitely up out of nowhere to make her way along the garden wall—plumelike tail erect, silky ruff floating about her high-held head, golden eyes gleaming—quite as if on cue, as Alissa said. "This is Miranda, come to say hello to you! *Isn't* she beautiful!" Alissa happily exclaimed. (For she seemed never to tire of remarking upon her cat's beauty—an innocent sort of narcissism, Mr. Muir supposed.) The usual praise, or flattery, was aired; the cat preened herself—fully conscious of being the center of attention—then leapt away with a violent sort of grace and disappeared down the steep stone steps to the river embankment. Mr. Muir thought then that he understood why Miranda was so uncannily *interesting* as a phenomenon: She represented a beauty that was both purposeless and necessary; a beauty that was (considering her pedigree) completely an artifice, and yet (considering she *was* a thing of flesh and blood) completely natural: Nature.

Though was Nature always and invariably—*natural?*

Now, as the white cat finished her meal (leaving a good quarter of it in the dish, as usual), Mr. Muir said aloud, in a tone in which infinite regret and satisfaction were commingled, "But beauty won't save you."

The cat paused to look up at him with her flat, unblinking gaze. He felt an instant's terror: Did she know? Did she know—already? It seemed to him that she had never looked more splendid: fur so purely, silkily white; ruff full as if recently brushed; the petulant pug face; wide, stiff whiskers; finely shaped ears so intelligently erect. And, of course, the eyes . . .

He'd always been fascinated by Miranda's eyes, which were a tawny golden hue, for they had the mysterious capacity to flare up, as if at will. Seen at night, of course—by way of the moon's reflection, or the headlights of the Muirs' own homebound car—they were lustrous as small beams of light. "Is that Miranda, do you think?" Alissa would ask, seeing the twin flashes of light in the tall grass bordering the road. "Possibly," Mr. Muir would say. "Ah, she's waiting for us! Isn't that sweet! She's waiting for us to come home!" Alissa would exclaim with childlike excitement. Mr. Muir—who doubted that the cat had even been aware of their absence, let alone eagerly awaited their return—said nothing.

Another thing about the cat's eyes that had always seemed to Mr. Muir somehow perverse was the fact that, while the human eyeball is uniformly white and the iris colored, a cat eyeball is colored and the iris purely black. Green, yellow, gray, even blue—the entire eyeball! And the iris so magically responsive to gradations of light or excitation, contracting to razor-thin slits, dilating blackly to fill almost the entire eye. . . . As she stared up at him now her eyes were so dilated their color was nearly eclipsed.

"No, beauty can't save you. It isn't enough," Mr. Muir said quietly. With trembling fingers he opened the screen door to let the cat out into the night. As she passed him—perverse creature, indeed!—she rubbed lightly against his leg as she had not done for many months. Or had it been years?

Alissa was twenty years Mr. Muir's junior but looked even younger: a petite woman with very large, very pretty brown eyes; shoulder-length blond hair; the upbeat if sometimes rather frenetic manner of a well-practiced ingenue. She was a minor actress with a minor ambition—as she freely acknowledged—for after all, serious professional acting is brutally hard work, even if one somehow manages to survive the competition.

"And then, of course, Julius takes such good care of me," she would say, linking her arm through his or resting her head for a moment against his shoulder. "I have everything I want, really, right here. . . ." By which she meant the country place Mr. Muir had bought for her when they were married. (Of course they also kept an apartment in Manhattan, two hours to the south. But Mr. Muir had grown to dislike the city—it abraded his nerves like a cat's claws raking against a screen—and rarely made the journey in any longer.) Under her maiden name, Howth, Alissa had been employed intermittently for eight years before marrying Mr. Muir; her first marriage—contracted at the age of nineteen to a well-known (and notorious) Hollywood actor, since deceased—had been a disaster of which she cared not to speak in any detail. (Nor did Mr. Muir care to question her about those years. It was as if, for him, they had not existed.)

At the time of their meeting Alissa was in temporary retreat, as she called it, from her career. She'd had a small success on Broadway but the success had not taken hold. And was it worth it, really, to keep going, to keep trying? Season after season, the grinding round of auditions, the competition with new faces, "promising" new talents. . . . Her first marriage had ended badly and she'd had a number of love affairs of varying degrees of worth (precisely how many Mr.

Muir was never to learn), and now perhaps it was time to ease into private life. And there was Julius Muir: not young, not particularly charming, but well-to-do, and well-bred, and besotted with love for her, and—*there.*

Of course Mr. Muir was dazzled by her; and he had the time and the resources to court her more assiduously than any man had ever courted her. He seemed to see in her qualities no one else saw; his imagination, for so reticent and subdued a man, was rich, lively to the point of fever, immensely flattering. And he did not mind, he extravagantly insisted, that he loved her more than she loved him—even as Alissa protested she *did* love him—would she consent to marry him otherwise?

For a few years they spoke vaguely of "starting a family," but nothing came of it. Alissa was too busy, or wasn't in ideal health; or they were traveling; or Mr. Muir worried about the unknown effect a child would have upon their marriage. (Alissa would have less time for him, surely?) As time passed he vexed himself with the thought that he'd have no heir when he died—that is, no child of his own—but there was nothing to be done.

They had a rich social life; they were wonderfully *busy* people. And they had, after all, their gorgeous white Persian cat. "Miranda would be traumatized if there was a baby in the household," Alissa said. "We really couldn't do that to her."

"Indeed we couldn't," Mr. Muir agreed.

And then, abruptly, Alissa decided to return to acting. To her "career" as she gravely called it—as if it were a phenomenon apart from her, a force not to be resisted. And Mr. Muir was happy for her—very happy for her. He took pride in his wife's professionalism, and he wasn't at all jealous of her ever-widening circle of friends, acquaintances, associates. He wasn't jealous of her fellow actors and actresses—Rikka, Mario, Robin, Sibyl, Emile, each in turn—and now Alban of the damp dark shiny eyes and quick sweet smile; nor was he jealous of the time she spent away from home; nor, if home, of the time she spent sequestered away in the room they called her studio, deeply absorbed in her work. In her maturity Alissa Howth had acquired a robust sort of good-heartedness that gave her more stage presence even as it relegated her to certain sorts of roles—the roles inevitable, in any case, for older actresses, regardless of their physical beauty. And she'd become a far better, far more subtle actress—as everyone said.

Indeed, Mr. Muir *was* proud of her, and happy for her. And if he felt, now and then, a faint resentment—or, if not quite resentment, a tinge of regret at the way their life had diverged into lives—he was too much a gentleman to show it.

"Where is Miranda? Have you seen Miranda today?"

It was noon, it was four o'clock, it was nearly dusk, and Miranda had not returned. For much of the day Alissa had been preoccupied with telephone calls—the phone seemed always to be ringing—and only gradually had she become aware of the cat's prolonged absence. She went outside to call her; she sent the servants out to look for her. And Mr. Muir, of course, gave his assistance, wandering about the grounds and for some distance into the woods, his hands cupped to his mouth and his voice high-pitched and tremulous: *"Kitty-kitty-kitty-kitty-kitty! Kitty-kitty-kitty—"* How pathetic, how foolish—how futile! Yet it had to be performed since it was what, in innocent circumstances, *would* be performed. Julius Muir, that most solicitous of husbands, tramping through the underbrush looking for his wife's Persian cat. . . .

Poor Alissa! he thought. She'll be heartbroken for days—or would it be weeks?

And he, too, would miss Miranda—as a household presence at the very least. They would have had her, after all, for ten years this autumn.

Dinner that night was subdued, rather leaden. Not simply because Miranda was missing (and Alissa did seem inordinately and genuinely worried), but because Mr. Muir and his wife were dining alone; the table, set for two, seemed almost aesthetically wrong. And how unnatural, the quiet . . . Mr. Muir tried to make conversation but his voice soon trailed off into a guilty silence. Midmeal Alissa rose to accept a telephone call (from Manhattan, of course—her agent, or her director, or Alban, or a female friend—an urgent call, for otherwise Mrs. Muir did not accept calls at this intimate hour) and Mr. Muir—crestfallen, hurt—finished his solitary meal in a kind of trance, tasting nothing. He recalled the night before—the pungent-smelling cat food, the grainy white poison, the way the shrewd animal had looked up at him, and the way she'd brushed against his leg in a belated gesture of . . . was it affection? Reproach? Mockery? He felt a renewed stab of guilt, and an even more powerful stab of visceral satisfaction. Then, glancing up, he chanced to see something white making its careful way along the top of the garden wall. . . .

Of course it was Miranda come home.

He stared, appalled. He stared, speechless—waiting for the apparition to vanish.

Slowly, in a daze, he rose to his feet. In a voice meant to be jubilant he called out the news to Alissa in the adjoining room: "Miranda's come home!"

He called out: "Alissa! Darling! Miranda's come home!"

And there Miranda was, indeed; indeed it *was* Miranda, peering into the dining room from the terrace, her eyes glowing tawny gold. Mr. Muir was trembling, but his brain worked swiftly to absorb the fact, and to construe a logic to accommodate it. She'd vomited up the poison, no doubt. Ah, no doubt! Or, after a cold, damp winter in the gardener's shed, the poison had lost its efficacy.

He had yet to bestir himself, to hurry to unlatch the sliding door and let the white cat in, but his voice fairly quavered with excitement: "Alissa! Good news! Miranda's come home!"

Alissa's joy was so extreme and his own initial relief so genuine that Mr. Muir—stroking Miranda's plume of a tail as Alissa hugged the cat ecstatically in her arms—thought he'd acted cruelly, selfishly—certainly he'd acted out of character—and decided that Miranda, having escaped death at her master's hands, should be granted life. He would *not* try another time.

* * *

Before his marriage at the age of forty-six Julius Muir, like most never-married men and women of a certain temperament—introverted, self-conscious; observers of life rather than participants—had believed that the marital state was unconditionally *marital*; he'd thought that husband and wife were one flesh in more than merely the metaphorical sense of that term. Yet it happened that his own marriage was a marriage of a decidedly diminished sort. Marital relations had all but ceased, and there seemed little likelihood of their being resumed. He would shortly be fifty-seven years old, after all. (Though sometimes he wondered: Was that truly *old*?)

During the first two or three years of their marriage (when Alissa's theatrical career was, as she called it, in eclipse), they had shared a double bed like any married couple—or so Mr. Muir assumed. (For his own marriage had not enlightened him to what "marriage" in a generic sense meant.) With the passage of time, however, Alissa began to complain gently of being unable to sleep because of Mr. Muir's nocturnal "agitation"—twitching, kicking, thrashing about, exclaiming aloud, sometimes even shouting in terror. Wakened by her he would scarcely know, for a moment or two, where he was; he would then apologize profusely and shamefully, and creep away into another bedroom to sleep, if he could, for the rest of the night. Though unhappy with the situation, Mr. Muir was fully sympathetic with Alissa; he even had reason to believe that the poor woman (whose nerves were unusually sensitive) had suffered many a sleepless night on his account without telling him. It was like her to be so considerate; so loath to hurt another's feelings.

As a consequence they developed a cozy routine in which Mr. Muir spent a half-hour or so with Alissa when they first retired for the night; then, taking care not to disturb her, he would tiptoe quietly away into another room, where he might sleep undisturbed. (If, indeed, his occasional nightmares allowed him undisturbed sleep. He rather thought the worst ones, however, were the ones that failed to wake him.)

Yet a further consequence had developed in recent years: Alissa had acquired the habit of staying awake late—reading in bed, or watching television, or even, from time to time, chatting on the telephone—so it was most practical for Mr. Muir simply to kiss her good-night without getting in bed beside her, and then to go off to his own bedroom. Sometimes in his sleep he imagined Alissa was calling him back—awakened, he would hurry out into the darkened corridor to stand by her door for a minute or two, eager and hopeful. At such times he dared not raise his voice above a whisper: "Alissa? Alissa, dearest? Did you call me?"

Just as unpredictable and capricious as Mr. Muir's bad dreams were the nighttime habits of Miranda, who at times would cozily curl up at the foot of Alissa's bed and sleep peacefully through to dawn, but at other times would insist upon being let outside, no matter that Alissa loved her to sleep on the bed. There was comfort of a kind—childish, Alissa granted—in knowing the white Persian was there through the night, and feeling at her feet the cat's warm, solid weight atop the satin coverlet.

But of course, as Alissa acknowledged, a cat can't be forced to do anything against her will. "It seems almost to be a law of nature," she said solemnly.

A few days after the abortive poisoning Mr. Muir was driving home in the early dusk when, perhaps a mile from his estate, he caught sight of the white cat in the road ahead—motionless in the other lane, as if frozen by the car's headlights. Unbidden, the thought came to him: *This is just to frighten her*—and he turned his wheel and headed in her direction. The golden eyes flared up in a blaze of blank surprise—or perhaps it was terror, or recognition— *This is just to redress the balance*, Mr. Muir thought as he pressed down harder on the accelerator and drove directly at the white Persian— and struck her, just as she started to bolt toward the ditch, with the front left wheel of his car. There was a thud and a cat's yowling, incredulous scream—and it was done.

My God! It *was* done!

Dry mouthed, shaking, Mr. Muir saw in his rearview mirror the broken white form in the road; saw a patch of liquid crimson blossoming out around it. He had not meant to kill Miranda, and yet he had actually done it this time—without premeditation, and therefore without guilt.

And now the deed was done forever.

"And no amount of remorse can undo it," he said in a slow, wondering voice.

Mr. Muir had driven to the village to pick up a prescription for Alissa at the drugstore—she'd been in the city on theater matters; had returned home late on a crowded commuter train and gone at once to lie down with what threatened to be a migraine headache. Now he felt rather a hypocrite, a brute, presenting headache tablets to his wife with the guilty knowledge that if she knew what he'd done, the severity of her migraine would be tenfold. Yet how could he have explained to her that he had not meant to kill Miranda this time, but the steering wheel of his car had seemed to act of its own volition, wresting itself from his grip? For so Mr. Muir—speeding home, still trembling and excited as though he himself had come close to violent death—remembered the incident.

He remembered too the cat's hideous scream, cut off almost at once by the impact of the collision—but not quite at once.

And was there a dent in the fender of the handsome, English-built car? There was not.

And were there bloodstains on the left front tire? There were not.

Was there in fact any sign of a mishap, even of the mildest, most innocent sort? There was not.

"No proof! No proof!" Mr. Muir told himself happily, taking the stairs to Alissa's room two at a time. It was a matter of some relief as well when he raised his hand to knock at the door to hear that Alissa was evidently feeling better. She was on the telephone, talking animatedly with someone; even laughing in her light, silvery way that reminded him of nothing so much as wind chimes on a mild summer's night. His heart swelled with love and gratitude. "Dear Alissa—we will be so happy from now on!"

* * *

Then it happened, incredibly, that at about bedtime the white cat showed up again. *She had not died after all.*

Mr. Muir, who was sharing a late-night brandy with Alissa in her bedroom, was the first to see Miranda: she had climbed up onto the roof—by way, probably, of a rose trellis she often climbed for that purpose—and now her pug face appeared at one of the windows in a hideous repetition of the scene some nights ago. Mr. Muir sat paralyzed with shock, and it was Alissa who jumped out of bed to let the cat in.

"Miranda! What a trick! What *are* you up to?"

Certainly the cat had not been missing for any worrisome period of time, yet Alissa greeted her with as much enthusiasm as if she had. And Mr. Muir—his heart pounding in his chest and his very soul convulsed with loathing—was obliged to go along with the charade. He hoped Alissa would not notice the sick terror that surely shone in his eyes.

The cat he'd struck with his car must have been another cat, not Miranda. . . . Obviously it had not been Miranda. Another white Persian with tawny eyes, and not his own.

Alissa cooed over the creature, and petted her, and encouraged her to settle down on the bed for the night, but after a few minutes Miranda jumped down and scratched to be let out the door: She'd missed her supper; she was hungry; she'd had enough of her mistress's affection. Not so much as a glance had she given her master, who was staring at her with revulsion. He knew now that he *must* kill her—if only to prove he could do it.

Following this episode the cat shrewdly avoided Mr. Muir—not out of lazy indifference, as in the past, but out of a sharp sense of their altered relations. She could not be conscious, he knew, of the fact that he had tried to kill her—but she must have been able to sense it. Perhaps she had been hiding in the bushes by the road and had seen him aim his car at her unfortunate doppelgänger, and run it down. . . .

This was unlikely, Mr. Muir knew. Indeed, it was highly improbable. But how otherwise to account for the creature's behavior in his presence—her demonstration, or simulation, of animal fear? Leaping atop a cabinet when he entered a room, as if to get out of his way; leaping atop a fireplace mantel (and sending, it seemed deliberately, one of his carved jade figurines to the hearth, where it shattered into a dozen pieces); skittering gracelessly through a doorway, her sharp toenails clicking against the hardwood floor. When, without intending to, he approached her out-of-doors, she was likely to scamper noisily up one of the rose trellises, or the grape arbor, or a tree; or run off into the shrubbery like a wild creature. If Alissa happened to be present she was invariably astonished, for the cat's behavior *was* senseless. "Do you think Miranda is ill?" she asked. "Should we take her to the veterinarian?" Mr. Muir said uneasily that he doubted they would be able to catch her for such a purpose—at least, he doubted *he* could.

He had an impulse to confess his crime, or his attempted crime, to Alissa. He had killed the hateful creature—*and she had not died.*

One night at the very end of August Mr. Muir dreamt of glaring, disembodied eyes. And in their centers those black, black irises like old-fashioned keyholes: slots opening into the Void. He could not move to protect himself. A warm, furry weight settled luxuriantly upon his chest . . . upon his very face! The cat's whiskery white muzzle pressed against his mouth in a hellish kiss and in an instant the breath was being sucked from him. . . .

"Oh, no! Save me! Dear God—"

The damp muzzle against his mouth, sucking his life's breath from him, and he could not move to tear it away—his arms, leaden at his sides; his entire body struck dumb, paralyzed . . .

"Save me . . . *save me!*"

His shouting, his panicked thrashing about in the bedclothes, woke him. Though he realized at once it had been only a dream, his breath still came in rapid, shallow gasps, and his heart hammered so violently he was in terror of dying: Had not his doctor only the other week spoken gravely to him of imminent heart disease, the possibility of heart failure? And how mysterious it was, his blood pressure being so very much higher than ever before in his life. . . .

Mr. Muir threw himself out of the damp, tangled bedclothes and switched on a lamp with trembling fingers. Thank God he was alone and Alissa had not witnessed this latest display of nerves!

"Miranda?" he whispered. "Are you in here?"

He switched on an overhead light. The bedroom shimmered with shadows and did not seem, for an instant, any room he knew.

"Miranda . . . ?"

The sly, wicked creature! The malevolent beast! To think that cat's muzzle had touched his very lips, the muzzle of an animal that devoured mice, rats—any sort of foul filthy thing out in the woods! Mr. Muir went into his bathroom and rinsed out his mouth even as he told himself calmly that the dream had been only a dream, and the cat only a phantasm, and that of course Miranda was *not* in his room.

Still, she had settled her warm, furry, unmistakable weight on his chest. She had attempted to suck his breath from him, to choke him, suffocate him, stop his poor heart. *It was within her power.* "Only a dream," Mr. Muir said aloud, smiling shakily at his reflection in the mirror. (Oh! To think that pale, haggard apparition was indeed *his* . . .) Mr. Muir raised his voice with scholarly precision. "A foolish dream. A child's dream. A woman's dream."

Back in his room he had the fleeting sense that something—a vague white shape—had just now scampered beneath his bed. But when he got down on his hands and knees to look, of course there was nothing.

He did, however, discover in the deep-pile carpet a number of cat hairs. White, rather stiff—quite clearly Miranda's. Ah, quite clearly. "Here's the evidence!" he said excitedly. He found a light scattering of them on the carpet near the door and, nearer his bed, a good deal more—as if the creature had lain there for a while and had even rolled over (as Miranda commonly did out on the terrace in the sun) and stretched her graceful limbs in an attitude of utterly pleasurable abandon. Mr. Muir had often been struck by the cat's remarkable *luxuriance* at such times: a joy of flesh (and fur) he could not begin to imagine. Even before relations between them had deteriorated, he had felt the impulse to hurry to the cat and bring the heel of his shoe down hard on that tender, exposed, pinkish-pale belly. . . .

"Miranda? Where are you? Are you still in here?" Mr. Muir said. He was breathless, excited. He'd been squatting on his haunches for some minutes, and when he tried to straighten up his legs ached.

Mr. Muir searched the room, but it was clear that the white cat had gone. He went out onto his balcony, leaned against the railing, blinked into the dimly moonlit darkness, but could see nothing— in his fright he'd forgotten to put on his glasses. For some minutes he breathed in the humid, sluggish night air in an attempt to calm himself, but it soon became apparent that something was wrong. Some vague murmurous undertone of—was it a voice? Voices?

Then he saw it: the ghostly white shape down in the shrubbery. Mr. Muir blinked and stared, but his vision was unreliable. "Miranda . . . ?" A scuttling noise rustled above him and he turned to see another white shape on the sharp-slanted roof making its rapid way over the top. He stood absolutely motionless—whether out of terror or cunning, he could not have said. That there was more than one white cat, more than one white Persian—more, in fact, than *merely one Miranda*—was a possibility he had not considered! "Yet perhaps that explains it," he said. He was badly frightened, but his brain functioned as clearly as ever.

It was not so very late, scarcely 1:00 a.m. The undertone Mr. Muir heard was Alissa's voice, punctuated now and then by her light, silvery laughter. One might almost think there was someone in the bedroom with her—but of course she was merely having a late-night telephone conversation, very likely with Alban—they would be chatting companionably, with an innocent sort of malice, about their co-actors and -actresses, mutual friends and acquaintances. Alissa's balcony opened out onto the same side of the house that Mr. Muir's did, which accounted for her voice (or *was* it voices? Mr. Muir listened, bemused) carrying so clearly. No light irradiated from her room; she must have been having her telephone conversation in the dark.

Mr. Muir waited another few minutes, but the white shape down in the shrubbery had vanished. And the slate-covered roof overhead was empty, reflecting moonlight in dull, uneven patches. He was alone. He decided to go back to bed but before doing so he checked carefully to see that he *was* alone. He locked all the windows, and the door, and slept with the lights on—but so deeply and with such grateful abandon that in the morning, it was Alissa's rapping on the door that woke him. "Julius? Julius? Is something wrong, dear?" she cried. He saw with astonishment that it was *nearly noon*: he'd slept four hours past his usual rising time!

Alissa said good-bye to him hurriedly. A limousine was coming to carry her to the city; she was to be away for several nights in succession; she was concerned about him, about his health, and hoped there was nothing wrong. . . . "Of course there is nothing wrong," Mr. Muir said irritably. Having slept so late in the day left him feeling sluggish and confused; it had not at all refreshed him. When Alissa kissed him good-bye he seemed rather to suffer the kiss than to participate in it, and after she had gone he had to resist an impulse to wipe his mouth with the back of his hand.

"God help us!" he whispered.

By degrees, as a consequence of his troubled mind, Mr. Muir had lost interest in collecting. When an antiquarian bookdealer offered him a rare octavo edition of the *Directorium Inquisitorum* he felt only the mildest tinge of excitement, and allowed the treasure to be snatched up by a rival collector. Only a few days afterward he responded with even less enthusiasm when offered the chance to bid on a quarto Gothic edition of Machiavelli's *Belfagor*. "Is something wrong, Mr. Muir?" the dealer asked him. (They had been doing business together for a quarter of a century.) Mr. Muir said ironically, "*Is* something wrong?" and broke off the telephone connection. He was never to speak to the man again.

Yet more decisively, Mr. Muir had lost interest in financial affairs. He would not accept telephone calls from the various Wall Street gentlemen who managed his money; it was quite enough for him to know that the money was there and would always be there. Details regarding it struck him as tiresome and vulgar.

In the third week of September the play in which Alissa was an understudy opened to superlative reviews, which meant a good, long run. Though the female lead was in excellent health and showed little likelihood of ever missing a performance, Alissa felt obliged to remain in the city a good deal, sometimes for a full week at a time. (What she did there, how she busied herself day after day, evening after evening, Mr. Muir did not know and was too proud to ask.) When she invited him to join her for a weekend (why didn't he visit some of his antiquarian dealers, as he used to do with such pleasure?) Mr. Muir said simply, "But why, when I have all I require for happiness here in the country?"

Since the night of the attempted suffocation Mr. Muir and Miranda were yet more keenly aware of each other. No longer did the white cat flee his presence; rather, as if in mockery of him, she held her ground when he entered a room. If he approached her she eluded him only at the last possible instant, often flattening herself close against the floor and scampering, snakelike, away. He cursed her; she bared her teeth and hissed. He laughed loudly to show her how very little he cared; she leapt atop a cabinet, our of his reach, and settled into a cat's blissful sleep. Each evening Alissa called at an appointed hour; each evening she inquired after Miranda, and Mr. Muir would say, "Beautiful and healthy as ever! A pity you can't see her!"

With the passage of time Miranda grew bolder and more reckless—misjudging, perhaps, the quickness of her master's reflexes. She sometimes appeared underfoot, nearly tripping him on the stairs or as he left the house; she dared approach him as he stood with a potential weapon in hand—a carving knife, a poker, a heavy, leatherbound book. Once or twice, as Mr. Muir sat dreaming through one of his solitary meals, she even leapt onto his lap and scampered across the dining room table, upsetting dishes and glasses.

"Devil!" he shrieked, swiping in her wake with his fists. "What do you want of me!"

He wondered what tales the servants told of him, whispered backstairs. He wondered if any were being relayed to Alissa in the city.

One night, however, Miranda made a tactical error, and Mr. Muir did catch hold of her. She had slipped into his study—where he sat examining some of his rarest and most valuable coins (Mesopotamian, Etruscan) by lamplight—having calculated, evidently, on making her escape by way of the door. But Mr. Muir, leaping from his chair with extraordinary, almost feline swiftness, managed to kick the door shut. And now what a chase! What a struggle! What a mad frolic! Mr. Muir caught hold of the animal, lost her, caught hold of her again, lost her; she raked him viciously on the backs of both hands and on his face; he managed to catch hold of her again, slamming her against the wall and closing his bleeding fingers around her throat. He squeezed, he squeezed! He had her now and no force on earth could make him release her! As the cat screamed and clawed and kicked and thrashed and seemed to be suffering the convulsions of death, Mr. Muir crouched over her with eyes bulging and mad as her own. The arteries in his forehead visibly throbbed. "Now! Now I have you! Now!" he cried. And at that very moment when, surely, the white Persian was on the verge of extinction, the door to Mr. Muir's study was flung open and one of the servants appeared, white faced and incredulous: "Mr. Muir? What is it? We heard such—" the fool was saying; and of course Miranda slipped from Mr. Muir's loosened grasp and bolted from the room.

After that incident Mr. Muir seemed resigned to the knowledge that he would never have such an opportunity again. The end was swiftly approaching.

It happened quite suddenly, in the second week of November, that Alissa returned home.

She had quit the play; she had quit the "professional stage"; she did not even intend, as she told her husband vehemently, to visit New York City for a long time.

He saw to his astonishment that she'd been crying. Her eyes were unnaturally bright and seemed smaller than he recalled. And her prettiness looked worn, as if another face—harder, of smaller dimensions—were pushing through. Poor Alissa! She had gone away with such hope! When Mr. Muir moved to embrace her, however, meaning to comfort her, she drew away from him; her very nostrils pinched as if she found the smell of him offensive. "Please," she said, not looking him in the eye. "I don't feel well. What I want most is to be alone . . . just to be alone."

She retired to her room, to her bed. For several days she remained sequestered there, admitting only one of the female servants and, of course, her beloved Miranda, when Miranda condescended to visit the house. (To his immense relief Mr. Muir observed that the white cat showed no sign of their recent struggle. His lacerated hands and face were slow to heal, but in her own grief and self-absorption, Alissa seemed not to have noticed.)

In her room, behind her locked door, Alissa made a number of telephone calls to New York City. Often she seemed to be weeping over the phone. But so far as Mr. Muir could determine—being forced, under these special circumstances, to eavesdrop on the line —none of her conversations were with Alban.

Which meant . . . ? He had to confess he had no idea: nor could he ask Alissa. For that would give away the fact that he'd been eavesdropping, and she would be deeply shocked.

Mr. Muir sent small bouquets of autumn flowers to Alissa's sickroom; bought her chocolates and bonbons, slender volumes of poetry, a new diamond bracelet. Several times he presented himself at her door, ever the eager suitor, but she explained that she was not prepared to see him just yet—not just yet. Her voice was shrill and edged with a metallic tone Mr. Muir had not heard before.

"Don't you love me, Alissa?" he cried suddenly.

There was a moment's embarrassed silence. Then: "Of course I do. But please go away and leave me alone."

So worried was Mr. Muir about Alissa that he could no longer sleep for more than an hour or two at a time, and these hours were characterized by tumultuous dreams. The white cat! The hideous smothering weight! Fur in his very mouth! Yet awake he thought only of Alissa and of how, though she had come home to him, it was not in fact to *him*.

He lay alone in his solitary bed, amidst the tangled bedclothes, weeping hoarsely. One morning he stroked his chin and touched bristles: He'd neglected to shave for several days.

From his balcony he chanced to see the white cat preening atop the garden wall, a larger creature than he recalled. She had fully recovered from his attack. (If, indeed, she had been injured by it. If, indeed, the cat on the garden wall was the selfsame cat that had blundered into his study.) Her white fur very nearly blazed in the sun; her eyes were miniature golden-glowing coals set deep in her skull. Mr. Muir felt a mild shock seeing her: What a beautiful creature!

Though in the next instant, of course, he realized what she was.

One rainy, gusty evening in late November Mr. Muir was driving on the narrow blacktop road above the river, Alissa silent at his side—stubbornly silent, he thought. She wore a black cashmere cloak and a hat of soft black felt that fitted her head tightly, covering most of her hair. These were items of clothing Mr. Muir had not seen before, and in their stylish austerity they suggested the growing distance between them. When he had helped her into the car she'd murmured "thank you" in a tone that indicated "Oh! Must you touch me?" And Mr. Muir had made a mocking little bow, standing bare-headed in the rain.

And I had loved you so much.

Now she did not speak. Sat with her lovely profile turned from him. As if she were fascinated by the lashing rain, the river pocked and heaving below, the gusts of wind that rocked the English-built car as Mr. Muir pressed his foot ever harder on the gas pedal. "It will be better this way, my dear wife," Mr. Muir said quietly. "Even if you love no other man, it is painfully clear that you do not love me." At these solemn words Alissa

started guiltily, but still would not face him. "My dear? Do you under-
stand? It will be better this way—do not be frightened." As Mr. Muir
drove faster, as the car rocked more violently in the wind, Alissa pressed her
hands against her mouth as if to stifle any protest; she was staring
transfixed—as Mr. Muir stared transfixed—at the rushing pavement.

Only when Mr. Muir bravely turned the car's front wheels in the di-
rection of a guardrail did her resolve break: she emitted a series of breathless
little screams, shrinking back against the seat, but made no effort to seize
his arm or the wheel. And in an instant all was over, in any case—the
car crashed through the railing, seemed to spin in midair, dropped to the
rock-strewn hillside and bursting into flame, turned end over end . . .

He was seated in a chair with wheels—a wheeled chair! It
seemed to him a remarkable invention and he wondered whose in-
genuity lay behind it.

Though he had not the capacity, being almost totally paralyzed,
to propel it of his own volition.

And, being blind, he had no volition in any case! He was quite
content to stay where he was, so long as it was out of the draft. (The
invisible room in which he now resided was, for the most part, cozily
heated—his wife had seen to that—but there yet remained unpredictable currents of cold air that assailed him from time to time.
His bodily temperature, he feared, could not maintain its integrity
against any sustained onslaught.)

He had forgotten the names for many things and felt no great
grief. Indeed, not knowing *names* relaxes one's desire for the *things*
that, ghostlike, forever unattainable, dwell behind them. And of
course his blindness had much to do with this—for which he was
grateful! Quite grateful!

Blind, yet not wholly blind: for he could see (indeed, could not
not see) washes of white, gradations of white, astonishing subtleties
of white like rivulets in a stream perpetually breaking and falling
about his head, not distinguished by any form or outline or vulgar
suggestion of an object in space. . . .

He had had, evidently, a number of operations. How many he

did not know; nor did he care to know. In recent weeks they had spoken earnestly to him of the possibility of yet another operation on his brain, the (hypothetical) object being, if he understood correctly, the restoration of his ability to move some of the toes on his left foot. Had he the capacity to laugh he would have laughed, but perhaps his dignified silence was preferable.

Alissa's sweet voice joined with the others in a chorus of bleak enthusiasm, but so far as he knew the operation had never taken place. Or if it had, it had not been a conspicuous success. The toes of his left foot were as remote and lost to him as all the other parts of his body.

"How lucky you were, Julius, that another car came along! Why, you might have *died*!"

It seemed that Julius Muir had been driving alone in a violent thunderstorm on the narrow River Road, high above the embankment; uncharacteristically, he'd been driving at a high speed; he'd lost control of his car, crashed through the inadequate guardrail, and over the side . . . "miraculously" thrown clear of the burning wreckage. Two-thirds of the bones in his slender body broken, skull severely fractured, spinal column smashed, a lung pierced. . . . So the story of how Julius had come to this place, his final resting place, this place of milk-white peace, emerged, in fragments shattered and haphazard as those of a smashed windshield.

"Julius, dear? Are you awake, or—?" The familiar, resolutely cheerful voice came to him out of the mist, and he tried to attach a name to it, *Alissa?* or, no, *Miranda?*—which?

There was talk (sometimes in his very hearing) that, one day, some degree of his vision might be restored. But Julius Muir scarcely heard, or cared. He lived for those days when, waking from a doze, he would feel a certain furry, warm weight lowered into his lap—"Julius, dear, someone very special has come to visit!"—soft, yet surprisingly heavy; heated, yet not disagreeably so; initially a bit restless (as a cat must circle fussily about, trying to determine the ideal position before she settles herself down), yet within a few minutes quite wonderfully relaxed, kneading her claws gently against his limbs and purring as she drifted into a companionable sleep. He would have liked to see, beyond the shimmering watery whiteness of his vision, her particular whiteness; certainly he would have liked to feel once again the softness, the astonishing silkiness, of that fur. But he could hear the deep-throated melodic purring. He could feel, to a degree, her warmly pulsing weight, the wonder of her mysterious *livingness* against his—for which he was infinitely grateful.

"My love!"

PART

II

The Model

1. The Approach of Mr. Starr

Had he stepped out of nowhere, or had he been watching her for some time, even more than he'd claimed, and for a different purpose?—she shivered to think that, yes, probably, she had many times glimpsed him in the village, or in the park, without really seeing him: him, and the long gleaming black limousine she would not have known to associate with him even had she noticed him: the man who called himself Mr. Starr.

As, each day, her eyes passed rapidly and lightly over any number of people both familiar to her and strangers, blurred as in the background of a film in which the foreground is the essential reality, the very point of the film.

She was seventeen. It was in fact the day after her birthday, a bright gusty January day, and she'd been running in the late afternoon, after school, in the park overlooking the ocean, and she'd just turned to head toward home, pausing to wipe her face, adjust her damp cotton headband, feeling the accelerated strength of her heartbeat and the pleasant ache of her leg muscles: and she glanced up, shy, surprised, and there he stood, a man she had never knowingly seen before. He was smiling at her, his smile broad and eager, hopeful, and he stood in such a way, leaning lightly on a cane, as to block her way on the path; yet tentatively too, with a gentlemanly, deferential air, so as to suggest that he meant no threat. When he spoke, his voice sounded hoarse as if from disuse. "Excuse me!— Hello! Young lady! I realize that this is abrupt, and an intrusion on your privacy, but I am an artist, and I am looking for a model, and I wonder if you might be interested in posing for me? Only here, I mean, in the park—in full daylight! I am willing to pay, per hour—"

Sybil stared at the man. Like most young people she was incapable of estimating ages beyond thirty-five—this strange person might have been in his forties, or well into his fifties. His thin, lank hair was the color of antique silver—perhaps he was even older. His skin was luridly pale, grainy, and rough; he wore glasses with lenses so darkly tinted as to suggest the kind of glasses worn by the blind; his clothes were plain, dark, conservative—a tweed jacket that fitted him loosely, a shirt buttoned tight to the neck, and no tie, highly polished black leather shoes in an outmoded style. There was something hesitant, even convalescent in his manner, as if, like numerous others in this coastal Southern California town with its population of the retired, the elderly, and the infirm, he had learned by experience to carry himself with care; he could not entirely trust the earth to support him. His features were refined, but worn; subtly distorted, as if seen through wavy glass, or water.

Sybil didn't like it that she couldn't see the man's eyes. Except to know that he was squinting at her, hard. The skin at the corners of his eyes was whitely puckered as if, in his time, he'd done a good deal of squinting and smiling.

Quickly, but politely, Sybil murmured, "No, thank you, I can't."

She was turning away, but still the man spoke, apologetically, "I realize this is a—surprise, but, you see, I don't know how else to make inquiries. I've only just begun sketching in the park, and—"

"Sorry!"

Sybil turned, began to run, not hurriedly, by no means in a panic, but at her usual measured pace, her head up and her arms swinging at her sides. She was, for all that she looked younger than her seventeen years, not an easily frightened girl, and she was not frightened now; but her face burned with embarrassment. She hoped that no one in the park who knew her had been watching—Glencoe was a small town, and the high school was about a mile away. Why had that preposterous man approached *her*!

He was calling after her, probably waving his cane after her— she didn't dare look back. "I'll be here tomorrow! My name is Starr! Don't judge me too quickly—please! I'm true to my word! My name is Starr! I'll pay you, per hour—" and here he cited an exorbitant sum, nearly twice what Sybil made babysitting or working as a librarian's assistant at the branch library near her home, when she could get hired.

She thought, astonished, "He must be mad!"

2. The Temptation

No sooner had Sybil Blake escaped from the man who called himself Starr, running up Buena Vista Boulevard to Santa Clara, up Santa Clara to Meridian, and so to home, than she began to consider that Mr. Starr's offer was, if preposterous, very tempting. She had never modeled of course but, in art class at the high school, some of her classmates had modeled, fully clothed, just sitting or standing about in ordinary poses, and she and others had sketched them, or tried to—it was really not so easy as it might seem, sketching the lineaments of the human figure; it was still more difficult, sketching an individual's face. But modeling, in itself, was effortless, once you overcame the embarrassment of being stared at. It was, you might argue, a morally neutral activity.

What had Mr. Starr said—*Only here, in the park. In full daylight. I'm true to my word!*

And Sybil needed money, for she was saving for college; she was hoping, too, to attend a summer music institute at U.C. Santa Barbara. (She was a voice student, and she'd been encouraged by her choir director at the high school to get good professional training.)

Her Aunt Lora Dell Blake, with whom she lived, and had lived since
the age of two years eight months, was willing to pay her way—
was determined to pay her way—but Sybil felt uneasy about accepting money from Aunt Lora, who worked as a physical therapist
at a medical facility in Glencoe, and whose salary, at the top of the
pay structure available to her as a state employee, was still modest
by California standards. Sybil reasoned that her Aunt Lora Dell could
not be expected to support her forever.

A long time ago, Sybil had lost her parents, both of them together, in one single cataclysmic hour, when she'd been too young
to comprehend what Death was, or was said to be. They had died
in a boating accident on Lake Champlain, Sybil's mother at the age
of twenty-six, Sybil's father at the age of thirty-one, very attractive
young people, a "popular couple" as Aunt Lora spoke of them, choosing her words with care, and saying very little more. *For why ask,*
Aunt Lora seemed to be warning Sybil—*you will only make yourself
cry.* As soon as she could manage the move, and as soon as Sybil was
placed permanently in her care, Aunt Lora had come to California,
to this sun-washed coastal town midway between Santa Monica and
Santa Barbara. Glencoe was less conspicuously affluent than either
of these towns, but, with its palm-lined streets, its sunny placidity,
and its openness to the ocean, it was the very antithesis, as Aunt
Lora said, of Wellington, Vermont, where the Blakes had lived for
generations. (After their move to California, Lora Dell Blake had
formally adopted Sybil as her child: thus Sybil's name was "Blake,"
as her mother's had been. If asked what her father's name had been,
Sybil would have had to think before recalling, dimly, "Conte.")
Aunt Lora spoke so negatively of New England in general and Vermont in particular, Sybil felt no nostalgia for it; she had no senti-
mental desire to visit her birthplace, not even to see her parents'
graves. From Aunt Lora's stories, Sybil had the idea that Vermont
was damp and cold twelve months of the year, and frigidly, impos-
sibly cold in winter; its wooded mountains were unlike the beautiful
snow-capped mountains of the West, and cast shadows upon its
small, cramped, depopulated and impoverished old towns. Aunt
Lora, a transplanted New Englander, was vehement in her praise of

California—"With the Pacific Ocean to the west," she said, "it's like a room with one wall missing. Your instinct is to look out, not back; and it's a good instinct."

Lora Dell Blake was the sort of person who delivered statements with an air of inviting contradiction. But, tall, rangy, restless, belligerent, she was not the sort of person most people wanted to contradict.

Indeed, Aunt Lora had never encouraged Sybil to ask questions about her dead parents, or about the tragic accident that had killed them; if she had photographs, snapshots, mementos of life back in Wellington, Vermont, they were safely hidden away, and Sybil had not seen them. "It would just be too painful," she told Sybil, "—for us both." The remark was both a plea and a warning.

Of course, Sybil avoided the subject.

She prepared carefully chosen words, should anyone happen to ask her why she was living with her aunt, and not her parents; or, at least, one of her parents. But—this was Southern California, and very few of Sybil's classmates were living with the set of parents with whom they'd begun. No one asked.

An orphan?—I'm not an orphan, Sybil would say. *I was never an orphan because my Aunt Lora was always there.*

I was two years old when it happened, the accident.

No, I don't remember.

But no one asked.

Sybil told her Aunt Lora nothing about the man in the park— the man who called himself Starr—she'd put him out of her mind entirely and yet, in bed that night, drifting into sleep, she found herself thinking suddenly of him, and seeing him again, vividly. That silver hair, those gleaming black shoes. His eyes hidden behind dark glasses. How tempting, his offer!—though there was no question of Sybil accepting it. Absolutely not.

Still, Mr. Starr seemed harmless. Well-intentioned. An eccentric, of course, but *interesting*. She supposed he had money, if he could offer her so much to model for him. There was something *not con-*

temporary about him. The set of his head and shoulders. That air about him of gentlemanly reserve, courtesy—even as he'd made his outlandish request. In Glencoe, in the past several years, there had been a visible increase in homeless persons and derelicts, especially in the oceanside park, but Mr. Starr was certainly not one of these.

Then Sybil realized, as if a door, hitherto locked, had swung open of its own accord, that she'd seen Mr. Starr before . . . somewhere. In the park, where she ran most afternoons for an hour? In downtown Glencoe? On the street?—in the public library? In the vicinity of Glencoe Senior High School?—in the school itself, in the auditorium? Sybil summoned up a memory as if by an act of physical exertion: the school choir, of which she was a member, had been rehearsing Handel's "Messiah" the previous month for their annual Christmas pageant, and Sybil had sung her solo part, a demanding part for contralto voice, and the choir director had praised her in front of the others . . . and she'd seemed to see, dimly, a man, a stranger, seated at the very rear of the auditorium, his features indistinct but his gray hair striking, and wasn't this man miming applause, clapping silently? *There. At the rear, on the aisle.* It frequently happened that visitors dropped by rehearsals—parents or relatives of choir members, colleagues of the music director. So no one took special notice of the stranger sitting unobtrusively at the rear of the auditorium. He wore dark, conservative clothes of the kind to attract no attention, and dark glasses hid his eyes. But there he was. *For Sybil Blake. He'd come for Sybil.* But at the time, Sybil had not seen.

Nor had she seen the man leave. Slipping quietly out of his seat, walking with a just perceptible limp, leaning on his cane.

3. The Proposition

Sybil had no intention of seeking out Mr. Starr, nor even of looking around for him, but the following afternoon, as she was headed home after her run, there, suddenly, the man was—taller than she recalled, looming large, his dark glasses winking in the sunlight, and his pale lips stretched in a tentative smile. He wore his clothes of the previous day except he'd set on his head a sporty plaid golfing cap that gave him a rakish yet wistful air, and he'd tied, as if in haste, a rumpled cream-colored silk scarf around his neck. He was standing on the path in approximately the same place as before, and leaning on his cane; on a bench close by were what appeared to be his art supplies, in a canvas duffel bag of the sort students carried. "Why, hello!" he said, shyly but eagerly, "—I didn't dare hope you would come back, but—" his smile widened as if on the verge of desperation, the puckered skin at the corners of his eyes tightened, "—I *hoped.*"

After running, Sybil always felt good: strength flowed into her legs, arms, lungs. She was a delicate-boned girl, since infancy prone to respiratory infections, but such vigorous exercise had made her strong in recent years; and with physical confidence had come a growing confidence in herself. She laughed, lightly, at this strange man's words, and merely shrugged, and said, "Well—this *is* my park, after all." Mr. Starr nodded eagerly, as if any response from her, any words at all, were of enormous interest. "Yes, yes," he said, "—I can see that. Do you live close by?"

Sybil shrugged. It was none of his business, was it, where she lived? "Maybe," she said.

"And your—name?" He stared at her, hopefully, adjusting his glasses more firmly on his nose. "—My name is Starr."

"My name is—Blake."

Mr. Starr blinked, and smiled, as if uncertain whether this might be a joke. " 'Blake'—? An unusual name for a girl," he said.

Sybil laughed again, feeling her face heat. She decided not to correct the misunderstanding.

Today, prepared for the encounter, having anticipated it for hours, Sybil was distinctly less uneasy than she'd been the day before: the man had a business proposition to make to her, that was all. And the park *was* an open, public, safe place, as familiar to her as the small neat yard of her Aunt Lora's house.

So, when Mr. Starr repeated his offer, Sybil said, yes, she was interested after all; she did need money, she was saving for college.

"For college?—really? So young?" Mr. Starr said, with an air of surprise. Sybil shrugged, as if the remark didn't require any reply. "I suppose, here in California, young people grow up quickly," Mr. Starr said. He'd gone to get his sketch pad, to show Sybil his work, and Sybil turned the pages with polite interest, as Mr. Starr chattered. He was, he said, an "amateur artist"—the very epitome of the "amateur"—with no delusions regarding his talent, but a strong belief that the world is redeemed by art—"And the world, you know, being profane, and steeped in wickedness, requires constant, ceaseless redemption." He believed that the artist "bears witness" to this fact; and that art can be a "conduit of emotion" where the heart is empty. Sybil, leafing through the sketches, paid little attention to Mr. Starr's tumble of words; she was struck by the feathery, uncertain, somehow *worshipful* detail in the drawings, which, to her eye, were not so bad as she'd expected, though by no means of professional quality. As she looked at them, Mr. Starr came to look over her shoulder, embarrassed, and excited, his shadow falling over the pages. The ocean, the waves, the wide rippled beach as seen from the bluff—palm trees, hibiscus, flowers—a World War II memorial in the park—mothers with young children—solitary figures huddled on park benches—cyclists—joggers—several pages of joggers: Mr. Starr's work was ordinary, even commonplace, but certainly earnest. Sybil saw herself amid the joggers, or a figure she guessed must be herself, a young girl with shoulder-length dark hair held off her face by a headband, in jeans and a sweatshirt, caught in midstride, legs and swinging arms caught in motion—it *was* herself, but so clumsily executed, the profile so smudged, no one would have known. Still, Sybil felt her face grow warmer, and she sensed Mr. Starr's anticipation like a withheld breath.

Sybil did not think it quite right for her, aged seventeen, to pass judgment on the talent of a middle-aged man, so she merely murmured something vague and polite and positive; and Mr. Starr, taking the sketch pad from her, said, "Oh, I *know*—I'm not very good, yet. But I propose to try." He smiled at her, and took out a freshly laundered white handkerchief, and dabbed at his forehead, and said, "Do you have any questions about posing for me, or shall we begin? We'll have at least three hours of daylight, today."

"Three hours!" Sybil exclaimed. "That long?"

"If you get uncomfortable," Mr. Starr said quickly, "—we'll simply stop, wherever we are." Seeing that Sybil was frowning, he added, eagerly, "We'll take breaks every now and then, I promise. And, and—" seeing that Sybil was still indecisive, "—I'll pay you for a full hour's fee, for any part of an hour." Still Sybil stood, wondering if, after all, she should be agreeing to this, without her Aunt Lora, or anyone, knowing: wasn't there something just faintly odd about Mr. Starr, and about his willingness to pay her so much for doing so little? And wasn't there something troubling (however flattering) about his particular interest in her? Assuming Sybil was correct, and he'd been watching her . . . aware of her . . . for at least a month. "I'll be happy to pay you in advance, Blake."

The name "Blake" sounded very odd, in this stranger's mouth. Sybil had never before been called by her last name only.

Sybil laughed nervously, and said, "You don't have to pay me in advance—thanks!"

So Sybil Blake, against her better judgment, became a model, for Mr. Starr.

And, despite her self-consciousness, and her intermittent sense that there was something ludicrous in the enterprise, as about Mr. Starr's intense, fussy, self-important manner as he sketched her (he was a perfectionist, or wanted to give that impression: crumpling a half-dozen sheets of paper, breaking out new charcoal sticks, before he began a sketch that pleased him), the initial session was easy, effortless. "What I want to capture," Mr. Starr said, "—is, beyond your beautiful profile, Blake—and you *are* a beautiful child!—the brooding quality of the ocean. That look to it, d'you see?—of it having consciousness of a kind, actually thinking. Yes, *brooding!*"

Sybil, squinting down at the white-capped waves, the rhythmic crashing surf, the occasional surfers riding their boards with their

remarkable amphibian dexterity, thought that the ocean was anything but *brooding.*

"Why are you smiling, Blake?" Mr. Starr asked, pausing. "Is
something funny?—am *I* funny?"

Quickly Sybil said, "Oh, no, Mr. Starr, of course not."

"But I *am,* I'm sure," he said happily. "And if you find me so,
please *do* laugh!"

Sybil found herself laughing, as if rough fingers were tickling
her. She thought of how it might have been . . . had she had a
father, and a mother: her own family, as she'd been meant to have.

Mr. Starr was squatting now on the grass close by, and peering
up at Sybil with an expression of extreme concentration. The charcoal stick in his fingers moved rapidly. "The ability to *laugh,*" he
said, "is the ability to *live*—the two are synonymous. You're too
young to understand that right now, but one day you will." Sybil
shrugged, wiping at her eyes. Mr. Starr was talking grandly. "The
world is fallen and profane—the opposite of 'sacred,' you know, *is*
'profane.' It requires ceaseless vigilance—ceaseless redemption. The
artist is one who redeems by restoring the world's innocence, where
he can. The artist gives, but does not take away, nor even supplant."

Sybil said, skeptically, "But you want to make money with your
drawings, don't you?"

Mr. Starr seemed genuinely shocked. "Oh, my, no. Adamantly,
no."

Sybil persisted, "Well, most people would. I mean, most people
need to. If they have any talent—" she was speaking with surprising
bluntness, an almost childlike audacity, "—they need to sell it,
somehow."

As if he'd been caught out in a crime, Mr. Starr began to stammer apologetically, "It's true, Blake, I—I am not like most people,
I suppose. I've inherited some money—not a fortune, but enough
to live on comfortably for the rest of my life. I've been traveling
abroad," he said, vaguely, "—and, in my absence, interest accu-
mulated."

Sybil asked doubtfully, "You don't have any regular profession?"

Mr. Starr laughed, startled. Up close, his teeth were chunky and irregular, slightly stained, like aged ivory piano keys. "But dear child," he said, "*this* is my profession—'redeeming the world'!"

And he fell to sketching Sybil with renewed enthusiasm.

Minutes passed. Long minutes. Sybil felt a mild ache between her shoulder blades. A mild uneasiness in her chest. *Mr. Starr is mad. Is Mr. Starr 'mad'?* Behind her, on the path, people were passing by, there were joggers, cyclists—Mr. Starr, lost in a trance of concentration, paid them not the slightest heed. Sybil wondered if anyone knew her, and was taking note of this peculiar event. Or was she, herself, making too much of it? She decided she would tell her Aunt Lora about Mr. Starr that evening, tell Aunt Lora frankly how much he was paying her. She both respected and feared her aunt's judgment: in Sybil's imagination, in that unexamined sphere of being we call the imagination, Lora Dell Blake had acquired the authority of both Sybil's deceased parents.

Yes, she would tell Aunt Lora.

After only an hour and forty minutes, when Sybil appeared to be growing restless, and sighed several times, unconsciously, Mr. Starr suddenly declared the session over. He had, he said, three promising sketches, and he didn't want to exhaust her, or himself. She *was* coming back tomorrow—?

"I don't know," Sybil said. "Maybe."

Sybil protested, though not very adamantly, when Mr. Starr paid her the full amount, for three hours' modeling. He paid her in cash, out of his wallet—an expensive kidskin wallet brimming with bills. Sybil thanked him, deeply embarrassed, and eager to escape. Oh, there *was* something shameful about the transaction!

Up close, she was able—almost—to see Mr. Starr's eyes through the dark-tinted lenses of his glasses. Some delicacy of tact made her glance away quickly but she had an impression of kindness—gentleness.

Sybil took the money, and put it in her pocket, and turned, to hurry away. With no mind for who might hear him, Mr. Starr called after her, "You see, Blake?—Starr is true to his word. Always!"

4. Is the Omission of Truth a Lie, or Only an Omission?

"Well!—tell me how things went with *you* today, Sybil!" Lora Dell Blake said, with such an air of bemused exasperation, Sybil understood that, as so often, Aunt Lora had something to say that really couldn't wait—her work at the Glencoe Medical Center provided her with a seemingly inexhaustible supply of comical and outrageous anecdotes. So, deferring to Aunt Lora, as they prepared supper together as usual, and sat down to eat it, Sybil was content to listen, and to laugh.

For it *was* funny, if outrageous too—the latest episode in the ongoing folly at the Medical Center.

Lora Dell Blake, in her late forties, was a tall, lanky, restless woman; with close-cropped graying hair; sand-colored eyes, and skin; a generous spirit, but a habit of sarcasm. Though she claimed to love Southern California— "You don't know what paradise is, unless you're from somewhere else" —she seemed in fact an awkwardly transplanted New Englander, with expectations and a sense of personal integrity, or intransigence, quite out of place here. She was fond of saying she did not suffer fools gladly, and so it was. Overqualified for her position at the Glencoe Medical Center, she'd had no luck in finding work elsewhere, partly because she did not want to leave Glencoe, and "uproot" Sybil while she was still in high school; and partly because her interviews were invariably disasters—Lora Dell Blake was incapable of being, or even seeming, docile, tractable, "feminine," hypocritical.

Lora was not Sybil's sole living relative—there were Blakes, and Contes, back in Vermont—but Lora had discouraged visitors to the small stucco bungalow on Meridian Street, in Glencoe, California; she had not in fact troubled to reply to letters or cards since, having been granted custody of her younger sister's daughter, at the time of what she called "the tragedy," she'd picked up and moved across the continent, to a part of the country she knew nothing about— "My intention is to erase the past, for the child's sake," she said, "and to start a new life."

And: "For the child, for poor little Sybil—I would make any sacrifice."

Sybil, who loved her aunt very much, had the vague idea that there had been, many years ago, protests, queries, telephone calls— but that Aunt Lora had dealt with them all, and really had made a new and "uncomplicated" life for them. Aunt Lora was one of those personalities, already strong, that is strengthened, and empowered, by being challenged; she seemed to take an actual zest in confrontation, whether with her own relatives or her employers at the Medical Center—anyone who presumed to tell her what to do. She was especially protective of Sybil, since, as she often said, they had no one but each other.

Which was true. Aunt Lora had seen to that.

Though Sybil had been adopted by her aunt, there was never any pretense that she was anything but Lora's niece, not her daughter. Nor did most people, seeing the two together, noting their physical dissimilarities, make that mistake.

So it happened that Sybil Blake grew up knowing virtually nothing about her Vermont background except its general tragic outline: her knowledge of her mother and father, the precise circumstances of their deaths, was as vague and unexamined in her consciousness as a childhood fairy tale. For whenever, as a little girl, Sybil would ask her aunt about these things, Aunt Lora responded with hurt, or alarm, or reproach, or, most disturbingly, anxiety. Her eyes might flood with tears—Aunt Lora, who never cried. She might take Sybil's hands in both her own, and squeeze them tightly, and, looking Sybil in the eyes, say, in a quiet, commanding voice, "But, darling, *you don't want to know.*"

So too, that evening, when, for some reason, Sybil brought up the subject, asking Aunt Lora how, again, exactly, *had* her parents died, Aunt Lora looked at her in surprise; and, for a long moment, rummaging in the pockets of her shirt for a pack of cigarettes that wasn't there (Aunt Lora had given up smoking the previous month, for perhaps the fifth time), it seemed almost that Lora herself did not remember.

"Sybil, honey—why are you asking? I mean, why *now?*"

"I don't know," Sybil said evasively. "I guess—I'm just asking."

"Nothing happened to you at school, did it?"

Sybil could not see how this question related to her own, but she said, politely, "No, Aunt Lora. Of course not."

"It's just that, out of nowhere—I can't help but wonder *why,*" Aunt Lora said, frowning, "—you should ask."

Aunt Lora regarded Sybil with worried eyes: a look of such suffocating familiarity that, for a moment, Sybil felt as if a band were tightening around her chest, making it impossible to breathe. *Why is my wanting to know a test of my love for you?—why do you do this, Aunt Lora, every time?* She said, an edge of anger to her voice, "I was seventeen years old last week, Aunt Lora. I'm not a child any longer."

Aunt Lora laughed, startled. "Certainly you're not a child!"

Aunt Lora then sighed, and, in a characteristic gesture, meaning both impatience and a dutiful desire to please, ran both hands rapidly through her hair, and began to speak. She assured Sybil that there was little to know, really. The accident—the tragedy—had happened so long ago. "Your mother, Melanie, was twenty-six years old at the time—a beautiful sweet-natured young woman, with eyes like yours, cheekbones like yours, pale wavy hair. Your father, George Conte, was thirty-one years old—a promising young lawyer, in his father's firm—an attractive, ambitious man—" And here as in the past Aunt Lora paused, as if, in the very act of summoning up this long-dead couple, she had forgotten them; and was simply repeating a story, a family tale, like one of the more extreme of her tales of the Glencoe Medical Center, worn smooth by countless tellings.

"A boating accident—Fourth of July—" Sybil coaxed, "—and I was with you, and—"

"You were with me, and Grandma, at the cottage—you were just a little girl!" Aunt Lora said, blinking tears from her eyes, "—and it was almost dusk, and time for the fireworks to start.

Mommy and Daddy were out in Daddy's speedboat—they'd been across the lake, at the Club—"

"And they started back across the lake—Lake Champlain—"

"—Lake Champlain, of course: it's beautiful, but treacherous, if a storm comes up suddenly—"

"And Daddy was at the controls of the boat—"

"—and, somehow, they capsized. And drowned. A rescue boat went out immediately, but it was too late." Aunt Lora's mouth turned hard. Her eyes glistening with tears, as if defiantly. "They drowned."

Sybil's heart was beating painfully. She was certain there must be more, yet she herself could remember nothing—not even herself, that two-year-old child, waiting for Mommy and Daddy who were never to arrive. Her memory of her mother and father was vague, dim, featureless, like a dream that, even as it seems about to drift into consciousness, retreats further into darkness. She said, in a whisper, "It was an accident. No one was to blame."

Aunt Lora chose her words with care. "No one was to blame."

There was a pause. Sybil looked at her aunt, who was not now looking at her. How lined, even leathery, the older woman's face was getting!—all her life she'd been reckless, indifferent, about sun, wind, weather, and now, in her late forties, she might have been a decade older. Sybil said, tentatively, "*No one* was to blame—?"

"Well, if you must know," Aunt Lora said, "—there was evidence he'd been drinking. They'd been drinking. At the Club."

Sybil could not have been more shocked had Aunt Lora reached over and pinched the back of her hand. "Drinking—?" She had never heard this part of the story before.

Aunt Lora continued, grimly, "But not enough, probably, to have made a difference." Again she paused. She was not looking at Sybil. "Probably."

Sybil, stunned, could not think of anything further to say, or to ask.

Aunt Lora was on her feet, pacing. Her close-cropped hair was disheveled and her manner fiercely contentious, as if she were arguing her case before an invisible audience as Sybil looked on.

"What fools! I tried to tell her! 'Popular' couple—'attractive' couple—lots of friends—too many friends! That Goddamned Champlain Club, where everyone drank too much! All that money, and privilege! And what good did it do! She—Melanie—so proud of being asked to join—proud of marrying *him*—throwing her life away! That's what it came to, in the end. I'd warned her it was dangerous—playing with fire—but would she listen? Would either of them listen? To Lora?—to *me*? When you're that age, so ignorant, you think you will live forever—you can throw your life away—"

Sybil felt ill, suddenly. She walked swiftly out of the room, shut the door to her own room, stood in the dark, beginning to cry.

So that was it, the secret. The tawdry little secret—drinking, drunkenness—behind the "tragedy."

With characteristic tact, Aunt Lora did not knock on Sybil's door, but left her alone for the remainder of the night.

Only after Sybil was in bed, and the house darkened, did she realize she'd forgotten to tell her aunt about Mr. Starr—he'd slipped her mind entirely. And the money he'd pressed into her hand, now in her bureau drawer, rolled up neatly beneath her underwear, as if hidden. . . .

Sybil thought, guiltily, I can tell her tomorrow.

5. The Hearse

Crouched in front of Sybil Blake, eagerly sketching her likeness, Mr. Starr was saying, in a quick, rapturous voice, "Yes, yes, like that!—yes! Your face uplifted to the sun like a blossoming flower! Just so!" And: "There are only two or three eternal questions, Blake, which, like the surf, repeat themselves endlessly: 'Why are we here?'—'Where have we come from, and where are we going?'—'Is there purpose to the universe, or merely chance?' These questions the artist seems to express in the images he knows." And: "Dear child, I wish you would tell me about yourself. Just a little!"

As if, in the night, some change had come upon her, some new resolve, Sybil had fewer misgivings about modeling for Mr. Starr, this afternoon. It was as if they knew each other well, somehow: Sybil was reasonably certain that Mr. Starr was not a sexual pervert, nor even a madman of a more conventional sort; she'd glimpsed his sketches of her, which were fussy, overworked, and smudged, but not bad as likenesses. The man's murmurous chatter was comforting in a way, hypnotic as the surf, no longer quite so embarrassing—for he talked, most of the time, not with her but at her, and there was no need to reply. In a way, Mr. Starr reminded Sybil of her Aunt Lora, when she launched into one of her comical anecdotes about the Glencoe Medical Center. Aunt Lora was more entertaining than Mr. Starr, but Mr. Starr was more idealistic.

His optimism was simpleminded, maybe. But it *was* optimistic.

For this second modeling session, Mr. Starr had taken Sybil to a corner of the park where they were unlikely to be disturbed. He'd asked her to remove her headband, and to sit on a bench with her head dropping back, her eyes partly shut, her face uplifted to the sun—an uncomfortable pose at first, until, lulled by the crashing surf below, and Mr. Starr's monologue, Sybil began to feel oddly peaceful, floating.

Yes, in the night some change had come upon her. She could not comprehend its dimensions, nor even its tone. She'd fallen asleep crying bitterly but had wakened feeling—what? Vulnerable, somehow. And wanting to be so. *Uplifted. Like a blossoming flower.*

That morning, Sybil had forgotten again to tell her Aunt Lora about Mr. Starr, and the money she was making—such a generous amount, and for so little effort! She shrank from considering how her aunt might respond, for her aunt was mistrustful of strangers, and particularly of men. . . . Sybil reasoned that, when she did tell Aunt Lora, that evening, or tomorrow morning, she would make her understand that there was something kindly and trusting and almost child-like about Mr. Starr. You could laugh at him, but laughter was somehow inappropriate.

As if, though middle-aged, he had been away somewhere, sequestered, protected, out of the adult world. Innocent and, himself, vulnerable.

Today, too, he'd eagerly offered to pay Sybil in advance for modeling, and, another time, Sybil had declined. She would not have wanted to tell Mr. Starr that, were she paid in advance, she might be tempted to cut the session even shorter than otherwise.

Mr. Starr was saying, hesitantly, "Blake?—can you tell me about—" and here he paused, as if drawing a random, inspired notion out of nowhere, "—your mother?"

Sybil hadn't been paying close attention to Mr. Starr. Now she opened her eyes, and looked directly at him.

Mr. Starr was perhaps not so old as she'd originally thought, nor as old as he behaved. His face was a handsome face, but oddly roughened—the skin like sandpaper. Very sallow, sickly-pale. A faint scar on his forehead above his left eye, the shape of a fish hook, or a question mark. Or was it a birthmark?—or, even less romantically, some sort of skin blemish? Maybe his roughened, pitted skin was the result of teenaged acne, nothing more.

His tentative smile bared chunky damp teeth.

Today Mr. Starr was bareheaded, and his thin, fine, uncannily silver hair was stirred by the wind. He wore plain, nondescript clothes, a shirt too large for him, a khaki-colored jacket with rolled-up sleeves. At close range, Sybil could see his eyes through the tinted lenses of his glasses: they were small, deep-set, intelligent, glistening. The skin beneath was pouched and shadowed, as if bruised.

Sybil shivered, peering so directly into Mr. Starr's eyes. As into another's soul, when she was unprepared.

Sybil swallowed, and said, slowly, "My mother is . . . not living."

A curious way of speaking!—for why not say, candidly, in normal usage, *My mother is dead.*

For a long painful moment Sybil's words hovered in the air between them; as if Mr. Starr, discountenanced by his own blunder, seemed not to want to hear.

He said, quickly, apologetically, "Oh—I see. I'm so sorry."

Sybil had been posing in the sun, warmly mesmerized by the sun, the surf, Mr. Starr's voice, and now, as if wakened from a sleep of which she had not been conscious, she felt as if she'd been touched—prodded into wakefulness. She saw, upsidedown, the fussy smudged sketch Mr. Starr had been doing of her, saw his charcoal stick poised above the stiff white paper in an attitude of chagrin. She laughed, and wiped at her eyes, and said, "It happened a long time ago. I never think of it, really."

Mr. Starr's expression was wary, complex. He asked, "And so—do you—live with your—father?" The words seemed oddly forced.

"No, I don't. And I don't want to talk about this any more, Mr. Starr, if it's all right with you."

Sybil spoke pleadingly, yet with an air of finality.

"Then—we won't! We won't! We certainly won't!" Mr. Starr said quickly. And fell to sketching again, his face creased in concentration.

And so the remainder of the session passed, in silence.

Again, as soon as Sybil evinced signs of restlessness, Mr. Starr declared she could stop for the day—he didn't want to exhaust her, or himself.

Sybil rubbed her neck, which ached mildly; she stretched her arms, her legs. Her skin felt slightly sun- or wind-burnt and her eyes felt seared, as if she'd been staring directly into the sun. Or had she been crying?—she couldn't remember.

Again, Mr. Starr paid Sybil in cash, out of his kidskin wallet brimming with bills. His hand shook just visibly as he pressed the money into Sybil's. (Embarrassed, Sybil folded the bills quickly and put them in her pocket. Later, at home, she would discover that Mr. Starr had given her ten dollars too much: a bonus, for almost making her cry?) Though it was clear that Sybil was eager to get away, Mr. Starr walked with her up the slope, in the direction of the Boulevard, limping, leaning on his cane, but keeping a brisk pace. He asked if Sybil—of course, he called her Blake: "Dear Blake"—would like to have some refreshment with him, in a café near by?—and, when Sybil declined, murmured, "Yes, yes, I understand—I suppose." He then asked if Sybil would return the following day, and, when Sybil did not say no, added that, if she did, he would like to increase her hourly fee in exchange for asking of her a slightly different sort of modeling—"A slightly modified sort of modeling, here in the park, or perhaps down on the beach, in full daylight of course, as before, and yet, in its way—" Mr. Starr paused nervously, seeking the right word, "—experimental."

Sybil asked doubtfully, " 'Experimental'—?"

"I'm prepared to increase your fee, Blake, by half."

"What kind of 'experimental'?"

"Emotion."

"What?"

"Emotion. Memory. Interiority."

Now that they were emerging from the park, and more likely to be seen, Sybil was glancing uneasily about: she dreaded seeing someone from school, or, worse yet, a friend of her aunt's. Mr. Starr gestured as he spoke, and seemed more than ordinarily excited. "—'Interiority.' That which is hidden to the outer eye. I'll tell you in more detail tomorrow, Blake," he said. "You *will* meet me here tomorrow?"

Sybil murmured, "I don't know, Mr. Starr."

"Oh, but you must!—please."

Sybil felt a tug of sympathy for Mr. Starr. He *was* kind, and courteous, and gentlemanly; and, certainly, very generous. She could not imagine his life except to see him as a lonely, eccentric man without friends. Uncomfortable as she was in his presence, she yet wondered if perhaps she was exaggerating his eccentricity: what would a neutral observer make of the tall, limping figure, the cane, the canvas duffel bag, the polished black leather shoes that reminded her of a funeral, the fine, thin, beautiful silver hair, the dark glasses that winked in the sunshine . . . ? Would such an observer, seeing Sybil Blake and Mr. Starr together, give them a second glance?

"Look," Sybil said, pointing, "—a hearse."

At a curb close by there was a long sleekly black car with dark-tinted, impenetrable windows. Mr. Starr laughed, and said, embarrassed, "I'm afraid, Blake, that isn't a hearse, you know—it's my car."

"Your car?"

"Yes. I'm afraid so."

Now Sybil could see that the vehicle was a limousine, idling at the curb. Behind the wheel was a youngish driver with a visored cap on his head; in profile, he appeared Oriental. Sybil stared, amazed. So Mr. Starr was wealthy, indeed.

He was saying, apologetically, yet with a kind of boyish pleasure, "I don't drive, myself, you see!—a further handicap. I did, once, long ago, but—circumstances intervened." Sybil was thinking that she often saw chauffeur-driven limousines in Glencoe, but she'd never known anyone who owned one before. Mr. Starr said, "Blake, may I give you a ride home?—I'd be delighted, of course."

Sybil laughed, as if she'd been tickled, hard, in the ribs.

"A ride? In that?" she asked.

"No trouble! Absolutely!" Mr. Starr limped to the rear door and opened it with a flourish, before the driver could get out to open it for him. He squinted back at Sybil, smiling hopefully. "It's the least I can do for you, after our exhausting session."

Sybil was smiling, staring into the shadowy interior of the car. The uniformed driver had climbed out, and stood, not quite knowing what to do, watching. He was a Filipino, perhaps, not young after all but with a small, wizened face; he wore white gloves. He stood very straight and silent, watching Sybil.

There was a moment when it seemed, yes, Sybil was going to accept Mr. Starr's offer, and climb into the rear of the long sleekly black limousine, so that Mr. Starr could climb in behind her, and shut the door upon them both; but, then, for some reason she could not have named—it might have been the smiling intensity with which Mr. Starr was looking at her, or the rigid posture of the white-gloved driver—she changed her mind and called out, "No thanks!"

Mr. Starr was disappointed, and hurt—you could see it in his downturned mouth. But he said, cheerfully, "Oh, I quite understand, Blake—I *am* a stranger, after all. It's better to be prudent, of course. But, my dear, I *will* see you tomorrow—?"

Sybil shouted, "Maybe!" and ran across the street.

6. The Face

She stayed away from the park. *Because I want to, because I can.*

Thursday, in any case, was her voice lesson after school. Friday, choir rehearsal; then an evening with friends. On Saturday morning she went jogging, not in the oceanside park but in another park, miles away, where Mr. Starr could not have known to look for her. And, on Sunday, Aunt Lora drove them to Los Angeles for a belated birthday celebration, for Sybil—an art exhibit, a dinner, a play.

So, you see, I can do it. I don't need your money, or you.

Since the evening when Aunt Lora had told Sybil about her parents' boating accident—that it might have been caused by drinking—neither Sybil nor her aunt had cared to bring up the subject again. Sybil shuddered to think of it. She felt properly chastised, for her curiosity.

Why do you want to know?—you will only make yourself cry.

Sybil had never gotten around to telling Aunt Lora about Mr. Starr, nor about her modeling. Even during their long Sunday together. Not a word about her cache of money, hidden away in a bureau drawer.

Money for what?—for summer school, for college.

For the future.

Aunt Lora was not the sort of person to spy on a member of her household, but she observed Sybil closely, with her trained clinician's eye. "Sybil, you've been very quiet, lately—there's nothing wrong, I hope?" she asked, and Sybil said quickly, nervously, "Oh, no! What could be wrong?"

She was feeling guilty about keeping a secret from Aunt Lora, and she was feeling guilty about staying away from Mr. Starr.

Two adults. Like twin poles. Of course, Mr. Starr was really a stranger—he did not exist in Sybil Blake's life, at all. Why did it feel to her, so strangely, that he did?

Days passed, and, instead of forgetting Mr. Starr, and strengthening her resolve not to model for him, Sybil seemed to see the man, in her mind's eye, ever more clearly. She could not understand why he seemed attracted to her, she was convinced it was not a sexual attraction but something purer, more spiritual, and yet—why? Why *her*?

Why had he visited her high school, and sat in on a choir rehearsal? Had he known she would be there?—or was it simply coincidence?

She shuddered, to think of what Aunt Lora would make of this, if she knew. If news of Mr. Starr got back to her.

Mr. Starr's face floated before her. Its pallor, its sorrow. That look of convalescence. Waiting. The dark glasses. The hopeful smile. One night, waking from a particularly vivid, disturbing dream, Sybil thought for a confused moment that she'd seen Mr. Starr, in the room—it hadn't been just a dream! How wounded he'd looked, puzzled, hurt. *Come with me, Sybil. Hurry. Now. It's been so long.* He'd been waiting for her in the park for days, limping, the duffel bag slung over his shoulder, glancing up hopefully at every passing stranger.

Behind him, the elegantly gleaming black limousine, larger than Sybil remembered; and driverless.

Sybil?—Sybil? Mr. Starr called, impatiently.

As if, all along, he'd known her real name. And she had known he'd known.

7. The Experiment

So, Monday afternoon, Sybil Blake found herself back in the park, modeling for Mr. Starr.

Seeing him in the park, so obviously awaiting her, Sybil had felt almost apologetic. Not that he greeted her with any measure of reproach (though his face was drawn and sallow, as if he hadn't been sleeping well), nor even questioned her mutely with his eyes *Where have you been?* Certainly not! He smiled happily when he saw her, limping in her direction like a doting father, seemingly determined not to acknowledge her absence of the past four days. Sybil called out, "Hello, Mr. Starr!" and felt, yes, so strangely, as if things were once again right.

"How lovely!—and the day is so fine!—'in full daylight'—as I promised!" Mr. Starr cried.

Sybil had been jogging for forty minutes, and felt very good, strengthened. She removed her damp yellow headband and stuffed it in her pocket. When Mr. Starr repeated the terms of his proposition of the previous week, restating the higher fee, Sybil agreed at once, for of course that was why she'd come. How, in all reasonableness, could she resist?

Mr. Starr took some time before deciding upon a place for Sybil to pose—"It must be ideal, a synthesis of poetry and practicality." Finally, he chose a partly crumbling stone ledge overlooking the beach in a remote corner of the park. He asked Sybil to lean against the ledge, gazing out at the ocean. Her hands pressed flat against the top of the ledge, her head uplifted as much as possible, within comfort. "But today, dear Blake, I am going to record not just the surface likeness of a lovely young girl," he said, "—but *memory*, and *emotion*, coursing through her."

Sybil took the position readily enough. So invigorated did she feel from her exercise, and so happy to be back, again, in her role as model, she smiled out at the ocean as at an old friend. "What kind of memory and emotion, Mr. Starr?" she asked.

Mr. Starr eagerly took up his sketch pad and a fresh stick of charcoal. It was a mild day, the sky placid and featureless, though, up the coast, in the direction of Big Sur, massive thunderclouds were gathering. The surf was high, the waves powerful, hypnotic. One hundred yards below, young men in surfing gear, carrying their boards lightly as if they were made of papier-mâché, prepared to enter the water.

Mr. Starr cleared his throat, and said, almost shyly, "Your mother, dear Blake. Tell me all you know—all you can remember —about your mother."

"My mother?"

Sybil winced and would have broken her position, except Mr. Starr put out a quick hand, to steady her. It was the first time he had touched her in quite that way. He said, gently, "I realize it's a painful subject, Blake, but—will you try?"

Sybil said, "No. I don't want to."

"You won't, then?"

"I *can't*."

"But why can't you, dear?—any memory of your mother would do."

"*No.*"

Sybil saw that as Mr. Starr was quickly sketching her, or trying to—his hand shook. She wanted to reach out to snatch the charcoal stick from him and snap it in two. How dare he! Goddamn him!

"Yes, yes," Mr. Starr said hurriedly, an odd, elated look on his face, as if, studying her so intently, he was not seeing her at all, "—yes, dear, like that. Any memory—any! So long as it's yours."

Sybil said, "Whose else would it be?" She laughed, and was surprised that her laughter sounded like sobbing.

"Why, many times innocent children are given memories by adults; contaminated by memories not their own," Mr. Starr said somberly. "In which case the memory is spurious. Inauthentic."

Sybil saw her likeness on the sheet of stiff white paper, upside-down. There was something repulsive about it. Though she was wearing her usual jogging clothes Mr. Starr made it look as if she were wearing a clinging, flowing gown; or, maybe, nothing at all. Where her small breasts would have been were swirls and smudges of charcoal, as if she were on the brink of dissolution. Her face and head were vividly drawn, but rather raw, crude, and exposed.

She saw too that Mr. Starr's silver hair had a flat metallic sheen this afternoon; and his beard was faintly visible, metallic too, glinting on his jaws. He was stronger than she'd thought. He had knowledge far beyond hers.

Sybil resumed her position. She stared out at the ocean—the tall, cresting, splendidly white-capped waves. Why was she here, what did this man want of her? She worried suddenly that, whatever it was, she could not provide it.

But Mr. Starr was saying, in his gentle, murmurous voice, "There are people, primarily women!—who are what I call 'conduits of emotion.' In their company, the half-dead can come alive. They need not be beautiful women or girls. It's a matter of blood-warmth. The integrity of the spirit." He turned the page of his sketch pad, and began anew, whistling thinly through his teeth. "Thus an icy-cold soul, in the presence of one so blessed, can regain something of his lost self. Sometimes!"

Sybil tried to summon forth a memory, an image at least, of her mother. *Melanie. Twenty-six at the time. Eyes . . . cheekbones . . . pale wavy hair.* A ghostly face appeared but faded almost at once. Sybil sobbed involuntarily. Her eyes stung with tears.

"—sensed that you, dear Blake—*is* your name Blake, really?—are one of these. A 'conduit of emotion'—of finer, higher things. Yes, yes! My intuition rarely misguides me!" Mr. Starr spoke as, hurriedly, excitedly, he sketched Sybil's likeness. He was squatting close beside her, on his haunches; his dark glasses winked in the sun. Sybil knew, should she glance at him, she would not be able to see his eyes.

Mr. Starr said, coaxingly, "Don't you remember anything—at all—about your mother?"

Sybil shook her head, meaning she didn't want to speak.

"Her name. Surely you know her name?"

Sybil whispered, "Mommy."

"Ah, yes: 'Mommy.' To you, that would have been her name."

"Mommy—went away. They told me—"

"Yes? Please continue!"

"—Mommy was gone. And Daddy. On the lake—"

"Lake? Where?"

"Lake Champlain. In Vermont, and New York. Aunt Lora says—"

" 'Aunt Lora'—?"

"Mommy's sister. She was older. Is older. She took me away. She adopted me. She—"

"And is 'Aunt Lora' married?"

"No. There's just her and me."

"What happened on the lake?"

"—it happened in the boat, on the lake. Daddy was driving the boat, they said. He came for me too but—I don't know if that was that time or some other time. I've been told, but I don't *know*."

Tears were streaming down Sybil's face now; she could not maintain her composure. But she managed to keep from hiding her face in her hands. She could hear Mr. Starr's quickened breath, and she could hear the rasping sound of the charcoal against the paper.

Mr. Starr said gently, "You must have been a little girl when —whatever it was—happened."

"I wasn't little to my*self*. I just *was*."

"A long time ago, was it?"

"Yes. No. It's always—there."

"Always where, dear child?"

"Where I, I—see it."

"See what?"

"I—don't *know*."

"Do you see your mommy? Was she a beautiful woman?—did she resemble you?"

"Leave me alone—I don't *know*."

Sybil began to cry. Mr. Starr, repentant, or wary, went immediately silent.

Someone—it must have been cyclists—passed behind them, and Sybil was aware of being observed, no doubt quizzically: a girl leaning forward across a stone ledge, face wet with tears, and a middle-aged man on his haunches busily sketching her. An artist and his model. An amateur artist, an amateur model. But how strange, that the girl was crying! And the man so avidly recording her tears!

Sybil, eyes closed, felt herself indeed a conduit of emotion—she *was* emotion. She stood upon the ground but she floated free. Mr. Starr was close beside her, anchoring her, but she floated free. A veil was drawn aside, and she saw a face—Mommy's face—a pretty heart-shaped face—something both affectionate and petulant in that face—how young Mommy was!—and her hair up, brown-blond lovely hair, tied back in a green silk scarf. Mommy hurried to the phone as it rang, Mommy lifted the receiver, Yes? yes? Oh hel*lo*—

for the phone was always ringing, and Mommy was always hurrying to answer it, and there was always that expectant note to her voice, that sound of hope, surprise—oh, hel*lo*.

Sybil could no longer maintain her pose. She said, "Mr. Starr, I am through for the day, I am *sorry*." And, as the startled man looked after her, she walked away. He began to call after her, to remind her that he hadn't paid her, but, no, Sybil had had enough of modeling for the day. She broke into a run, she escaped.

8. A Long Time Ago . . .

A girl who'd married too young: was that it?

That heart-shaped face, the petulant pursed lips. The eyes widened in mock-surprise: Oh, Sybil what have you *done* . . . ?

Stooping to kiss little Sybil, little Sybil giggling with pleasure and excitement, lifting her chubby baby arms to be raised in Mommy's and carried in to bed.

Oh honey, you're too big for that now. Too heavy!

Perfume wafting from her hair, loose to her shoulders, pale golden-brown, wavy. A rope of pearls around her neck. A low-cut summer dress, a bright floral print, like wallpaper. Mommy!

And Daddy, where *was* Daddy?

He was gone, then he was back. He'd come for her, little Sybil, to take her in the boat, the motor was loud, whining, angry as a bee buzzing and darting around your head, so Sybil was crying, and someone came, and Daddy went away again. She'd heard the motor rising, then fading. The churning of the water she couldn't see from where she stood, and it was night too, but she wasn't crying and no one scolded.

She could remember Mommy's face, though they never let her see it again. She couldn't remember Daddy's face.

Grandma said, You'll be all right, poor little darling you'll be all right, and Aunt Lora too, hugging her tight. Forever now you'll be all right, Aunt Lora promised. It was scary to see Aunt Lora crying: Aunt Lora never cried, did she?

Lifting little Sybil in her strong arms to carry her in to bed but it wasn't the same. It would never be the same again.

9. The Gift

Sybil is standing at the edge of the ocean.

The surf crashes and pounds about her . . . water streams up the sand, nearly wetting her feet. What a tumult of cries, hidden within the waves! She feels like laughing, for no reason. *You know the reason: he has returned to you.*

The beach is wide, clean, stark, as if swept with a giant broom. A landscape of dream-like simplicity. Sybil has seen it numberless times but today its beauty strikes her as new. *Your father: your father they told you was gone forever: he has returned to you.* The sun is a winter sun, but warm, dazzling. Poised in the sky as if about to rapidly descend. Dark comes early because, after all, it is winter here, despite the warmth. The temperature will drop twenty degrees in a half hour. *He never died: he has been waiting for you all these years. And now he has returned.*

Sybil begins to cry. Hiding her face, her burning face, in her hands. She stands flat-footed as a little girl and the surf breaks and splashes around her and now her shoes are wet, her feet, she'll be shivering in the gathering chill. *Oh, Sybil!*

When Sybil turned, it was to see Mr. Starr sitting on the beach. He seemed to have lost his balance and fallen—his cane lay at his feet, he'd dropped the sketch pad, his sporty golfing cap sat crooked on his head. Sybil, concerned, asked what was wrong—she prayed he hadn't had a heart attack!—and Mr. Starr smiled weakly and told her quickly that he didn't know, he'd become dizzy, felt the strength go out of his legs, and had had to sit. "I was overcome suddenly, I think, by your emotion!—whatever it was," he said. He made no effort to get to his feet but sat there awkwardly, damp sand on his trousers and shoes. Now Sybil stood over him and he squinted up at her, and there passed between them a current of—was it understanding? sympathy? recognition?

Sybil laughed to dispel the moment and put out her hand for Mr. Starr to take, so that she could help him stand. He laughed too, though he was deeply moved, and embarrassed. "I'm afraid I make too much of things, don't I?" he said. Sybil tugged at his hand (how big his hand was! how strong the fingers, closing about hers!) and, as he heaved himself to his feet, grunting, she felt the startling weight of him—an adult man, and heavy.

Mr. Starr was standing close to Sybil, not yet relinquishing her hand. He said, "The experiment was almost too successful, from my perspective! I'm almost afraid to try it again."

Sybil smiled uncertainly up at him. He was about the age her own father would have been—wasn't he? It seemed to her that a younger face was pushing out through Mr. Starr's coarse, sallow face. The hook-like quizzical scar on his forehead glistened oddly in the sun.

Sybil politely withdrew her hand from Mr. Starr's, and dropped her eyes. She was shivering—today, she had not been running at all, had come to meet Mr. Starr for purposes of modeling, in a blouse and skirt, as he'd requested. She was bare-legged and her feet, in sandals, were wet from the surf.

Sybil said, softly, as if she didn't want to be heard, "I feel the same way, Mr. Starr."

They climbed a flight of wooden steps to the top of the bluff, and there was Mr. Starr's limousine, blackly gleaming, parked a short distance away. At this hour of the afternoon the park was well populated; there was a gay giggling bevy of high school girls strolling by, but Sybil took no notice. She was agitated, still; weak from crying, yet oddly strengthened, elated too. *You know who he is. You always knew.* She was keenly aware of Mr. Starr limping beside her, and impatient with his chatter. Why didn't he speak directly to her, for once?

The uniformed chauffeur sat behind the wheel of the limousine, looking neither to the right nor the left, as if at attention. His visored cap, his white gloves. His profile like a profile on an ancient coin. Sybil wondered if the chauffeur knew about her—if Mr. Starr talked to him about her. Suddenly she was filled with excitement, that someone else should *know*.

Mr. Starr was saying that, since Sybil had modeled so patiently that day, since she'd more than fulfilled his expectations, he had a gift for her—"In addition to your fee, that is."

He opened the rear door of the limousine, and took out a square white box, and, smiling shyly, presented it to Sybil. "Oh, what *is* it?" Sybil cried. She and Aunt Lora rarely exchanged presents any longer, it seemed like a ritual out of the deep past, delightful to rediscover. She lifted the cover of the box, and saw, inside, a beautiful purse; a shoulder bag; kidskin, the hue of rich dark honey. "Oh, Mr. Starr—thank you," Sybil said, taking the bag in her hands. "It's the most beautiful thing I've ever seen." "Why don't you open it, dear?" Mr. Starr urged, so Sybil opened the bag, and discovered money inside—fresh-minted bills—the denomination on top was a twenty. "I hope you didn't overpay me again," Sybil said, uneasily, "—I haven't modeled for three hours yet. It isn't fair." Mr. Starr laughed, flushed with pleasure. "Fair to whom?" he asked. "What is 'fair'?—*we* do what *we* like."

Sybil raised her eyes shyly to Mr. Starr's and saw that he was looking at her intently—at least, the skin at the corners of his eyes was tightly puckered. "Today, dear, I insist upon driving you home," he said, smiling. There was a new authority in his voice that seemed to have something to do with the gift Sybil had received from him. "It will soon be getting chilly, and your feet are wet." Sybil hesitated. She had lifted the bag to her face, to inhale the pungent kidskin smell: the bag was of a quality she'd never owned before. Mr. Starr glanced swiftly about, as if to see if anyone was watching; he was still smiling. "Please do climb inside, Blake!— you can't consider me a stranger, now."

Still, Sybil hesitated. Half teasing, she said, "*You* know my name isn't Blake, don't you, Mr. Starr?—how do you know?"

Mr. Starr laughed, teasing too. "*Isn't* it? What is your name, then?"

"Don't you know?"

"Should I know?"

"Shouldn't you?"

There was a pause. Mr. Starr had taken hold of Sybil's wrist; lightly, yet firmly. His fingers circled her thin wrists with the subtle pressure of a watchband.

Mr. Starr leaned close, as if sharing a secret. "Well, I did hear you sing your solo, in your wonderful Christmas pageant at the high school; I must confess, I'd sneaked into a rehearsal too—no one questioned my presence. And I believe I heard the choir director call you—is it 'Sybil'?"

Hearing her name in Mr. Starr's mouth, Sybil felt a sensation of vertigo. She could only nod, mutely, yes.

"*Is* it?—I wasn't sure if I'd heard correctly. A lovely name, for a lovely girl. And 'Blake'—is 'Blake' your surname?"

Sybil murmured, "Yes."

"Your father's name?"

"No. Not my father's name."

"Oh, and why not? Usually, you know, that's the case."

"Because—" And here Sybil paused, confused, uncertain what to say. "It's my mother's name. Was."

"Ah, really! I see," Mr. Starr laughed. "Well, truly, I suppose I *don't*, but we can discuss it another time. Shall we—?"

He meant, shall we get into the car; he was exerting more pressure on Sybil's wrist, and, though kindly as always, seemed on the edge of impatience. His grip was unexpectedly hard. Sybil stood flat-footed on the sidewalk, wanting to acquiesce; yet, at the same time, uneasily thinking that, no, she should not. Not yet.

So Sybil pulled away, laughing nervously, and Mr. Starr had to release her, with a disappointed downturning of his mouth. Sybil thanked him, saying she preferred to walk. "I hope I will see you tomorrow, then?—'Sybil'?" Mr. Starr called after her. "Yes?"

But Sybil, hugging her new bag against her chest, as a small child might hug a stuffed animal, was walking quickly away.

* * *

Was the black limousine following her, at a discreet distance?

Sybil felt a powerful compulsion to look back, but did not.

She was trying to recall if, ever in her life, she'd ridden in such a vehicle. She supposed there had been hired, chauffeur-driven limousines at her parents' funerals, but she had not attended those funerals; had no memory of anything connected with them, except the strange behavior of her grandmother, her Aunt Lora, and other adults—their grief, but, underlying that grief, their air of profound and speechless shock.

Where is Mommy, she'd asked, where is Daddy, and the replies were always the same: Gone away.

And crying did no good. And fury did no good. Nothing little Sybil could do, or say, or think did any good. That was the first lesson, maybe.

But Daddy isn't dead, you know he isn't. You know, and he knows, why he has returned.

10. "Possessed"

Aunt Lora was smoking again!—back to two packs a day. And Sybil understood guiltily that she was to blame.

For there was the matter of the kidskin bag. The secret gift. Which Sybil had hidden in the farthest corner of her closet, wrapped in plastic, so the smell of it would not permeate the room. (Still, you could smell it—couldn't you? A subtle pervasive smell, rich as any perfume?) Sybil lived in dread that her aunt would discover the purse, and the money; though Lora Dell Blake never entered her niece's room without an invitation, somehow, Sybil worried, it *might* happen. She had never kept any important secret from her aunt in her life, and this secret both filled her with a sense of excitement and power, and weakened her, in childish dread.

What most concerned Lora, however, was Sybil's renewed interest in *that*—as in, "Oh, honey, are you thinking about *that* again? *Why?*"

That was the abbreviated euphemism for what Lora might more fully call "the accident"—"the tragedy"—"your parents' deaths."

Sybil, who had never shown more than passing curiosity about *that* in the past, as far as Lora could remember, was now in the grip of what Lora called "morbid curiosity." That mute, perplexed look in her eyes! That tremulous, sometimes sullen, look to her mouth! One evening, lighting up a cigarette with shaking fingers, Lora said, bluntly, "Sybil, honey, this tears my heart out. What *is* it you want to know?"

Sybil said, as if she'd been waiting for just this question, "Is my father alive?"

"What?"

"My father. George Conte. *Is* he—maybe—alive?"

The question hovered between them, and, for a long, pained moment, it seemed almost that Aunt Lora might snort in exasperation, jump up from the table, walk out of the room. But then she said, shaking her head adamantly, dropping her gaze from Sybil's, "Honey, no. The man is not alive." She paused. She smoked her cigarette, exhaled smoke vigorously through her nostrils; seemed about to say something further; changed her mind; then said, quietly, "You don't ask about your mother, Sybil. Why is that?"

"I—believe that my mother is dead. But—"

"But—?"

"My—my father—"

"—isn't?"

Sybil said, stammering, her cheeks growing hot, "I just want to *know*. I want to see a, a—grave! A death certificate!"

"I'll send to Wellington for a copy of the death certificate," Aunt Lora said slowly. "Will that do?"

"You don't have a copy here?"

"Honey, why would I have a copy here?"

Sybil saw that the older woman was regarding her with a look of pity, and something like dread. She said, stammering, her cheeks warm, "In your—your legal things. Your papers. Locked away—"

"Honey, no."

There was a pause. Then Sybil said, half sobbing, "I was too young to go to their funeral. So I never saw. Whatever it was—I never *saw*. Is that it? They say that's the reason for the ritual—for displaying the dead."

Aunt Lora reached over to take Sybil's hand. "It's one of the reasons, honey," she said. "We meet up with it all the time, at the medical center. People don't believe that loved ones are dead—they know, but can't accept it; the shock is just too much to absorb at once. And, yes, it's a theory, that if you don't see a person actually dead—if there isn't a public ceremony to define it—you may have difficulty accepting it. You may—" and here Aunt Lora paused, frowning, "—be susceptible to fantasy."

Fantasy! Sybil stared at her aunt, shocked. *But I've seen him, I know. I believe him and not you!*

The subject seemed to be concluded for the time being. Aunt Lora briskly stubbed out her cigarette, and said, "I'm to blame—probably. I'd been in therapy for a couple of years after it happened and I just didn't want to talk about it any longer, so when you'd asked me questions, over the years, I cut you off; I realize that. But, you see, there's so little to say—Melanie is dead, and *he* is dead. And it all happened a long time ago."

That evening, Sybil was reading in a book on memory she'd taken out of the Glencoe Public Library: *It is known that human beings are "possessed" by an unfathomable number of dormant memory-traces, of which some can be activated under special conditions, including excitation by stimulating points in the cortex. Such traces are indelibly imprinted in the nervous system and are commonly activated by mnemonic stimuli—words, sights, sounds, and especially smells. The phenomenon of déjà vu is closely related to these experiences, in which a "doubling of consciousness" occurs, with the conviction that one has lived an experience before. Much of human memory, however, includes subsequent revision, selection, and fantasizing . . .*

Sybil let the book shut. She contemplated, for the dozenth time, the faint red marks on her wrist, where Mr. Starr—the man who called himself Mr. Starr—had gripped her, without knowing his own strength.

Nor had Sybil been aware, at the time, that his fingers were so strong; and had clasped so tightly around her wrist.

11. "Mr. Starr"—or "Mr. Conte"

She saw him, and saw that he was waiting for her. And her impulse was to run immediately to him, and observe, with childish delight, how the sight of her would illuminate his face. *Here! Here I am!* It was a profound power that seemed to reside in her, Sybil Blake, seventeen years old—the power to have such an effect upon a man whom she scarcely knew, and who did not know her.

Because he loves me. Because he's my father. That's why.

And if he isn't my father—

It was late afternoon of a dull, overcast day. Still, the park was populated at this end: joggers were running, some in colorful costumes. Sybil was not among them, she'd slept poorly the previous night, thinking of—what? Her dead mother who'd been so beautiful?—her father whose face she could not recall (though, yes surely, it was imprinted deep, deep in the cells of her memory)?—her Aunt Lora who was, or was not, telling her the truth, and who loved her more than anyone on earth? And Mr. Starr of course.

Or Mr. Conte.

Sybil was hidden from Mr. Starr's gaze as, with an air of smiling expectancy, he looked about. He was carrying his duffel bag and leaning on his cane. He wore his plain, dark clothes; he was bareheaded, and his silvery hair shone; if Sybil were closer, she would see light winking in his dark glasses. She had noticed the limousine, parked up on the Boulevard a block away.

A young woman jogger ran past Mr. Starr, long-legged, hair flying, and he looked at her, intently—watched her as she ran out of sight along the path. Then he turned back, glancing up toward the street, shifting his shoulders impatiently. Sybil saw him check his wristwatch.

Waiting for you. You know why.

And then, suddenly—Sybil decided not to go to Mr. Starr, after all. The man who called himself Starr. She changed her mind at the last moment, unprepared for her decision except to understand that, as, she quickly walked away, that it must be the right decision: her heart was beating erratically, all her senses alert, as if she had narrowly escaped great danger.

12. The Fate of "George Conte"

On Mondays, Wednesdays, and Fridays Lora Dell Blake attended an aerobics class after work, and on these evenings she rarely returned home before seven o'clock. Today was a Wednesday, at four: Sybil calculated she had more than enough time to search out her aunt's private papers, and to put everything back in order, well before her aunt came home.

Aunt Lora's household keys were kept in a top drawer of her desk, and one of these keys, Sybil knew, was to a small aluminum filing cabinet beside the desk, where confidential records and papers were kept. There were perhaps a dozen keys, in a jumble, but Sybil had no difficulty finding the right one. "Aunt Lora, please forgive me," she whispered. It was a measure of her aunt's trust of her that the filing cabinet was so readily unlocked.

For never in her life had Sybil Blake done such a thing, in violation of the trust between herself and her aunt. She sensed that, unlocking the cabinet, opening the sliding drawers, she might be committing an irrevocable act.

The drawer was jammed tight with manila folders, most of them well-worn and dog-eared. Sybil's first response was disappointment —there were hundreds of household receipts, financial statements, Internal Revenue records dating back for years. Then she discovered a packet of letters dating back to the 1950's, when Aunt Lora would have been a young girl. There were a few snapshots, a few formally posed photographs—one of a strikingly beautiful, if immature-looking, girl in a high school graduation cap and gown, smiling at the camera with glossy lips. On the rear was written "Melanie, 1969." Sybil stared at this likeness of her mother—her mother long before she'd become her mother—and felt both triumph and dismay: for, yes, here was the mysterious "Melanie," and, yet, *was* this the "Melanie" the child Sybil knew?—or, simply, a high school girl, Sybil's own approximate age, the kind who, judging from her looks and self-absorbed expression, would never have been a friend of Sybil's?

Sybil put the photograph back, with trembling fingers. She was half grateful that Aunt Lora had kept so few mementos of the past —there could be fewer shocks, revelations.

No photographs of the wedding of Melanie Blake and George Conte. Not a one.

No photographs, so far as Sybil could see, of her father "George Conte" at all.

There was a single snapshot of Melanie with her baby daughter Sybil, and this Sybil studied for a long time. It had been taken in summer, at a lakeside cottage; Melanie was posing prettily, in a white dress, with her baby snug in the crook of her arm, and both were looking toward the camera, as if someone had just called out to them, to make them laugh—Melanie with a wide, glamorous, yet sweet smile, little Sybil gaping open-mouthed. Here Melanie looked only slightly more mature than in the graduation photo- graph: her pale brown hair, many shades of brown and blond, was shoulder-length, and upturned; her eyes were meticulously outlined in mascara, prominent in her heartshaped face.

In the foreground, on the grass, was the shadow of a man's head and shoulders—"George Conte," perhaps? The missing person.

Sybil stared at this snapshot, which was wrinkled and faded. She did not know what to think, and, oddly, she felt very little: for was the infant in the picture really herself, Sybil Blake, if she could not remember?

Or did she in fact remember, somewhere deep in her brain, in memory-traces that were indelible?

From now on, she would "remember" her mother as the pretty, self-assured young woman in this snapshot. This image, in full color, would replace any other.

Reluctantly, Sybil slid the snapshot back in its packet. How she would have liked to keep it!—but Aunt Lora would discover the theft, eventually. And Aunt Lora must be protected against knowing that her own niece had broken into her things, violated the trust between them.

The folders containing personal material were few, and quickly searched. Nothing pertaining to the accident, the "tragedy"?—not even an obituary? Sybil looked in adjacent files, with increasing desperation. There was not only the question of who her father was, or had been, but the question, nearly as compelling, of why Aunt Lora had eradicated all trace of him, even in her own private files. For a moment Sybil wondered if there had ever been any "George Conte" at all: maybe her mother had not married, and that was part of the secret? Melanie had died in some terrible way, terrible at least in Lora Dell Blake's eyes, thus the very fact must be hidden from Sybil, after so many years? Sybil recalled Aunt Lora saying, earnestly, a few years ago, "The only thing you should know, Sybil, is that your mother—and your father—would not want you to grow up in the shadow of their deaths. They would have wanted you—your mother especially—to be *happy*."

Part of this legacy of happiness, Sybil gathered, had been for her to grow up as a perfectly normal American girl, in a sunny, shadowless place with no history, or, at any rate, no history that concerned her. "But I don't want to be *happy*, I want to *know*," Sybil said aloud.

But the rest of the manila files, jammed so tightly together they were almost inextricable, yielded nothing.

So, disappointed, Sybil shut the file drawer, and locked it.

But what of Aunt Lora's desk drawers? She had a memory of their being unlocked, thus surely containing nothing of significance; but now it occurred to her that, being unlocked, one of these drawers might in fact contain something Aunt Lora might want to keep safely hidden. So, quickly, with not much hope, Sybil looked through these drawers, messy, jammed with papers, clippings, further packets of household receipts, old programs from plays they'd seen in Los Angeles—and, in the largest drawer, at the very bottom, in a wrinkled manila envelope with

MEDICAL INSURANCE carefully printed on its front, Sybil found what she was looking for.

Newspaper clippings, badly yellowed, some of them spliced together with aged cellophane tape—

WELLINGTON, VT., MAN SHOOTS WIFE, SELF
SUICIDE ATTEMPT FAILS

AREA MAN KILLS WIFE IN JULY 4 QUARREL
ATTEMPTS SUICIDE ON LAKE CHAMPLAIN

GEORGE CONTE, 31, ARRESTED FOR MURDER
WELLINGTON LAWYER HELD IN SHOOTING DEATH OF WIFE, 26

CONTE TRIAL BEGINS
PROSECUTION CHARGES "PREMEDITATION"
FAMILY MEMBERS TESTIFY

So Sybil Blake learned, in the space of less than sixty seconds, the nature of the tragedy from which her Aunt Lora had shielded her for nearly fifteen years.

Her father was indeed a man named "George Conte," and this man had shot her mother "Melanie" to death, in their speedboat on Lake Champlain, and pushed her body overboard. He had tried to kill himself too but had only critically wounded himself with a shot to the head. He'd undergone emergency neurosurgery, and recovered; he was arrested, tried, and convicted of second-degree murder; and sentenced to between twelve and nineteen years in prison, at the Hartshill State Prison in northern Vermont.

Sybil sifted through the clippings, her fingers numb. So this was it! This! Murder, attempted suicide!—not mere drunkenness and an "accident" on the lake.

Aunt Lora seemed to have stuffed the clippings in an envelope in haste, or in revulsion; with some, photographs had been torn off, leaving only their captions—"Melanie and George Conte, 1975," "Prosecution witness Lora Dell Blake leaving courthouse." Those photographs of George Conte showed a man who surely did resemble "Mr. Starr": younger, dark-haired, with a face heavier in the jaws and an air of youthful self-assurance and expectation. *There. Your father. "Mr. Starr." The missing person.*

There were several photographs, too, of Melanie Conte, including one taken for her high school yearbook, and one of her in a long, formal gown with her hair glamorously upswept—"Wellington woman killed by jealous husband." There was a wedding photograph of the couple looking very young, attractive, and happy; a photograph of the "Conte family at their summer home"; a photograph of "George Conte, lawyer, after second-degree murder verdict"—the convicted man, stunned, downlooking, being taken away handcuffed between two grim sheriff's men. Sybil understood that the terrible thing that had happened in her family had been of enormous public interest in Wellington, Vermont, and that this was part of its terribleness, its shame.

What had Aunt Lora said?—she'd been in therapy for some time afterward, thus did not want to relive those memories.

And she'd said, *It all happened a long time ago.*

But she'd lied, too. She had looked Sybil full in the face and lied, lied. Insisting that Sybil's father was dead when she knew he was alive.

When Sybil herself had reason to believe he was alive.

My name is Starr! Don't judge me too quickly!

Sybil read, and reread, the aged clippings. There were perhaps twenty of them. She gathered two general things: that her father George Conte was from a locally prominent family, and that he'd had a very capable attorney to defend him at his trial; and that the community had greatly enjoyed the scandal, though, no doubt, offering condolences to the grieving Blake family. The spectacle of a beautiful young wife murdered by her "jealous" young husband, her body pushed from an expensive speedboat to sink in Lake Champlain—who could resist? The media had surely exploited this tragedy to its fullest.

Now you see, don't you, why your name had to be changed. Not "Conte," the murderer, but "Blake," the victim, is your parent.

Sybil was filled with a child's rage, a child's inarticulate grief—
Why, why! This man named George Conte had, by a violent act,
ruined everything!

According to the testimony of witnesses, George Conte had been
"irrationally" jealous of his wife's friendship with other men in their
social circle; he'd quarreled publicly with her upon several occasions,
and was known to have a drinking problem. On the afternoon of
July Fourth, the day of the murder, the couple had been drinking
with friends at the Lake Champlain Club for much of the afternoon,
and had then set out in their boat for their summer home, three
miles to the south. Midway, a quarrel erupted, and George Conte shot
his wife several times with a .32 caliber revolver, which, he later con-
fessed, he'd acquired for the purpose of "showing her I was serious."
He then pushed her body overboard, and continued on to the cottage
where, in a "distraught state," he tried to take his two-year-old
daughter, Sybil, with him, back to the boat—saying that her mother
was waiting for her. But the child's grandmother and aunt, both relatives of the murdered woman, prevented him from taking her, so he
returned to the boat alone, took it out a considerable distance onto the
lake, and shot himself in the head. He collapsed in the idling boat, and
was rescued by an emergency medical team and taken to a hospital in
Burlington where his life was saved.

Why, why did they save *his* life?—Sybil thought bitterly.

She'd never felt such emotion, such outrage, as she felt for this
person George Conte: "Mr. Starr." He'd wanted to kill her too, of
course—that was the purpose of his coming home, wanting to get
her, saying her mother wanted her. Had Sybil's grandmother and
Aunt Lora not stopped him, he would have shot her too, and
dumped her body into the lake, and ended it all by shooting
himself—but not killing himself. A bungled suicide. And then, after
recovering, a plea of "not guilty" to the charge of murder.

A charge of second-degree murder, and a sentence of only between twelve to nineteen years. So, he was out. George Conte was
out. As "Mr. Starr," the amateur artist, the lover of the beautiful
and the pure, he'd found her out, and he'd come for her.

And you know why.

13. "Your Mother Is Waiting for You"

Sybil Blake returned the clippings to the envelope so conspicuously marked MEDICAL INSURANCE, and returned the envelope to
the very bottom of the unlocked drawer in her aunt's desk. She
closed the drawer carefully, and, though she was in an agitated state,
looked about the room, to see if she'd left anything inadvertently
out of place; any evidence that she'd been in here at all.

Yes, she'd violated the trust Aunt Lora had had in her. Yet Aunt
Lora had lied to her too, these many years. And so convincingly.

Sybil understood that she could never again believe anyone, fully.
She understood that those who love us can, and will, lie to us; they
may act out of a moral conviction that such lying is necessary, and
this may in fact be true—but, still, they *lie.*

Even as they look into our eyes and insist they are telling the
truth.

Of the reasonable steps Sybil Blake might have taken, this was
the most reasonable: she might have confronted Lora Dell Blake with
the evidence she'd found and with her knowledge of what the tragedy had been, and she might have told her about "Mr. Starr."

But she hated him so. And Aunt Lora hated him. And, hating
him as they did, how could they protect themselves against him, if
he chose to act? For Sybil had no doubt, now, her father had returned
to her, to do her harm.

If George Conte had served his prison term, and been released
from prison, if he was free to move about the country like any other
citizen, certainly he had every right to come to Glencoe, California.
In approaching Sybil Blake, his daughter, he had committed no
crime. He had not threatened her, he had not harassed her, he had
behaved in a kindly, courteous, generous way; except for the fact (in
Aunt Lora's eyes this would be an outrageous, unspeakable fact) that
he had misrepresented himself.

"Mr. Starr" was a lie, an obscenity. But no one had forced Sybil
to model for him, nor to accept an expensive gift from him. She had

done so willingly. She had done so gratefully. After her initial timidity, she'd been rather eager to be so employed.

For "Mr. Starr" had seduced her—almost.

Sybil reasoned that, if she told her aunt about "Mr. Starr," their lives would be irrevocably changed. Aunt Lora would be upset to the point of hysteria. She would insist upon going to the police. The police would rebuff her, or, worse yet, humor her. And what if Aunt Lora went to confront "Mr. Starr" herself?

No, Sybil was not going to involve her aunt. Nor implicate her, in any way.

"I love you too much," Sybil whispered. "You are all I have."

To avoid seeing Aunt Lora that evening, or, rather, to avoid being seen by her, Sybil went to bed early, leaving a note on the kitchen table explaining that she had a mild case of the flu. Next morning, when Aunt Lora looked in Sybil's room, to ask her worriedly how she was, Sybil smiled wanly and said she'd improved; but, still, she thought she would stay home from school that day.

Aunt Lora, ever vigilant against illness, pressed her hand against Sybil's forehead, which did seem feverish. She looked into Sybil's eyes, which were dilated. She asked if Sybil had a sore throat, if she had a headache, if she'd had an upset stomach or diarrhea, and Sybil said no, no, she simply felt a little weak, she wanted to sleep. So Aunt Lora believed her, brought her Bufferin and fruit juice and toast with honey, and went off quietly to leave her alone.

Sybil wondered if she would ever see her aunt again.

But of course she would: she had no doubt, she could force herself to do what must be done.

Wasn't her mother waiting for her?

A windy, chilly afternoon. Sybil wore warm slacks and a wool pull-over sweater and her jogging shoes. But she wasn't running today. She carried her kidskin bag, its strap looped over her shoulder.

Her handsome kidskin bag, with its distinctive smell.

Her bag, into which she'd slipped, before leaving home, the sharpest of her aunt's several finely honed steak knives.

Sybil Blake hadn't gone to school that day but she entered the park at approximately three forty-five, her usual time. She'd sighted Mr. Starr's long elegantly gleaming black limousine parked on the street close by, and there was Mr. Starr himself, waiting for her.

How animated he became, seeing her!—exactly as he'd been in the past. It seemed strange to Sybil that, somehow, to him, things were unchanged.

He imagined her still ignorant, innocent. Easy prey.

Smiling at her. Waving. "Hello, Sybil!"

Daring to call her that—"Sybil."

He was hurrying in her direction, limping, using his cane. Sybil smiled. There was no reason not to smile, thus she smiled. She was thinking with what skill Mr. Starr used that cane of his, how practiced he'd become. Since the injury to his brain?—or had there been another injury, suffered in prison?

Those years in prison, when he'd had time to think. Not to repent—Sybil seemed to know he had not repented—but, simply, to think.

To consider the mistakes he'd made, and how to unmake them.

"Why, my dear, hello!—I've missed you, you know," Mr. Starr said. There was an edge of reproach to his voice but he smiled to show his delight. "—I won't ask where *were* you, now you're *here*. And carrying your beautiful bag—"

Sybil peered up at Mr. Starr's pale, tense, smiling face. Her reactions were slow at first, as if numbed; as if she were, for all that she'd rehearsed this, not fully wakened—a kind of sleepwalker.

"And—you *will* model for me this afternoon? Under our new, improved terms?"

"Yes, Mr. Starr."

Mr. Starr had his duffel bag, his sketch pad, his charcoal sticks. He was bareheaded, and his fine silver hair blew in the wind. He wore a slightly soiled white shirt with a navy blue silk necktie and his old tweed jacket; and his gleaming black shoes that put Sybil in mind of a funeral. She could not see his eyes behind the dark lenses of his glasses but she knew by the puckered skin at the corners of his eyes that he was staring at her intently, hungrily. She was his model, he was the artist, when could they begin? Already, his fingers were flexing in anticipation.

"I think, though, we've about exhausted the possibilities of this park, don't you, dear? It's charming, but rather common. And so *finite*," Mr. Starr was saying, expansively. "Even the beach, here in Glencoe. Somehow it lacks—amplitude. So I was thinking—I was hoping—we might today vary our routine just a bit, and drive up the coast. Not far—just a few miles. Away from so many people, and so many distractions." Seeing that Sybil was slow to respond, he added, warmly, "I'll pay you double, Sybil—of course. You know you can trust me by now, don't you? Yes?"

That curious, ugly little hook of a scar in Mr. Starr's forehead —its soft pale tissue gleamed in the whitish light. Sybil wondered if that was where the bullet had gone in.

Mr. Starr had been leading Sybil in the direction of the curb, where the limousine was waiting, its engine idling almost soundlessly. He opened the rear door. Sybil, clutching her kidskin bag, peered inside, at the cushioned, shadowy interior. For a moment, her mind was blank. She might have been on a high board, about to dive into the water, not knowing how she'd gotten to where she was, or why. Only that she could not turn back.

Mr. Starr was smiling eagerly, hopefully. "Shall we? Sybil?"

"Yes, Mr. Starr," Sybil said, and climbed inside.

PART

III

Extenuating Circumstances

Because it was a mercy. Because God even in His cruelty will sometimes grant mercy.

Because Venus was in the sign of Sagittarius.

Because you laughed at me, my faith in the stars. My hope.

Because he cried, you do not know how he cried.

Because at such times his little face was so twisted and hot, his nose running with mucus, his eyes so hurt.

Because in such he was his mother, and not you. Because I wanted to spare him such shame.

Because he remembered you, he knew the word *Daddy*.

Because watching TV he would point to a man and say, *Daddy*—?

Because this summer has gone on so long, and no rain. The heat lightning flashing at night, without thunder.

Because in the silence, at night, the summer insects scream.

Because by day there are earthmoving machines and grinders operating hour upon hour razing the woods next to the playground. Because the red dust got into our eyes, our mouths.

Because he would whimper *Mommy?*—in that way that tore my heart.

Because last Monday the washing machine broke down, I heard

a loud thumping that scared me, the dirty soapy water would not drain out. Because in the light of the bulb overhead he saw me holding the wet sheets in my hand crying *What can I do? what can I do?*

Because the sleeping pills they give me now are made of flour and chalk, I am certain.

Because I loved you more than you loved me even from the first when your eyes moved on me like candleflame.

Because I did not know this yet; yes I knew it but cast it from my mind.

Because there was shame in it. Loving you knowing you would not love me enough.

Because my job applications are laughed at for misspellings and torn to pieces as soon as I leave.

Because they will not believe me when listing my skills. Because since he was born my body is misshapen, the pain is always there.

Because I see that it was not his fault and even in that I could not spare him.

Because even at the time when he was conceived (in those early days we were so happy! so happy I am certain! lying together on top of the bed the corduroy bedspread in that narrow jiggly bed hearing the rain on the roof that slanted down so you had to stoop being so tall and from outside on the street the roof with its dark shingles looking always wet was like a lowered brow over the windows on the third floor and the windows like squinty eyes and we would come home together from the University meeting at the Hardee's corner you from the geology lab or the library and me from Accounting where my eyes ached because of the lights with their dim flicker no one else could see and I was so happy your arm around my waist and mine around yours like any couple, like any college girl with her boy friend, and walking *home*, yes it was *home*, I thought always it was *home*, we would look up at the windows of the apartment laughing saying who do you think lives there? what are their names? who are they? that cozy secret-looking room under the eaves where the roof came down, came down dripping black runny water I hear now drumming on this roof but only if I fall asleep during the day with my clothes on so tired so exhausted and when I wake up there is no rain, only the earthmoving machines and grinders in the woods so I must acknowledge *It is another time, it is time*) yes I knew.

Because you did not want him to be born.

Because he cried so I could hear him through the shut door, through all the doors.

Because I did not want him to be *Mommy*, I wanted him to be *Daddy* in his strength.

Because this washcloth in my hand was in my hand when I saw how it must be.

Because the checks come to me from the lawyer's office not from you. Because in tearing open the envelopes my fingers shaking and my eyes showing such hope I revealed myself naked to myself so many times.

Because to this shame he was a witness, he saw.

Because he was too young at two years to know. Because even so he knew.

Because his birthday was a sign, falling in the midst of Pisces.

Because in certain things he *was* his father, that knowledge in eyes that went beyond me in mockery of me.

Because one day he would laugh, too, as you have done.

Because there is no listing for your telephone and the operators will not tell me. Because in any of the places I know to find you, you cannot be found.

Because your sister has lied to my face, to mislead me. Because she who was once my friend, I believed, was never my friend.

Because I feared loving him too much, and in that weakness failing to protect him from hurt.

Because his crying tore my heart but angered me too, so I feared laying hands upon him wild and unplanned.

Because he flinched seeing me. That nerve jumping in his eye.

Because he was always hurting himself, he was so clumsy falling off the swing hitting his head against the metal post so one of the other mothers saw and cried out *Oh! oh look your son is bleeding*! and that time in the kitchen whining and pulling at me in a bad temper reaching up to grab the pot handle and almost overturning the boiling water in his face so I lost control slapping him shaking him by the arm *Bad! bad! bad! bad!* my voice rising in fury not caring who heard.

Because that day in the courtroom you refused to look at me your face shut like a fist against me and your lawyer too, like I was dirt beneath your shoes. Like maybe he was not even your son but you would sign the papers as if he was, you are so superior.

Because the courtroom was not like any courtroom I had a right to expect, not a big dignified courtroom like on TV just a room with a judge's desk and three rows of six seats each and not a single window and even here that flickering light that yellowish-sickish fluorescent tubing making my eyes ache so I wore my dark glasses giving the judge a false impression of me, and I was sniffing, wiping my nose, every question they asked me I'd hear myself giggle so nervous and ashamed even stammering over my age and my name so you looked with scorn at me, all of you.

Because they were on your side, I could not prevent it.

Because in granting me child support payments, you had a right to move away. Because I could not follow.

Because he wet his pants, where he should not have, for his age.

Because it would be blamed on me. It *was* blamed on me.

Because my own mother screamed at me over the phone. She could not help me with my life she said, no one can help you with your life, we were screaming such things to each other as left us breathless and crying and I slammed down the receiver knowing that I had no mother and after the first grief I knew *It is better, so.*

Because he would learn that someday, and the knowledge of it would hurt him.

Because he had my hair coloring, and my eyes. That left eye, the weakness in it.

Because that time it almost happened, the boiling water overturned onto him, I saw how easy it would be. How, if he could be prevented from screaming, the neighbors would not know.

Because yes they would know, but only when I wanted them to know.

Because you would know then. Only when I wanted you to know.

Because then I could speak to you in this way, maybe in a letter which your lawyer would forward to you, or your sister, maybe over the telephone or even face to face. Because then you could not escape.

Because though you did not love him you could not escape him.

Because I have begun to bleed for six days quite heavily, and will then spot for another three or four. Because soaking the blood in wads of toilet paper sitting on the toilet my hands shaking I think of you who never bleed.

Because I am a proud woman, I scorn your charity.

Because I am not a worthy mother. Because I am so tired.

Because the machines digging in the earth and grinding trees are a torment by day, and the screaming insects by night.

Because there is no sleep.

Because he would only sleep, these past few months, if he could be with me in my bed.

Because he whimpered, *Mommy!*—*Mommy don't!*

Because he flinched from me when there was no cause.

Because the pharmacist took the prescription and was gone such a long time, I knew he was telephoning someone.

Because at the drugstore where I have shopped for a year and a half they pretended not to know my name.

Because in the grocery store the cashiers stared smiling at me and at him pulling at my arm spilling tears down his face.

Because they whispered and laughed behind me, I have too much pride to respond.

Because he was with me at such times, he was a witness to such.

Because he had no one but his Mommy and his Mommy had no one but him. Which is so lonely.

Because I had gained seven pounds from last Sunday to this, the waist of my slacks is so tight. Because I hate the fat of my body.

Because looking at me naked now you would show disgust.

Because I *was* beautiful for you, why wasn't that enough?

Because that day the sky was dense with clouds the color of raw liver but yet there was no rain. Heat lightning flashing with no sound making me so nervous but no rain.

Because his left eye was weak, it would always be so unless he had an operation to strengthen the muscle.

Because I did not want to cause him pain and terror in his sleep.

Because you would pay for it, the check from the lawyer with no note.

Because you hated him, your son.

Because he was *our* son, you hated him.

Because you moved away. To the far side of the country I have reason to believe.

Because in my arms after crying he would lie so still, only one heart beating between us.

Because I knew I could not spare him from hurt.

Because the playground hurt our ears, raised red dust to get into our eyes and mouths.

Because I was so tired of scrubbing him clean, between his toes and beneath his nails, the insides of his ears, his neck, the many secret places of filth.

Because I felt the ache of cramps again in my belly, I was in a panic my period had begun so soon.

Because I could not spare him the older children laughing.

Because after the first terrible pain he would be beyond pain.

Because in this there is mercy.

Because God's mercy is for him, and not for me.

Because there was no one here to stop me.

Because my neighbors' TV was on so loud, I knew they could not hear even if he screamed through the washcloth.

Because you were not here to stop me, were you.

Because finally there is no one to stop us.

Because finally there is no one to save us.

Because my own mother betrayed me.

Because the rent would be due again on Tuesday which is the first of September. And by then I will be gone.

Because his body was not heavy to carry and to wrap in the down comforter, you remember that comforter, I know.

Because the washcloth soaked in his saliva will dry on the line and show no sign.

Because to heal there must be forgetfulness and oblivion.

Because he cried when he should not have cried but did not cry when he should.

Because the water came slowly to boil in the big pan, vibrating and humming on the front burner.

Because the kitchen was damp with steam from the windows shut so tight, the temperature must have been 100°F.

Because he did not struggle. And when he did, it was too late.

Because I wore rubber gloves to spare myself being scalded.

Because I knew I must not panic, and did not.

Because I loved him. Because love hurts so bad.

Because I wanted to tell you these things. Just like this.

Don't You Trust Me?

This occurred early in the second year of The Edict, when the first wave of arrests, fines and imprisonments, and frequent deaths had run their course; and all but the most desperate women were likely to accept the new conditions, and have their babies, as The Moral Law of The Land decreed.

Except: *she* had no choice. She was a student, she had no money, no hope of employment before graduation. Her mother, divorced and very poor, would be devastated. She simply could not have a baby, and she would not. "I know what must be done"—her resolve gave her a fierce, determined courage, and kept terror at bay.

Yet weeks passed, as, fearfully, obliquely, she made inquiries about where she might find a doctor willing to perform the outlaw procedure. She spoke only with those female friends whom she believed she could trust. Under The Maternal Statute, even making such inquiries was punishable as a misdemeanor. She could be fined a thousand dollars, and expelled from college.

Nor could she trust the young man who had impregnated her —her lover who was not really her lover, hardly more than an acquaintance. She avoided him, now. He knew nothing of her condition. The mistake, jointly theirs, she would accept as solely hers.

Rumors were rife, too, of men turned informers to The Bureau of Medical Ethics, who betrayed even their own wives, out of malice. And greed: informers were paid as much as five hundred dollars for information leading to arrests.

Even so, with friends, she hid her desperation and spoke in careful, detached terms: "I have a friend who made a mistake, and who really needs help . . ."

In this way she was led, at the start of her second trimester, to Dr. Knight.

I can't go through with this, she thought—*no: in an hour it will be over, and I'll be free.* Climbing the rickety wooden outdoor stairs to Dr. Knight's office, at the rear of a row house on South Main Street. It was ten-thirty p.m. on a weekday. In her bag were sanitary napkins, a change of underwear, and eight hundred dollars cash. She'd borrowed from virtually everyone she knew.

She rang a buzzer. After a moment the door was unbolted, and opened, and there stood Dr. Knight—"Come in. Hurry. You've brought the money?"

She stepped inside, and Dr. Knight shut the door behind her and bolted it. He'd been smoking—the air stung her eyes. And there was a close, stale, faintly sweet odor as of garbage, stopped drains.

She saw to her surprise that there was no waiting room, nor any nurse or attendant. What appeared to be a kitchen table had been placed in the center of the drafty, dim-lit room, beneath a powerful light hanging from the ceiling; in a corner, on the linoleum floor, was a mound of damp, soiled towels. Dr. Knight was tall and fattily muscular in the torso, with dyed-looking shiny black hair, horn-rimmed tinted glasses, a gauze mask hiding the lower half of his face. He wore a long white apron badly stained with blood, and smooth, tight-fitting surgical gloves.

"Here. Disrobe, and put it on. Hurry." Dr. Knight handed her a soiled cotton smock, and turned away, to count his money.

She did as instructed. Terrified, her hands shaking so badly she could hardly undress, no she was resolved, she'd made her decision and knew herself fortunate: *in an hour I'll be free.* Trying not to gag at the odors, nor to notice the linoleum floor with its dark starburst stains. Trying not to hear Dr. Knight humming to himself as, at a sink, he washed his hands briskly—his gloved hands.

He beckoned her to the table, which had a chipped porcelain top, also stained. Stirrups had been attached to one end. She sat at this end, facing Dr. Knight and an aluminum stand bearing gleaming gynecological and surgical instruments. Panicked, she thought, *The instruments are shiny, that must mean they're clean.*

Of course, "Knight" was not the man's name. He had a real name, he was a real doctor, no doubt attached to one of the medical clinics in the city; very likely a member of the politically powerful PFF—Physician Friends of the Fetus. He had not come so highly recommended as a "Dr. Swan" and a "Dr. Dugan," but his fee was considerably lower.

She'd begun to sweat, and shiver. Now lying back on the cold table top, her feet in the stirrups, and her legs spread. Unasked, she told Dr. Knight how long it had been since her last period. She thought to impress him by being precise. Dr. Knight made a chuckling sound, looming over her, his eyes shadowed inside the tinted glasses, his curly graying hair given an aureole by the powerful light beyond his head. The gauze mask was damp with spittle, covering both his nose and mouth. He said, "Can't wait to get rid of it, eh?"

This was meant to be a joke—a bit gruff, but not at all hostile.

He *was* a kindly man, Dr. Knight. She was sure.

More seriously, he said, "It's a simple medical procedure, no big deal. In and out in eight minutes." But when he began to insert the cold, sharp tip of a dilating instrument into her vagina she panicked, and skidded back on the table, whimpering. Dr. Knight swore, and said, "D'you want this, or not?—it's up to you. But no refund."

She could not hear, quite. Her teeth were chattering convulsively.

She whispered, "Could I have some—anesthetic?"

"You gave me eight hundred dollars. That's all."

Chloroform, an option, would have been another three hundred;

she'd believed it would be too much of a risk, anyway—rumors were spreading that as many women were dying of carelessly administered chloroform as of hemorrhaging and infection. Now, terrified, she wished she'd borrowed the extra money.

No: stay awake. As soon as it's over, walk out free.

Dr. Knight said again it was a simple medical procedure, vacuum suction, a minimum of pain and blood and he had appointments through the night so did she want to cooperate, or not— "Don't you trust me? Eh?" There was something touchingly sulky and even hurt in his manner, beneath the masculine annoyance. *Don't you trust me?* had been her lover's query too, forgotten until this moment.

She forced herself to slide back down the table, and gripped the sides hard. Feet in the stirrups which were somewhat wobbly and bare, shivery legs spread wide. She licked her lips and whispered, "Yes."

And shut her eyes tight.

The Guilty Party

Jocko was in the habit of waking her most mornings but this morning his attack was fierce, his voice penetrating. She saw his black shiny-button eyes through the bedclothes she'd pulled over her head.

"Momma wake *up*. Momma don't *hide*. You *know* what day this is—don't you?"

She did. She did. Through the warm weight of the bedclothes that needed changing, in a voice like fur, she protested, "No. Oh please. Leave me alone."

Jocko, her child. For whom she'd suffered an eleven-hour labor of excruciating pain, having refused, for principle's sake, a cesarian. Jocko who was only two years old and scarcely out of diapers yet capable of speech, and of such cruel and uncompromising speech, she, the mother, the agent responsible, wondered what a force she'd loosed upon the world.

Mornings when she slept later than Jocko thought permissible he'd slam open the bedroom door and clamber onto the bed as he did now, straddling her with his fattish little knees and pounding on her in a tattoo of rapid-fire fists as if kneading bread dough—the pain caused seems but incidental. His voice was shrill and right-eous as a trumpet, his black bulging eyes the eyes of those terrible cherubs who are God's special creatures in the most militant of Renaissance paintings. Issued from Jocko's mouth, "Momma" was a word like a weapon.

"Momma damn you don't try to *hide*, you can't hide from *me*, damn dumb bitch don't you know who I *am*! And I'm *hungry*!"

Faintly she protested, "You're always hungry."

He tugged the bedclothes rudely away from her, exposing her so hastily she pulled up one of the straps of her nightgown to hide her flat slack bruised breast that had never recovered from Jocko's furious sucking. She gave a little scream and tried to kick him loose but he straddled her more tightly: he was too strong, and too mean. And smiling at her with what appeared to her astonished eyes a full set of white wet-glistening teeth, alarming to contemplate. Do all mothers, she wondered, look upon their offspring thinking, *Am I responsible?*

There had been a father, too, of course but the man had slipped from her, betrayed her. Before, even, Jocko was born.

Jocko was chiding her, now more pityingly, telling her she must get up, must make her plans, she'd let too many days pass until this was the final day and she hadn't any choice now—"By midnight tonight it's gonna be over."

"No. I'm not ready."

"You *are* ready."

"No!"

"*Yes!*"

"*Leave me alone!*"

She dragged at her eyes with her fists wanting to erase the vision of her son from them but this vision was too bright, too terrible, pulsing like neon, too deeply imprinted in her soul—Jocko was clearly here to stay.

"Momma where's your *pride*!"

They lived, the two of them, mother and son, in a flat in a brick row house in an aging industrial city on the mid-Atlantic seaboard, in contemporary times. The woman had not been prepared to be a mother and was still dazed, so long after the birth of her son, that she *was* a mother: herself, yet also a mother: for how she had become pregnant given her characteristic caution, which mounted at times to paranoia, and the caution and paranoia of her former lover, she simply could not comprehend. To prevent the conception of just such a presence in her life as little Jocko, she'd systematically sub-jected herself to a biochemical method of contraception that held the threat of stroke, blood clots, pulmonary embolus, endometrical cancer, and mental depression, and this threat she had lived with uneasily for the duration of her active sexual life, which was now apparently concluded. (Since the dissolution of her love and the de-parture of her lover she had some genuine difficulty imagining her-self as a physical being, still less a woman not yet in the prime of her life. And, as Jocko said, not with an air of juvenile menace but simply as if stating a self-evident fact, "Now *I'm* here, Momma, you can shut down business.")

The woman's former lover, whom she called, in her imagination, "X," being incapable any longer of uttering his name even to herself, had bitterly rejected her claim that Jocko's conception had been accidental and not her fault; and had coldly dissociated himself from her when she delayed having an abortion until it was too late—though he would have left her, she knew, in any case.

What a brief memory passion has!—and its consequences, if it has consequences, invariably make of us fools.

The woman, who had believed herself an independent woman, and had, in fact, a career, tried to see her predicament as impersonal: a symptom of contemporary times. An unmarried mother, her child. The father of the child absent. (Though he continued to live in the same city, and kept the same job—in the large complex of office and laboratory buildings in which the woman herself worked.) She tried to see that it was pointless and childish to assign blame, to speak of trust betrayed, love betrayed, "the guilty party" as Jocko insisted upon calling X, "—the son of a bitch that's got to be punished."

Jocko was no-nonsense, his attitude was direct and primitive, even in the woman's womb he'd counseled *You've had enough humiliation, it's justice we're gonna get* but she tried not to listen, or to hear.

At breakfast, gripping a soup spoon in his fist and spooning thick clots of steaming oatmeal into his mouth, Jocko mused, "*He* wanted me dead before I could even draw breath, fucker wanted me vacuum-sucked out of you the way you vacuum-suck dustballs and hairs out of a cruddy corner," chewing his food hungrily, chuckling to himself, "—*he* won't know what hits him, fucker. Tonight by midnight."

The woman, the mother, holding a cup of black coffee in her shaking fingers, said, "Oh Jocko I don't think so, really. Oh no."

"Eye for an eye, tooth for a tooth."

Smiling to show her, again, and even more resplendently now in the bright kitchen light, his strong white teeth that were slightly large for baby teeth, and of an apparently thicker texture than baby teeth usually were.

"He hadn't wanted a baby, he'd warned me beforehand—in a way, he was entirely innocent. I don't think we can blame him really. And—"

"Wanting *me* sucked up some tube and dumped into a toilet, like shit! *Me!*"

"Oh but Jocko he didn't know it would be *you*—"

"And you, did you know?—darling 'Momma'?"

"I—I didn't know at first. But—eventually—I did."

" 'Cause I took over, that's why. Damn dumb bitch don't know her ass from a hole in the ground half the time. Huh!"

"Jocko, you're too hard. Oh don't say such things!"

Jocko, eating, scowled into his sunny-yellow cereal bowl that was decorated with smiling faces. For months he'd refused his high chair and insisted upon sitting at the table with her, propped up precariously on two telephone directories and several volumes of the *World Book Encyclopedia.* Just the past week he'd begun drinking coffee, which the woman was sure was bad for his nerves since it was clearly bad for *her* nerves, yet, if she drank coffee, drank coffee in fact through most of the morning, how could she reasonably deny it to Jocko?—and how? When she tried weakly to discipline him he merely laughed, sometimes winked, as if there were a joke between them: maybe the joke of her motherhood and his babyhood? But what did that joke mean?

There were frightening moments when the woman saw Jocko, whom she loved, as a miniature man. Since X's betrayal, she was not certain that she could tolerate men, that she wanted to share the world with them. She even saw him as a prodigy, a freak, a medical horror—she'd read of a certain terrible illness, a hormonal imbalance, which causes a child (usually male) to age rapidly; to overtake his parents and die before their astonished eyes. Was Jocko so afflicted? When she took him to the pediatrician, Jocko lapsed into the style of a typical two-year-old; somehow he managed even to *look* like a two-year-old. Dr. Monk was impressed with the boy's evident sharpness and intelligence, and never failed to compliment the mother on his "physical well-being," as he called it, but he seemed to take no notice of Jocko's development otherwise; certainly he saw nothing amiss. And, in any case, so oddly—yet so characteristically!—Jocko played the role of a toddler so perfectly, down to charming little motor uncoordinations and lisping halting monosyllabic speech, his mother herself might have been deceived. Almost.

"Jocko" with its sound of brash masculine buoyancy was not a name the woman would have chosen for her son, in fact she'd chosen "Allen," after her deceased father, but "Jocko" was the name Jocko himself wanted: he'd screamed furiously as an infant if he were called anything else. "Jocko *here!*" "Jocko want *this!*" "Jocko hungry *now!*" X had come to see Jocko only three times and each time he'd been just perceptively repelled. He had not held his own son in his arms, still less had he kissed him. Tall, long-boned, with receding hair and glasses, X was not a man physically at ease in his body; his training was in biochemistry and mathematics, and he saw the world, the woman gathered, in terms of equations. Certainly he had been unable to see anything of himself in Jocko who, even as a newborn infant, had had so ruddy a face, so striking a head of spiky dark hair, and such shiny-black penetrating eyes, he could be said to resemble no one except himself. "Jocko."

Now two years old, Jocko had a chunky upper body shaped like an old-fashioned washboard. His face was round, and chunky too, but acquired at times an anxious, calculating, adult angularity; his babyish forehead sometimes furrowed cruelly with thought. His legs were foreshortened, not at all stunted, yet suggested those of a dwarf; they were chubby but muscular beneath, like his arms, and his torso. And his eyes—Jocko's remarkable thirstily intense eyes—what of them? And his genitalia, that swollen bunchy fruit distending the front of his elastic-band white cotton underpants?

What to make of Jocko except he was *here*. The sign of a new era, or a new life, of the next century perhaps.

"Whatcha looking at, Momma?" Jocko said irritably.

"At—nothing."

"Huh! I'd of said I was *something!*"

The woman had been staring at her little boy, unable to concentrate on his words (at such times, early in the morning, Jocko frequently kept up a brisk rambling monologue as if thinking aloud for both himself and her), holding her coffee cup in front of her face. Now she set it down clumsily, and rubbed her fists again into her eyes, beginning to cry, though well knowing how crying infuriated Jocko, "Oh please. I'm afraid. I can't go through with it. My own blood, Jocko, that I lost when you were born—that's enough."

Days were exterior matters. She navigated them skillfully because they were not entirely real; not as Jocko, and Jocko's father, and the wound her body bore, were real.

Mechanically, yet with impeccable taste, she dressed for work: flannel suit with a snugly fitting stylish jacket, sheer stockings and good lizard pumps; a red silk scarf for a bit of color. Jocko scolded her if her long brooding face was too pale—"No need to look older and homelier than you *are*, Momma." He'd long ago outgrown his need to be dressed by her, whistling as he zipped up his crimson silk jacket with the fire-breathing green-scaled dragon stitched on the back, stomped on his leather boots, tugged the red wool cap she'd knitted for him down over his head to about the level of his eyebrows. It was an overcast April morning, rain and icy pellets blown against the windows, so Jocko insisted they both dress warmly—there was an adult's economics in his belief that being sick and "out of action" was a stupid waste of time.

He went to get her car keys for her, and rattled them.

"C'mon Momma, haul your ass!"

"You watch your mouth, you—I'm *coming!*"

Five days a week the woman dropped Jocko off at the Little Beavers Child Care Center, where, so far as she could determine, he behaved like any normally robust child of his approximate age. It was a mystery to her how he accomplished the transformation, but clearly he enjoyed it: "yukking it up with the kiddies" was even more of a challenge than playing a toddler's role with Dr. Monk. When his mother brought Jocko into the Center and handed him over to Junie, a smiling big-breasted woman with braided hair, the child seemed actually to shrink a bit in height and girth; his shiny quick-darting eyes took on a quality of innocence; even his spiky hair lightened in tone, with a look too of childlike innocence. Most of all, Jocko's manner changed: when his mother murmured, "Bye, dear, be good, honey, I'll see you later," kissing him goodbye as always, Jocko hugged her in return and mashed his warm face against hers and said, "Momma, don't go." It was just a moment's lapse as if in some mysterious way Jocko *was* only a two-year-old with a working mother and no father at all, terrified of being abandoned.

At the Little Beavers Child Care Center, Jocko had a reputation for being mature for his age; sometimes "unsociable and belligerent," sometimes "sweet, shy, withdrawn." His great talent, to his mother's surprise, was for painting—big splashy posters in primary colors of sunflowers, grinning balloon faces, and hallucinogenic planets, which were tacked up prominently on the walls of the Center. He seemed to have some friends there but he expressed no desire to visit their homes nor did he, to his mother's relief, want anyone to visit him.

Drolly he'd observed, more than once, "The company of small children is fucking *fatiguing*."

That morning when the woman kissed Jocko goodbye he hugged her more adamantly than usual, and said, in a childish pleading voice, "Don't forget, Momma! Don't forget to come back! *Don't forget what today is!*"

"Oh Jocko," his mother said nervously, aware of Junie looking on, "—how could I forget?"

And what precisely was today?—the eve of X's departure from the city.

The last day he would be in his office at the complex, the last day as regional supervisor of the SPE Program (Special Projects, Engineering) at Bell Laboratories, the last day (and night) he would be spending in his apartment approximately four miles across the city from the woman's apartment before the moving van came to collect his possessions in the morning to bear them away to Cleveland, Ohio—X had been promoted to head a larger SPE Program at the Cleveland division of Bell Labs, and he was very proud of himself, and eager to be gone.

These humiliating facts the woman knew without having been told by X, of course; or by anyone in particular. Somehow, simply, she *knew*. And so did Jocko with his extraordinary powers of ferreting out her secrets.

As Jocko had been saying, nudging, for weeks, "Your time's running out, bimbo. Be sure *he's* marking off the days on his calendar."

The day, which was a Friday at the very end of the month, passed in erratic surges, like a flotilla of clouds. Like April storm clouds puffed and puckered with thought. Like a semi-drunken procession of brains. The woman tried to concentrate on her work for after all this was her public life, her exterior life, as valuable a life as any in the capitalist-consumer society in which she'd discovered herself living out her years, as the century itself waned and dwindled to a close, not probably the blazing apocalypse in which her generation had pretended to believe, but, yes, certainly, a close, an end, and a "new" century to follow on the calendar, plowing ours under with the impatience of all that is new, young, vigorous, and hungry. Jocko would be only twelve years old in 2000: already he belonged to the next century.

She hoped he would not forget her too quickly.

Impulsively, she telephoned X in his office—his office which was in another building, a space of mazes, escalators, and cul-de-sacs away—but was told by his secretary (who recognized the woman's voice perhaps) that X was "unavailable." The woman thanked her, and hung up quietly without leaving a message. Her pride would not allow her to leave any more messages when so many had gone unanswered these past twenty-four months.

Twenty-four months! Had it been that long?

The intolerable space of time, of X's betrayal!

In fact, as the woman well knew, it had been longer since X had so callously broken off all relations with her before their baby's birth; the space of time following their split was now considerably larger than the space of time when they'd been lovers. At first X had been apologetic, guilty, or guilty-seeming, he'd offered to pay for the abortion of course, and offered her money generally, the sums of money gradually increasing as his desperation to be free of her (and of Jocko, in the womb) increased; but the woman had refused. I love you, she said. We have brought life into the world by way of our love and we dare not extinguish it, you know that, but X hadn't seemed to hear her words, nor had he been swayed by the intense almost mystical rapture underlying her words, even as the presence in her womb urged her *Yes! yes! like that! keep on going like that, the bastard has got to listen!*

He had not listened, though. He'd simply broken off with her as other men in the past had, abruptly, outrageously, broken off with her; the difference being that now the woman was pregnant and she was not going to have an abortion—the presence in her womb would not allow her. *I want to be born, I want sunshine and I want a real mouth damn you bitch nobody's gonna stand in my way* and this was true, or became true. X could not hear their baby's urgent words nor could he be induced to press his ear against the woman's belly, not even to caress her there, to gain a sense of the life within, the miraculous life within, the life that was not to be denied. Variously X said, "Look: I'm truly sorry, can't we be friends?" and, "I guess there was a profound misunderstanding between us—if so, I'm sorry," and, less patiently, "Please leave me alone, will you? This is embarrassing for both of us," and, "Goddamn it you know I can't be the father of that child *so please leave me alone!*" and at last he'd hung up the telephone when the woman called him; and, at Bell, he'd hurry to elude her when he saw her approaching; she believed he'd made an arrangement with his director so that his office hours were ingeniously rescheduled so that the woman could never calculate when they were and wait for him in the parking lot. She visited his apartment building several times but was rebuffed. She sent him any number of letters of course, most of them dictated by Jocko. The last one, at Christmas, was terse and elliptical as a poem: *Guilt festers to blight even the innocent, thus beware!*

To none of the woman's letters had X replied.

Naturally, relations between them had totally deteriorated.

Yet the woman continued with her work at which she was highly competent and for which she was reasonably well paid: she had an advanced degree in English, and it was her responsibility at Bell to assist certain valued employees—engineers, physicists, chemists, mathematicians—prepare reports for their division supervisors and for the Department of Defense in Washington, D.C. Some of the men (they were all men) were foreign-born and needed special assistance, particularly the Japanese; all, even the native-born, seemed to have trouble expressing their ideas in coherent and fluid structures. This task the woman accomplished without knowing, or needing to know, what it was the reports meant to report; if there were elaborate requests for funding from the Pentagon, or detailed accounts of how funds had been implemented, she could type them up on the word processor swiftly and serenely, with very little sense of her subject, let alone its ontological status in the high-tech world as *hard-* or another sort of *-ware.*

As Jocko somewhat cruelly observed, "Anyway, *there,* you know what you're doing. Even if you don't know what you're doing."

Though he could be supportive too, in a more tender mood, "You do a damn good job and they know it—*just keep in control Momma, O.K.?"*

Momma agreed. O.K.

Still, late that afternoon, when most of the division staff had gone home, the woman laid her head on her arms, on her desk, and wept; or tried to weep. She muttered, "—He might still love me, he might forgive me and take me back," and for some minutes there was no response, only silence, or the humming of the fluorescent lights overhead, "—he might change his mind and take us to Cleveland with him, he *might,*" but she couldn't cry because she'd cried too many times and her tear ducts were exhausted, and in any case she wasn't in fact alone and the silence was broken by Jocko's voice sudden and staccato in her ear: *Momma why resist? You know what's your destiny, Goddamn why not fulfill it?*

The woman hadn't been home an hour after picking her little boy up at the Little Beavers Child Care Center when, curious at his whereabouts, she walked into the kitchen and saw a sight she hadn't wanted to see.

But calmly she asked, "Where did you get those knives, Jocko?"

Jocko signaled for her to be quiet, he was thinking.

He stood on a chair arranging a half dozen knives on the orange-Formica kitchen counter. Not apparently in terms of size but in terms of degrees of sharpness.

"Jocko? Those knives?"

"Don't play dumb, Momma."

The woman's hands were shaking badly, as if the entire building were vibrating. She'd drunk too many cups of coffee that day and her vision wasn't altogether reliable; driving home, she'd had a close call swerving into a lane of oncoming traffic. She would have walked out of the kitchen and left Jocko to his game but as if reading her mind he reached out swiftly and clamped his steely little fingers around her wrist.

She said faintly, "Oh—I won't *touch*," but already she'd lifted one of the knives, the one Jocko had pushed a little out of line from the others, and was weighing it in her hand.

A carving knife, made in Taiwan, with a ten-inch blade of stainless steel; finely honed, razor sharp. The plastic simulated wood handle was perfectly suited for the woman's hand.

"When did I buy this?—I never bought this."

"At the Christmas sale at Sears, Momma."

"I never did!"

"Then who, Momma?"

"Yes, but I'm not going out with it. I'm not going anywhere with it."

"Not until dark."

"When?"

"Around nine, Momma: not too early and not too late."

"I'm not."

"Sure you are."

"I'm not going alone."

"Momma, of course you're not going alone."

"I'm—not?"

"You don't go anywhere alone, Momma, do you? Anymore?"

And Jocko, balanced on the kitchen chair, of a height with his mother, smiled his sweetest and least coercive smile; the smile that, so often when, these past months, she'd wanted to die, had lifted her heart and made her impassioned as a wild young girl to *live*.

Jocko slid his arms around the woman's neck, and gave her a childish hug, and a wet warm kiss, and said again, "Momma, you know you don't go anywhere alone, anymore ever!"

*   *   *

At X's apartment building the woman would have taken the
elevator up to the ninth floor but sharp-eyed Jocko tugged at her
arm and urged her to the stairs. They didn't want any witnesses to
their visit, did they?

It was a late hour in civilization. As Jocko many times observed,
"With any guilty party—you can't just wait for God to punish."

By the time the woman and Jocko had ascended to the ninth
floor the woman was breathing quickly and shallowly and sparks of
excitement coursed along her veins. In her shoulder bag was the ten-
inch carving knife; at her side, taking the stairs more deftly than
she, with his short strong legs, was little Jocko, the fruit of her
womb. It seemed fitting and just, the woman thought, that, since
X had so rarely brought her to this place, and his own son not at
all, the two of them should be coming to see him now. And no
going back.

He'd come instead to her home, to *her*. He'd eaten the food she'd
lovingly prepared for him. Like others. Like others of his sex. He'd
spoken of loving her, he'd anointed her tense hopeful body with his
kisses. Under his tutelage she'd become beautiful hadn't she?

She had opened her woman's soul to him with no thought of
how, a man's passion spent, her very soul might be returned to her
soiled and crumpled—in Jocko's sneering words, "Like a Kleenex
the bastard's blown his nose in."

But never again.

On X's floor Jocko pushed open the staircase door an inch or so
and peered out cautiously. Saw the corridor was empty, motioned
the woman out. Whispering, "Momma *move*. C'mon." The woman
fumbled with her shoulder bag. Her vision seemed askew: she'd had
several glasses of wine, and a large white pellet-pill to calm her
nerves, before setting out. She crouched to whisper to Jocko, "Just
don't leave me, honey—promise you'll keep the door ajar?" Jocko
pushed at her legs, said impatiently, "Jesus, Momma! Of course!"
Then she was walking, swaying in her good lizard pumps through
a benign haze counting doors, locating 9-G which was X's apart-

ment, wiping at her eyes which kept filling with tears, and she drew a long deep breath to steady herself and pressed her forefinger to the doorbell, hard, so there was no going back.

Remembering how, long ago, newly pregnant and sick, and terrified, she'd telephoned X—she was certain it had been X, no matter what the man later claimed—and heard his telephone ringing ringing ringing like her life's blood remorselessly draining away and in her womb the voice spoke for the first time infinitely consoling and wondrous as God in His ancient wrath *Someday they will all pay, those guilty—only be patient* and damn right she'd been patient, ringing the doorbell a second time and hearing footsteps approaching. So there was no going back?

At the far end of the lengthy dim-lit corridor Jocko awaited her, just beyond the fire exit door he awaited her but when she squinted in that direction she saw only the blank front of the door, the door shut tight, and a near-invisible fibrillation of the air between herself and the door, a flickering quivering sensation in the corridor as if the very building, perhaps even the earth beneath, had begun to shake, which the woman, who was after all a rational person, supposed could not really be happening, or happening in any sense that had to do with her.

In any case, she was here. And so, now the door was opened, was X.

The
Premonition

Christmas was on a Wednesday this year. On the preceding Thursday, at dusk, as Whitney drove across the city to his brother Quinn's house, he had a premonition.

Not that Whitney was a superstitious man. He wasn't.

Nor was he one to interfere in others' domestic affairs, especially his elder brother's. It could be dangerous even offering Quinn unsolicited advice.

But Whitney had had a call from their youngest sister who'd had a call from another sister who'd had a call from an aunt who'd been visiting with their mother—Quinn had started drinking again, he'd threatened his wife, Ellen, and perhaps their daughters too, it was a familiar story, and depressing. For the past eleven months Quinn had been attending AA meetings, not regularly, and with an attitude of embarrassed disdain, but, yes, he'd attended meetings, and had quit drinking, or, at any rate—and here opinions differed depending upon which family member you spoke with—he'd cut down substantially on his drinking. For a man of Quinn's wealth and local prominence, the eldest of the Paxton sons, it was far more difficult, everyone agreed, than it would be for an ordinary man, to join AA, to admit he had a drinking problem; to admit he had a problem with his temper.

Whitney had had a premonition the night before, and a feeling of unease through the day, that Quinn might lose control: might this time seriously injure Ellen, even his daughters. Quinn was a big man, in his late thirties, trained at the Wharton School, with an amateur expert's knowledge of corporate law, socially gregarious, good-natured, yet, as Whitney well knew from their boyhood, very much a physical person: he used his hands to express himself, and sometimes those hands hurt.

Several times that day Whitney had called his brother's house but no one answered the telephone. A click, and the familiar husky tone of the answering tape, *Hello! This is the Paxton residence! We regret that we cannot come to the phone right now. But*—The voice was Quinn's, hearty and exuberant yet with an undercurrent of threat.

When Whitney called Quinn's office, Quinn's secretary said only that he wasn't available. Though Whitney identified himself each time as Quinn's brother, and though the secretary surely knew who he was, she refused to give out any more information. "Is Quinn at home? Is he out of town? Where *is* he?" Whitney had asked, trying not to sound upset. But Quinn's secretary, one of his faithful allies, said only, quietly, "I'm sure Mr. Paxton will be in touch with you over the holidays."

Christmas Day at the elder Paxton's enormous house on Grandview Avenue, amid all the relatives!—in such a frenetic atmosphere, how could Whitney take Quinn aside to speak with him? By then, too, it might be too late.

So, though he wasn't the type to interfere in others' marriages, still less in his brother's private life, Whitney got in his car, and drove across the city, out of the modestly affluent neighborhood of condominiums and single-family homes where he'd lived, for years, his unambitious bachelor's life, and into the semi-rural neighborhood of million-dollar homes where Quinn had moved his family a few years ago. The area was known as Whitewater Heights, all the houses were large, luxurious, and screened from the road by trees and hedges; none of the lots was smaller than three acres. Quinn's house was his own design: an eclectic mixture of neo-Georgian and contemporary, with an indoor pool, sauna, an enormous redwood deck at the rear. Whitney never drove his Volvo up the curving gravel drive, parked it in front of the three-car garage, approached the front door to ring the doorbell without feeling that he was trespassing, and he'd be made to pay, even when invited.

So he felt, now, distinctly uneasy. He rang the doorbell, he waited. The foyer was darkened, and so was the living room. He'd noticed that the garage door was shut and neither Quinn's nor Ellen's car was in the driveway. Was no one home? But did he hear music?—a radio? He was thinking that the girls had school the next day; the holiday recess wouldn't begin until Monday. It was a school night, then. Shouldn't they be home? And Ellen, too?

Waiting, he drew a deep breath of the cold night air. It was below freezing, yet no snow had yet fallen. Apart from the Christmas lights of a few houses he'd passed entering Whitewater Heights, he had no sense of an imminent holiday; he could see no Christmas decorations inside Quinn's and Ellen's house. Not even an evergreen wreath on the front door. . . . No Christmas tree? At the elder Paxton's house on Grandview Avenue, an enormous fir tree would be erected in the foyer, and there was always quite a ceremony, trimming it. The annual ritual was still celebrated, though Whitney no longer attended. One of the privileges of adulthood, he thought, was keeping your distance from the font of discomfort and pain. He *was* thirty-four years old now.

Of course, he would spend Christmas Day with the family. Or part of the day. Impossible to avoid, so long as he continued to live in the city of his birth. Yes, and he'd deliver his share of expensively wrapped presents, and receive his share; he'd be gracious as always with his mother, and courteous with his father; he understood that he'd disappointed them by failing to grow into the kind of son Quinn had grown into, but, amid holiday festivities, so many people and so much cheerful noise, the hurt would be assuaged. Whitney had lived with it so long, perhaps it was no longer actual hurt but merely its memory.

He rang the doorbell again. He called out, cautiously, "Hello? Isn't anybody home?" He could see, through the foyer window, a light or lights burning toward the rear of the house; the music seemed to have stopped. In the shadowy foyer, at the foot of the stairs, were boxes—or suitcases? Small trunks?

Was the family going on a trip? At such a time, before Christmas?

Whitney recalled a rumor he'd heard a few weeks ago, that Quinn had spoken of traveling to some exorbitantly costly exotic place, the Seychelles, with one of his women friends. He'd discounted the rumor, believing that Quinn, for all his arrogance and his indifference to his wife's feelings, would never behave so defiantly; their father would be furious with him, for one thing. And Quinn was sensitive, too, of his local reputation, for he'd toyed with the idea, over the years, of one day running for public office. Their great-grandfather Lloyd Paxton had been a popular Republican congressman and the name Paxton was still a revered one in the state. . . . The bastard wouldn't dare, Whitney thought.

Still, he felt a tinge of fear. A further premonition. What if Quinn had done something to Ellen and the girls, in a fit of rage? An image flashed to Whitney's mind of Quinn in his blood-smeared chef's apron, barbecuing steaks on the sumptuous redwood deck at the rear of the house. Quinn, last Fourth of July. A double-pronged fork in one hand, his electric carving knife in the other. The whirring of the electric gadget, the deadly flash of the blades. Quinn, flush-faced, annoyed at his younger brother for having come late, had waved him up onto the deck with the strained ebullience of a man who is on the verge of drunkenness but determined not to lose control. How masterful Quinn had seemed, six feet three inches tall, two hundred pounds, his pale blue eyes prominent in his face, his voice ringing! Whitney had obeyed him, at once. Quinn in his comical apron tied tight around his spreading waist, the wicked-looking carving knife extended toward Whitney in a playful gesture: a mock-handshake.

Whitney shuddered, remembering. The other guests had laughed. Whitney himself had laughed. Only a joke, and it *was* funny. . . . If Ellen had seen, and shuddered too, Whitney had not noticed.

This image, Whitney tried to push out of his mind.

Thinking, though, that it isn't just desperate, impoverished men who kill their families; not just men with histories of mental illness. The other day Whitney had read an appalling news item about a middle-aged insurance executive who had shotgunned his estranged wife and their children. . . . But, no, better not think of that, now.

Whitney tried the doorbell another time. It *was* working: he could hear it. "Hello? Quinn? Ellen? It's me, Whitney—" How weak, how tremulous, his voice! He was convinced that something was wrong in his brother's household, yet, at the same time, how Quinn would scorn him, if Quinn were home, for interfering; how furious Quinn would be, in any case. The Paxtons were a large, gregarious, but close-knit clan, and little sympathy was felt for those who stirred up trouble, poked their noses where they weren't wanted. Whitney's relations with Quinn were cordial at the present time, but, two years ago, when Ellen had moved out of this house and begun short-lived divorce proceedings, Quinn had accused Whitney of conspiring with Ellen behind his back; he'd even accused Whitney of being one of the men with whom Ellen had been unfaithful. "Tell the truth, Whit! I can take it! I won't hurt her, or you! Just tell the truth, you cowardly son of a bitch!" —so Quinn had raged. Yet, even in his rage, there had seemed an air of pretense, for of course Quinn's suspicions were unfounded. Ellen had never loved anyone but Quinn, the man was her life.

Not long afterward, Ellen had returned to Quinn, bringing their daughters with her. She'd dropped the divorce proceedings. Whitney had been both disappointed, and relieved—disappointed, because Ellen's bid for freedom had seemed so necessary, and so right; relieved, because Quinn, his family restored to him, his authority confirmed, would be placated. He'd had no further reason to be angry with his younger brother, only, as always, mildly contemptuous.

"Of course I wasn't serious, suspecting *her* with *you*," Quinn had said, "—I must have been drunk out of my mind."

And he'd laughed, as if even that prospect had been unlikely.

Since then, Whitney had kept a discreet distance from Quinn and Ellen. Except when they were thrown together, unavoidably, at Paxton family occasions, like Christmas Day.

Now Whitney was shivering, wondering if he should go around to the back of the house and try the door there; peer inside. But, if Quinn was home, and something *was* wrong, might not Quinn be —dangerous? The man owned several hunting rifles, a shotgun, even a revolver for which he had a permit. And, if he'd been drinking . . . Whitney recalled that policemen are most frequently shot when investigating domestic quarrels.

Then, vastly relieved, he saw Ellen approaching the door—*was* it Ellen? There appeared to be something wrong with her—this was Whitney's initial, though confused impression, which he would recall long afterward—for she was walking hesitantly, almost swaying, as if the floor were tilting beneath her; she was vigorously wringing her hands, or was she wiping them, on an apron; clearly she was anxious about the doorbell, whoever was waiting on the stoop. Whitney called out, "Ellen, it's just me, Whitney!" and saw her look of profound childlike relief.

Was she expecting Quinn? Whitney wondered.

It was flattering to Whitney, how quickly Ellen switched on the foyer lights, and how readily she opened the door to him.

Ellen exclaimed, softly, "Whitney!"

Her eyes were wide and moist and the pupils appeared dilated; there was a look of fatigue in her face, yet something feverish, virtually festive, as well. She seemed astonished to see her brother-in-law, gripping his hand hard, swaying slightly. Whitney wondered if she'd been drinking. He had watched her now and then at parties, sipping slowly, even methodically, at a glass of wine, as if willing herself to become anesthetized. Never had he seen her intoxicated, nor even in such a peculiar state as she appeared to be in now.

Whitney said, apologetically, "Ellen, I'm sorry to disturb you, but—you haven't been answering your phone, and I was worried about you."

"Worried? About me?" Ellen blinked at him, smiling. The smile began as a quizzical smile, then widened, broadened. Her eyes were shining. "About *me?*"

"—and the girls."

"—the *girls?*"

Ellen laughed. It was a high-pitched, gay, melodic laugh of a kind Whitney had never heard from her before.

Swiftly, even zestfully, Ellen shut the door behind Whitney, and bolted it. Leading him into the hall by the hand—her own hand was cool, damp, strong-boned, urgent—she switched off the foyer light again. She called out, "It's Uncle Whitney, girls!—it's Uncle Whitney!" Her tone suggested vast relief, and a curious hilarity beneath the relief.

Whitney gazed down upon his sister-in-law, perplexed. Ellen was wearing stained slacks, a smock, an apron; her fair brown hair was brushed back indifferently from her forehead, exposing her delicate ears; she wore no makeup, not even lipstick, thus looked younger, more vulnerable than Whitney had ever seen her. In public, as Quinn Paxton's wife, Ellen was unfailingly glamorous—a quiet, reserved, beautiful woman who took obsessive care with grooming and clothes, and whose very speech patterns seemed premeditated. Quinn liked women in high heels—good-looking women, at least —so Ellen rarely appeared in anything other than stylishly high heels, even at casual gatherings.

In flat-heeled shoes of the kind she was wearing this evening, she seemed smaller, more petite than Whitney would have guessed. Hardly taller than her elder daughter Molly.

As Ellen led Whitney through the house, to the kitchen at the rear—all the rooms were darkened, and in the dining room, as in the foyer, there were boxes and cartons on the floor—she spoke to him in that bright, high-pitched voice, as if she were speaking, and drawing him out, for others to hear. "You say you were worried, Whitney?—about me, and the girls? But why?"

"Well—because of Quinn."

"Because of Quinn! Really!" Ellen squeezed Whitney's hand, and laughed. "But why 'because of Quinn,' and why now?—tonight?"

"I'd been speaking to Laura, and she told me—he'd started drinking again. He'd been threatening you, again. And so I thought—"

"It's kind of you, and of Laura, to care about me and the girls," Ellen said, "—it's so unlike the Paxtons! But then you and Laura aren't really Paxtons yourselves, are you. You're—" She hesitated, as if the first word that came to mind had to be rejected, "—on the periphery. You're . . ." And here her voice trailed off into silence.

Whitney asked the question most urgent to him, hoping he didn't betray the apprehension he felt, "Is—Quinn here?"

"Here? No."

"Is he in town?"

"He's gone."

"Gone—?"

"On a business trip."

"Oh, I see." Whitney breathed more deeply. "And when is he coming back?"

"He's going to send for us, in Paris. Or maybe Rome. Wherever *we* are, when he finishes up his business, when he has time for us."

"Do you mean you're going away, too?"

"Yes. It's all very recent. I was running around all morning, getting the girls' passports validated. It will be their first time out of the country, except for Mexico; we're all very excited. Quinn wasn't enthusiastic at first, he had complicated business dealings in Tokyo, you know Quinn, always negotiating, always calculating, his brain never *stops*—" But here Ellen paused, laughing, as if startled. "Well—you know Quinn. You are his brother, you've lived in his shadow, how could you not know Quinn. No need to anatomize Quinn!"

And Ellen laughed again, squeezing Whitney's hand. She appeared to be leaning slightly against him, as if for balance.

Whitney had to admit, he was profoundly relieved. The thought that his brother was in no way close at hand, in no way an active threat to him—this restored Whitney's composure considerably.

"So. Quinn has flown off, and you and the girls are following him?"

"He has his business dealings, you see. Otherwise, we'd all have gone together. Quinn wanted us to go together." Ellen spoke more precisely now, as if repeating memorized words. "Quinn *wanted* us to go together, but—it wasn't practical, under the circumstances. After Tokyo he thought he might have to fly to—I think it's Hong Kong."

"So you're going to miss Christmas here? All of you?"

"I've done my Christmas shopping, though! I won't feel guilty about not participating. The girls and I just won't be at your parents' to watch our presents being opened," Ellen said cheerfully, with a peculiar emphasis, as if she were trying not to slur her words. "Of course, we're going to miss you all. Oh, terribly! Your dear father, your lovely mother, *all* Quinn's family—yes, we're going to miss you terribly. And so will Quinn."

Whitney asked, "When did you say Quinn left, Ellen?"

"Did I say?—he left last night. On the Concorde."

"And you and the girls are leaving—?"

"Tomorrow! Not on the Concorde, of course. Just regular coach. But we're tremendously excited, as you can imagine."

"Yes," Whitney said guardedly. "I can imagine."

Whitney deduced that Quinn *had* gone off with his latest woman friend, to the Seychelles, or wherever; he'd managed to convince his credulous wife that he was on one of his "confidential" business trips, and she seemed satisfied by—grateful for?—the explanation.

How women crave being lied to—being deluded! Poor Ellen.

Whitney thought, I'm not the one to enlighten her.

"How long did you say you're going to be gone, Ellen?"

"*Did* I say?—I don't remember, if I did!" Ellen laughed.

And she pushed gaily through the swinging doors into the kitchen, leading Whitney by the hand, as if in triumph.

"It's Uncle Whitney!" Molly cried.

"Uncle Whit-ney!" Trish cried, clapping her rubber-gloved hands.

The kitchen was so brightly lit, the atmosphere so charged, gay, frenetic, Whitney halfway thought he'd stepped into a celebration of some kind. This too he would remember, afterward.

Ellen helped him remove his overcoat as his pretty nieces beamed upon him, giggly and breathless. Whitney had not seen them in six months, and it seemed to him that each had grown. Molly, fourteen years old, was wearing a slovenly shirt, jeans, and an apron knotted around her thin waist; white plastic-framed sunglasses with amethyst lenses hid her eyes. (Was one of the eyes blackened?—shocked, Whitney tried not to stare.) Trish, eleven years old, was similarly dressed, but with a baseball cap reversed on her head; when Whitney entered the kitchen she'd been squatting, wiping something up off the floor with a sponge. She wore oversized yellow rubber gloves which made a sticky, sucking sound as she clapped her hands.

Whitney was fond, very fond, of his young nieces. Their girlish mock-rapturous delight in his visit made him blush, but he was flattered. "Great to see you, Uncle Whitney!" they cried in unison, and, giggling, "Great to see *you*, Uncle Whitney!"

As if, Whitney thought, they'd been expecting someone else?

He frowned, wondering if perhaps Quinn had not gone, after all.

Ellen was hurriedly removing her stained apron. "It's ideal that you've dropped by tonight, Whit," she said warmly, "—you are the girls' favorite uncle by far. We were all thinking how sad it is, we wouldn't be seeing you on Christmas Day!"

"And I'll be sorry not to see *you*."

A distinctly female atmosphere in the room, Whitney thought; with an undercurrent of hysteria. A radio was tuned to a popular music station, and from it issued the simplistic, percussive, relentlessly shrill music young Americans loved, though Whitney could not see how Ellen tolerated it. All the overhead lights were on, glaring. Surfaces gleamed, as if newly scrubbed. The fan above the stove was turned up high, yet the kitchen still smelled—of something rich, damp, sour-sweet, cloying. The very air was overheated, as if steamy. Scattered about were empty cans of Diet Coke and crusts of pizza; on the counter near a stack of gift-wrapped packages was a bottle of California red wine. (So Ellen *had* been drinking!—Whitney saw that her eyes were glassy, her lips slack. And she too had a bruise, or bruises, just above her left eye.) What was remarkable was that most of the available space in the kitchen, including the large butcher block table at the center, was taken up with packages and Christmas wrapping paper, ribbons, address labels—Whitney was astonished to realize that, on the very eve of their ambitious trip abroad, his sister-in-law and nieces had given themselves up to a frenzy of Christmas preparations. How like women, to be thinking of others at such a time! No wonder their faces were so bright and feverish, their eyes glittering manic.

Ellen offered Whitney a drink, or would he prefer coffee?— "It's so cold out! And you'll have to go back out in it!" Ellen said, shivering. The girls shivered too, and laughed. What *was* so funny, Whitney wondered? He accepted the offer of a cup of coffee if it wasn't too much trouble, and Ellen said, quickly, "Of course not! Of course not! Nothing is too much trouble *now*!"

And again the three of them laughed, virtually in unison.

Do they know? Whitney wondered. That Quinn has betrayed them?

As if reading Whitney's thoughts, Trish said suddenly, "Daddy is going to the Sea Shell Islands. That's where he's going."

Molly said, with a little laugh, "No, silly—Daddy is going to Tokyo. Daddy is *in* Tokyo. On business."

"—Then he's going to meet us. On the Sea Shell Islands. 'A tropical paradise in the Indian Ocean.' " Trish ripped off her stained rubber gloves and tossed them onto a counter.

"The Seychelle Islands," Ellen said, "—but we're not going there, any of us." She spoke pointedly to Trish, voice slightly raised. She was making coffee with quick deft motions, scarcely paying attention to the movements of her hands. "*We're* going to Paris. Rome. London. Madrid."

" 'Paris. Rome. London. Madrid.' " The girls toned in near-unison.

The fan whirred loudly above the stove. But the close, steamy air of the kitchen was very slowly dispelled.

Ellen chattered about the upcoming trip, and Whitney saw that the bruises on her forehead were purplish-yellow. If he were to ask her what had caused them, she would no doubt say she'd bumped her head in an accident. Molly's blackened eye—no doubt that was an accident too. Whitney recalled how, many years ago, at a family gathering on the lawn of the Paxtons' estate, Quinn had suddenly and seemingly without provocation slapped his young wife's head —it had happened so swiftly few of the guests had noticed. Red-faced, incensed, Quinn said loudly, for the benefit of witnesses, "Bees! Goddam bees! Trying to sting poor Ellen!"

Eyes smarting with tears, Ellen recovered her poise, and, deeply embarrassed, hurried away into the house. Quinn did not follow.

No one followed.

No one spoke of the incident to Quinn. Nor did they, so far as Whitney ever knew, speak of it to one another.

Whitney uneasily anticipated the comments that would be made, on Christmas Day, when Quinn and his family were absent —willfully absent, it would seem. He wondered, but did not want to ask, if Ellen had spoken with his mother yet, to explain, and to apologize. Why hadn't they waited until January, to take a vacation? Quinn and his woman friend too?

No, better not ask. For it was none of Whitney Paxton's business.

Ellen gave Whitney his coffee, offered him cream and sugar, handed him a teaspoon, but the spoon slipped from her fingers and fell clattering to the damp, polished floor. Double-jointed Trish stooped to pick it up, tossed it high in the air behind her back and caught it over her shoulder. Ellen said crossly, "Trish!" and laughed. Molly, wiping her overheated face on her shirt, laughed too.

"Don't mind Trish, she's getting her period," Molly said wickedly.

"Molly—!" Ellen cried.

"Damn you—!" Trish cried, slapping at her sister.

Whitney, embarrassed, pretended not to hear. Was little Trish really of an age when she might menstruate? Was it possible?

He raised the coffee cup to his lips with just perceptibly shaking fingers, and sipped.

* * *

So many presents!—Ellen and the girls must have been working for hours. Whitney was touched, if a bit bemused, by their industry; for how like women it was, buying dozens of gifts which in most cases no one really wanted, and, in the case of the affluent Paxtons, certainly did not need; yet fussily, cheerfully, wrapping them in expensive, ornate wrapping paper, glittering green and red Christmas paper, tying big ornate bows, sprinkling tinsel, making out cards—*To Father Paxton, To Aunt Vinia, To Robert* were a few that caught Whitney's eye—with felt-tip pens. Whitney saw that most of the packages had been wrapped, and neatly stacked together; no more than a half-dozen remained to be wrapped, ranging in size from a small hatbox to an oblong container made of some lightweight metal measuring perhaps three feet by two. One unwrapped present appeared to be a gift box of expensive chocolates, in a gilt-gleaming cannister, metallic too. Everywhere on the counters and the butcher block table were sheets and strips of wrapping paper, ribbon remnants, Scotch tape rolls, razor blades, scissors, even gardening shears. On a section of green plastic garbage bag on the floor, as if awaiting removal to the garage, or disposal, was a heterogenous assortment of tools— claw-headed hammer, pliers, another gardening shears, a butcher knife with a broken point, Quinn's electric carving knife.

"Uncle Whitney, don't peek!"

Molly and Trish tugged at Whitney's arms, greatly excited. Of course, Whitney realized, they didn't want him to discover his own Christmas present.

Yet he said, teasing, "Why don't I take my own present tonight, and save you the trouble of mailing it? If, that is, you have one for me."

"Of course we have one for you, Whit dear!" Ellen said reprovingly. "But we can't give it to you now."

"Why not?" He winked at the girls. "I promise not to open it till Christmas Day."

"Because—we just can't."

"Even if I promise, cross my heart and hope to die?"

Ellen and the girls exchanged glances, eyes shining. How like their mother the daughters were, Whitney was thinking, with a pang of love, and loss—these three attractive, sweet-faced women, like benign Fates, his brother Quinn's family and not, not ever, *his*. The girls had Ellen's fair, delicate skin, and her large, somber, beautiful gray eyes; there was little of Quinn, or of the Paxtons, in them, only a twisty sort of curl to their hair, a pert upper lip.

They were all giggling. "Uncle Whitney," Molly said, "we just *can't*."

The remainder of the visit passed quickly. They talked of neutral matters, of travel in general, of Whitney's undergraduate year in London; they did not speak of, or even allude to, Quinn. Whitney sensed that, for all their high spirits, and their obvious affection for him, they were eager to be alone again, to finish preparations. And Whitney was eager to be gone.

For this *was* Quinn's house, after all.

Like the kitchen, the guest bathroom had been freshly cleaned; the sink, the toilet bowl, the spotless white bathtub fairly sparkled, from a thorough scrubbing with kitchen cleanser. And the fan whirred energetically overhead, turned to high.

And there was that peculiar odor—a cloying, slightly rancid odor, as of blood. Washing his hands, Whitney puzzled over it, uneasily, for it reminded him of something—but what?

Suddenly, then, the memory returned: many years ago, as a child at summer camp in Maine, Whitney had seen the cook cleaning chickens, whistling loudly as she worked—ducking the limp carcasses in steaming water, plucking feathers, chopping and tearing off wings, legs, feet, scooping out, by hand, moist slithery innards. Ugh! The sight and the smell had so nauseated Whitney, he had not been able to eat chicken for months.

With a thrill of repugnance, he wondered, now, if the blood-heavy odor had to do after all with menstruation.

His cheeks burned. He didn't want to know, really.

Some secrets are best kept by females, among females. Yes?

* * *

Then, as Whitney was about to leave, Ellen and the girls surprised him: they gave him his Christmas present, after all.

"Only if you promise not to open it before Christmas!"

"Only if you pro-mise!"

Ellen pressed it upon him, and, delighted, Whitney accepted it:
a small, agreeably lightweight package, beautifully wrapped in red
and gilt paper, of about the size of a box containing a man's shirt
or sweater. *To Uncle Whitney with love—Ellen, Molly, Trish.* Quite
pointedly, Quinn's name had been omitted, and Whitney felt satisfaction that Ellen had taken revenge of sorts upon her selfish husband, however petty and inconsequential a revenge.

Ellen and the girls walked with Whitney to the front door,
through the darkened house. He noticed slipcovers on the living
room furniture, rolled-up carpets, and, again, in the shadowy foyer,
a number of boxes, suitcases, and small trunks. These were preparations not for a brief vacation but for a very long trip; apparently
Quinn had tricked Ellen into agreeing to some sort of wild plan, to
his own advantage, as always. What this might be, Whitney could
not guess, and was not about to inquire.

They said goodbye at the door. Ellen, Molly, and Trish kissed
Whitney, and he kissed them in turn, and, breath steaming, feeling
robust and relieved, Whitney climbed into his car, setting the present in the seat beside him. Girlish voices called after him, "Remember, you promised not to open it till Christmas! Remember, you
promised!" and Whitney called back laughingly, "Of course—I
promise." An easy promise to make, for he had virtually no interest
in whatever they'd bought for him; there was the sentiment, of
course, which he appreciated, but so little interest did he have in
these annual rituals of gift giving, he arranged for his own presents
to be sent out gift-wrapped from a department store, for all occasions
requiring gifts; if items of clothing given him didn't fit, he rarely
troubled to exchange them.

Driving back home across the city, Whitney felt pleased, however, with the way things had turned out. He'd been brave to go to
Quinn's house—Ellen and the girls would always remember. *He*
would always remember. He glanced at the present beside him,

pleased too that they'd given it to him tonight, that they'd trusted him not to open it prematurely.

How characteristic of women, how sweet, that they trust us as they do, Whitney was thinking; and that, at times at least, their trust is not misplaced.

Phase Change

Who is it? Did he follow me in here, or was he waiting just inside the door? Julia Matterling sensed rather than saw the man watching her. She had not yet looked at him, had not confronted him. He stood motionless to her extreme left (against a wall?), at the very periphery of her vision; it seemed that he exerted a palpable gravitational tug. Julia was alert rather than alarmed, or even apprehensive, for, in this public place, she was certainly in no danger—in the County Clerk's office in the basement of the Broome County Courthouse, on a busy weekday afternoon. She had come to get her and her husband's updated passports and was now about to leave, having given a check to the woman behind the counter and having slipped the passports and the receipt into her handbag. Turning, with a studied casualness, Julia glanced at the man she believed had been watching her—seeing, to her surprise, that he was in uniform!—he was one of the numerous sheriff's deputies stationed at intervals in the courthouse. And, with an unsettling bluntness, he *was* watching her.

Do I know him?—impossible. Does he know me?

A swarthy-skinned man in his mid-thirties, with deep-set derisive eyes, lank graying-brown hair, an ironic mouth. He had a coarse, country-boy attractiveness, but had grown thick-bodied, beefy. His gunmetal-gray uniform with blue trim fitted him snugly at the torso; Julia could see, or believed she could see, the bulge of his shiny black leather holster and the grip of his revolver, above his left thigh. He was a stranger, and could not possibly know Julia Matterling or her husband, Norman, yet, rudely, he continued to stare at her as if they were acquainted.

No. Stop. I don't know you.

Their eyes met, and held, for several seconds. Then, confused, blushing, Julia looked pointedly away, and walked quickly out of the Clerk's office. She wondered at the womanly instinct to feel guilt for arousing male interest—as if there could be any reasonable grounds for *her* complicity!

What a dreary place, the Broome County Courthouse! Julia was eager to be gone but hesitated between taking the stairs back up to the first floor, or the elevator. She had taken the stairs down, but the stairway was grimy and dim-lit, not very pleasant. (She had recently learned that a friend from college, a woman executive at CBS, had been raped and badly beaten in a stairwell in some presumably safe building in New York City. What horror!) The elevator was a safer prospect, Julia thought, so she punched the *up* button, and waited.

Is he watching?—following me?—no.

She glanced covertly over her shoulder, but saw only an elderly black woman and a boy entering the County Clerk's office. The sheriff's deputy was nowhere in sight. *My imagination! Ridiculous.* For Julia Matterling was not a young woman—she was thirty-seven years old. Even as a girl, in the prime of her small-boned, dark-eyed prettiness, she had not been one to feel eyes drawn irresistibly to her as she entered a room or walked down a street; nor had she wanted such attention. For what in fact does such abstract male interest mean, does it hold a promise, or a threat?

The elevator was maddeningly slow. Like the courthouse generally, it was old, even antiquated. Julia pressed the *up* button again and waited, trying to forestall nervousness. How eager she was, like a silly, frightened child, to be gone!

The Matterlings, Julia and Norman, lived in the suburban village of Queenston, twenty miles away; like most Queenston residents, they rarely visited the grimy industrial city that was the county seat, except on unavoidable official business. Julia had not been here for years; Norman, perhaps, had never been here. He held the title of Distinguished Research Fellow at the Center for Advanced Study in the Sciences at Queenston, and when, grudgingly, he agreed to travel at all, it was usually thousands of miles, to scientific conferences in distant parts of the globe. So absorbed in his work! So preoccupied, like an overgrown child! Even when, during dinner, Norman frowned at his plate, chewing slower and slower, the man was busy, he was *working*, and Julia had learned not to interrupt.

She had a job as an assistant curator at a privately endowed art museum in Queenston, but she attended to all of the household chores and local errands, like getting her and Norman's passports updated. (Norman was scheduled to give an important paper on phase changes in the early universe, in Tokyo, next month; Julia hoped to accompany him.) She did not mind being responsible for the practical, domestic side of their lives; she had never minded. She had no children to care for, and no dependents (except Norman).

A contract between the practical and the celestial?—between the ordinary and the extraordinary?

At last the elevator arrived: the door opened, and Julia automatically stepped inside.

Seeing, too late, even as the door slid shut behind her, that there was a single other passenger in the car: *the sheriff's deputy.*

Julia stared at him, too surprised at first to be frightened. It *was* him! But how had he slipped past her, to get to another floor of the building? He was smiling at her, baring his uneven, yellowed teeth in a sniggering grimace. He shook his head, brusque as a dog, flicking a strand of greasy hair out of his eyes.

Julia whispered, "What are you—? Who are—?"

Even as he moved toward her. At her. As Julia gave a little scream and pushed at him with her handbag, the deputy took hold of her by both shoulders, shoved her back against the wall of the elevator so that she cried out in pain; pressed himself against her in a lewd, grinding manner. "No! Stop! Help!"—Julia's words were cut off as her assailant jammed the palm of his hand against her mouth.

Seen so closely, the man's skin was roughly textured, as if pitted; his eyes were damp, cruel, derisive; an oily sheen covered his face. Julia could no longer cry aloud, her protests were silent, interior, *Don't! Don't hurt me! Who are you!* as the elevator rose in drunken lurches—past the first floor—past the second—past the third—and now her assailant, laughing, panting, had pulled the skirt of Julia's beige linen suit up past her hips, crudely he'd unzipped his trousers, with no mind for how he was hurting her, slamming her back against the wall, he thrust his penis at her, between her legs, and then into her, *or was he thrusting the barrel of his revolver into her*, Julia screamed behind his hand *No! Not me!* as a sensation of scalding water splashed over her, centered in her loins, coursing rapidly through her body, and—

Julia woke, terrified, panting. Desperate to free herself from something twisted between her legs. Bedclothes? Was she in *bed*?

Dazed, she groped beside her to feel a presence in the bed: dark, warm, heavy, inert: her husband, asleep.

"Thank God! Oh, thank God!" Julia whispered aloud.

What an ugly dream! how vivid, lifelike! and what shame to it!

But Norman had not been disturbed. He lay on his back, a damp hoarse rattle in his throat. Oblivious of Julia's anguish.

It must have been about four o'clock in the morning. Julia lay shivering in her sweat-soaked nightgown, stiffly, on her side of the bed, drifting in and out of a troubled sleep for the remainder of the night. She was grateful for Norman's uninterrupted sleep, which was like that of a great infant: Norman sometimes worked through the night, and slept fitfully during the day; but when he slept at night, it was this enviable sleep of oblivion, as if the very particles of his being were in dissolution, like that of the early universe which was his life's work. *He will never know.*

By the time the room lightened with dawn, Julia had forgotten most of her dream. When, examining her face in the bathroom mirror, next morning, she noticed a plumlike bruise on her throat, she had no idea what might have caused it—she'd forgotten even the struggle of her dream, her abrupt wrenching into consciousness.

Next morning, after Norman left for the Center, Julia drove to the Broome County Courthouse, as she'd planned. How odd, how . . . uncanny . . . as she parked her car, approached the building, began climbing the stairs, she began to feel a curious sensation of apprehension and excitement. How familiar the old courthouse was, outside and in, how familiar its very odor, as if she'd been there only recently!—when, in fact, she had not been there for years. Julia took the elevator to the basement, hurried to the County Clerk's office, picked up her and Norman's passports, paid the fee, without incident. Yet, to her embarrassment, her hands shook visibly as she made out a check. She looked around the room—seeing only strangers, clerks behind the counter, a sheriff's deputy stationed beside the door; no one taking the slightest notice of Julia Matterling.

She knew herself as an attractive woman past the bloom of her youth, but not strikingly attractive. Norman had once believed her beautiful—telling her, shyly, clumsily, as if it were a modest truth that might be refuted with uneasy laughter on Julia's part. (It had not been. Deeply moved, willing to believe that, in Norman's inexperienced eyes, she *was* beautiful, Julia had remained silent.) This morning, wearing her tailored beige linen suit and tasteful shoes with a modest heel, pearl button-earrings in her ears, Julia would surely not have expected, nor indeed welcomed, any attention from strangers; and it seemed quite fitting that, passing through the Broome County Courthouse on her perfunctory errand, she drew no one's attention at all—as if she were invisible.

Like one of Norman's quarks. Or—is it leptons? hadrons? gluons? squarks? passing invisibly, by magic, through a vacuum?

Julia noticed several sheriff's deputies in their smart gray uniforms with blue trim stationed at intervals around the building. There seemed little need for them, at the present time; but Julia supposed that, when a trial was in session, there might be the threat of sudden violence. How bored some of them looked, like museum guards! She wondered idly, a curious thought for her, whether, in their enforced lethargy, they dreamt with their eyes open.

When Julia left by the front door of the courthouse, one of the deputies, a swarthy-skinned man with lank graying-brown hair, politely pushed the door open for her, murmuring, "Exit here, ma'am!"—but even he scarcely glanced at her.

Yet—how good Julia Matterling felt, her morning's errand completed, and her quick return to Queenston, and the solace of her weekday schedule before her, before her! The sensation of dread and excitement was already beginning to lift.

What is happening to me, what change is coming over me? And why at this time?

The visit to the courthouse was on a Tuesday. Three days later, slipping into a seat at the rear of a crowded amphitheater at the Center for Advanced Study at Queenston, where a symposium on the structure of the universe was in session, Julia felt again that uncanny sensation: a dread so extreme as to be almost nausea, overlaid with a childlike excitement and yearning.

She had hurried to the Center from the art museum in which she worked, not wanting to be late for the four-thirty session; or, if late, which was seemingly unavoidable, hoping not to be conspicuous in her lateness. Norman would surely not notice—Norman was not a man to notice such trivial matters—but others, his colleagues and their wives, would see, and disapprove. Julia entered the room breathless, sat quickly, tried to collect her thoughts. *Why is my heart beating so fast? Am I going to faint?* For the fourteen years of her marriage to Norman Matterling, Julia had been attending professional sessions to hear her distinguished husband speak; surely she had no reason to feel, this afternoon, a wife's anxiety?

On a raised platform at the front of the room, a panel of five male scientists, prominent among them Norman Matterling with his silvery-blond wispy hair and his thick-lensed glasses, was discussing a problem of some urgency. Julia strained to hear: such terms as "radius of curvature," "supersymmetry," "phase change," "horizon problem," were being uttered. These were teasingly familiar to Julia: had not her husband tried to explain them to her, many times?— for we are living in a revolutionary epoch, Norman Matterling believed, and it is a pity, if not a tragedy, for anyone to be left behind.

Julia saw with pride how everyone in the amphitheater, rows and rows of men and women, leaned forward intently as the panelists debated the significance of recent laboratory experiments in which, astonishingly, the conditions of the early universe—*the universe as it was when it was a mere one ten-billionth of a second old*—had been simulated, by way of machines that accelerated two beams of protons to nearly the speed of light, then let them collide head-on; in these collisions, temperatures were raised to the probable levels of that point in time when the weak and the electromagnetic forces in the universe unified. "Therefore," Norman Matterling said in a quavering voice, "—it is possible to theorize—"

Julia winced to see that Norman was wearing the bulky, frayed, hunter-green corduroy jacket she was certain she had thrown out years ago; and that his wispy hair rose from his scalp as if charged with static electricity. Why didn't he wet it down! When Norman was in earnest, as he was now, rising clumsily from his seat to hurry to the blackboard, to scrawl a lengthy, illegible equation, he began to stammer; spittle flew from his lips; he had the look of a bear on its hind legs, gaze turned inward with the effort of keeping its balance. Yet—with what respect the other panelists turned to him! With what hushed interest the entire audience listened! Norman was promulgating a theory about an early phase change of the universe, which occurred at a time so immediately after the Big Bang as to defy comprehension by any means other than mathematical: 10^{-35} seconds. (Which was represented by a decimal point, thirty-four zeros, and then a one.) Prior to this, apparently, "quarks had frozen into hadrons."

Julia smiled uneasily. Had she known that?

A phase change was a change from one state to another, as when gas changes to liquid, liquid to solid, solid to gas, the seemingly whole into the infinitely fragmented. A phase change was not deducible but only to be experienced. A phase change was/was not irrevocable.

Norman Matterling was speaking of supersymmetrical particles forming a mirror-image of the observed world; from this, one could deduce an entire shadow universe, a mirror of the universe we inhabit—"Interacting with ours," Norman said excitedly, "only through the force of gravity. So—" At this, another panelist, an astrophysicist from Cal Tech, rudely interrupted, and strode to the blackboard to scribble an unintelligible equation of his own.

Julia was deeply absorbed in the exchange, even as, heart pounding as if she were approaching a crisis of which she had no conscious awareness, she slipped quietly out of her seat, needing to find a lavatory.

How many times had she attended meetings and social gatherings at the Center, yet, to her frustration, she invariably had difficulty locating a women's room. (Perhaps, in this monastic place so primarily male, there were in fact few facilities for women?) And the maze of corridors, flights of stairs, glass cul-de-sacs overlooking empty Japanese gardens—what did it remind her of but the phenomenon of the rapidly expanding universe? *Faintness means farness. And madness.*

But Julia was not thinking of such things. Gripping her handbag so tightly her knuckles turned white, she was thinking only of the weakness in her bowels.

And then—what relief! She found a women's lavatory just around a corner from the Center's kitchen facilities.

She used a toilet; then stood at a sink splashing cold water onto her face. At an adjacent sink stood a plump, plain-faced woman with gray hair wrapped in braids around her head, washing her hands vigorously. Julia said, with forced vivacity, wiping her face, "I wish I could understand them, don't you? I know they hold the secrets to the universe—the *real* universe, not *ours*. Actually, I got A's in high school physics and calculus, I'm not an ignorant person, but I can't remember anything I've ever learned, and it's getting worse. Dozens of times I've been told what a 'quark' is, what a 'black hole' is, what 'omega' means—but I never remember, I never *know*. Sometimes I just wish it would all go away! Just—*vanish!*" Julia laughed, expecting the woman to join in; but the woman merely stared at her coldly, wiped her hands on a towel, and left the room. Julia realized belatedly, to her extreme embarrassment, that the woman was none other than Elsa Heisenberg, a relative of the great Werner Heisenberg, and a renowned astronomer at Palomar Observatory.

Julia caught her own blurry gaze in the mirror above the sink. "Aren't you a fool, mistaking *her* for *you!*"

She did not want to miss any more of the symposium, but, in her haste to return to the amphitheater, apparently she took a wrong turn, and lost her way. She found herself wandering in an airless, overheated corridor; turned a corner, and found herself at the rear of the Center's kitchen area, where several workers, husky young black men in white uniforms, were lounging around a table, smoking cigarettes. (Marijuana? Hashish? Julia's nostrils pinched at the sweet, acrid, piercing odor.) As soon as the black men saw Julia their eyes opened wide, and their postures stiffened perceptibly.

Shyly Julia said, "Excuse me, but I—I seem to be lost. How do I get back to the amphitheater?"

The men continued to stare at her, as if they had never seen anyone quite like her. They were now standing, as if at attention. The youngest, a lanky brown-skinned youth with a bizarre flattop haircut and woolly hair shaved and sculpted around the base of his head, giggled shrilly and hid his cigarette behind his back. Another, squat and thick-necked, with a broad, brutal, purplish-black-skinned face and lips that looked swollen, grinned at Julia suggestively.

Do they know me? Do I know them?

Were they waiting for me, at this juncture of time and space and contingency?

There were four black men, in dazzling white waiter's uniforms. White teeth, white smiles. Gold fillings glittering amid those smiles. Several gold earrings in the left ear of the youngest . . . if these constituted a code, what did the code mean? Julia saw that the men were exchanging glances; easing slyly forward. One, surely no less than six feet seven inches tall, with a glaring ebony-black skin, had sidestepped adroitly to the right, blocking Julia's path should she try to flee.

Julia gripped her handbag tight in both hands. She stood tall and with as much authority as she could summon. Very frightened, faintness washing over her, but she tried to speak calmly, reasonably. "I—I seem to have taken a wrong turn. Can you help me, please? Which way is—" she paused, wondering if these uncouth men would know what the word "amphitheater" meant, "—the foyer? The front of the building?" The men's eyes widened yet further, and glittered with mirth. Their lips twitched. "I'm attending the symposium on the structure of the universe, in fact my husband is one of the participants, so I don't want to miss a word. The secrets of the universe are being revealed! Mankind's conception of the heavens is being revolutionized totally! So, if you could help me, please—" Julia was backing away, even as the black men were advancing upon her; springy and lithe on their feet as great supple black predator cats.

Suddenly panicked, Julia turned to run; turned her ankle, and nearly fell; her handbag went flying. The youngest black man caught her, his fingers strong as steel, long enough to encircle her rib cage. "No! Please! Let me go! Oh, please!" she begged. "I've never been a prejudiced woman, I swear! I know that Queenston is a—a white enclave—but I don't share in the—prejudices of my neighbors! I am the wife of—" The young black man squealed with laughter, shoving Julia roughly at one of his friends, who caught her by the upper arm, and shut his fist in her hair, and gave her head a cruel shake. Julia drew breath to scream, but could not. She was groveling, panting, whispering, "*I am the wife of*—"

But her mind had gone blank. She could not remember her husband's name, nor even her own.

I am not here, then, am I? Or, if here—who?

Julia Matterling struggled courageously with her assailants, even as, cruelly outnumbered and overpowered as she was, so petite and terrified a woman, she must have known it was hopeless to resist. She could not scream except inwardly, silently—*No! no! please! Don't you know who I am?* Disgusting rude lips mashed against hers, a slap to the side of her head made her ears ring. Her breasts were being fondled, squeezed, pinched. Her buttocks were being kneaded like doughy white bread. *No! please! not me! not here!* The men towered over her, laughing shrilly, exuding a smell of primal male sweat— horrible! Julia was being shoved this way, and that; passed from one man to another as if this were a game, and she a living basketball or football—no matter how she wept, thrashed from side to side, pleaded *No! don't! have mercy!*

But the black men in their dazzling-white waiters' uniforms had no mercy for Julia Matterling.

In the very building in which her distinguished husband was speaking on the subject of the structure of the universe, its probable origin and its probable end, Julia Matterling was being dragged into the steamy interior of a kitchen; her wrists gripped tight, as by steel manacles; the nape of her neck gripped, too; she was flung like a carcass over a table, as, with prudent dexterity, black hands quickly shoved aside trays of fruit cup and dinner salads (for a banquet for the two hundred participants of the symposium was shortly to be-gin); now nearly hysterical crying *Help! no! please!* as the skirt of her navy blue serge suit was yanked up, her panties dragged down, fingers poked her private parts as on all sides the black men giggled and grunted and cried in piping high-pitched voices *Uh-oh!* and *Mmmm! white-meat cunt!* and *Eeeeeyyyh! man!* and Julia blinked dazed at the floor seeing blood dripping from her nose onto the linoleum tile, and had one of her teeth come loose?—*No! no! have mercy! oh, please!* but there was no mercy for Julia Matterling, their hands on her now-naked squirming body pinning her fast to the table, one of them straddling her, hot and harsh and pitiless as a jackhammer, what excruciating pain, his gigantic blood-swollen black penis, pushing its way between the cheeks of her unprotected buttocks, into her anus, into the tender interior of the woman's being where no man, certainly not that husband whose name she had forgotten, had ever penetrated—

Now Julia Matterling did draw breath to scream, and screamed and screamed.

And woke, another time, in her bed, in the dark, amid tangled sweat-smelling bedclothes.

I am not here, then, am I? Or, if here—who?

How shameful. Unspeakable.

Julia was revulsed by the dream—so vivid, *had* it been a dream?—and did her best to forget. Yet, the following day, and the following, even as details rapidly faded, the horror stayed with her —as if, somehow, it continued to exist in some other dimension of the universe.

Of course Julia was determined to hide her agitation from Norman, who would have been confused and upset, if he knew. *Can one inhabit madness, yet not be mad?* Julia wondered if madness might pass through a human being, like those subatomic particles whose name she could never quite recall, neurons? neutrinos?—passing through solid matter, bearing chaos, yet causing not so much as a ripple on the surface of the observed world.

He will never know. Will he?

Julia could not remember the details, nor the very outline, of her dream (except to know that it had taken place at the Center, of all unlikely settings for a nightmare); but she understood guiltily, with a sense of womanly shame, that, another time, she had had a lethal effect upon a man. Or men.

Touching her, a man, or men, *vanished*.

She smiled. No, she was not smiling—she was concerned. Disturbed.

Am I a "fatal" woman, then? Without my knowing?

She knew it was all absurd; sheerly fantasy; yet, days passed, and nights, and she dreaded sleep, dreaded its power over her. Norman noticed nothing—fortunately! Julia was fiercely protective of him, the way a mother might be with a gifted child obscurely handicapped, disabled. *He will never know. Must never.* When Julia kissed him, in greeting, or as he was about to leave the house, he frequently smiled at her startled and pleased, and hugged her, indeed like a child: "Dear Julia! I love you!" he would murmur.

Julia was equally determined to keep *whatever the horror was, of which she must not think* separate from her work at the Queenston Art Museum. For she was a professional woman, after all: wasn't she?

Yet it happened, to Julia's dismay, that she began to feel, even in the museum, that sense of anticipation and dread she'd felt elsewhere; even in the sanctuary of her office. *What is happening to me? What is this change coming upon me?* Suddenly one morning, a few days after the Symposium on the Structure of the Universe, hosted by the Center for Advanced Study at Queenston (for indeed there had been a symposium), Julia realized, at her desk, that her pulse was unnaturally fast; and that she was startled by the most innocuous of things—her ringing telephone, the sound of voices in the corridor, the museum's curator summoning her into his office. (The curator, a man of self-consciously vigorous middle age, was subtly, yet unmistakably, gay; with absolutely no erotic interest in Julia Matterling, or in any other woman.)

Passing by the museum guards, as she'd done countless times, Julia felt strangely dizzy; did not dare glance up at them, still less smile and greet them by name as she normally did. *No. Don't look. It's better not to know.* The thought haunted her, since that last, incompletely recalled nightmare (the kitchen of the Center? but why the *kitchen?*—and had there been more than one assailant?), that, without her wish, she had the curious power to destroy: for, when men advanced upon her, when actually they dared touch her, they were punished severely, by imploding: *vanishing.*

Which was what they deserved. Animals.

Yes, but Julia did not want that sort of thing, that violence, to occur, certainly she did not want it to occur. She was not a vindictive woman. She was not a hysterical woman.

That morning, the curator had arranged for Julia to meet with a Hawaiian-born sculptor whose work the museum was considering for an exhibit. As Julia nervously examined slides of the man's sculptures through a viewer, and asked questions of him meant to be friendly, polite, she became acutely aware of him staring at her; frowning at her; sitting at the edge of his chair, head thrust forward in a way that could only be belligerent. (Or was the man shy? awkward? socially disadvantaged?) Julia blinked at the massive, ugly, teasingly obscene hulks of scrap metal that constituted the sculptor's "art" and had no idea what to think, or to say. Her mind was going blank. Evaporating. Waves of panic stirred in her belly. She moved her arm, and the sculptor moved his, as in a mirror. Mocking? His features were Oriental, yet Caucasian; his skin dark, as if tanned; his eyes hooded. *Who are you? Do I know you? Do you know me?*

Julia had asked the sculptor about his background, and he had answered gruffly, in monosyllables, then fell silent, staring at her. On Julia's desk was a brass lamp, small but heavy; covertly, her fear increasing, she measured the distance between the lamp and her right hand. *If you dare. Threaten me.* Now her pulse was racing erratically and she understood that the sculptor was well aware of her distress. When she wiped moisture from her upper lip, in a gesture intended to be unobtrusive, the sculptor mirrored it, mockingly, by sighing, and wiping his forehead on the sleeve of his denim jacket. Then, their eyes met.

No. Not again. Never again.

As the sculptor was about to lunge forward—as Julia sensed he was about to lunge forward—she stood suddenly, snatched up the lamp to defend herself, and stammered, "Thank you! You can leave now! You've said enough! Please take your slides!" The sculptor gaped up at her, all mockery and masculine arrogance drained from his face; the very swarthiness of his skin draining pale.

"Just leave! Now! Quickly! Before there's danger!" Julia cried.

And so, quickly, sweeping his slides into a duffel bag, the sculptor did.

Julia looked around her, at the walls, the windows, the familiar dimensions of the room. Nothing had changed. All was as it had been. She remained where she was. Exactly where she was. (Trembling, behind her desk, the heavy brass lamp pressed against her breasts.)

I am not here, then, am I. Or, if here—who?

She was sobbing, she had lost all shame opening her heart to one who would help. "Doctor, I'm so frightened of losing my mind! I believe I'm approaching a nervous breakdown—madness!"

Dr. Fitz-James smiled sympathetically, yet doubtfully. " 'Approaching,' Julia?"

Julia stared at him, blinking. Was it a poor word choice? One approached a point in time, or in space; one approached, for instance, an abyss. But could one approach anything so intangible as a nervous breakdown? She said, stammering, "Doctor, I have such dreams! Such ugly, hateful, obscene dreams! And now they're spilling over into real life—that's what I fear most." She paused, pressing a tissue against her eyes, conscious of Dr. Fitz-James' thoughtful look. He was a much-admired Queenston doctor; not a psychiatarist, nor a psychoanalyst, but an internist with a reputation for being kindly, informative, up-to-date, intuitively shrewd—with a particular gift for understanding women. Quite coincidentally, Dr. Fitz-James resembled Norman Matterling, in build and physical appearance, though not manner: where Norman was abstract and dreamy, Dr. Fitz-James was alert, almost unsettlingly watchful. Julia felt that he anticipated her very words as she spoke. "And the dreams aren't my own, really—they seem to be the dreams of another person. A madwoman."

"Indeed, Julia! But how do you know?"

"How do I—know?"

Patiently, bringing the tips of his blunt, stubby fingers together, Dr. Fitz-James said, "When human beings dream, they are not conscious; thus they cannot know anything with certainty, not even that they are not conscious." He smiled, as if addressing a young child, or a very slow-witted person. "It's a familiar conundrum—how do we know we are awake, when we *are* awake?—where is the evidence? The material world seems to us real—" he struck the top of his desk smartly with his knuckles, so that Julia, whose nerves were strung tight as a bow, started, "—and so, no doubt, it *is*. But—are we in it, as we think we are? And who are *we?*" He paused, for dramatic effect. Julia was beginning to feel quite helpless. "And when we wake, Julie—excuse me: Julia—and consciousness floods back, the dreaming self vanishes, irretrievable. So—how can we have knowledge of that other self? of the dreams it engenders?"

How like Norman Matterling the man was: the wisps of graying hair, the broad, somewhat heavy face, the pale blue eyes behind polished lenses, the sense he communicated of absolute and unwavering logic, irrefutable! But Dr. Fitz-James was several years younger than Norman Matterling, his big body more muscular than fatty; there was a masculine edge to his voice that comforted Julia, yet also disturbed her. For, possessed of logic as the internist was, was he also possessed of truth?

Julia wiped at her eyes, and said, weakly, yet stubbornly, "Whatever it is, Doctor, whether I *know* or not, I'm terribly upset. I dread falling asleep; I've had a kind of flu, and have been running a temperature; I had a, a—misunderstanding at the museum where I work, and have taken sick leave for a while. It's all I can do to get through the day—running our household without Norman suspecting that anything is wrong. He'd be devastated if he knew, he depends upon me so completely." Now this fact was uttered, Julia understood it was a fact; perhaps the central fact of her existence as a wife. Dr. Fitz-James nodded, in apparent agreement. Julia said, shuddering, "And what I think I can remember of my dreams—so ugly! Repulsive! Hideous!"

Julia wept. Laughed. Hid her face.

But Dr. Fitz-James said, in the same sympathetic yet skeptical voice, rising from his desk to lead Julia into an examination room, "Now, Julia, you women should remember that certain 'facts' are no more than passing moods, a jangle of neurons—sheer ephemera. Your dreams, my dear, and the disgust they engender, are not 'real'—thus not important."

Julia entered the examination room, which was brightly lit, with a clinical chill. Since childhood she had dreaded physical examinations; even as she understood their necessity. *If I am good, if I obey, will I be helped? loved?* She whispered, "—Not important?"

Dr. Fitz-James laughed. "Not set beside *physical facts.*"

To this, Julia could make no objection. She began to undress, with trembling fingers; removing her outer garments, then, shivering, her brassiere and panties—grateful that Dr. Fitz-James was averting his eyes. On the examination table lay an oversized paper smock into which Julia quickly slipped. *If I am good? if I obey?* As she had told the doctor, she was slightly feverish; had not slept more than a few hours in the past several nights; nor had she any appetite. How she hoped Dr. Fitz-James might find a physical disorder underlying her malaise!—for which she might take pills, the most efficient of solutions.

Julia lay on the examination table, her bare feet in the stirrups and her thighs wide spread. Dr. Fitz-James murmured, "Move up just a bit, June—Julia!" and she felt the warmth of his breath against her skin. *If I am good, good, good. If I obey.* There was no disguising the fact that Julia was shivering with anticipation: excitement, or dread: her entire pubic region was exposed to the chill, unsparingly bright air of the examination room, and to Dr. Fitz-James' professional scrutiny. (Why was there no nurse in attendance?—but Julia was grateful there was none.) Her eyelids fluttered. The overhead lights and the ceiling beyond shimmered, as if on the brink of dissolution. Dr. Fitz-James murmured, in a muffled, choked-sounding voice, "Now, my dear, this may tickle a little— just a routine check for growths." With rubber-gloved hands he began to press, squeeze, massage Julia's pelvic region, her lower abdomen, her stomach, her breasts; Julia drew in her breath sharply, and held it. "Oh! oh!"—she might have laughed shrilly, or cried. "Oh—Doctor!"

So thorough was the internist, he did the entire procedure a second time, yet more forcibly.

"Oh!—Doctor!" Julia cried, biting her lower lip.

"Very fine, very fine," Dr. Fitz-James said. He was perspiring; his balloon face, looming above Julia, had an oily sheen. "Now, do relax—we'll look at your uterus, and do a Pap smear." Julia made an effort to relax, even as she anticipated discomfort, pain. She saw, to her horror, a tray of glittering instruments on a table close by: several scalpels, one of them the length of a steak knife; a device that uncannily resembled an ice-cream scoop; another that resembled an egg-beater; still another, with an expandable head, to dilate the vagina. *Obey. If I obey. Will I be loved? saved?* She had stiffened, gripping the sides of the examination table tight. Her knees, with no support, were badly trembling; Julia's instinct was to bring them together, even as, gently, yet firmly, Dr. Fitz-James spread them apart.

"Now, my dear, this *may* hurt a little: just a little," he said, selecting, from the tray of instruments, the ice-cream scoop; and disappearing from Julia's view behind her outspread knees.

Julia held her breath. She felt a finger-probe around the lips of her vagina—no pain, really, yet she stiffened at once. Dr. Fitz-James chided her, in a muffled voice, "Dear, do relax! It will be so much better for you, if you do." She could hear him breathing, which reminded her of Norman when his sinuses were congested; she made an effort to obey. *Don't touch. Don't dare. Who am I, here?* There was a pause; then the touch of cold metal; then, even as Julia drew breath to scream, yet could not scream, a sudden piercing pain, in her vagina, in the birth canal, of an intensity she had never before felt in her life.

No! no!—Julia tried to slide away from Dr. Fitz-James, but with his left hand he was gripping her buttocks so tightly she could not move. Even as Julia struggled, the cruel instrument plunged deeper; a nova of pain filled her body; and, scarcely knowing what she did, Julia reached out for something with which to defend herself—and there was the knife-size scalpel suddenly in her fingers, so deftly so lethally fitted to her fingers, she was screaming *Now! now! this is happening now!* as, in a frenzy, she slashed and stabbed at the astonished man whose name she no longer knew, bright blood at once splashing his white outfit, blood on his face, blood on his flailing hands, blood pouring from a severed artery in his throat, *I warned you: and now! now!* her assailant stumbling backward with that look

of rapt and utter astonishment on his face, colliding with the table
bearing the tray of gleaming instruments, and—

And vanished.

And Julia Matterling awoke another time, dazed and terrified,
to find herself—where?

In her bed, in her bedroom of many years, amid tangled bedclothes that gave off a reek of panic. Pain throbbed in her loins and
the nipples of both breasts were raw—how had it happened?

Night. She was alone. Switching on her bedside lamp with badly
shaking fingers (were they bloodstained? no), Julia saw that it was
three-twenty a.m. Norman was awake, elsewhere in the house,
working.

I am not here, then, am I? Or, if here—who?

It was the night following the day of the embarrassment at the
art museum. The misunderstanding involving the Hawaiian-born
sculptor who had, or had not, made "threatening" gestures toward
Julia Matterling. . . . All had agreed, a sick-leave might be advised.

Shakily, Julia rose from bed (was it bloodstained? no); ran a bath
in the adjoining bathroom, water as steamily hot, as cleansing, as
she could bear. She could not recall the ugly dream that had wakened
her but she seemed to know that her assailant had been someone
she knew, clad in white. He had hurt her badly, and then he'd been
destroyed: vanished: like the others.

Julia was stiff with pain, but she smiled. *Gone where?*

Startled, then, she glanced up as the door was pushed open, and
there stood Norman, perplexed, disapproving, his hair standing up
in wispy tufts. "Julia, what are you doing?—at this hour of the
morning?" Surely he had every right to be annoyed: Norman Matterling, fresh from the isolation of his work amid galaxies, stars,
atoms, quarks, leptons, primal cosmic soup, ready at last for bed.
And where was his wife?

How strangely he was staring at her. Julia in her nakedness, a
sight he rarely saw. Her shimmering-pale body, her delicate frame,
breasts gleaming damp, the shadowy pubic hair at the base of her

belly, scarcely visible. And, how strangely too, Julia smiled up at him: a taunting, provocative, sexual smile: lifting her arms to him, yes and her knees raised too.

Julia heard herself say, in a low, suggestive voice, "What do you think I'm doing, Norman?"

PART

IV

Poor Bibi

Were you ever awakened from a deep satisfying sleep to the sound of another's hoarse, strangulated breathing? It isn't a very pleasant experience, I can tell you!

My husband and I were so awakened, one night not long ago, by Bibi, poor thing—and when we discovered him, not in his pile of rags in the warmest snuggest corner of the cellar but in a far, dark corner, it seemed we were already too late, and Bibi was dying.

Poor thing!—he'd been ailing for weeks. Since he first came to live in our house Bibi had been susceptible to respiratory infections, a genetic weakness for which some ancestor was to blame, but what good are accusations at such a time?

Bibi himself was very much to blame. One of us, my husband or I, would notice that Bibi was behaving oddly, coughing, wheezing, pushing his food aside in a gesture of revulsion, and say, Maybe we should take Bibi to be examined?—and the other would agree, Yes, we should. But cunning Bibi overheard, and understood, and managed to improve, for a few days. And since it was disruptive to the entire household to force Bibi to do anything against his will— I still have a scar, on the back of my left hand, from one such episode, last spring!—we kept postponing the task.

And it did seem, for weeks I swear—Bibi *was* holding his own.

Of course, with Bibi, it was easy to be deceived. That had been one of the problems with Bibi from the start.

In the beginning, though it was long ago, I can remember we were very happy. It had been promised to my bridegroom and me that we would be very happy all the days of our lives. I believe this would be so, still, had we not weakened, and out of loneliness brought Bibi home to live with us. We were *two* then, and with the recklessness of youth thought we would expand our happiness to *three*.

How many years ago has it been, since Bibi first came to live in our household?—the happiest, most energetic, most innocent and delightful creature imaginable! All marveled at his frisky antics, his unflagging high spirits. Many were frankly envious. Darling Bibi! —the miraculous flame of life itself danced in him, unquenchable. In those early days his eyes were clear and shining; lovely, faintly iridescent, shifting shades of amber. His pert little "button" nose was pink, damp, and cool—how I shivered, when he nuzzled it against my bare legs! His ears pricked up erect, his pelt crackled with static electricity when we brushed it, his small, sharp teeth were glistening and white—no, you would not want to tease Bibi too roughly, in the vicinity of those teeth.

Bibi! Bibi! we would cry, clapping as Bibi raced around the lawn yipping and squealing like a maddened creature. (How we laughed, though perhaps it was not always amusing!) Inside the house, though it was forbidden, Bibi made a game of scrambling up the staircase and tumbling head-first down again, his sharp nails clicking and scraping against the polished parquet. Bibi, naughty boy!—oh, aren't you *darling*!

We forgave him, we had not the heart to seriously discipline him, as our wise elders urged us; when he pushed his heated little face against us, frantic to know how we loved him, and only him.

As, of course, in those early years, we did.

* * *

Then, it seemed with cruel abruptness, Bibi was no longer young, and no longer in good health. And no longer our darling naughty boy.

If he snapped at us—if his teeth caught in our flesh, drawing blood—forgiveness didn't come so readily.

If he refused his food, or, indeed, gobbled it down in a way disgusting to see, and vomited it, in dribbles, through the house— are we to be blamed for relegating him more and more to the cellar, and out of our sight?

(Not that the cellar was a dank, damp, unhealthy place. In the warm snug corner near the furnace, where Bibi's bed of rags lay, it was really most comfortable. It was really quite nice.)

We did not neglect him, even so. Indeed it was impossible to ignore him!—with his whining, whimpering, and clawing at the cellar door, and the loathsome messes he made which one of us (more often, I) would have to clean up each morning.

Yet it was impossible to be angry with Bibi for long. When he lay on his back and rolled awkwardly over, showing his belly, as if in a memory of play, when he gazed up at us, his master and mistress, with eyes rimmed in mucus, that look of mute animal sorrow, animal hurt, animal terror—we saw that, yes, we loved him still.

And how painful, such love!

For it became ever more obvious, Bibi's time had come.

We can't let him suffer, one of us said. And the other, We can't, may God have mercy we *can't*.

And wept in each other's arms, as Bibi gazed mutely and fearfully up at us.

So it happened that, on that night we were awakened so rudely from our sleep, my husband and I made our decision. Stealing silently into the cellar before the sun had fully risen, to surprise Bibi where he lay, out of spite I believe, in his dark, cold corner. Quickly, we wrapped him in an old blanket, binding his limbs to keep him from struggling. Fortunately, he'd grown too feeble to put up much resistance.

We then carried him out to the car, and I held him in my lap
as my husband drove to Family Pet Veterinary Hospital and Emergency Clinic several miles away. This was an establishment we had
passed numerous times, noting that it boasted 24-HOUR EMERGENCY
SERVICE.

Bibi, good Bibi, sweet Bibi, I murmured, everything will be all
right! Trust us! But Bibi was whining, and whimpering, and growling, and drooling; and his mucus-clotted eyes rolled in his head in
a way distressful to see.

When we arrived at Family Pet Veterinary Hospital and Emergency Clinic we were astonished to see that the large parking lot,
so very unexpectedly for this early hour (not yet seven a.m.), was
nearly full. Inside, the barnlike waiting room was so crowded, not
a single seat was free! Fortunately, as we gave our names to the
receptionist, a couple was called into the waiting room, and two
seats became available.

How disagreeably busy it was in the pet hospital!—how warm,
airless, and oppressive the atmosphere. Bibi began to whimper and
squirm, but was too weak to cause any mischief.

Nor, apparently, had he eaten for some time; a blessing since,
in panic, or out of spite, he might have vomited on us—or
worse!

So we sat, and waited. I had had the foresight to wrap Bibi in
his blanket so that only the very tips of his ears showed. I meant to
protect the poor, dying thing against the prurient stares of
strangers—how I loathed them, staring at my husband and me, with
our feebly squirming burden.

So many men and women, married couples like ourselves, were
seated in the waiting room, with their ailing, fretting creatures.
What a din! Yips, barks, whining, cries, groans, shrieks, pitiful to
hear. There was a feverish pulse to the air, and such a combination
of smells! The waiting room was vast, larger than one might have
predicted from the outside; in the unwinking fluorescent glare, rows
of seats stretched virtually out of sight.

My husband whispered, Shall I hold Bibi for a while? and I
assured him, Oh no, the poor thing isn't heavy any longer. My

husband wiped at his eyes, and said, He's being very brave, isn't he? and I said, carefully, for I was on the verge of bursting into tears, We are all being very brave.

Finally our names were called. As we rose, Bibi put up a last, faint struggle, but I gripped him tight. Everything will be all right, Bibi, soon!—I promised. Have faith in us!

Strangers' eyes followed us as we went into the examining room. But I had made certain that Bibi was wrapped up snug in his blanket, and shielded from them. Poor darling! And so *brave*!

A young female assistant in a blood- or excrement-smeared uniform led us briskly into the examination room, which was windowless, with grim, gray, unadorned concrete walls and floor; a high ceiling; harsh fluorescent lighting; and a searing odor of disinfectant. This young woman behaved with bright, mechanical efficiency, instructing us to lay Bibi—"your patient"—on a metal table in the center of the room, which we did; and to remove his blanket, which we did. At that moment, the doctor appeared, entering the room whistling thinly, and I thought rudely, through his teeth; he was wiping his hands on a paper towel which he crumpled and tossed carelessly in the direction of an overflowing trash basket. He was young, and the assessing look he gave us, my husband and me, before turning to Bibi, was one of shocking impertinence.

By this time, my husband and I were exhausted, and our tempers wearing thin. We explained to the doctor that we'd been waiting for hours to see him; we'd hurried to this place in the hope that Bibi might be granted a quick, merciful end to his suffering, but, so far, he'd only suffered more.

Bibi was lying, quivering, on the cold metal table, his slack, hairless belly exposed; ribs and pelvic bones protruding obscenely. I had not realized the poor thing had lost so much flesh, and felt a twinge of shame—as if I were to blame. His eyes were encrusted with dried mucus, yet shifted nervously in their sockets, so it was clear that the poor thing heard, and surely understood, everything that was being said about him.

Doctor, my husband and I pleaded—just look at him! Will you help us?

The young doctor had been staring at Bibi, rooted to the spot. His whistling had ceased abruptly.

Doctor—?

Still, the doctor stood staring at Bibi. Yes, it was true that Bibi looked piteous, but surely a doctor has seen worse, far worse? Why did he stare at Bibi so—incredulously?

At last, turning to my husband and me, he said, his voice trembling, Is this some sort of joke?

My husband, who is a forthright man, faltered beneath the doctor's glare. Joke?—what on earth do you mean, Doctor?

The doctor said, regarding us with an expression of disbelief and revulsion, What do *you* mean, coming to me with *this*? Are you mad?

My husband and I were utterly baffled, and becoming desperate. We said, Why, Doctor, we would like a—merciful end to poor Bibi's suffering. Can't you see, he's suffering terribly, he's past all hope—

But the doctor said rudely, My God! I can't believe this!

Doctor?—what do you mean? Can't you put him to—to sleep?

All this while, it breaks my heart to report that poor Bibi was lying helpless before us on the table. Panting, shivering, a frothy line of drool on his discolored lips. I saw with a shock that his eyes were not amber any longer, but a sickly yellow, as with jaundice. The insides of his ears, that had once been so pink and clean, were yellow too, and encrusted with scum. How unspeakably cruel, that he should be a witness to such a scene!

The doctor and his assistant were conferring together, in whispers. The young woman too had been staring aghast at Bibi—as if she had any right to judge.

My husband dared interrupt, for he was losing his patience. Doctor?—what on earth is wrong? We're going to pay you, after all. You do this simple procedure for others all the time—*why not for us?*

But the doctor had turned resolutely away from Bibi, as from my husband and me, as if he could not bear our presence another moment. Impossible, he said. Just take it—him—out of here, at once. Of course we don't do such things.

Stubbornly, angrily, my husband repeated, You do this for others, Doctor—*why not for us?*

And I joined in, my eyes flooded with tears, Oh Doctor yes, please—*why not for us?*

But the young doctor had had enough of us. He simply strode out of the room, and shut the door behind him. Our words hung in the air like shameful gaseous odors. How could anyone in a position of authority, to whom others have come begging for help, behave so cruelly?—so unprofessionally?

My husband and I stared at each other, and at Bibi. We *two* who had lost all innocence by becoming *three*. What was wrong? Was there some error?—some terrible misunderstanding?

But there was only Bibi there on the cold metal table, in mortal agony, beneath the unwinking fluorescent lights, watching us, hearing every word.

The doctor's assistant handed us Bibi's soiled blanket as if it were contaminated, and said, with an air of righteous disgust, You may leave by this door, into the parking lot. Please.

And so (I know you are preparing to judge us harshly, too) we did it ourselves. We did what had to be done.

For, after all, society failed us. What choice had we!

Fifty feet behind the pet hospital was a deep drainage ditch filled with brackish, ill-smelling water, in which there floated, like shards of dreams, threads of detergent scum. Trembling, sick at heart, blinking back tears, my husband and I carried Bibi to the ditch, resolved to put the poor thing out of his misery.

We hadn't needed, even, to confer. No, there was no possibility of our bringing Bibi back home with us. We simply couldn't go through all that again!

For we, too, have grown, if not old, older. We, too, have lost our hope and high spirits, along with our youth.

We, too, to whom it was promised we would live happily forever have had quite enough of suffering.

And yet: not in our very worst dreams could we have anticipated such an ending to our beloved Bibi. So heartbreaking a task, yes and physically demanding and repulsive an ordeal—forcing poor Bibi into that cold, foul water, and pushing his head under! And how fiercely, how savagely he fought us!—he, who had pretended to be so feeble!—he, our darling Bibi, who had lived with us for so many years, transformed into a stranger, an enemy—a beast! Causing us to think afterward that *Bibi had been hiding his deepest, most secret self from us.* Never had we truly known him.

Bibi, no! we cried.

Bibi, *obey!*

Naughty Bibi! Bad boy! *Obey!*

The appalling struggle lasted at least ten minutes. I will never, never forget. I, who'd loved Bibi so, was forced to become his executioner, in the interest of mercy. And my poor, dear husband, the most refined and civilized of men, imagine him suddenly provoked to rage—for Bibi would not die for the longest time—grunting, cursing, ugly veins standing out in his forehead as he held the thrashing, squirming, frantic creature beneath the surface of ditch water in a suburban field, one weekday morning. Imagine!

For we soon forget what we do, in the human desperation of doing it.

And you, you damned hypocrites—what will you do with yours?

Thanksgiving

Father spoke quietly. "We'll do the shopping for your mother, the turkey and all. You know she isn't feeling well."

At once I asked, "What's wrong with her?"

I thought I knew. Probably. It had been three days now. But the question was what any father would have expected of any daughter of thirteen.

My voice, too, was a thirteen-year-old's. A scrawny sort of voice, drawling, skeptical.

Father seemed not to hear. Hitched up his trousers, rattled the keys to the pick-up as a man does who likes the feel of keys, the noisy rattle. "We'll just do it. We'll surprise her. Then it will be done." He counted on his fingers, smiling. "Thanksgiving is on Thursday, day after tomorrow. We'll surprise her so she can get started early." Yet there was a vagueness in his pebble-colored eyes, that moved upon me scarcely seeing me; as if, standing before him, a long-legged skinny girl all elbows and knees and pimples gritty as sand scattered across her forehead, I was no more to him than the horizon of scrub pine a short distance away or the weatherworn fake-beige-brick asphalt siding on our house.

Father nodded, grim and pleased. "Yes. She'll see."

With a sigh he climbed up into the truck on the driver's side, and I climbed up into the truck on the passenger's side. It was just getting dark when he turned on the ignition. You needed to make a quick escape from our place, before the dogs rushed out yammering to be taken along—and sure enough, hearing us slam the truck doors, there came running Foxy, Tiki, Buck, hounds with some terrier blood in them, barking and whining after us. Foxy was my favorite, the one who loved me best, hardly more than a year old but long-bodied and showing her ribs, big wet staring eyes like I'd broken her heart going away without her, but what the hell, you have to go to school without the damn dogs and sometimes to church and sure enough you want to go to town without people smiling at you behind your back, figuring you as a country hick with dogs trailing after. "Go on back!" I yelled at the dogs, but they only yipped and fussed louder, running right alongside the pick-up as Father took it out the drive tossing up gravel in our wake. What a racket! I hoped Mother would not hear.

I was feeling guilty, seeing Foxy left behind, so I poked Father, and asked, "Why don't we take them along, in the back?" and Father said, in a voice like he was talking to some fool, "We're going grocery shopping for your mother, where's your sense?"

Now we were out on the road, and Father had the gas pedal pressed down flat. The fenders of the old truck rattled. That weird high vibration started in the dashboard like a cricket none of us could ever find to stop it.

For the longest time, the dogs ran after us, Buck in the lead, and Foxy second. Long ears flapping, tongues out, like it was warm weather and not an almost-freezing November day. A strange feeling came over me, hearing the dogs barking like that—loud and anxious as they'd bark if they thought we were never coming back. Like I wanted to laugh, but to cry too. Like when you're tickled so hard it begins to hurt and whoever's doing it, tickling you, doesn't know the difference.

Not that I was tickled any more, that old. I don't guess I'd been tickled in years.

The dogs fell farther and farther behind, till I couldn't see them any more in the rear view mirror. Their barking faded too. Still,

Father was driving hard. The damn road was so rutted, my teeth rattled in my head. I knew better, though, than to tell Father to slow down, or even to switch on his headlights. (Which he did anyway, a few minutes later.) There was a mix of smells about him—tobacco and beer and that harsh-smelling steel-gray soap he used to get the worst of the grease off his hands. And another smell too, I couldn't name.

Father was saying, like I'd been arguing with him, "Your mother is a good woman. She'll pull out of this."

I didn't like that kind of talk. The age I was, you don't want to hear adults talk about other adults to you. So I made some kind of low, impatient mumble. Not that Father heard, anyway—he wasn't listening.

It was eleven miles to town and once we got on the paved highway Father kept the speedometer needle right at sixty miles per hour. Still, it seemed to take us a long time. Why would it take such a long time? I'd come out without my jacket, just wearing jeans and a plaid wool shirt, and boots; so I was shivering. The sky was on fire, behind the foothills and the mountains in the west. We had to drive over the long shaky bridge across the Yewville River that used to scare me so when I was little, I'd shut my eyes tight until we were on solid land. Except now I wouldn't let myself shut my eyes, I was too old for such cowardice.

I think I knew that something was going to happen. In town, maybe. Or when we returned home.

Father drove straight down the middle of the high wrought-iron vibrating old bridge. Lucky no one was coming in the left lane. I could hear him mumbling to himself, like thinking aloud. "—coupons? In the drawer? Jesus. Forgot to look." I didn't say a word because it made me mad, either of them talking to themselves in my presence. Like somebody picking his nose and not seeing you're there.

(And I knew what Father was talking about too: Mother kept shopping coupons in a kitchen drawer, she'd never go to the A & P without taking a batch of them along in her purse. Claimed she'd saved hundreds of dollars over the years—! What I'd come to think

was, grown-up women liked to fuss clipping coupons out of the
newspaper ads or shoving their hands up to the elbows in some giant
box of detergent or dog chow to fish out a coupon worth twelve
cents. You figure it.

For Thanksgiving, though, there'd be a lot of food coupons. "Big
savings" on the turkey, plus all the extras. But this year there was
nobody in our house to take the time to notice them, let alone cut
them out of the ads and file them away.)

Driving to town is driving downhill, mainly. Into the valley.
Out of the foothills where it always seemed colder. On the far side
of the river, Yewville looked squeezed in, steep streets dropping
down to the river, flat-looking, almost vertical, at a distance. I was
starting to get that nervous feeling I'd get sometimes when we came
to town, and I guessed I wasn't dressed right, or didn't look right
—my face, my snarly-frizzy hair. Father made a wrong turn off the
bridge ramp before I could stop him so we had to drive through a
neighborhood that didn't look familiar: tall narrow row houses built
to the sidewalk, some of them boarded-up and empty, and not much
traffic on the street; here and there, old rusted tireless hulks of cars
at the curbs. There was a thickness to the air as of smoke, and a
smell of scorch. All that remained of the fiery sunset was a thin
crescent in the west, very far away. The night coming on so fast
made me shiver more. And there was the A & P but—what had
happened? The smell of smoke and scorch was strong here, you could
see that the front of the store was blackened and the plate glass
windows that ran the length of it had plywood inserts here and there.
The posters advertising special bargains BACON BANANAS TURKEY
CRANBERRY MIX EGGS PORTERHOUSE STEAK had begun to peel off
the glass and the building itself looked smaller, not as high, as if
the roof was sinking in. But there was movement inside. Lights were
on, flickering and not very bright, but they were on, and people
were inside, shopping.

Father whistled through his teeth, "Well, hell." But pulled into
the parking lot. "We'll do it, and get it done." There were only five
or six cars in the lot, which looked different from what I
remembered—more like raw earth, with weeds growing in cracks,

tall thistles. Beyond the parking lot there wasn't anything familiar, no other buildings, or houses, just dark. I whispered, "I don't want to go in there, I'm afraid," but Father already had his door open, so I opened mine too, and jumped down. The smell of smoke and burn was so strong here my nostrils pinched and tears came into my eyes. There was another smell beneath it—wet earth, decomposing matter, garbage.

Grimly, grinning, Father said, "We'll have Thanksgiving like always. Nothing will change that."

The automatic doors were not operating, so we had to open the ENTER door by hand, which took some effort. Inside, cold damp air rushed at us—a smell as of the inside of a refrigerator that hadn't been cleaned in a long time. I stifled an impulse to gag. Father sniffed cautiously. "Well, hell!" he murmured again, as if it was a joke. The rear of the store was darkened but there were lighted areas near the front where a few shoppers, most of them women, were pushing carts. Of the eight check-out counters, only two were open. The cashiers were women who looked familiar but they appeared older than I'd remembered, white-lipped and frowning.

"Here we go!" Father said with a broad forced smile, extricating a cart from a snarl of carts. "We'll do this in record time."

One of the cart's wheels stuck every few rotations but Father pushed it hard and impatiently in the direction of the brightest-lit part of the store, which happened to be the fresh produce section, where Mother always shopped first. How it was changed, though! —most of the bins and counters were bare, and some of them were broken; the aisles were partly blocked by mounds of decaying debris and plywood crates. There were puddles on the floor. Flies buzzed groggily. A flush-faced man in a soiled white uniform, a porkpie hat jaunty on his head declaring, in red letters, BARGAIN HOLIDAY BUYS! was snatching heads of lettuce out of a crate and dumping them in a bin so carelessly that some of the heads fell onto the filthy floor at his feet.

Father pushed our cockeyed cart over to this man, and asked

him what the hell had happened here, a fire?—but the man just
smiled at him without looking at him, a quick angry smile. "No
sir!" he said, shaking his head. "Business as usual!"

Rebuffed, Father pushed the cart on. I could see his face
reddening.

Of all things, a man hates to be treated rudely by another man
in the presence of one of his children.

Father asked me how many people Mother would be cooking for
on Thanksgiving, and between us we tried to count. Was it eight?
eleven? fifteen? I remembered, or thought I remembered, that Mother's older sister was coming this year with her family (husband, five
children), but Father said no, they were *not* invited. Father said that
Uncle Ryan would be sure to show up, like every year, but I told
him no, didn't he remember, Uncle Ryan was dead.

Father blinked, and drew his hand over his stubbly jaw, and
laughed, his face reddening still more. "Jesus. I guess so."

So we counted, using all our fingers, but couldn't decide. Father
said we would have to buy food for the largest number, then, in
case they all showed up. Mother would be so upset if something
went wrong.

Mother always shopped with a list neatly written in pencil: she'd
keep it in plain view in her hand, sending me around the store
getting items, up and down the aisles, while she followed more
slowly behind, getting the rest, examining prices. It was important
to examine prices, she said, because they changed from week to
week. Some items were on special, and marked down; others were
marked up. But a bargain was not a bargain if it was spoiled or
rotten, or just on the brink of being so. Suddenly, with no warning,
Father gripped my arm. "Did you bring the list?" he asked. I told
him no and he pushed at me, as a child might do. "Why didn't
you!" he said.

Father's face in the flickering light was oily, smudged. As if,
despite the cold, he was sweating inside his clothes.

"I never saw any list," I said, meanly. "I don't know about any
damn list."

We had to get lettuce, though, if Mother was going to make a green salad. We had to get potatoes to be mashed, and yams to be baked, and cranberries for the sauce, and a pumpkin for pie, and apples for applesauce; we had to get carrots, lima beans, celery . . . but the best heads of lettuce I could find were wilted and brown and looked as if insects had been chewing on them. "Put them in the cart, and let's get a move on," Father said, wiping his mouth on his sleeve. "I'll tell her it's the goddamn best we could do." Then he sent me running around, slipping on the wet, puddled floor, trying to find a dozen decent potatoes in a bin of mostly blackened ones, a pumpkin that wasn't soft and beginning to stink, apples that weren't wizened and wormy.

A plump-faced woman with bright orange lipstick and trembling hands was reaching for one of the last good pumpkins but I slipped in under her arm and snatched it away. Open-mouthed, the woman turned to stare at me. Did she know me? Did she know Mother? I pretended not to notice, and hauled the pumpkin to our cart.

The rear of the fresh produce section was blocked off because part of the floor had collapsed, so we had to turn around and retrace our route. Father cursed the grocery cart, which was sticking worse. What else did Mother need? Vinegar, flour, cooking oil, sugar, salt? Bread for the turkey stuffing? I shut my eyes tight trying to envision our kitchen, the inside of the refrigerator that needed cleaning, the cupboard shelves where ants scurried in the dark. They were empty, weren't they, or nearly—it had been many days since Mother had shopped last. But the quavering lights of the A & P were distracting. A sound of dripping close by. And Father speaking to me, his voice loud. "—This aisle? Anything? We need—" His breath was expelled in short steaming pants. He squinted into the semi-darkness where the way was partly blocked by stacks of cartons spilling cans and packages.

I told Father, "I don't want to," and Father told me, "Mother is counting on you, girl," and I heard myself sobbing, an angry-ugly sound, "Mother is counting on *you*." But he gave me a nudge and off I went slip-sliding on the floor where water lay in pools two or three inches deep. My breath was steaming, too. I groped quickly for things on the shelves, anything we might need, Mother would want canned applesauce since we wouldn't be bringing her fresh apples, yes and maybe creamed corn, too, maybe canned spinach? beets? pineapple? green beans? And there, on a nearly empty shelf, were cans of tuna fish, bloated and leaking giving off a powerful stink—maybe I should take a few of these, too, for next week? And a big can of Campbell's Pork and Beans: that Father loved.

"Hurry up! What's wrong! We haven't got all night!" Father was calling at me through cupped hands, from the far end of the aisle. I gathered up the canned goods as best I could, hugging them to my chest, but some fell, I had to stoop to pick them up out of the smelly water. "Goddamn you, girl! I said hurry *up!*" I could hear the fear in Father's voice, that I had never heard before.

Shivering, I ran back to Father and dropped the cans in the cart, and we pushed forward.

The next aisle was darkened and partly blocked by loosely strung twine . . . there was a gaping hole in the floor about the size of a full-grown horse. Overhead, part of the ceiling was missing, too: you could look up into the interior of the roof, at the exposed girders. Rust-colored drops of water fell from the girders, heavy as shot. Here were fairly well-stocked shelves of detergent, dish washing soap, toilet cleanser, aerosol insect sprays, ant traps. A woman in a green windbreaker was reaching beyond the blocked-off area to try to get a box of something, teetering on the edge of the hole, but her reach wasn't long enough, she had to give up. I hoped that Father wouldn't make me go down that aisle but, yes, he was pointing, he was determined, "—she'll want soap I guess, for dishes, laundry: go on—" so I knew I hadn't any choice. I slid along sideways as best I could, around the edge of the hole, one foot and then the other, trying to make myself skinnier than I was, not daring to breathe. The rust-colored drops fell in my hair, on my face and hands. *Don't look down. Don't.* I leaned over as far as I could, stretching my arm, my fingers, reaching for a box of detergent. There was regular, economy, giant, jumbo, jumbo-giant: I took the economy because it was closest at hand, and not too heavy. Though it *was* heavy.

I managed to get a box of dish washing soap too, and made my way back to Father who stood leaning against the cart, pressing a hand against his chest where he'd opened his jacket. I was clumsy dropping the detergent into the cart, so it broke, and a fine silvery acid-smelling powder spilled out onto the lettuce. Father cursed me and cuffed me so hard on the side of the head my ear rang and I wondered if my eardrum had broken. Tears flooded into my eyes but I'd be damned if I'd cry.

I wiped my face on my shirt sleeve and whispered, "She doesn't want any of this shit. You know what she wants."

Father slapped me again, on the mouth this time. I rocked back on my heels and tasted blood. *"You're* the little shit," he said, furious.

Father gave the cockeyed cart an angry push, and it lurched forward on three wheels; the fourth wheel was permanently stuck. I wiped my face again and followed after, thinking what choice did I have, Mother *was* counting on me, maybe. If she was counting on anyone at all.

Next was flour, sugar, salt. And next, bakery products: where the shelves were mainly empty, but, on the floor, a few loaves of bread were lying, soggy from the wet. Father grunted in resignation and we picked them up and dropped them in the cart.

Next then was the dairy products section, where a strong smell of spoiled milk and rancid butter prevailed. Father stared at pools of milk underfoot; his mouth worked, but he couldn't speak. I held my nose and plunged in gathering up whatever I could find that wasn't spoiled, or anyway wasn't spoiled too badly. Mother would need milk, yes and cream, yes and butter, and lard. And eggs: we didn't raise chickens any longer, a chicken-flu had carried them all away the previous winter, so we needed eggs, yes but I couldn't find a carton of one dozen eggs that was whole. I squatted on my haunches breathing in little steamy spurts examining eggs, taking a good egg, or anyway what looked like a good egg, from one carton and putting it in another. I wanted at least twelve and this took time and Father was standing a few yards away so nervous waiting I could hear him talking to himself but not his actual words.

I hoped Father was not praying. It would have made me disgusted to hear. The age I was, you don't want to hear any adult, let alone your father, yes and your mother, maybe most of all your mother, praying aloud to God to help them because you know, when you hear such a prayer, there won't be any help.

Next to the dairy products was the frozen food section where it looked as if some giant had smashed things down under his boot. The insides of the refrigerating units were exposed and twisted and gave off an ammonia-like stink. A young mother, fattish, tears on her cheeks, three small children in tow, was searching through mounds of frozen food packages, ice cream packages, while the children fretted and bawled. The cartons of ice cream were mainly melted, flat. The frozen-food dinners must have been thawed. Yet the young mother was stooped over the packages fussing and picking among them, sobbing quietly. I wondered should I look too—we all liked ice cream, and the freezer at home was empty. The ice cream cartons lay in pools of melted ice cream amid something black that seemed to be quivering and seething, like rippling oil. I went to look closer, nudged a quart of raspberry ripple ice cream with my foot, and saw, underneath, a shiny scuttling of cockroaches. The young mother, panting, snatched up a carton of chocolate chip ice cream, shaking off cockroaches, with a sound of disgust; but she put the carton in her shopping cart, along with some others. She looked at me, and smiled, the kind of helpless-angry smile that means, What can you do? I grinned back at her, wiping my sticky hands on my jeans. But I didn't want any of the ice cream, thank you.

Father hissed impatiently, "Come on!" He was shifting his weight from one leg to the other, like he had to go to the bathroom.

So I brought the dairy things back, best as I could, and put them in our cart, which was getting filled at last.

Next, the meat department. Where we had to get our Thanksgiving turkey, if we were going to have a real Thanksgiving. This section, like the frozen foods section, seemed to have been badly damaged. The counters spilled out onto the floor in a mess of twisted metal, broken glass, and spoiling meat—I saw chicken carcasses, coils of sausage like snakes, fat-marbled steaks oozing blood. Here too the smell was overwhelming. Here too roaches were scuttling about. Yet the butcher in his white uniform stood behind the remains of a glass counter, handing over a bloody package of meat to a woman with carrot-red hair and no eyebrows, a high school friend of Mother's whose name I did not know, who made a fool of herself, thanking him so profusely. Father was the next customer, so he stepped up to the counter, asking in a loud voice where was the turkey, and the butcher smirked at him as if he'd asked a fool question, and Father said, louder yet, "Mister, we'd like a good-size bird, twenty pounds at least. My wife—" The butcher was the store's regular butcher, familiar to me, yet changed: a tall, cadaverous man with sunken cheeks, part of his jaw missing, a single beady eye bright with derision. His uniform was filthy with blood and he, too, wore a jaunty porkpie hat with red letters proclaiming BARGAIN HOLIDAY BUYS!

"Turkey's all gone," the butcher said, meanly, with satisfaction, "—except what's left, back in the freezer." He pointed to a wall, beyond a smashed meat counter, where there was a gaping hole; a kind of tunnel. "You want to climb in there and get it, mister, you're welcome to it." Father stared at the hole and worked his mouth but no sound came. I crouched, pinching my nostrils shut with my fingers, and tried to see inside where it was shadowy, and dripping, and there were things (slabs of meat? carcasses?) lying on a glistening floor, and something, or someone, moving.

Father's face was dead-white and his eyes had shrunk in their sockets. He didn't speak, and I didn't speak, but we both knew he couldn't squeeze through a hole that size, even if he tried. Even I would have difficulty.

So I drew a breath, and I said to Father, "Okay. I'll get the damn old turkey." Screwing up my face like a little kid to hide how frightened I was, so he needn't know.

I stepped over some debris and broken glass, got down on my hands and knees—ugh! in that smelly mess!—and poked my head inside the opening. My heart was beating so hard I couldn't get my breath and it scared me to think that I might faint, like Mother. But at the same time I knew I wasn't the kind of girl to faint, I'm strong.

The opening was like a tunnel into a cave, how large the cave was you couldn't see because the edges dissolved out into darkness. The ceiling was low, though, only a few inches above my head. Underfoot were puddles of bloody waste, animal heads, skins, intestines, but also whole sides of beef, parts of a butchered pig, slabs of bacon, blood-stippled turkey carcasses, heads off, necks showing gristle and startlingly white raw bone. I thought that I would vomit, but I managed to control myself. There was one other shopper in here, a woman Mother's age with steely-gray hair in a bun, a good cloth coat with a fur collar and the coat's hem was trailing in the mess but the woman didn't seem to notice. She examined one turkey, rejected it and examined another, rejected that and examined another, finally settling upon a hefty bird which, with a look of grim triumph, she dragged back through the hole. Which left me alone in the cave, shaky, sickish, but excited. I could make out only three or four turkey carcasses remaining. I tried to sniff them wondering were they beginning to go bad? Was one of them still fresh enough to be eaten?—squatting in bloody waste to my ankles. All my life that I could remember up to then, helping Mother in the kitchen, I'd been repulsed by the sight of turkey or chicken carcasses in the sink: the scrawny headless necks, the loose-seeming pale-pimpled skin, the scaly clawy feet. And the smell of them, the unmistakable smell.

Spooning stuffing rich with spices into the bird's scooped-out body, sewing the hole shut, basting with melted fat, roasting. As dead-clammy meat turns to edible meat. As revulsion turns to appetite.

How is it possible you ask, the answer is it *is* possible.

The answer is it *is*.

The smells in the cave were so strong, I couldn't really judge which turkey was fresher than the others so I chose the biggest bird remaining, a twenty-pound bird at least, panting now, half-sobbing with effort I dragged it to the opening, shoved it through, and crawled after it myself. The lights in the store that had seemed dim before now seemed bright, and there was Father standing close by hunched over the grocery cart waiting for me, his mouth agape, a twitchy smile at the corners of his lips. He was so surprised at something, the size of the turkey maybe, or just the fact of it, the fact that I'd done what I'd done, blinking up grinning at him, wiping my filthy hands on my jeans as I stood to my full height, he couldn't even speak at first, and was slow to help me lift the turkey into the cart.

Then, weakly, he said, "Well, *hell*."

The store was darkening, only one cashier remained to ring up our purchases. Outside, it was very dark; no moon, and a light snow falling, the first snowfall of the year. Father carried the heavier grocery bags, I carried the lighter, to the truck, where we placed them in the rear, and dragged a tarpaulin over them. Father was breathing harshly, his face still unnaturally white, so I wasn't surprised when he told me he wasn't feeling all that good and maybe shouldn't drive home. This was the first time ever I'd been a witness to any adult saying any such thing but somehow I wasn't surprised and when Father gave me the key to the ignition I liked the feel of it in my hand.

We climbed up into the truck. Father in the passenger's seat pressing his fist against his chest; me in the driver's seat, behind the high wheel. I was only just tall enough to see over the wheel and the hood. I'd never driven any vehicle before but I'd watched them, him and her, over the years. So I knew how.

Blind

Sometime during the night which is a terrible dark here in the country on moonless nights the electricity went off.

I was wakened by it, I think. I was asleep, and suddenly wakened. A low rumbling sound like the sound of collapse. And a harsh pelting rain drumming on the roof over my head which is a low ceiling and a low roof of rotting shingles close over my head. And blown slantwise against the windows so I sat up terrified hearing the *hiss! hiss!* of the rain seeking entry.

I did not speak to *him*, nor even wake *him*.

Let the old fool slumber, let them all sleep. Snoring and snuffling and a rattle in their throats. At that age, what can you expect?

I am not a fearful woman, in truth I am a strong and practical-minded woman with the experience of years. Overseeing the household in our other house, and here—in our retirement. (*His* retirement: how is it mine?) Thus I am not fearful of storms except in a practical way, you must use your common sense in a household, one member of the household at least. Hearing the rain like that streaming down the window as it was streaming down the walls of the house vertical and plunging because the eaves gutters had not yet been cleaned, and were overflowing, thus the water runs down the house to the old stone foundation and into the cellar, oh God.

That was my fear. That, and not the storm itself. Because of course *he* had not gotten around to cleaning the gutters, no matter how I reminded him.

One day soon, now it was April at last in this cold windy place, I would drag the aluminum step-ladder out of the barn myself, to rid the eaves of rotted leaves and other debris to shame him. That old man. But I had neglected to do so, yet—and now, too late. And now the *hiss! hiss!* of the rain seeking entry.

It was then that I attempted to switch on the bedside light but the power was off. The room so utterly dark I could not see my hand in front of my face. Groping for the lamp, and almost knocking it over blundering against the shade, muttering to myself but to no avail the power was off. (Did *he* hear my distress?—snoring and snuffling the ratchety noise of phlegm in his throat? Never!) Several times during the winter the power had gone off, once it was off for eighteen hours, and when I telephoned to complain the girl said in a smirky little voice, The company is doing all it can, ma'am, power will be restored as soon as possible. And each time I called, the girl said in a smirky little voice, The company is doing all it can, ma'am, power will be restored as soon as possible. Until at last I shouted into the phone, You're a liar! You are all liars! We pay for our electricity and we want better service! And there was silence, I believed I had gained the little snip's respect at last, but then said the smirky little voice, I could all but see the red lipstick pursing in mockery of decent respect for one's elders, Ma'am, I have told you —the company is doing all it can.

So in fury I slammed the receiver down. So hard, it clattered to the floor. Hairline cracks in the cheap plastic.

I tried then to see the time. Peering into the dark where the clock should be. But even the green-luminescent numerals were gone, it was so dark. But I judged (by the pressure on my bladder: I am wakened regularly each night by this discomfort) that it was between three a.m. and three-thirty a.m. The very middle of the night so you would know the electric company would be slow to get a repair crew out, and use that as an excuse.

I was breathing hard now in exasperation and worry, and had to use the bathroom, and in this pitch dark!—swinging my legs (which are slightly swollen, the ankles especially) off the bed and rising unsteady on bare feet. Where were my slippers?—I groped for them, but could not find them.

I sighed and may have murmured to myself, as I acknowledge it is my habit to do, where once I addressed the cat and in other years the canary, *he* being deaf when it suited him, murmuring aloud, God have mercy! though from my tone you would judge God is no friend of mine any longer. Not for many years you may be sure. But *he* did not hear slumbering on, no doubt lying on his back his jaw drooping and a strand of spittle leaking across his cheek I did not doubt.

I am not a heavy woman, still less fat. I have grown a bit stout, which puts pressure on the legs and back. Sometimes I grow short of breath, as with natural impatience.

In my place, I tell my daughters, when rarely they call, you would be no different. Oh don't you tell *me*!

Slowly then, painstakingly I groped my way to the bathroom, for my bladder *was* pinched, and I was in near-distress. Had I shut my eyes I might have been unerring, for the room, the entire house, is memorized in my mind, but I tried to see which is in such circumstances a mistake. Thus stubbing my toe, thus bumping against the bureau, groping for the door which did not seem to be where I knew it must be, but a few feet to one side. Panting, muttering to myself, for at my age you come to expect more respect from the world of objects if not from the world of humankind, but of course *he* did not hear, lost in selfish slumber.

Fortunately the bathroom is in the hall right outside the bedroom. So I had not far to go.

Inside, forgetting the lights were off, I fumbled for the wall switch, so strong is the force of habit.

I was able to use the toilet with little trouble, though. Noting that the bathroom was, I thought, darker somehow than the bedroom and the hall; though there is a window behind the toilet overlooking a steep-sloped roof and an old overgrown pasture. (Bathed in moonlight many times these past twelve years since moving to this place I had stood at the window, looking out. To see what? In expectation of what?) But now the window too was lost in darkness. Utter blackness. You would not have believed a window was there at all, except for the pelting rain, the noise and damp.

I flushed the toilet once, twice, a third time before the mechanism took hold. Cursing the plumbing as many times in the past, for something was always breaking down in this old house and who then would call the plumber?—and who make out the check, to pay the bill? And my daughters saying, Why do you nag Daddy, why don't you let Daddy alone you know his nerves poor Daddy they say, or used to say. As if the little fools knew—.

Well it was my fault I suppose. Agreeing so readily in fact so vehemently to sell our old house, to move *here*. Leaving our house in the college town where we'd lived for forty-three years, to move *here*. This farmland and monotony of trees that held a memory for *him* (because when he was a boy, his family had taken him to visit some relatives here in the summer—happiest memories of his life he said) but not for *me*. Leaving my three women friends without saying goodbye because they'd slighted me, took me for granted and I would not tolerate it so moving away was my revenge and I took it. And too late to regret it now.

I groped my way back to bed in the terrible black hearing the rain louder than before, that *hiss*! against the windowpanes and drumming on the roof. *He* wasn't snoring so loud now, or the wind was loud enough to drown him out; he'd never stirred when I got out of bed, I could have had an attack or fit or fallen down the stairs in the pitch black and would he take notice?—don't make me laugh. Lowering myself into bed, and the box springs creaked. Still, *he* never stirred.

So I tried not to think about the rain, and the cellar. The overflowing eaves. I tried to calm my mind seeing waves of black water move toward me, shallow waves, where I might rise, and float, as I'd learned to float at the pool, on my back, what a surprise I could float so easy and feel no fear when the younger women had trouble, the skinny ones had the worst time of all. When it's so easy. You just give yourself up to it. And float.

But my mind wouldn't rest. It was like knitting—the steely needles clicking and flashing.

All the years *he* locked himself away in his study not to be disturbed typing over his lecture notes, always the same lecture notes, working on his scholarly articles, his single book—the source of some ancient Greek tragedy no one ever read who hadn't been assigned to. Well we were proud of him I suppose, his wife and daughters I suppose, there is natural pride in us all thus we must be proud of something I suppose! And of course his salary as a professor of classics supported us, I grant that. Poor fool sucking on that pipe of his not knowing what it was, he sucked. None of them do. And when he was forbidden actual smoke he sucked on the unlit pipe like a baby with a rubber nipple, now that *is* pathetic. They held the retirement party in the classics common room just sweet red wine and cheese cubes on toothpicks, a few toasts, the chairman praising and *him* rising to thank, tears gleaming in his eyes while the younger professors exchanged smirks and even the senior professors, next to go, swallowed yawns like swallowing pits almost too big to go down. Now that was funny to observe!

All toasts to Professor Emeritus, and *him* raising his wineglass so solemnly. Never knowing. Poor vain fool never guessing what it was the first thing to come into *my* mind, about that occasion.

Yet, then, in a weakness of my own, seeking revenge on my only friends, I let him talk me into moving out here.

His retirement: how is it mine?

I tried to sleep but the rain continued hard as before, and the thunder began to come nearer like something huge rolling across the countryside aimed for this very house so my eyes flew open in terror as the thing, it was a gigantic round object, *rolled over the house* and away across the fields to disappear. But no lightning! Not before, or after. The night was dark as any night I had ever seen.

Now I tried to wake *him*. Seized his shoulder, shook *him*.

Wake up! Help us! Something terrible has happened!

My voice climbed high as a mad soprano's yet had no effect

upon *him*. In this pitch black I could not see *him*, not so much as a blur, a glimmer.

Yet I was certain it must be *him*, my husband of fifty-one years lying beside me slack and heavy as a bag of fertilizer, the mattress sagging beneath him. I groped feeling his whiskery jaws, his thin hair and the bony skull beneath. I groped feeling his eyes, which were wide open like my own.

Myron! What is it! What has happened to you!

Yet he lay there unmoving. And now a dank sickish odor arose from the bedclothes pinching my nostrils hard.

I realized I had not heard his breathing for some minutes. That snoring-snuffling, that rattle in his throat.

Anger rose in me in clots like phlegm. Sucking that pipe of his not knowing what he sucked, hadn't the doctor warned him!—and I, and his doting daughters, warned him!

But, no: Professor's mind was off in the ancient world, or poking about in the stars (for the universe was one of his "interests").

Wake up! Wake up! Wake up! How dare you leave me, at such a time!—and I struck his shoulder hard, with my fist.

Did *he* groan, or was it my imagination?—drowned out in any case by a sudden swelling of thunder again, rolling over the countryside and the house so I whimpered for mercy like a child. And still there was no lightning, not the briefest of flashes!

Which was not natural, I knew. For thunder must be preceded by lightning, for thunder is precipitated by lightning splicing the sky in pieces, that fact I *knew*.

Unless the sound was not of thunder at all but something else?

Suddenly I was in the grip of a panic seizing me from the outside as from the dark, I pushed *him* from me as of no further use, for had *he* known who I was, or so much as looked at me these many years?—the thought coming to me, *No one can help anyone now, this is the dark of the very beginning, and the end.*

That would have been about four a.m., by my subsequent calculations. At the time, in my panicked state, in the first knowledge that *he* was dead, and that I should get help, I was not able to absorb the significance of such wisdom. Knowing only that I was alone, oh and so terrified! my heart beating like a wild creature's so terrified! That *he* had abandoned me at the very start of this siege, this terror abroad in the world beyond my knowledge.

I climbed out of our common bed desperate to be gone as from a grave.

The ceiling was leaking?—the bedclothes were damp, something sticky on the coverlet. That foul sickish-sweet odor in the air despite the fresh smell of the rain. Oh I blamed *him*! I blamed *him*! Fumbling for the telephone in the dark, overturning a lamp, and I shrieked, oh I screamed, and began sobbing like a young bride having lost *him*, whose face I had not truly seen for a long time, though not so long a time as *he* had not seen mine.

Once, my elder daughter had discovered me, in the kitchen of our old house in University Heights, and said, shocked, Why Mother, why are you crying?—and I hid my face from her young eyes murmuring in anger and shame, Because your father and I are no longer husband and wife, we have not loved each other in twenty years, and my daughter drew in her breath sharply as if she had heard an obscenity from this middle-aged woman, her mother's lips, and said, Oh Mother!—I don't believe that!—turning away from me in distaste for she meant instead, as they all mean, the children who spring from our bodies and stride away quick and brisk as they can, I don't want to hear such a thing from *you*.

And now *he* was dead, and I must get help, except, on my hands and knees groping for the fallen telephone, I understood that, if *he* was dead, it was for the same reason that the power was out; if the power was out, it was for the same reason that *he* was dead—thus beyond all human help.

And did I want strangers coming into this room, even should they be able to find this house, this room, in the pitch-black night?

My fingers scrambled against the coarse material of the carpet but I could not locate the plastic telephone, nor hear its dial tone which meant, I realized, that the telephone lines too were down; all communication with the outside world had ceased.

That foul sickish odor. *His. Him.* Suddenly it was unbearable, cooped up in here with *him*. A wildness came over me, that I had to escape.

I crawled on hands and knees in the direction of the door, whispering to myself yes! yes! like this! have courage! There was a kerosene lamp on the bureau, and matches, for just such emergencies, but I seemed to know that I would not be able to find it, still less light the wick with my trembling fingers.

So it was, on hands and knees trailing my nightgown stinking of the grave I escaped.

Slowly, painstakingly, panting with strain, I descended the steep stairs into the dark.

So many steps!—I had never counted them before, and, descending them now, lost count at twenty.

I grasped the bannister (which was not very steady) with my left hand and groped along the wall with my right hand. My eyes were dry of tears now and wide open staring seeing nothing below me except the dark, blunt and depthless as a smear of black paint. I understood that there was something mysterious about this dark which was like no other dark of my life.

I must see, I must have light to see.

I was desperate to get downstairs, to get the flashlight out of the cupboard; to light candles. In my haste I had forgotten my bathrobe, my slippers. I could not have said which year it was, nor where *I* was, which house this was of the houses I had lived in. Oh, a woman of my age, coarse gray hair trailing down between her shoulder blades, heavy flaccid breasts, hips, thighs, belly flaccid too, panting like a dog, and sweating, even on these drafty stairs sweating, barefoot and ungainly, how my former friends would stare in pity, how my daughters would sneer! Never do you dream as a young woman that, one day, this will be *you*.

The rain and the thunder continued, but still there was no lightning. Except for the pull of gravity I did not seem to be going *down* until suddenly, lowering a foot to the next step, I discovered there was no next step, I had come to the end of the stairs.

I was trembling badly, crouched as if to ward off an attack. But the darkness was empty.

And here the foul odor of that upper room was dissipated. I could still smell it—it clung to my flannel nightgown, my hair— but less strongly. A sharp smell of rain and earth prevailed, a smell I associated with spring. The rains of spring, and the thaw after the long winter. Each year the thaw seems to come later in the season, thus it is more welcome. On gusty days, when the sun shines, such smells can make you feel as if you are *alive*.

I was clutching at the newel post trying to get my bearings. To my right was the parlor, to my left the kitchen. It was the kitchen I sought.

Like stepping off into black water then I groped in the direction of the kitchen yet colliding at once with a chair (but who had left a chair in such a place?) and knocking the side of my head against the sharp edge of something (a shelf?—*there?*), finally entering the kitchen knowing it was that room by the odor of cooking and grease and the cold linoleum beneath my feet.

Here too I fumbled for the light switch on the wall—so strong is the force of habit.

But no light of course. The darkness remained steady and depthless.

It crossed my mind here to attempt the telephone another time, for there was need to get help, a terrible need wasn't there?—though memory was blurred, as to exactly why. But the telephone, on the wall beside the sink, was on the far side of the expanse of floor black and fearful as deep water, and my bowels clenched at the risk. And *what if I was not alone? What if something waited for me to make a false move?* All unexpectedly I found myself at the refrigerator, the door open, cold wafting out, ravenous with hunger suddenly I reached blindly yet unerringly for a piece of frosted cinnamon coffee cake I had wrapped in cellophane yesterday morning, a quart container of milk, able to see in my mind's eye as I could not see in the dark. And shameless and trembling with animal appetite I stood there, the door open wastefully, devouring cake until the last crumb was gone and drinking milk so greedily some dribbled on my night-gown. Then, appetite sated, I felt the disgust of my behavior, and the folly, quickly shutting the door to conserve the precious cold.

The electricity being off, and who knows when it might be restored, perishables in the refrigerator and the freezer were in danger of spoilage. Of course a freezer will keep certain foods (for instance meat) for hours before defrosting begins but once the process starts it cannot be reversed, under threat of food poisoning.

I was in dread of being without food if the storm continued, if the roads were out and I dared not leave the house for days. For the telephone was of no use for even should my call go through, I would be greeted by mockery and derision. I would be provoked into screaming curses, and then they would know my name.

I had to have light, now in a panic ravenous for light as for food I groped my way to the cupboard where the flashlight was kept, groping amid the cannisters and aerosol spray cans but where was the flashlight?—had *he* misplaced it?—in my haste knocking an object to the floor where it shattered, a cup perhaps, shattering at my feet and now the added danger of stepping in broken glass with my poor bare feet, oh God have mercy! So distraught now whimpering aloud *Why? why? help me!* seeking the lost flashlight I wondered if unknowingly in my past I had committed some terrible sin for which I must now be punished, some meanness or hardness of the heart committed not willfully perhaps but in the absence of will or conscious intention as in our blind lives we perform so many actions only half thinking, half *seeing* the effects of our behavior. And if so, may You forgive me!

(Yet I could not believe I had truly committed any such sin, for I remembered nothing. As if the electrical failure here had erased all memory too. As if, in absolute dark, there need be no time save absolute Now.)

And then in my desperation trying an adjacent cupboard, where the flashlight had never once been, I discovered it!—snatched it up at once and pushed the little switch with my thumb, but, though it clicked on at once, *there came no light.*

How was it possible? Was the battery dead? And yet, I had used the flashlight only recently, down in the cellar—in the dark alcove where my canned fruits are kept.

And yet: *there came no light.*

Sobbing aloud now in frustration and despair I took a step unwisely and my foot came down on a splinter of glass. Fortunately I had not put my full weight upon the foot, yet the cut stung, and was surely bleeding.

Carefully then as I could, trying to control my sobbing (for I am as I have said a practical-minded woman, the capable wife of this and previous households for beyond a half-century), I groped my way to the far side of the kitchen, located the counter beside the sink, the drawer beneath, where loose candles and matches were kept for such emergencies, and moving my lips in prayer to You for mercy (I, who had cast off in disdain my belief in You so many years ago!) struck matches holding them with trembling fingers against a candle's invisible wick, and how vexing! how much trickier a task than lighting a candle when you can see! finally after numerous clumsy attempts I succeeded, I swear, for one of the matches *did* catch fire, and I smelled sulphur—but I saw *no flame.*

Then it was clear and irrefutable to me, what I had only suspected previously—that there was something mysterious about this dark, this night; something that made it unlike any other dark or any other night. For it was not the mere absence of light (which is of course derived from our Sun) but *the presence of dark itself thick and opaque as any matter.*

Thus I realized it could have no visible effect whether a match was "lighted"—whether a candle wick "burned." What would have been light under normal circumstances was immediately sucked away, vanished, as if it had no existence. For indeed it had no existence.

If I could bear this, till dawn—!

With dawn, surely all would be well? (The storm seemed to be abating. Yet even if the rain continued, and the sky remained overcast, there *would* be light—for what evil force could withstand the strength of our Sun?)

I did not believe in God, but I believed in our Sun. Though never listening with much attention when *he* would prattle on reading to me out of one of his science magazines, the billion-billion-billion age of the Sun, or size of the universe, or whether time might be collapsed into something small enough to fit in my thimble!— as if, sighing with my housewifely tasks, I had the patience for such.

How exhausted I was suddenly, my search for light so futile, and my dignity rent, I turned in haste to grope my way back out into the hall thinking in my confusion that I would climb the stairs and return to bed not remembering in my confusion what it was that had usurped my bed, thus my sleep, how I abhorred it, what wickedness it sought to inflict upon me, and another time I stepped upon glass this time cutting my foot more severely. Fool! fool! fool! I cried feeling the blood slippery against the linoleum floor; yet, spared of seeing it, unexpectedly I seemed hardly to care.

I groped, stumbled, blundered my way into the hall, and into the parlor, sobbing aloud in anger, and if anything or anyone awaited me in that dark smelling of mildew and dust (had I not cleaned in that room, vacuumed and polished, only last week?) I did not care in the slightest—I did not. So exhausted now my legs were as water beneath me, I groped for the sofa, a handsome old leather sofa of *his* purchase as I recalled it, smooth to the touch but fine-cracked in places with age, and cold. But by now I did not care what sort of thing it was, I lay down in. I wanted only to shut my eyes, and sleep.

And did I sleep, indeed?—was it sleep I slipped into, or a greater, bottomless dark, whimpering and moaning to myself, unable to find a position on the sofa that did not pinch my neck, distend my spine?—release formless terrors to my brain?

I did not dream. I "saw" nothing. Until waking at last to the sun, I "saw" myself waking eager and smiling to the new day, a pale but unmistakable sunlight eking through the lacy curtains of the parlor window—At last! at last!

Except, cruelly, this *was* a dream—and when I sat up blinking and dazed, I found myself staring into the dark, as before; the unchanged, hideous dark. For long minutes I simply could not grasp what had happened, where I was, for I was *not* in my bed, nor in any bed I knew; calling out, so great was my confusion, Myron! Myron! Where are you! What has happened to us!

And then, as if a black tide swept upon me, and swept me away with it, I remembered. I knew.

Should you track me to my hiding place supposing me, a woman of my age, alone, thus vulnerable, you would be mistaken. For the darkness in this place is so complete, none of you will ever penetrate it.

And I have driven in three-inch spikes, to seal the door from within.

I am in no danger of running out of provisions. I have stocked all I could of fresh and canned goods from the kitchen; I have here, in the cellar, dozens of jars of preserves—pears, cherries, tomatoes, rhubarb, even pickles; and there is an apple bin, and a sack of Idaho potatoes. Devoured raw, some foods are more delicious than cooked.

(The preserves I had prepared out of a need to keep busy, here in the country where I knew no one, and cared to know no one. Even as *he* went about shaking hands, smiling in *his* hope, poor fool, of being accepted as one of you. And which of us now stands vindicated?)

I am no longer fearful of the dark. For here, in this place, it is *my* dark.

When it was exactly, that I understood what had happened and how, with no more delay, I must hide, I cannot recall—it may have been the equivalent of a month, it may have been only a few hours ago. In perpetual night, Time does not apply.

I do remember though long months through the preceding winter when the sky was overcast and the sun, burning through, had a look of tarnished pewter; the many evenings the lights in the house would dim, and flicker. My complaints to the power company fell on deaf ears—of course.

Then came the storm: the actual attack.

And when I woke to dawn it was to night though hearing certain faint but unmistakable sounds—the cries of birds close about the house—understanding that it *was* dawn; yet without the sun.

And the rain had ceased. And the thunder.

Groping to a window in what was the parlor I pressed both hands against the pane feeling, yes, the warmth of the sun, it *was* the sun, though invisible. As, earlier, there had been the struck flame of a match and a candle's burning wick. But the change was upon the world, *there could be no light*.

I had not time then to comprehend what had happened, what disaster of nature, knowing only that I must act quickly! Home-owners like myself would have to protect themselves against looting, burning, rape and pillage of every kind—for the world would now divide itself into those *with* shelter and provisions and those *without*.

Those *with* a secure hiding place, and those *without*.

So I have barricaded myself here. In the cellar, in the dark. Where I require no eyes.

I have memorized all this space by touch. Never can I be enticed to leave. Thus do not appeal to me, do not threaten me, do not even approach. I know nothing of *before* the catastrophe, and have no interest. Should any of you claim to be kin of mine, even to be my daughters, be advised: I am not the woman you once knew, *nor any woman at all*.

In *his* prattle *he* once marveled at certain dangers to the Earth from outer space, a warning, or was it a prophecy, that one day a malevolent celestial body (comet? asteroid?) would strike Earth with an impact equivalent to the release of numberless nuclear explosions, thus rocking Earth off its natural course, raising pulverized rock and dust to block all sunlight henceforth casting sinful mankind into perpetual night. If this is Your wish, so it is Your wish. It is the end of the old world yet not the end to those of us who were prepared.

Even now I hear sirens in the distance. I am sure that that foul, acrid smell is a smell of smoke.

But I have no curiosity, I have made my own peace.

As I've said I have provisions to last for many months—for the remainder of my life. I have food, and water; not water out of the well but water fresh enough for me, dank, earthy-smelling but plenteous here in the cellar darkness where it lies in some areas to a depth of four or five inches; and, when rain returns, it will trickle freely down the rock walls where I can lap it delightedly with my tongue.

The Radio Astronomer

For Jeremiah Ostriker

There was this old Professor Emeritus from the college, in his late eighties, who'd had a stroke and needed a live-in nurse so I was hired, had a nice tidy little room down the hall from the old man's bedroom in one of those big brick houses near the college and the days were routine mostly but sometimes at night he'd wake up not knowing where he was and get excited and want to go home so I'd say gently, You *are* home, Professor Ewald, I am Lilian here to care for you, let me help you back to bed?—and he'd stare at me half-blind with his sad runny eyes like egg yolks, his lips quivering, not remembering me exactly but knowing why I was there and he should cooperate if he didn't want things to get worse. Usually they cooperate, a stroke victim has a memory like a dream I suppose of how things were at the time of the collapse and at the hospital, anything is better than that so they cooperate. Professor Ewald should have been in a nursing home by then but that was between him and his children (grown-up children older than me, one of them a professor himself in Chicago), none of my business for sure. I hate those places, hospitals yet more where it's forms and procedure and people bossing you around and spying on you. I didn't blame the Professor for trying to live in his house as long as he could, he'd lived here he said for fifty years!—and that's all elderly people want, to live at home as long as possible, as long as there's money for it, who can blame them?

Even the smart ones like Professor Ewald who'd been chair of the Astronomy Department at the college and director of the Fine Observatory (as I was told many times, to impress me I suppose, yes I *was* impressed) have this idea their condition is only temporary, they'll be back to their old selves if they hang on, do the therapy and take the medication and have faith. And you tell them that's so, you assure them. That's your job. An old man or woman in a diaper, bars up on their bed like a crib but if they can talk you'll hear they're planning how when they go back home, when they're on their feet again, it's maybe a pet cat out of the kennel, or a golf game with somebody who's probably been dead ten years. You never contradict them or scare them, that's your job.

And sometimes they reward you, with nobody else to know. Jewelry, a fancy black-and-gold Parker Pen, outright cash. That's just between you and them.

Professor Ewald had his good days and his rough days but all in all he wasn't bad. Except for people not visiting him much he rarely complained. He had old papers he'd sift through, computer print-outs with weird signs and equations but I don't believe he could see them that well even with his magnified glasses. He'd work on these papers, he'd talk and fuss to himself, but also for me to overhear, I believe, so I'd know he was *working*. The kind of man he was, even at eighty-six or -seven, it was important for him to be *working*.

He'd tell me how he'd been a radio astronomer for more than sixty years, did I know what a radio astronomer was, I said I knew what an astronomer was, a man looking at stars through a big tel-escope, so he explained he hadn't just looked but listened too, radio waves meaning radiation not radio stations as on earth and some of them coming from billions of light-years away . . . but I have to admit I wasn't listening to every word, and the words I did hear like *light-year* I did not comprehend, because you can't, no point in trying, it's like you're the dead wife or husband to them, the chil-dren who never stay long when they visit, or don't visit at all, they aren't really talking to *you*. Professor Ewald had a way of talking too, like he was lecturing, in a large room, when his voice lifted in a certain way I knew he was making a joke, yes and he *was* funny sometimes, I could see he'd been a popular lecturer so all I needed to do was laugh, nod and laugh and say, Is that so! or, My goodness! while I helped him dress or undress, onto the toilet or up from it, in or out of the tub (where we had a wooden stool he could sit on and I'd operate the shower and lather him up real good). On sunny days he'd be so eager to sit in the sun porch he'd walk there himself just using his walker, he'd sit in his chair dozing and listening to the classical music station on the radio, wake up thinking he'd heard some other kind of noise, static, or interference, or maybe a telephone ringing, but no it was nothing most of the time, No Professor: nothing, don't be upset.

Lilian, I am not upset, he said, enunciating each syllable as if I was the one hard of hearing and not him, but smiling to show he wasn't angry—I am *hopeful*.

I'd been in the hire of Professor Emeritus Ewald for maybe seven weeks when one day, a cold November day but the sun was wonderful and warm streaming through the windows in the sun porch, he opened his eyes from what I'd thought was a nap, and said, When did you come here, and what is your name? so I told him, I kept on with my knitting unperturbed, for there was nothing hostile in his voice, only questioning. And when will you leave? he asked.

Now I did falter a bit with the needles, then picked up the stitch again and continued. My hands are the kind of hands that must keep busy at all times, even in my sleep I will be dreaming of doing something useful though I am not a nervous woman, and never have been. I said, Professor Ewald, I don't know: I guess I'll be here as long as I'm needed.

That seemed to satisfy him so nothing more was said on the subject.

He got to talking about the sun, now you'd think there wasn't much to be said about such a thing, but he was always one to come out with the darndest things: D'you know, Lilian, the sun we see isn't the actual sun, it takes eight minutes for the sun's rays to get to earth, the sun could be dead and gone and we wouldn't know for eight minutes, and I gave one of my shivery little laughs not glancing up from my knitting, Is that so!—and where would the sun go if it was gone, Professor? but he didn't hear, asking, Did I know what *lookback time* is, and I said, Well I guess you told me, Professor, but I kinda forgot, so he lectures me on *lookback time* for many minutes, asking did I realize the stars I saw in the night sky were all in *lookback time* meaning they weren't really there, long dead and gone, so I laughed and said, Whew! that's one on me I guess, *I* never knew any better! though he'd told me all this before, or things like it. His voice went sharp asking what was so funny, why did I think that was funny, and I saw how he was looking at me with those runny yellow eyes that had a kind of light in them, and I remembered how I'd been told the old man had been pretty well known at one time, what you'd call famous in his line of work, a long time ago, and I felt my face burn, yes I was embarrassed, mumbling, Oh it's so hard to think about things like that, it almost hurts a person's brain to think about things like that, and I thought this would let me off the hook but Professor Emeritus just stares at me and says, Yes but can't you for God's sake *try*.

Like all his life he'd been dealing with the ignorant like me, and he was weary of it.

Yet: his left hand was all stiff and bent like a bird's talons, his left leg dragged and the left side of his face fell away like collapsed putty from the right side, what of *that*, I wanted to ask him, Professor Emeritus you're so damned smart.

But always when they try to boss you, or turn mean and sarcastic, you can hear the pleading beneath, the voice quavering. No purpose then in getting angry.

Yes and you know you'll outlive them too. No purpose in getting the least little-bit angry.

*   *   *

So things changed then, like a day that starts out warm then the temperature drops. That afternoon he was excitable and wouldn't take his medication, and refused to lie down for his nap, and the evening meal was all sulking and childish-nasty behavior (like spitting out a mouthful of mushy food) but I didn't let any of it bother me, I never do, it's my job. Then around seven-thirty there was a telephone call that was a wrong number, just my luck damn it, that set him raving saying it had been his daughter but I'd kept him from her, and so on and so forth, you know how they get. I reasoned with him suggesting why didn't he just call his daughter back, I'd make the call for him, but he just fumed and fussed talking to himself, then at bedtime he said, Nurse I'm sorry, I could see he'd forgotten my name and I smiled assuring him it was all right but after we got him undressed and about to climb into bed he started crying, he took hold of my wrist and started crying, I should say here that I do not like to be touched by anybody, no I do not, but I tried not to show it listening to the old man rave how they made him retire at the peak of his powers, they promised him time on the telescope, all the time he wanted, they lied to him refusing him time, this was the very radio telescope he'd been the one to design and helped raise funds to make, his enemies were jealous of his reputation and fearful that his new research would refute theirs. . . . He'd spent eleven years after his retirement until he'd gotten sick listening for signals, unnatural patterns that might mean radio communication from another galaxy, did I know what that meant? and I said yes, I was kind of impatient wanting to get him to bed, I didn't like the way he was squeezing my wrist in his skinny, strong fingers like claws, I said yes maybe, and he said, spittle showing on his lips, There is no more important work for science than the search for other intelligence in the universe, time is running out for us, we must know we are not alone, and I said, Yes Professor, oh yes trying to humor the old man, helping him into bed, except he kept on saying how many years he'd wasted sifting through other men's data, now he had a direct approach using his own powers with no gadgets interfering, one night last year he'd picked up a clear and orderly signal *dot dash dot dot dash dot dot dot dash dot dot dot dot dash dot dot dot dot dot dash dot* from somewhere in the Hyades, in the constellation Taurus, billions of light-years away, an unmistakable radio communication not noise but before he could record it static interfered, and on other occasions when he'd heard signals from distant galaxies they were interrupted by static, a terrible buzzing and ringing in his head. I said, Yes Professor it sure is a shame, but maybe you should take your medication? try to sleep? and he said, Nurse you could go to the newspapers with the story, it would be the story of the century, you could help all of mankind if you just would, and I finally pried his fingers off my wrist, I do not appreciate being touched, saying, as if the old fool had been joking with me and not bawling like a baby, Yes Professor but if there's life on other planets like in the movies how d'you know they might not be evil, maybe they'd come to earth and eat us all up? and he just looked at me, blinking, and said, stammering, But—if there was intelligent life elsewhere it would confirm our hope, and I said, helping him in bed and settling him back on his pillows, Hope of what? and he said, Mankind's hope of—not being alone, and I said, with a little snort, Some of us, we're not alone enough.

And switched off the light.

And that would have been the end of it for one night I thought, except I was in my bed later and on the edge of falling asleep, like slipping over a ravine, that feeling you have more precious than any even sex, even love, for you can live without sex and love, as I have done for half my life, but you sure can't live without sleep, and there's a crashing noise in the Professor's bedroom down the hall and I get out of bed and grab my bathrobe and run in hoping he hasn't had another attack, I switched on the light and the weirdest thing—there's Professor Ewald in his pajamas crouching in a corner of the room beyond his bed, he'd knocked over his aluminum bedside stand, he was shielding his head from me screaming, You're Death aren't you! You're Death! Go away! I want to go home! and I stood there pretending not to see him, out of breath myself and excited but maintaining calm as you must do, tying my bathrobe snug around me, you learn to do with them like they are children, like it's a game, hide-and-seek and the old man is peeping at me through his fingers whimpering and begging, No! no! you're Death! no! I want to go home! so I pretended to be surprised seeing him back there in the corner, and smoothed his pillows for him, and said, Professor, you *are* home.

Accursed
Inhabitants of
The House of Bly

In life she'd been a modest girl, a sensible and sane young woman whose father was a poor country parson across the moors in Glyngden. How painful then to conceive of herself in this astonishing new guise, an object of horror, still less an object of disgust. Physical disgust if you saw her. Spiritual disgust at the thought of her. Condemned to the eternal motions of washing the mud-muck of the Sea of Azof off her body, in particular the private parts of her marmoreal body, with fanatic fastidiousness picking iridescent-shelled beetles out of her still-lustrous black hair with the stubborn curl her lover had called her "Scots curl" to flatter her—for the truth, too, can be flattery, uttered with design. And not only he, her lover, Master's valet, but Master himself had flattered her, so craftily: "*I* would trust *you*, ah! with any responsibility!"

She, twenty-year-old Miss Jessel, interviewed by Master in Harley Street, wearing her single really good dark cotton-serge dress, how hot her face, how brimming with moisture her eyes, how stricken with shyness at the rush of love, its impact scarcely less palpable than a slap in the buttocks would have been. And, later, in the House of Bly, so stricken-shy of love, or love's antics, Master's valet Peter Quint burst into laughter (not rude exactly, indeed affectionate, but indeed laughter) at the cringing nakedness of her, the shivers that rippled across her skin, the lovely smoky-dark eyes downcast, blind in maidenly shame. Oh, ridiculous! Now Jessel, as she bluntly calls herself, has to bite her lips to keep from howling with laughter like a beast at such memories; has to stop herself short imagining the sharp tug of a chain fixed to a collar tight around her neck, for otherwise she might drop to all fours to scramble after prey (terrified mice, judging from the sound of their tiny squeals and scurrying feet) here in the catacombs.

The catacombs!—as, bemusedly, bitterly, they call this damp, chill, lightless place with its smell of ancient stone and sweetly-sour decay to which *crossing over* has brought them: in fact, unromantically, their place of refuge is a corner, an abandoned storage area, in the cellar of the great ugly House of Bly.

By night, of course, they are free to roam. If compulsion overcomes them (she, passionate Jessel, being more susceptible than he, the coolly appalled Quint), they venture forth in stealthy forays even during the day. But nights, ah! nights! lawless, extravagant! by wind-ravaged moonlight Quint pursues Jessel naked across the very front lawn of Bly, lewd laughter issuing from his throat, he, too, near-naked, crouched like an ape. Jessel is likely to be in a blood-trance when at last he catches her on the shore of the marshy pond, he has to pry her delicate-boned but devilishly strong jaws open to extricate a limp, bloody, still-quivering furry creature (a baby rabbit?—Jessel dreads to know) caught between her teeth.

Are the children watching, from the house? Are their small, pale, eager faces pressed to the glass? What do little Flora and little Miles see, that the accursed lovers themselves cannot see?

In interludes of sanity Jessel considers: how is it possible that, as a girl, in the dour old stone parsonage on the Scots border, she'd been incapable of eating bread dipped in suet, gravy was repugnant to her as a thinly disguised form of blood, she'd eaten only vegetables, fruits, and grains with what might be called a healthy appetite; yet, now, scarcely a year later, in the catacombs of the House of Bly, she experiences an ecstatic shudder at the crunch of delicate bones, nothing tastes so sweet to her as the warm, rich, still-pulsing blood, her soul cries *Yes! yes! like this! only let it never end!* in a swoon of realization that her infinite hunger might be, if not satisfied, held at bay.

In life, a good pious scared-giggly Christian girl, virgin to the tips of her toes.

In death, for why mince words?—a ghoul.

Because, in a fury of self-disgust and abnegation, she'd dared to take her own life, is that the reason for the curse?—or is it that in taking her own life, in that marshy-mucky pond the children call the Sea of Azof, she'd taken also the life of the ghostly being in her womb?

Quint's seed, planted hot and deep. Searing flame at the conception and sorrow, pain, rage, defiance, soul-nausea to follow.

Yet there had seemed to Jessel no other way. An unwed mother, a despoiled virgin, a figure of ignominy, pity, shame—no other way.

Indeed, in that decent Christian world of which the great ugly House of Bly was the emblem, there *was* no other way.

Little Flora, seven years old at the time of her governess's death, was wild with grief, and mourns her still. *Her* Miss Jessel!

And I love you too, dear Flora, Jessel wills her words to fly, in silence, into the child's sleep—*please forgive me that there was no other way.*

Do children forgive?—of course, always.

Being children, and innocent.

Orphaned children, like little Flora, and little Miles, above all.

More strangely altered than Jessel, in a sense, by the rude shock of *crossing over,* is Master's flamey-haired and -whiskered valet Peter Quint—"That hound!" as Mrs. Grose calls him still, with a shiver of her righteous jowls.

In the old, rough, careless days, the bachelor days of a dissolute and protracted youth, Quint had cared not a tuppence for conscience;

tall, supple-muscled, handsome in a redhead's luminous pale-skinned way, irresistible to weakly female eyes in certain purloined vests, tweeds, riding breeches and gleaming leather boots of Master's, he'd had his way, indeed his myriad-wallowing ways, with half the household staff at Bly. (Even Mrs. Grose, some believed. Yes, even Mrs. Grose, who now hates him with a fury hardly mitigated by the man's death.) It was rumored, or crudely boasted, that babes born to one or another of the married women belowstairs at Bly were in fact Quint's bastards, whether accursed by tell-tale red hair, or not; yes, and in the Village as well, and scattered through the county.

Hadn't Master, himself livened by drink, been in the habit of regaling Quint, one fellow to another, "Quint, my man, *you* must do my living for me, eh?"—all but nudging his valet in the ribs.

At which times the shrewd Quint, knowing how aristocrats may play at forgetting their station in life, as if to tempt another to forget, fatally, his own, maintained a servile propriety, commensurate with his erect posture and high-held head, saying, quietly, "Yes, sir. If you will explain how. I am at your command, sir."

But Master had only laughed, a sound as of wet gravel being roughly shoveled.

And now, how unexpected, in a way how perverse: Quint finds himself considerably sobered by his change of fortune. His death, unlike poor Jessel's, was not deliberate; yet, a drunken misstep, a fall down a rocky slope midway between The Black Ox (a pub in the Village of Bly) and the House of Bly in the eerie pre-dawn of a morning shortly after Jessel's funeral, it was perhaps not accidental, either.

In the catacombs, where time, seemingly, has stopped, the fact of Quint's death is frequently discussed. Jessel muses, "You need not have done it, you know. No one would have expected it of you," and Quint says, with a shrug of irritation, "I don't do what is expected of me, only what I expect of myself."

"Then you do love me?" —the question, though reiterated often, is quaveringly posed.

"We are both accursed by love, it seems," Quint says, in a flat, hollow tone, stroking his bearded chin (and how unevenly trimmed his beard, once the pride of his manly bearing), "—for each other, and, you know, damn them—little Flora, and little Miles."

"Oh! don't speak so harshly. They are all we have."

"But we don't, you know, precisely 'have' them. They are still—" Quint hesitates, with a fastidious frown, "—they have not yet *crossed over*."

Jessel's luminous, mad eyes glare up at him, out of the sepulchral gloom. "Yes, as you say—not *yet*."

Little Flora, and little Miles!—the living children, not of the lovers' union, but of their desire.

Quint would not wish to name it thus, but his attachment to them, as to Jessel, is that of a man blessed (some might say, accursed) by his love of his family.

Jessel, passionate and reckless now, as, in life, she'd been stricken by shyness as by a scarlet rash of the skin (a "nerve" rash, which had indeed afflicted her occasionally), spoke openly— "Flora is my soul, and I will not give her up. No, nor dear little Miles, either!"

Since *crossing over*, since the deaths, and alarms, and funerals, and hushed conversations from which the children were banned, Flora and Miles have grieved inwardly; forbidden to so much as speak of the "depraved, degenerate sinners"—as all in the vicinity of Bly call the dead couple—they have had to contemplate Miss Jessel and Peter Quint, if at all, only at distances, and in their dreams.

The unhappy children, now eight and ten years old, were, years ago, tragically orphaned when their parents died of mysterious tropical diseases in India. Their uncle-guardian, Master of the House of Bly, resident of sumptuous bachelor's digs in Harley Street, London, always professes to be very, very fond of his niece and nephew, indeed devoted to them—their well-being, their educations, their "moral, Christian selves"; even as, when he speaks of them, his red-veined eyes glaze over.

Tremulous twenty-year-old Miss Jessel with the staring eyes, interviewed by the Master of Bly in his Harley Street townhouse, clasped her fingers so tightly in her cotton-serge lap, the bony knuckles glared white. She, a poor parson's daughter, educated at a governess's school in Norfolk, had never in her life been in such a presence!—gentlemanly, yet manly; of the landed aristocracy in bearing, if not in actual lineage, yet capable, a bit teasingly, of plain talk. It is a measure of the young governess's trust in her social superiors that she did not think it strange that the Master glided swiftly, indeed cursorily, over her duties as a governess, and over the bereaved children themselves, but reiterated several times, with an inscrutable smile that left her breathless, that the "prime responsibility" of her employment would be that she must never, under any circumstances, trouble him with problems.

In a sort of giddy daze Miss Jessel heard herself giggle, and inquire, almost inaudibly, "—*any* circumstances, sir?" and Master loftily and smilingly replied, "I would trust *you*, ah! with any responsibility!"

And so the interview, which required scarcely half an hour, came to an end.

Little Flora was Miss Jessel's delight. Miss Jessel's angel. Quite simply—so the ecstatic young woman wrote home, to Glyngden— the most beautiful, the most charming child she'd ever seen, with pale blond curls like silk, and thick-lashed blue eyes clear as washed glass, and a sweet melodic voice. Shy, initially—ah, tragically shy! —as if seemingly abandoned by her parents, and only barely tolerated by her uncle, Flora had no sense of her human worth. When first Miss Jessel set eyes upon her, introduced to her by the housekeeper Mrs. Grose, the child visibly shrank from the young woman's warm scrutiny. "Why, hello, Flora! I'm Miss Jessel: I am to be your friend," Miss Jessel said. She, too, was afflicted by shyness, but in this case gazed upon the perfect child with such a look of rapture that Flora must have seen, yes, here was her lost young mother restored to her, at last!

Within the space of a few blissful days, Miss Jessel and little Flora became inseparable companions.

Together they picnicked on the grassy bank of the pond—the "Sea of Azof," as Flora so charmingly called it. Together they walked white-gloved hand in hand to church a mile away. Together they ate every meal. Flora's organdy-ruffled little bed was established in a corner of Miss Jessel's room.

On bare Presbyterian knees, beside her own bed, in the dark, Miss Jessel fiercely prayed: *Dear God, I vow to devote my life to this child!—I will do far, far more than he has so much as hinted of my doing.*

No need, between Miss Jessel and an omniscient God, to identify this Olympian *he.*

Days and weeks passed in an oblivion of happiness. For what *is* happiness, save oblivion. The young governess from Glyngden with the pale, rather narrow, plain-pretty face and intense dark eyes, who had long forbade herself fantasy as a heathen sort of indulgence, now gave herself up in daydreams of little Flora, and Master, and, yes, she herself. (For, at this time, little Miles was away at school.) *A new family, the most natural of families, why not?* Like every other young governess in England, Miss Jessel had avidly read her *Jane Eyre.*

These were the oblivious days before Peter Quint.

Little Miles, as comely and angelic a boy as his sister was perfection as a girl, was under the guidance, when at Bly, of Peter Quint, his uncle's trusted valet. The more censorious among the servants, in particular Mrs. Grose, thought this an unfortunate situation: cunning Quint played the gentleman at Bly and environs, a dashing figure (if you liked the type) in purloined clothes belonging to the Master, but, born of coarse country folk in the Midlands, without education or breeding, he was a "base menial—a hound" as Mrs. Grose sniffed.

He had a certain reputation as a ladies' man. Excepting of course, as the clumsy riposte went, Quint's ladies were hardly *ladies.*

Infrequently, on unpredictable weekends, Master came by train to Bly—"To my country retreat"—with a flushed, sullen look of, indeed, a gentleman in retreat. (From amorous mishaps?—gambling debacles? Not even his valet knew.) He paid scant attention to the quivering Miss Jessel, whom, to her chagrin, he persisted in calling by the wrong name; he paid virtually no attention at all to poor little Flora, beaming with hope like an angel and dressed in her prettiest pink frock. He did make it a point to speak with Peter Quint in private, bringing up the unexpected subject of his little nephew Miles, enrolled at Eton—"I want, you know, Quint, this boy of my poor dear fool of a brother to be a boy; and not, you know," here he paused, frowning, "—*not* a boy. D'you see?" Master's face flushed brick-red with discomfort and a sort of choked anger.

Politic Quint murmured a polite, "Yes sir. Indeed."

"These boys' schools—notorious! All sorts of—" Another pause, a look of distaste. A nervous stroking of his moustache— "Antics. Best not spoken aloud. But you know what I mean."

Quint, who had not had the privilege of attending any public boys' school, let alone the distinguished one in which little Miles was enrolled, was not sure that he did know; but could guess. Still, the gentleman's man hesitated, now stroking his own whiskery chin.

Seeing Quint's hesitation, and interpreting it as a subtle refinement of his own distaste, Master continued, hurriedly, "Let me phrase it thus, Quint: I require that those for whom I am responsible subscribe to decent standards of Christian behavior, that's to say normal standards of human behavior. D'you see? That is not much to ask, but it is everything."

"Certainly, sir."

"A nephew of mine, blood of my blood, bred to inherit my name, the bearer of a great English lineage—he must, he *will*, marry, and sire children to continue the line to—" Another pause, and here a rather ghastly slackening of the mouth, as if the very prospect sickened, "—perpetuity. D'you see?"

Quint mumbled a vague assent.

"Degenerates will be the death of England, if we do not stop them in the cradle."

"In the cradle, sir?"

"For, y'know, Quint, just between us two, man to man: I would rather see the poor little bugger dead, than *unmanly*."

At this Quint started, and so forgot himself as to look the Master of Bly searchingly in the face; but the gentleman's eyes were red-veined, with a flat, opaque cast that yielded little light.

The interview was over, abruptly. Quint bowed to Master, and took his leave. Thinking, *My God! the upper classes are more savage than I had guessed.*

Yet little Miles, though blood of Master's blood, and bred to the inheritance not merely of a revered English lineage but a good deal of wealth, was a child starved for affection—a sweet-natured, sometimes a bit mischievous, yet always sunnily charming boy; fair-skinned like his sister, but with honey-brown hair and eyes, and, though small-framed, with an inclination toward heart palpitations and breathlessness, indefatigably high-spirited when others were around. (Alone, Miles was apt to be moody and secretive; no doubt he mourned his parents, whom, unlike Flora, he could recall, if confusedly. He had been five at the time of their deaths.) However quick and intelligent he was, Miles did not like school, or, in any case, his more robust classmates at Eton. Yet he rarely complained, and, in Peter Quint's presence, as in the presence of any adult male of authority, it seemed resolute in the child that he *not* complain.

From the start, to Quint's astonishment, Miles attached himself to him with childish affection, hugging and kissing him, even, if he was able, clambering onto Quint's lap. Such unguarded demonstrations of feeling both embarrassed the valet, and flattered him. Quint tried to fend off Miles, laughingly, rather red-faced, protesting, "Your uncle would not approve of such behavior, Miles!—indeed, your uncle would call this 'unmanly.' " But Miles persisted; Miles was adamant; Miles wept if pushed forcibly away. It was a habit of his to rush at Quint if he had not seen him in a while and seize him around the hips, burrowing his flushed little face into the elder man as a kitten or puppy might, blindly seeking its mother's teats. Miles would plead, "But, you know, Quint, Uncle doesn't love me. *I only want to be loved.*" Taking pity on the child, Quint would caress him, awkwardly, bend over to kiss the top of his head, then push him away, in a nervous reflex. "Miles, dear chap, this is really not what we want!" he laughed.

But Miles held tight, laughing too, breathless and defiant, pleading, "Oh, but isn't it, Quint?—*isn't* it?—*isn't it?*"

As Miss Jessel and little Flora were inseparable companions, so
too were Peter Quint and little Miles, when Miles was home from
school. And, as the children were intensely, one might almost say
desperately, attached to each other, the shy, plain-pretty governess
from Glyngden and the coarser valet from the Midlands were very
often in each other's company.

Damned hard to pride oneself on one's feral good looks when a
man is forced to shave with a dull razor in a cracked looking glass,
and when his clothes, regardless of how "smart," are covered with a
patina of grime; when, drifting into a thin, ragged sleep as the moon
seems on windy nights to be sailing through a scrim of cloud, he
wakes with a a start of terror. *As if*, thinks Quint, *I am not even dead
yet: and the worst is yet to come.*

Poor Jessel!—whom *crossing over* has humbled yet more egre-
giously!

In puddles of dirty water the once-chaste young governess with
the lustrous "Scots curl" tries repeatedly, compulsively, to cleanse
herself. The brackish mud-muck of Flora's Sea of Azof clings to her
underarms, the pit of her belly, the hot dark crevice between her
legs with its own brackish odor; a particular sort of spiny iridescent
beetle that breeds copiously in the earthy damp of the cellar is attracted to hair, and sticks tight as snarls. Her single good dress,
which, out of defiance, she'd worn as she waded into the water, is
stiff with filth, and her petticoats, once white, are striated with mud,
and not yet fully dry. She rages, she weeps, she claws at her cheeks
with her broken nails, she turns against her lover, demanding why,
if he'd known she was hysterically inclined, he'd made love to her
at all.

Quint protests. Guiltily. A man is a man, a pronged creature destined to impregnate: how, given their attraction to each other, in the romantically sequestered countryside of Bly, could he, lusty Peter Quint, *not* have made love to her? How could he have known she was "hysterically inclined" and would take her own, dear life, in an excess of shame?

Not that Miss Jessel's desperate act was solely a consequence of shame: it was pragmatic, practical. Word had come from Harley Street (fed, of course, by tales told by Mrs. Grose and others) that Miss Jessel was dismissed from Bly, commanded at once to vacate her room, disappear.

Where, then, could she have gone?—back to the Glyngden parsonage?

A ruined woman, a despoiled woman, a humiliated woman, a fallen woman, a woman made incontrovertibly a *woman*.

Jessel says tartly that all virgins of this time and place are "hysterically inclined"—little Presbyterian governesses above all. If, in life, she'd had the luck to have been born a man, she'd have avoided such pathetic creatures like the plague.

Quint laughs irritably. "Yes, but, dear Jessel, you know—*I love you.*"

The statement hovers in the air, forlorn and accusing.

Here is perversity: in this twilit realm to which *crossing over* has brought the accursed lovers, Jessel seems, in Quint's eyes, far more beautiful than she'd been in life; Quint, to Jessel, despite her anger, quite the most attractive man she has ever seen—touching in his vanity even now, in grimy and tattered vests, shirts, and breeches, his rooster's-crest of brick-red hair threaded with gray, his jaws covered in wiry stubble. The most manly of men!—graced now with sobriety and melancholy. Yearning for each other, moaning in frustration, they grasp each other's hands, they slip their arms around each other, they stroke, squeeze, kiss, bite, sighing when their "material beings" turn immaterial as vapor—and Quint's arms shut around mere air, a shadow, and Jessel paws wildly at him, her fingers in his hair, her mouth pressed against his, except, damnably, Quint too is a shadow: an apparition.

"We are not 'real,' then?—any longer?" Jessel asks, panting.

"If we can love, if we can desire—who is more 'real' than we?" Quint demands.

But of course, why mince words, Quint's a man, he's chagrined at *impotence*.

Yet, sometimes, they can make love. Of a kind. If they act swiftly, spontaneously. If they don't articulate, in conscious thought, what they are about to do, they can, almost, with luck, do it.

At other times, by some mysterious law of decomposition, though unpredictably, the molecules that constitute their "bodies" shift in density, and become porous. But not inevitably at the same time: so that Jessel, reaching out to touch Quint with a "real" hand, might recoil in horror as her "real" hand passes through his insubstantial body. . . . How the lovers yearn for those days, not so very long ago, when they inhabited wholly ordinary "human bodies" they had not understood were miracles of molecular harmony!

Flesh of our flesh, blood of our blood. Dear Flora, dear Miles.

How to leave Bly?—Jessel and Quint cannot give up their little charges, who have no one but them. Their days and nights are passed in drifting, brooding . . . how, next, to make contact with the children. Time passes strangely in these catacombs, as a night of intermittent dreams passes for the living, during which hours are pleated, or protracted, or reduced to mere seconds. Sometimes, in a paroxysm of despair, Jessel believes that time, for the dead who are linked to the world by desire, thus insufficiently dead, cannot pass. Suffering is infinite *and will never diminish.* "Quint, the horror of it is: we're frozen forever at a single point of time, the ghastly point of our *crossing over*," Jessel says, her eyes dilated, all pupil, "—and nothing will, nothing *can*, change for us," and Quint says quickly, "Dear girl, time *does* pass. Of course it does! You went first, remember, and I followed; there were our funerals (swiftly and a bit cursorily performed, indeed); we hear them, upstairs, speak of us less and less frequently, where once the damned prigs spoke of nothing else. Miles has been away at school and will, I think, shortly be home again for Easter recess. Flora's eighth birthday was last week . . ."

"And we dared not be with her, but had to watch through the window, like lepers," Jessel says hotly.

"And there is this new governess expected tomorrow, I've heard—your replacement."

Jessel laughs. Harsh, scratchy-throated, brief laughter, without mirth. *"My* replacement! *Never."*

"Dun-colored, and so plain! Skin the color of curdled milk! And the eyes so squinty and small!—the forehead so *bony!"*

Jessel is incensed. Jessel is quivering with rage. Quint would admonish her, but that would only make things worse.

From the summit of the square tower to the east, that overlooks the drive, the accursed lovers regard the newly hired governess as she steps down, not very gracefully, with a scared smile, from the carriage. Mrs. Grose has little Flora by the hand, urging the child forward to be introduced. How eager she is, fattish Grose!—who'd once been Miss Jessel's friend, and had then so cruelly rejected her. The new governess (as Quint overheard, from Ottery St. Mary, Devonshire—a rural village as obscure and provincial as Glyngden) is a skinny broomstick of a girl, in a gray bonnet that does not flatter her, and a badly wrinkled gray traveling cloak; her small, pale, homely face is lit from within by a hope, a prayer, of "succeeding"—Jessel recoils, recalling such, in herself. Jessel mutters, half-sobbing, "Quint, how could he! Another! To take my place with Flora! *How dare he!"*

Quint assures her, "No one will take your place with Flora, dear girl. You know that."

As the new governess stoops over Flora, all smiles and delight, Jessel sees, with a trip of her heart, how the child glances over her

shoulder, stealthily, to ascertain that Miss Jessel is somewhere near.
Yes, dear Flora. Your Jessel is always somewhere near.

So it begins, the bitter contest.

The struggle for little Flora, and little Miles.

"That woman is one of *them*," Jessel says, her fist jammed against
her mouth, "—the very worst of *them*." Quint, who would like to
stay clear of his mistress's fanatic plots, that turn, and turn, and
turn upon the hope, to his skeptical mind not very likely, of re-
uniting the four of them someday, says, with a frown, "The very
worst of—?" Jessel replies, her eyes brimming with tears, "A vicious
little—Christian! A Puritan! You know the sort: one who hates and
fears life in others. Hates and fears joy, passion, love. All that *we've*
had."

There is a moment's silence. Quint is thinking of certain slum-
berous summer afternoons, heat lightning flashing in the sweetly
bruised sky, a weeping Miss Jessel cradled in his arms, the smell of
tall grasses and the calls of rooks and little Flora and little Miles
approaching through the grove of acacia trees calling softly, slyly,
happily, *Oh, Miss Jessel! Oh, Mr. Quint! Where are you hiding? May
we see?*

Quint shivers, recalling. He understands that Jessel, too, is
thinking of those lovely lost afternoons.

Of course, it has also irked Quint that Master has hired a new
governess for little Flora, yet, to be reasonable, would there not have
to be a new governess, soon? So far as the world knows, Miss Jessel
is dead, and has departed to where all the dead go. Master would
have hired a new governess within twenty-four hours of the death
of the old, had decorum not forbade it.

Yes, and there is a new valet, too: but this gentleman's man,
Quint has heard, will live in Harley Street, and will never meet
little Miles.

Quint has wondered, *Did Master know?—not just of Jessel and me,
but of the children, too?*

Quint asks Jessel, "You see all that, darling? In the poor pinched thing's face?"

"Of course! Can't you?"

Jessel's mad beautiful eyes, her skin gleaming with the ferocity of moonlight. Her mouth is a wound. To gaze upon it, Quint thinks, succumbing, is to be aroused.

Quint appears to the new governess first. He must confess, there is something in the young woman's very bearing, the thin, stiff little body inside the clothes, the nervously high-held head, the quick-darting steely gray eyes, that both repels and attracts him. Unlike Flora, who is capable of staring in a trance of mystic contentment at her Miss Jessel (who will appear to Flora, for instance, across the pond, as the new governess, her back to the pond, chatters to her little charge in complete ignorance), and occasionally at Peter Quint as well (for Quint sometimes appears with Jessel, arms entwined), the new governess reacts with a shock, an astonishment, a naked terror, that is immensely gratifying to a man.

A man of still-youthful vigor and lusts, deprived by this damn-able *crossing over* of his manhood.

Quint ascends the square tower to the west, dashing up the spiral stairs to the crenelated top, bodiless, thus weightless, and feeling quite good. The "battlements" of the House of Bly are architectural fancies not unlike manufactured fossils, for they were added to the house in a short-lived romantic-medieval revival of a decade or so ago, touchingly quaint, yet, who can deny it?—wonderfully atmospheric. Quint sees that the governess is approaching below on the path, she is alone, meditative, exciting in her maiden vulnerability, he preens his feathers glancing down the lean length of himself liking what he sees, he *is* a damned fine figure of a man. The vagrant late-afternoon wind dies down; the rooks cease their fretful, ubiquitous cries; there is an unnatural "hush"—and Quint feels with a shudder of delight the governess's shock as she lifts her eyes to the top of the tower, to the machicolated ledge, to *him*. Ah, bliss!

For some dramatic seconds, protracted as minutes, Quint and the governess stare at each other: Quint coolly and severely, with his "piercing" eyes (which few women, inexperienced young virgins or no, would be likely to forget); the governess with an expression of alarm, incredulity, terror. The poor thing takes an involuntary step backward. She presses a tremulous hand to her throat. Quint gives her the full, *full* impact of his gaze—he holds her fast there below on the path, he wills her to stand as if paralyzed. For this performance, Quint has pieced together an attractive costume that does not altogether embarrass him. Trousers still holding their crease, a white silk shirt kept in readiness for just such an occasion, that elegant coat of Master's, and the checked vest—another's things, but put to superior use on Quint's manly body. His beard is freshly trimmed, which gives him a sinister-romantic dash; he's hatless, of course—that virile-red rooster's crest of hair must be displayed.

"The Devil," as Quint remarked to Jessel, "—who is, you know, as you women prefer it, also a Dandy."

So indeed the governess stands rooted to the spot, her small pale face disguising nothing of the turbulent emotions she feels. With the studied nonchalance of a professional actor, though such a "visitation," so calibrated, is entirely new to him, Quint walks slowly along the ledge, continuing to stare at the governess: *You do not know me, my dear girl, but you can guess who I am. You have been forewarned.*

Cunning Quint, as the governess stares up at him like a transfixed child, strolls to the farther curve of the tower, *disappears.*

Thinking afterward, in the golden-erotic glow of a wholly satisfactory experience, *How otherwise to know what power we wield, except to see it in another's eyes?*

*   *   *

Excitedly, extravagantly, Jessel predicts that her "replacement" will flee Bly immediately— "*I* should do so, under such circumstances!"

"Seeing a ghost, do you mean?" Quint asks, bemused, "—or seeing *me*?"

Yet, to Jessel's surprise, and extreme disappointment, the governess from Ottery St. Mary, Devonshire, does not flee Bly; but seems to be digging in, as for a siege. She is intimidated, surely, but also wary, and alert. She exudes an air of—what? A Puritan's prim, punitive zeal?—a Christian martyr's stubborn resolve? The second time Quint appears to her, the two of them, alone, no more than fifteen feet apart, separated by a pane of glass, the young woman draws herself up to her full height (she lacks Jessel's stature, is no more than five feet two inches tall) and stares unwaveringly at Quint for a long tense moment.

Quint frowns severely. *You know who I am! You have been forewarned!*

The governess is so frightened that the blood drains from her face, turning it a ghastly waxen color; her fists are clenched, white-knuckled, against her flat bosom. Yet, staring at Quint, she seems to challenge him. *Yes, I know who you are. But, no, I will not give in.*

When Quint releases her, she does not run to hide in her room, but, again most unexpectedly, bounds out of the house, and rushes around to the terrace, where, if Quint were a flesh-and-blood man, a "real" man, he would have stood to peer through the window. Of course, no one is there. A scattering of bruised forsythia blossoms on the terrace beneath the window lies undisturbed.

The governess, white-faced, yet arrogant, peers about with the nervous intensity of a small terrier. Clearly, she *is* frightened; yet, it seems, fear alone is not enough to deter her. (Her behavior is the more courageous in that it is Sunday, and most of the household, including the ever-vigilant Mrs. Grose, are at church in the Village of Bly.) Quint has retreated to a hedgerow a short distance away, where, joined by a somber Jessel, he contemplates the governess in her plain, prim, chaste Sunday bonnet and provincial costume: how defiant the gawky little thing is! Jessel gnaws at a thumbnail, murmuring, "How can it be, Quint! A normal woman, thinking she'd seen a ghost—or, indeed, thinking she'd seen, in such circumstances, an actual man—would have run away screaming for help." Quint says, annoyed, "Maybe, love, I'm not so formidable as we think." Jessel says, worriedly, "Or *she* is not a normal woman."

Afterward, Quint recalls the episode with, beyond annoyance and chagrin, a stir of sexual arousal. It excites him that there is a new, young, willful woman at Bly; homely as a pudding, and with a body flat, bosom and buttocks, as a board. Certainly she lacks Jessel's passion, as she lacks Jessel's desperation. Yet she is *alive*, and poor dear Jessel is *dead*.

Quint makes himself snake-slender, incorporeal: yet gifted with a prodigious red-skinned erection: an incubus: insinuating himself into the governess's bedroom, and into her bed, and, despite her faint flailing protests, into her very body.

When he groans aloud, shuddering, Jessel pokes him with a sharp little fist.

"Are you having a nightmare, Quint?" she asks ironically.

And then, an unexpected development: poor little Miles has been expelled from Eton!

Quint and Jessel contrive to overhear the governess and Mrs. Grose as they discuss the subject, and the mystery embedded in it, repeatedly; obsessively. The governess, quite shocked, and puzzled, reads the headmaster's letter of dismissal to Mrs. Grose; together, the women dissect the chill, blunt, insultingly formal sentences, which present the expulsion as a *fait accompli*, about which there can be no negotiations. It seems, simply, that Eton "declines" to keep little Miles as a student. That is all.

Jessel, crouched beside Quint, murmurs in a low, sensuous voice, "Delightful for you, Quint, to have your boy back again, eh? The four of us will be reunited soon!—I know it."

But Quint, who has a notion that he knows why Miles has been expelled, says, gravely, "But, poor Miles! He *must* go to school, after all; he can't hang about here like his sister. His uncle will be furious when he learns. The old bugger wants nothing but that Miles grow up to be a 'manly man' like himself."

"Oh, what do we care for *him*?" Jessel asks. "He is the worst of the enemy, after all."

A day later, Miles appears. He is much the same as Quint recalls, perhaps an inch or so taller, a few pounds heavier; fair-skinned, clear-eyed, with that slightly feverish flush to his cheeks and that air of startled breathlessness that Quint found so appealing—finds appealing still. A sweet, clever, circumspect lad of ten, but far, far older than his years, Miles wins the heart of the new governess at their first meeting; forestalls, by his very innocence, any awkward questions about Eton; and, that night, when he should have been in bed, slips past the door of the governess's room (which little Flora shares) and wanders out into the deep, shifting shadows of the park, seeking—who, or what?

Moonlight cascades over the slated roofs of the great ugly House of Bly. The cries of nocturnal birds sound in a rhythmic, staccato pulse.

Quint observes dear little Miles, in pajamas, barefoot, making his way across the slope of the lawn, and back beyond the stables, to one of their old trysting places: there the child throws himself, with an air of abandon, on the dewy grass, as if to declare *I am here, where are you?* When Quint died, little Miles was said to have been "stony-cold"—not a tear shed. So Quint overheard the servants talking. When Miss Jessel drowned, little Flora was said to have been "heartbroken"—inconsolable for days. Quint approves of Miles's stoicism.

Hidden close by the restive child (Miles is looking impatiently about, pulling at blades of grass), Quint observes him with fond, guilty eyes. In life, Quint's passion was for women; his affection for little Miles was in reaction to little Miles's affection for him, thus not a true passion, perhaps. Quint wonders is it fair to the child, the secret bond between them?—the attachment, of such tender, wordless intimacy, even Quint's abrupt *crossing over* seems not to have weakened it?

In the moonlit silence the child's voice is low, fearful, quavering with hope. "Quint? Damn you, Quint, *are* you here?"

Quint, choked with emotion suddenly, does not reply. He sees the child's beautiful eyes, glittering as with a fever. What a tragedy, to be orphaned at the age of five!—no wonder the child grasped Quint's knee as a drowning person a lifeboat.

It had been Miles's habit, charming, and touching, perhaps a bit pitiful, to seek out the lovers Quint and Miss Jessel in just such trysting places, if he could find them; then, silky hair disheveled and eyes dilated as with an opiate, he would hug, burrow, twist, groan with yearning and delight—who could resist him, who could send him away? And little Flora, too.

"Quint?" Miles whispers, glancing nervously about, his rapt, eager face luminous as a lily, "—I know you're here, you couldn't, could you, *not* be here! It has been so damnably long."

Those happiest of times. Because most unexpected, uncalculated of times.

And what a dreamy infinity of time, at Bly: the Bly of lush rural England: unimaginable, indeed, in the bustle of London and the stern verticality of Harley Street.

Miles continues, more desperate, and demanding, "Quint, damn you! I know you're here—somewhere." Indeed, the boy is staring, with a frown that creases his perfect little forehead like crumpled paper, at Quint—without seeming to see him. "Not 'dead'—" Miles's perfect mouth twists in distaste, "—not you. She has seen you, eh?—the new, the supremely awful governess? 'St. Ottery,' I call her—aren't I clever? Quint? *Has* she seen you? She doesn't let on, of course, she's far too cunning, but Flora has guessed. There's been such a tedious prattle of the 'purity' of childhood, and the need to 'be good, starting with clean *hands*.' " Miles laughs shrilly.

"Quint? They've sacked me, you know—sent me down—as you'd worried—warned. *I'm* to blame, I suppose—what a fool!— telling only two or three boys about it—boys I liked, oh! ever so much—and who liked me, I know—they vowed never to tell, and yet—somehow—it all came out—there was a nasty hue and cry— Quint, how I hate them all!—they are the enemy, and they are so many! Quint? I love only you."

And I love only you, dear Miles.

Quint appears before Miles, a tall, glimmering shape, taller than he had been in life. Miles gapes up at him, astonished; then, on hands and knees he crawls to Quint, now weeping, "Quint! Quint!" groaning in a delirium of joy as he tries to hug the phantom flesh —legs, thighs. The porousness of Quint's being does not deter him, perhaps in his excitement he does not comprehend, "I knew! I knew! I knew!—you would not abandon me, Quint!"

Never, dear boy: you have my word.

Then, horribly, there comes an abrupt call, nasal, reedy, scolding— "Miles? You naughty boy, where are you?"

It is the governess from Ottery St. Mary: a diminutive, stubborn figure, just rounding the corner of the stable some thirty feet away, holding aloft a lighted candle: groping, yet persistent, bravely undaunted by the night and by the feeble, flickering radius of the candle-flame: *her!*

"—Miles? *Miles*—?"

So the tryst ends, rudely interrupted. Quint, swearing, retreats. Miles in his pajamas, so charmingly barefoot, rises, rueful, brushing at himself, composing a face, a child's angelic face, untwisting his mouth, with no recourse but to say, "Here I am."

But who is guiding us, Quint, if not ourselves?—is there Another whose face we cannot see and whose voice we cannot hear, except as it echoes in our own thoughts?

Jessel fairly spits the words, her lovely mouth turned ugly— "I despise her! *She* is the ghoul. If only we could destroy her outright!"

As rarely in the past she'd done, coaxed by the child's urgent need, Jessel appears to little Flora in emboldened daylight, daring to "materialize" on the farther shore of the placid Sea of Azof. A cloudless afternoon in early summer, a vertigo of honeysuckle in the air, and, so suddenly, out of nowhere, there appears, on the grassy bank, a somber yet beautiful figure, hair shockingly undone, darkly lustrous, falling past her shoulders, her face alabaster pale: an heraldic figure, one might think, out of an ancient legend, or a curse. And the child's doll-like figure in the foreground, blond curls, an angel's profile, pinafore brightly yellow as the buttercups that grow in happy profusion in the surrounding grass—is not little Flora in her innocence, as in her need, necessary to the vision?

And, on a stone bench close by the child, busily knitting, yet keeping a watchful and jealous eye on her—"St. Ottery," as Miles has wittily dubbed her.

So like a Fate, indeed!

A common jailer.

Eyes like ditch-water, scanty fair lashes, brows; the small brave chin, sparrow body, skin stretched tight as the skin of a drum. The narrow face is too small for the head, and the head is too small for the body, the body too small for such long, angular feet. The shoulder blades are painfully prominent beneath the dark cotton of her governess's dress, like folded wings.

Flora is playing, quite absorbedly it seems, on the bank of the pond, humming a nonsensical little tune as she cradles her newest doll in her arms, and an exquisitely beautiful, life-like doll it is, from France, Flora's guardian-uncle's gift to her on the occasion of her eighth birthday (which, to Uncle's regret, he could not attend), her head is lowered, yet she is gazing, staring fixedly, through her eyelashes, at beloved Miss Jessel on the other bank. How the child's heart beats, in yearning! *Take me with you, Miss Jessel, oh please! I am so lonely here* the child mutely begs, *I am so unhappy, dear Miss Jessel, since you went away!* and Jessel's heart too beats in yearning, in love, for Flora *is* her own little girl, the babe cruelly drowned in her womb, hers and Quint's, in this very pond.

Jessel fixes her gaze upon Flora, across the pond: Jessel would comfort the child, as a hypnotist might. *Dear Flora, dear child, you know I love you: you know we will be together soon, and never again apart. My darling—*

But, then, the rude interruption, in a most shrill, reedy voice: "Flora, is something wrong?—what is it?"

The terrier "St. Ottery" leaps to her feet and hurries to Flora, glancing level, myopic eyes narrowed, to the opposite bank—seeing the figure of her predecessor, whom perhaps she recognizes; an apparition of the most sorrowful beauty; yet more frightful, in its very solemnity, than the other, the man. (For the man, in his sexually aggressive, self-conscious posture, might have been interpreted as, simply, a *man*; this creature, "St. Ottery" shrewdly sees, can be nothing but a *ghoul*.)

The governess grips little Flora by the arm, with unconscious force, crying, appalled, "My God, what a—horror! Hide your eyes, child! Shield yourself!"

Flora protests, in tears. Dazed and blinking as if slapped, insists she sees nothing, there *is* nothing. Even as Jessel stares in impotent rage, the governess swiftly, indeed rather brutally, leads the whimpering child away, pulling her by both arms, murmuring words of reproachful comfort: "Don't look at her, Flora! The horrid, obscene thing! You're safe now."

Horrid, obscene thing. When, in life, she'd been so sweetly modest a girl, impeccably groomed in ways spiritual no less than material; yes, and a Christian, of course; and a virgin—of course.

That ticklish scuttling in her hair?—a hard-shelled beetle falls to the ground.

Fanatic Jessel, stung to the core of her being, begins to lose control. Ever more carelessly by day she prowls the House of Bly seeking her darling girl alone, if only for a few snatched moments. "It seems *I* am haunted," Jessel laughs despairingly, "but what's to be done? Flora is my soul." Yet the jealous and vindictive "St. Ottery" hovers over the child every waking hour; she has pulled Flora's pretty little bed up snug beside her own, for safekeeping at night.

(Since the upset on the bank of the pond, neither the governess nor her agitated, feverish charge is capable of sleeping for more than a few minutes at a time.)

Flora pleads: *Miss Jessel, help me! Come to me! Hurry!*

And Jessel: *Flora, my darling, I will come. Soon.*

But the vigilant young woman from Ottery St. Mary refuses to allow the shutters in her and Flora's room to be opened! Nor the shutters in the adjoining nursery. In Miss Jessel's reign, when she and the red-bearded Quint were lovers, how these rooms were flooded with sunshine!—yes, and with moonlight, too! The very air pulsed with their love, humid and languorous; the baroque silver sconces on the walls trembled with their love-cries. Now the air is stale and sour, fresh linen laid upon the beds turns soiled within minutes.

Pushing her authority, as there is no one here at Bly to oppose it, "St. Ottery" tries to insist that the windows in poor Miles's bedroom be permanently shuttered as well; but, being a boy, and a most willful boy, whose angelic face belies his precocious soul, little Miles resists. "What are windows for, pray, you silly old thing—" for so Miles has affected a gay, jocose, just slightly taunting flirtatious tone with the terrible woman, "—if not, you know, to look *out* of?"

To which the reply is a grim-jawed, "Miles, I will put that question to *you*."

As if shutters, of mere wood, can keep at bay love's most violent yearnings.

Poor damned soul: by now, all of the household staff has seen her.

Drifting through the house, now upstairs, now down, now at the French windows opened upon a profusion of sticky-petaled glaring-white clematis . . . that wailing sound is hers, a sigh torn from her . . . woman sighing for her lost child, or her own soul as it nears extinction. How is it "St. Ottery" is always between her and Flora—always! Most recently, the New Testament in her hand.

This morning, Jessel finds herself exhausted at her old desk in the schoolroom. A soft moan escapes her. Her arms slumped on the desk and head heavy with sorrow resting on her arms, her face hidden, eyes brimming hot with tears of hurt, bewilderment, rage, *How am I, who is love, evil?* and a footfall behind her, a sharp intake of breath, rouse her to wakefulness, and she stands, swaying, and turns, to see her enemy confronting her hardly six feet away: "St. Ottery" bent at the waist like a crippled woman, her arms upraised as if to ward off the devil, but the colorless eyes narrowed in loathing, and the certitude of that loathing, the pale, prominent forehead, the thin lips— "Go away, out of here! This is no place for you!—vile, unspeakable horror!"

Where once Jessel would have stood her ground, now, seeing the revulsion in the other's eyes, she is sickened, defenseless. She cannot protest, she feels herself dissolving, surrendering the field to her enemy, who calls after her, in ecstatic triumph, a shrill reedy voice wholly without pity— "And never return! Never, never dare return!"

Now, with more concentrated zeal, the fierce "St. Ottery" interrogates poor Flora, mercilessly. "Flora, dear, is there something you would like to tell me?" and, "Flora, dear, you *can* tell me, you know: I've seen the dreadful thing, I'm aware." And, most cruelly: "My child, you may as well confess! I've spoken with your 'Miss Jessel,' and *she* has told *me*."

Jessel is a witness, albeit an invisible and powerless witness, when a bubble bursts at last in Flora's brain. Her sobs might be those of countless children, reverberating horribly in the catacombs beneath the great ugly House of Bly. Flora screams, "No no no *no*! I didn't! I don't! I don't know what you mean! I hate you!"

Jessel is powerless to interfere even as she sees the hysterical child caught up in Mrs. Grose's arms.

What more bitter irony, that Jessel should find herself grateful for, of all people, her old enemy Mrs. Grose.

* * *

I will be extinct by daylight: it's time. I have been only a memory of night.

The old house rings, down to the very catacombs, with the mad child's howls, her guttural little barks of profanity, obscenity. Mrs. Grose and another woman servant, accompanying Flora on the journey to London, where she will be put under the supervision of a noted child physician, are obliged numerous times to clap their hands over their ears, for shame.

Mrs. Grose asks tearfully, "Where did that angel pick up such *language?*"

"St. Ottery" remains behind, of course, to care for little Miles. She is shaken—saddened-baffled—infuriated—by the loss of little Flora, but she is determined not to lose Miles.

She, too, the virgin daughter of a country parson, a Methodist. On her knees, praying to Our Father for strength against the Devil. She reads the New Testament for solace, and for a girding of the loins. Did not Our Savior cast out evil demons from the afflicted? —did not He, when He chose, have the power of raising the dead? In such a universe, of fiercely contending spirits, all things are possible.

"Miles, dear! Where are you? Come, it's time for your lessons!"

Far below, in the dank-dripping catacombs, heartsick with mourning his beloved Jessel (Quint was no husband, but feels a husband's loss: half his soul torn from him), Peter Quint hears the governess hurrying from room to room, surprisingly heavy on her heels. Her call is like a rook's, shrill, persistent. "Miles? Miles—"

Quint, with trembling fingers, readies himself for the final confrontation. He perceives himself as a figure in a drama, or it may be an equation, there is Good, there is Evil, there is deception, there must be deception, for otherwise there would be no direction in which to move. . . . Squinting at his sallow reflection in a shard of mirror, plucking at his graying beard to restore, or to suggest, its old virility; recalling, with a swoon in the loins, poor Miles hugging him about the knees, mashing his heated face against him.

How is it evil, to give, as to receive, love's comforts?

Jessel has vanished. Dissolved, faded: as the morning mist, milkily opaque at dawn, fades in the gathering light. His beloved Jessel!—the girl with the "Scots curl," and the hymen so damnably hard to break! A mere cloud of dispersing molecules, atoms?

For that dispersal is Death. To which *crossing over* is but an overture. It was desire that held them at Bly, the reluctance of love to surrender the beloved. Desire holds Quint here, still. The fact stuns him. Mere molecules, atoms? When we love so passionately? He sees Miles's yearning face, feels Miles's shyly-bold groping caress.

Readying himself for the enemy.

Panting like a beast, feet damp with dew, Quint peers through the dusty windowpane. Inside, poor Miles has been tracked down at last, discovered by "St. Ottery" hidden away, suspiciously, and cozily, in a wingback chair turned to face a corner in the library—a vault-like room on the first floor of the house, into which no one (including Master on one of his rare visits) has stepped foot for some time. It is a gentleman's place, a mausoleum of a kind, its dark-grained oak panelings hung with portraits of patriarchs long since dissolved to dust, and forgotten; twelve-foot bookshelves rear to the ceiling, crammed with aged and mildewed books, great leather-bound and gilt-etched tomes that look as if they have not been opened in centuries. How incongruous, in such gloom, the fresh-faced ten-year-old Miles with the quick, seemingly carefree smile!

White-lipped "St. Ottery" asks, hands on her hips, why Miles has "crept away" here, why, hidden in a chair, legs drawn up beneath him, so *still?*— "When, you know, I've been calling and *call*ing you?"

Miles glances toward the window, the merest flicker of a glance, even as he says, gaily, "I was just so lost in this, you see—!" showing the governess an absurdly heavy, antique tome on his knees—the *Directorium Inquisitorum*. "St. Ottery" says dryly, "And since when, my boy, do you read Latin for pleasure?" and Miles giggles charmingly, "My dear, I read Latin as everyone does—for *pain*."

"St. Ottery" would remove the *Directorium Inquisitorum* from Miles's knees but, prankishly, the boy spreads them, and the heavy book crashes to the floor in a cloud of dust. Miles murmurs, "Oh! Sorry."

Again, Miles glances toward the window. *Quint, are you here?*

Quint strains forward, hoping to lock eyes with the boy, but the damnable governess moves between them. How he wishes he could strangle her, with his bare hands! She falls to interrogating Miles at once, sternly, yet with an air of pleading, "Tell me, Miles: your sister *did* commune with that ghastly woman, didn't she? My predecessor here? That is why Flora is so terribly, tragically ill, isn't it?" But cunning Miles denies this at once, denies even knowing what "St. Ottery" is talking about. He reverts to the behavior of a much younger child, grimacing and wriggling about, eluding "St. Ottery" as she reaches for him. Again, his eyes snatch at the window. *Quint, damn you, where are you? Help me!*

"St. Ottery," snake-quick, seizes his arm. Her no-color myopic eyes shine with a missionary's good intentions. "Miles, dear, only tell the truth, you know, and don't lie: you will break Jesus's heart, and *my* heart, if you lie. Poor Flora was seduced by 'Miss Jessel,' is that it?—and you, what of you and 'Peter Quint'? There is nothing to fear from him, you know, if you tell *me*."

Miles's laughter is wild and skittering. He simply denies all, everything: "I don't know a thing of what you say. Flora isn't ill, Flora has gone to visit our uncle in London. I know nothing of Miss Jessel, who died when I was away at school. And Peter Quint—why," his flushed face creasing in distaste, "—the man is *dead*."

"Dead, yes! But here with us, at Bly, constantly!" the governess cries, with the aggrieved air of a betrayed lover, "—as, Miles, I think, *you* know."

" 'Here with us'? 'Constantly'? What do you mean? Where?" The boy's face, struck blank, is so dazzling an image of innocence Quint stares in wonder. "Damn you, *where?*"

In triumph "St. Ottery" turns, and points to the windowpane against which Quint presses his yearning face. Surely, the woman cannot have known Quint is there, yet with fanatic certainty she whirls about, points her accusatory finger, directing Miles's terrified gaze. "There!—as you've known all along, you wicked, wicked boy!"

Yet, it seems, Miles, though staring straight at Quint, cannot see him. "What?" he cries. " 'Peter Quint'—where?"

"There, I say—*there!*" In a fury, the governess taps against the glass, as if to break it. Quint shrinks away.

Miles gives an anguished cry. His face has gone dead-white, he appears on the verge of a collapse, yet, when "St. Ottery" tries to secure him in her arms, he shoves her away. "Don't touch me, leave me alone!" he shouts. *"I hate you."*

He runs from the room, leaving "St. Ottery" behind.

Leaving "St. Ottery" and Peter Quint to regard each other through the window, passionless now, spent as lovers who have been tortured to ecstasy in each other's arms.

We must have imagined that, if Evil could be made to exist, Good might exist as rightfully.

Into the balmy-humid night the child Miles runs, runs for his life, damp hair sticking to his forehead, and his heart, that slithery fish, thumping against his ribs. Though guessing it is futile, for the madwoman was pointing at nothing, Miles cries, in a hopeful, dreading voice, "Quint?—*Quint?*"

The wind in the high trees, a night sky pierced with stars. No answer of course.

Miles hears, with a smile, bullfrogs in the pond. Every year at this time. Those deep guttural urgent rhythmic croaks. Comical, yet with dignity. And so many! The night air is warmly moist as the interior of a lover's mouth. The bullfrogs have appropriated it. Their season has begun.

Martyrdom

A sleek tiny baby he was, palpitating with life and appetite as he emerged out of his mother's birth canal, and perfectly formed: twenty miniature pink toes intact, and the near-microscopic nails already sharp; pink-whorled tiny ears; the tiny nose quivering, already vigilant against danger. The eyes were relatively weak, in the service of detecting motion rather than figures, textures, or subtleties of color. (In fact, he may have been color blind. And since this deficiency was never to be pointed out to him, he was arguably "blind" in a secondary, metaphysical sense.) His baby's jaws, lower and upper, were hinged with muscle, and unexpectedly strong. And the miniature teeth set in those jaws—needle-sharp, and perfectly formed. (More of these teeth, soon.) And the quizzical curve of the tail, pink, hairless, thin as a mere thread. And the whiskers, no more than a tenth of an inch long, yet quivering, and stiff too, like the bristles of a tiny tiny brush.

2.

What a beautiful baby *she* was, Babygirl the loving parents called her, conceived in the heat of the most tender yet the most erotic love, fated to be smothered with love, devoured with love, an American Babygirl placed with reverent fingers in her incubator. Periwinkle blue eyes, fair silk-soft blond hair, perfect rosebud lips, tiny pug nose, uniform smoothness of the Caucasian skin. A call went out to nursing mothers in ghetto neighborhoods requesting milk from their sweet heavy balloon-breasts, mother's milk for pay, since Babygirl's own mother failed to provide milk of the required richness. Her incubator filtered out contaminated air and pumped pure oxygen into her lungs. She had no reason to wail like other infants, whose sorrow is so audible and distracting. In her incubator air, humid and warm as a tropical rain forest, Babygirl thrived, glowed, prospered, *grew*.

3.

And how *he* grew, though nameless even to his mother! How *he* doubled, trebled, quadrupled *his* weight, within days! Amid a swarm of siblings he fended his way, shrewd and driven, ravenous with hunger. Whether he was in the habit of gnawing ceaselessly during his waking hours, not only edible materials but such seemingly inedible materials as paper, wood, bone, metal of certain types and degrees of thinness, and so on, because he was ravenously hungry or because he simply liked to gnaw, who can say? It is a fact that his incisors grew at the rate of between four and five inches a year, so he had to grind them down to prevent their pushing up into his brain and killing him. Granted the higher cognitive powers generated by the cerebral cortex, he might have speculated upon his generic predicament: is such behavior voluntary or involuntary; where survival is an issue, what *is* compulsion; under the spell of Nature, who can behave *unnaturally*?

4.

Babygirl never tormented herself with such questions. In her glass-topped incubator she grew ounce by ounce, pound by pound, feeding, dozing, feeding, dozing—no time at all before her dimpled knees pressed against the glass, her breath misted the glass opaque. Her parents were beginning to be troubled by her rapid growth, yet proud too of her rosy female beauty, small pointed breasts, curving hips, dimpled belly and buttocks and crisp cinnamon-colored pubic hair, lovely thick-lashed eyes with no pupil. Babygirl had a bad habit of sucking her thumb so they painted her thumb with a foul-tasting fluorescent-orange iodine mixture and observed with satisfaction how she spat, and gagged, and writhed in misery, tasting it. One mild April day, when a winey-red trail of clotted blood was detected in the incubator, issuing from between Babygirl's plump thighs, we were all quite astonished and disapproving, but what's to be done? Babygirl's father said, Nature cannot be overcome, nor even postponed.

5.

So many brothers and sisters he had, an alley awash with their wriggling bodies, a warehouse cellar writhing and squeaking with them, he sensed himself multiplied endlessly in the world, thus not likely to die *out*. For of all creaturely fears it is believed the greatest is the fear of, not merely dying, but dying *out*. Hundreds of thousands of brothers and sisters related to him by blood which was a solace, yes but also a source of infinite anxiety for all were ravenous with hunger, the *squeak! squeak! squeak!* of hunger multiplied beyond accounting. He learned, on his frantic clicking toenails, to scramble up sheer verticals, to run to the limits of his endurance, to tear out the throats of his enemies, to leap, to fly—to throw himself, for instance, as far as eleven feet into space, from one city rooftop to an adjacent rooftop—thus thwarting his pursuers. He learned to devour, when necessary, the living palpitating flesh of prey while on the run. The *snap!* of bones radiated pleasure through his jaws, his small brain thrummed with happiness. He never slept. His heartbeat was fever-rapid at all times. He knew not to back himself into corners, nor to hide in any space from which there was no way out. He was going to live forever!—then one day his enemies set a trap for him, the crudest sort of trap, and sniffing and squeaking and quivering with hunger he lunged for the moldy bread-bait and a spring was triggered and a bar slammed down across the nape of his neck snapping the delicate vertebrae and nearly severing his poor astonished head.

6.

They lied to her, telling her it was just a birthday party—for the family. First came the ritual bath, then the anointing of the flesh, the shaving and plucking of certain undesirable hairs, the curling and crimping of certain desirable hairs, she fasted for forty-eight hours, she was made to gorge herself for forty-eight hours, they scrubbed her tender flesh with a wire brush, they rubbed pungent herbs into the wounds, the little clitoris was sliced off and tossed to the clucking hens in the yard, the now-shaven labia were sewed shut, the gushing blood was collected in a golden chalice, her buckteeth were forcibly straightened with a pliers, her big hooked nose was broken by a quick skilled blow from the palm of a hand, the bone and cartilage grew back into more desirable contours, then came the girdle-brassiere to cinch in Babygirl's pudgy twenty-eight-inch waist to a more desirable seventeen-inch waist, so her creamy hips and thighs billowed out, so her gorgeous balloon-breasts billowed out, her innards were squeezed up into her chest cavity, she had difficulty breathing at first, and moist pink-tinted bubbles issued from her lips, then she got the knack of it, reveling in her classic "hour-glass" figure and new-found power over men's inflammable imaginations. Her dress was something fetching and antique, unless it was something sly and silky-slinky, a provocative bustline, a snug-fitting skirt, she was charmingly hobbled as she walked her dimpled knees chafing together and her slender ankles quivering with the strain, she wore a black lace garter belt holding up her gossamer-transparent silk stockings with straight black seams, in her spike-heeled pointed-toed white satin shoes she winced a bit initially until she got the knack and very soon she got the knack, the shameless slut. Giggling and brushing and making little fluttery motions with her hands, wriggling her fat ass, her nipples hard and erect as peanuts inside the sequined bosom of her dress, her eyes glistened like doll's eyes of the kind that shut when the doll's head is thrust back, the periwinkle-blue had no pupils to distract, Babygirl was not one of those bitches always thinking plotting calculating how to take advantage of some poor jerk, she came from finer stock, you could check her pedigree, there were numerals tattooed into her flesh (the inside of the left thigh), she could be neither lost nor mislaid, nor could the cunt run away, and lose herself in America the way so many have done, you read about it all the time. They misted her in the most exquisite perfume—one whiff of it, if you were a man, a normal man, there's a fever in your blood only one act can satisfy, they passed out copies of the examining physician's report, she *was* clean of all disease venereal or otherwise, she *was* a virgin, no doubt of that though tripping in her high heels and grinning and blushing peering through her fingers at her suitors she sometimes gave the wrong impression, poor Babygirl: those lush crimson lips of such fleshy contours they suggested, even to the most gentlemanly and austere among us, the fleshy vaginal labia.

7.

Filthy vermin! obscene little beast! they were furious at him for *being* as if, incarnated thus, he'd chosen his species, and took a cruel pleasure in carrying the seeds of typhus in his guts, bubonic plague virus in his saliva, poisons of all kinds in his excrement. They wanted him dead, they wanted all of his kind extinct, nothing less would satisfy them firing idle shots at the town dump as, squeaking in

terror, he darted from one hiding place to another, reeking garbage
exploding beside him as the bullets struck, they blamed him for the
snap! of poultry bones in predators' jaws, they had no evidence but
they blamed him for a litter of piglets devoured alive, and what
happened to that baby in the ground floor apartment on Eleventh
Street left unattended for twenty minutes when its mother slipped
out to buy cigarettes and milk at the 7-Eleven store a block away
—*Oh my God! Oh oh oh don't tell me, I don't want to know*—and a fire
that started and blazed out of control in the middle of a frigid
January night because insulation around some electrical wires had
been gnawed through, but how was that his fault, how *his*, where
was the proof amidst hundreds of thousands of his siblings, each
possessed by a voracious hunger and a ceaseless need to gnaw? Pur-
suing him with rocks, a gang of children, whooping and yodeling
across the rooftops injuring him as in desperation he scrambled up
the side of a brick wall, yes but he managed to escape even as his
toenails failed him and he slipped, fell—fell sickeningly into space
—down an air shaft—five storeys—to the ground below—high-
pitched squeaky shrieks as he fell—plummeted downward thrashing
and spiraling in midair, red eyes alight in terror for such creatures
know terror though they do not know the word "terror," they em-
body terror, that's to say em*body* it, though every cell in his body
strained to live, every luminous particle of his being craved immor-
tality, even as you and me. (Of the suffering of living things through
the millennia, it is wisest not to think, Darwin advises.) So he fell
off the edge of the roof, down the air shaft, the equivalent of approximately one hundred seventy times his size measured from nose
to rump (but excluding his tail which, uncurled, straight and stiff,
is longer than his length—eight inches!) so we were watching smiling in the knowledge that the dirty little bugger would be squashed
flat, thus imagine our indignation and outrage to see him land on
his feet! a tiny bit shaken, but uninjured! untouched! a fall that
would have broken every bone in our Goddamn bodies and *he* shakes
his whiskers and furls up his tail and scampers away! And the rancid
night parted like black water to shield him.

8.

It was the National Guard Armory, rented for the night at discount price, a slow season, and in the cavernous smoke-filled gallery fresh-groomed men sat attentive in rows of seats, their faces indistinct as dream-faces, their eyes vague and soft as molluscs focused on Babygirl, fingers fat as cigars poking in their crotches, genitalia heavy as giant purplish-ripe figs straining at the fabric of their trousers. Yes but these are carefully screened and selected gentlemen. Yes but these are serious fellows. Most of them pointedly ignore the vendors hawking their wares in the Armory, now's hardly the time for beer, Coke, hotdogs, caramel corn, the men's eyes are hotly fixed on Babygirl my God get a load of *that*. To find a worthy wife in today's world is no simple task. An old-fashioned girl is the object of our yearning, the girl that married old dead dad is our ideal, but where is she to be found?—in today's debased world. So Babygirl tossed her shimmering cinnamon curls and prettily pouted, revealed her dazzling white smile, in a breathy sing-song she recited the sweet iambic verse she had composed for this very occasion. So Babygirl twirled her gem-studded baton. Flung her baton spinning up into the rafters of the Armory where at the apogee of its flight it seemed for a magic instant to pause, then tumbled back down into Babygirl's outstretched fingers—the rows of staring seats burst into spontaneous applause. So Babygirl curtsied, blushed, ducked her head, paused to straighten the seams of her stockings, adjusted an earring, adjusted her girdle that cut so deeply into the flesh of her thighs there would be angry red indentations there for days, Babygirl giggled and blew kisses, her lovely skin all aglow, as the auctioneer strutted about hamming it up with his hand-held microphone, Georgie Bick's his name, cocky and paunchy in his tux with the red cummerbund, Hey whooee do I hear 5000, do I hear 8000, gimme 10-, 10-, 10,000, in a weird high-pitched incantatory voice so mesmerizing that bidding begins at once, a Japanese gentleman signaling a bid by touching his left ear lobe, a swarthy turbanned gentleman signaling with a movement of his dark-glittering eyes, Hey whooee do I hear 15,000, do I hear 20,000, do I hear 25-,

25-, 25,000, thus a handsome moustached Teutonic gentleman cannot resist Yes, a Mediterranean gentleman, a gentleman with a
shaved blunt head, a gentleman from Texas, a heavyset perspiring
gentleman rubbing at the tip of his flushed pug nose, Do I hear
30,000, do I hear 35,000, do I hear 50,000, winking and nudging
Babygirl, urging her to the edge of the platform, C'mon sweetie
now's not the time for shyness, c'mon, honey, we all know why
you're here tonight don't be coy you cunt, clumsy cow-cunt, gentlemen observe those dugs, those udders, and there's *udder* attractions
too, hardee-har-har! And from up in the balcony, unobserved till
now, a handsome white-haired gentleman signals with his white-
gloved hand Yes.

9.

He was battle-weary, covered in scabs, maggot-festering little
wounds stippling his body, his once-proud tail was gangrenous, the
tip rotted away, yet he remained stoic and uncomplaining gnawing
through wood, through paper, through insulation, through thin
sheets of metal, eating with his old appetite, the ecstasy of jaws,
teeth, intestines, anus, as if the time allotted to him were infinite
as his hunger it's certain he *would* gnaw his way through the entire
world and excrete it behind him in piles of moist dark dense little
turds. But Nature prescribes otherwise: the species into which he
was born grants on the average only twelve months of survival—if
things go well. And this May morning things are decidedly not
going well here on the fourth floor of the partly empty ancient brick
building on Sullivan Street housing on its first floor the Metropole
Bakery, most acclaimed of local bakeries, "Wedding Cakes Our Spe-
cialty Since 1949," he has nested in a nook in a wall, he has been
nibbling nervously on a piece of something theoretically edible (the
hardened flattened remains of a sibling struck by a vehicle in the
street, pounded into two dimensions by subsequent vehicles) sniffing
and blinking in an agony of appetite: on the fourth floor, with his
many thousands of fellows, since, it's one of Nature's quiddities,

when BROWN and BLACK species occupy a single premise, BROWN (being larger and more aggressive) inhabit the lower levels while BLACK (shyer, more philosophical) are relegated to the upper levels where food foraging is more difficult. So he's eating, or trying to eat, when there's a sound as of silk being torn, and a furry body comes flying at him, snarling, incisors longer and more deadly than his own, claws, hind legs pummeling like rotor blades, every flea and tick on his terror-struck little body is alert, every cell of his being cries out to be spared, but Sheba with her furry moon face has no mercy, she's a beautiful silver tabby much adored by her owners for her warm affectionate purring ways but here on this May morning in the ancient brick building housing the Metropole Bakery she is in a frenzy to kill, to tear with her jaws, to eat, the two of them locked in the most intimate of embraces, yowling, shrieking, he'd go for her jugular vein but, shrewd Sheba, she has already gone for his jugular vein, they are rolling crazily together in the filth, not just Sheba's terrible teeth but her maniac hind legs are killing him, yes but he's putting up a damned good fight yes he has ripped a triangular patch of flesh out of her ear, yes but it's too late, yes you can see that Sheba's greater weight will win the day, even as he squeaks and bites in self-defense Sheba has torn out his throat, she has in fact disemboweled him, his hapless guts in slimey ribbons now tangled in her feet, what a din! what a yowling! you'd think somebody was being killed! and he's dying, and she begins to devour him, warm-gushing blood is best, twitchy striated muscle is best, pretty Sheba shuts her jaws on his knobby little head and crushes his skull, his brains inside his skull, and he goes *out*. Just goes *out*. And the greedy tabby (who isn't even hungry: her owners keep her sleek and well fed, of course) eats him where they've landed, snaps his bones, chews his gristle, swallows his scaly tail in sections, his dainty pink-whorled ears, his rheumy eyes, his bristly whiskers, as well as his luscious meat. And afterward washes herself, to rid herself of his very memory.

10.

Except: wakened rudely from her post-prandial nap by a sickish stirring in her guts, poor Sheba is suddenly wracked by vomiting, finds herself reeling ungracefully and puking on the stairs, descending to the rear of the Metropole Bakery, mewing plaintively but no one hears as, teetering on a rafter above one of the giant vats of vanilla cake batter, poor Sheba heaves out her guts, that's to say *him*, the numerous fragments and shreds of *him*: a convulsive gagging and choking that concludes with the puking-up of his whiskers, which are now broken into half- and quarter-inch pieces. Poor puss!—runs home meek and plaintive and her adoring mistress picks her up, cuddles, scolds, Sheba where have you *been*! And Sheba's supper comes early that evening.

11.

Madly in love, Mr. X is the most devoted of suitors. And then the most besotted of bridegrooms. Covering Babygirl's pink-flushed face with kisses, hugging her so tight she cries *Oh!* and all of the wedding company, her own daddy in particular, laugh in delight. Mr. X is a dignified handsome older gentleman. He's the salt of the earth. He leads Babygirl out onto the polished dance floor as the band plays "I Love You Truly" and how elegantly he dances, how masterfully he leads his bride, blood-red carnation in his lapel, chips of dry ice in his eyes, wide fixed grinning-white dentures, how graceful the couple's dips and bends, Babygirl in a breathtakingly beautiful antique wedding gown worn by her mother, her grandmother, and her great-grandmother in their times, an heirloom wedding ring as well, lilies of the valley braided in the bride's cinnamon curls, Babygirl laughs showing the cherry-pink interior of her mouth, she squeals *Oh!* as her new husband draws her to his bosom, kisses her full on the lips. His big strong fingers stroke her shoulders, breasts, rump. There are champagne toasts, there are gay drunken speeches lasting well into the evening. The Archbishop himself intones a blessing. Babygirl on Mr. X's knee being fed strawberries and wedding cake by her bridegroom, and feeding her bridegroom strawberries and wedding cake in turn, each sucking the other's fingers, amid kisses and laughter. Chewing her wedding cake Babygirl is disconcerted to discover something tough, sinewy, bristly in it, like gristle, or fragments of bone, or tiny bits of wire, but she is too well-bred and embarrassed to spit the foreign substance, if it is a foreign substance, out: discreetly pushes it with her tongue to the side of her mouth, behind her molars, for safe-keeping. For his part, Mr. X, a gentleman, washes his mouthfuls of wedding cake down with champagne, swallows everything without blinking an eye, This is the happiest day of my life he whispers into Babygirl's pink-whorled ear.

12.

It was an experiment in behavioral psychology, in the phenomenon of conditioning, to be published in *Scientific American*, and there to cause quite a stir, but naturally *he* wasn't informed, poor miserable bugger, nor did he give consent. Semi-starved in his wire mesh cage, compulsively gnawing on his own hind legs, he quickly learned to *react* to the slightest gesture on the part of his torturers, his monitored heartbeat raced in panic, his jaundiced eyeballs careened in their sockets, a metaphysical malaise permeated his soul like sulphur dioxide, after only a few hours. Yet his torturers persisted for there were dozens of graphs and charts to be filled out; dozens of young assistants involved in the experiment. In the gauging of "terror" in dumb beasts of his species they shocked him with increasing severity until virtual puffs of smoke issued from the top of his head, they singed his fur with burning needles, poked burning needles into his tender anus, lowered his cage over a Bunsen burner, wiped their eyes laughing at his antics, shaking and rattling his cage, spinning his cage at a velocity of ninety miles an hour, they marveled at how he was conditioned to respond not just to their gestures but to their words as if he could understand them and then, most amazing of all—this would be the crux of the controversial article in *Scientific American*—after forty-eight hours he began to react unerringly to the mere *thought* that the torture would be resumed. (Provided the experimenters consciously "thought" their thoughts inside the laboratory, not outside.) A remarkable scientific discovery!—unfortunately, after his death, never once to be duplicated. Thus utterly worthless as science and a bit of a joke in experimental psychology circles.

13.

How Mr. X adored his Babygirl!—lovingly bathing her in her fragrant bubble bath, brushing and combing her long wavy-curly cinnamon hair that fell to her hips, cooing to her, poking his tongue in her, bringing her breakfast in bed after a fevered night of marital love, insisting upon shaving, with his own straight razor, the peachy-fuzzy down that covered her lovely body, and the stiff "unsightly" hairs of underarms, legs, and crotch. Weeks, months. Until one night his penis failed him and he realized he was frankly bored with Babygirl's dimpled buttocks and navel, her wide-open periwinkle-blue eyes, the flattering *Oh!* of her pursed rosebud lips. He realized that her flat nasal voice grated against his sensitive nerves, her habits disgusted him, several times he caught her scratching her fat behind when she believed herself unobserved, she was not so fastidious as to refrain from picking her nose, frequently the bathroom stank of flatulence and excrement after she emerged from it, her menstrual blood stained the white linen heirloom sheets, her kinky hairs collected in drains, her early-morning breath was rancid as the inside of his own oldest shoes, she gazed at him with big mournful questioning cow-eyes, Oh what is wrong dearest, oh! don't you love me any longer? What did I *do*! lowering her bulk onto his knees, sliding her pudgy arms around his neck, exhaling her meaty breath in his face, so, cruelly, he parted his knees and Babygirl fell with a graceless thud to the floor. As she stared at him speechless in astonishment and hurt he struck her with the backside of his hand, bloodying her nose, Oh you will, bitch, will you! he grunted, will you! Eh!

14.

Mating, and mating. Mating. A frenzy of mating. In the prime of his maleness he fathered dozens, hundreds, thousands of off-spring, now they're scurrying and squeaking everywhere, little buggers everywhere underfoot, nudging him aside as he feeds, ganging up on him, yes a veritable gang of them, how quickly babies grow up, it's amazing how quickly babies grow up, one day an inch long, the next day two inches long, the next day four inches long, those tiny perfect toes, claws, ears, whiskers, graceful curved tails, incisors, ravenous appetite *And the horror of it washed over me suddenly: I cannot die, I am multiplied to infinity.* It was not his fault! His enemies are even now setting out dollops of powdery-pasty poison, to rid the neighborhood of him and his offspring, but it was not his fault! A fever overtook him, him and certain of his sisters, almost daily it seemed, yes daily, maybe hourly, no time to rest, no time for contemplation, a two-inch thing, a sort of a knob of flesh, a rod, hot and stiff with blood, piston-quick, tireless, unfurling itself out of the soft sac between his hind legs, yes and he was powerless to resist, it was more urgent even than gnawing, more excruciatingly pleasurable, *he* was but an appendage! thus innocent! But his enemies, plotting against him, don't give a damn, they're cruel and cold-blooded setting out dollops of this most delicious poison, sugary, pasty, bread-moldy, delicious beyond reckoning, he should know better (shouldn't he?) but he's unable to resist, pushing his way into the sea of squeaking quivering young ones, seething sea, dark waves, wave upon wave eating in a delirium of appetite, a single feeding organism you might think, it's a diabolical poison however that doesn't kill these poor buggers on the premises but induces violent thirst in them thus shortly after feeding he and his thousands of sons and daughters are rushing out of the building, in a panic to find water, to drink water, to alleviate this terrible thirst, they're drawn to the dockside, to the river, there are screams as people see them emerge, the dark wave of them, glittering eyes, whiskers, pink near-hairless tails, they take no notice of anyone or anything in their need to get to water, there in the river a number of them drown, others drink and drink and drink until, as planned, their poor bodies bloat, and swell, and *burst*. And city sanitation workers wearing gas masks complain bitterly as they shovel the corpses, small mountains of corpses, into a procession of Dumpster trucks, then they hose down the sidewalks, streets, docks. At a fertilizer plant he and his progeny will be mashed down, ground to gritty powder and sold for commercial/residential use. No mention of the poison of course.

15.

Grown increasingly and mysteriously insensitive to his wife's feelings, Mr. X, within their first year of marriage, began to bring home "business associates" (as he called them) to ogle Babygirl, to peek at her in her bath, to whisper licentious remarks in her ears, to touch, fondle, *molest*—as Mr. X, often smoking a cigar, calmly watched! At first Babygirl was too astonished to comprehend, then she burst into tears of indignation and hurt, then she pleaded with the brute to be spared, then she flew into a tantrum tossing silky garments and such into a suitcase, then she was lying in a puddle on the bathroom floor, nights and days passed in a delirium, her keeper fed her grudgingly and at irregular intervals, there were promises of sunshine, greenery, Christmas gifts, promises made and withheld, then one day a masked figure appeared in the doorway, in leather military regalia, gloved hands on his hips, brass-studded belt, holster and pistol riding his hip, gleaming black leather boots the toes of which Babygirl eagerly kissed, groveling before him, twining her long curly-cinnamon hair around his ankles. Begging, Have mercy! don't hurt me! I am yours! in sickness and in health as I gave my vow to God! And assuming the masked man was in fact Mr. X (for wasn't this a reasonable assumption, in these circum-stances?) Babygirl willingly accompanied him to the master bedroom, to the antique brass four-postered bed, and did not resist his wheezing, straining, protracted and painful lovemaking, if such an act can be called lovemaking, the insult of it! the pain of it! and not till the end, when the masked figure triumphantly removed his mask, did Babygirl discover that he was a stranger—and that Mr. X himself was standing at the foot of the bed, smoking a cigar, calmly observing. In the confusion of all that followed, weeks, months, there came a succession of "business associates," never the same man twice, as Mr. X grew systematically crueler, hardly a gentleman any longer, forcing upon his wife as she lay trussed and helpless in their marriage bed a man with fingernails filed razor-sharp who lacerated her tender flesh, a man with a glittering scaly skin, a man with a turkey's wattles, a man with an ear partly missing, a man with a stark-bald head and cadaverous smile, a man with infected draining sores like exotic tattoos stippling his body, and poor Babygirl was whipped for disobedience, Babygirl was burnt with cigars, Babygirl was slapped, kicked, pummeled, near-suffocated and near-strangled and near-drowned, she screamed into her saliva-soaked gag, she thrashed, convulsed, bled in sticky skeins most distasteful to Mr. X who then punished her additionally, as a husband will do, by withholding his affection.

16.

So light-headed with hunger was he, hiding in terror from his enemies beneath a pile of bricks, he began to gnaw at his own tail —timidly at first, then more avidly, with appetite, unable to stop, his poor skinny tail, his twenty pink toes and pads, his hind legs, choice loins and chops and giblets and breast and pancreas and brains and all, at last his bones are picked clean, the startling symmetry and beauty of the skeleton revealed, now he's sleepy, contented and sleepy, washes himself with fastidious little scrubbing motions of his paws then curls up in the warm September sun to nap. A sigh ripples through him: exquisite peace.

17.

Except: two gangling neighborhood boys creep up on him dozing atop his favorite brick, capture him in a net and toss him squeaking in terror into a cardboard box, slam down the lid that's pocked
with air holes, he's delivered by bicycle to a gentleman with neatly
combed white hair and a cultivated voice who pays the boys five
dollars each for him, observes him crouched in a corner of the box,
rubbing his hands delightedly together chuckling softly, Well!
you're a rough-looking fella aren't you! To his considerable surprise,
the white-haired gentleman feeds him; holds him up, though not
unkindly, by the scruff of his neck, to examine him, the sleek perfectly formed parts of him, the rakish incisors most particularly.
Breathing audibly, murmuring, with excited satisfaction, Yes. I believe you will do, old boy.

18.

No longer allowed out of the house, often confined to the bedroom suite on the second floor, poor Babygirl nonetheless managed
to adjust to the altered circumstances of her life with commendable
fortitude and good humor. Spending most of her days lying lan-
guorously in bed, doing her nails, devouring gourmet chocolates
brought her by one or another of Mr. X's business associates, sometimes, in a romantic mood, by the unpredictable Mr. X himself, she
watched television (the evangelical preachers were her favorites),
complained to herself in the way of housewives in America, tended
to her wounds, clipped recipes from magazines, gossiped over the
telephone with her female friends, shopped by catalogue, read her
Bible, grew heavier, sullen, apprehensive of the future, plucked her
eyebrows, rubbed fragrant creams into her skin, kept an optimistic
attitude, made an effort. Of the disturbing direction in which her
marriage was moving she tried not to think for Babygirl was not
the kind of wife to whine, whimper, nag, not Babygirl so imagine
her surprise and horror when, one night, Mr. X arrived home and

ran upstairs to the bedroom in which, that day, she'd been confined, tied to the four brass posts of the marital bed by white silken cords, and in triumph threw open his camel's hair coat, See what I've brought for you, my dear! unzipping his trousers with trembling fingers and as Babygirl stared incredulous out *he* leapt—squeaking, red-eyed, teeth bared and glistening with froth, stiff curved tail erect. Babygirl's screams were heartrending.

19.

Mr. X and his (male) companions observed with scientific detachment the relationship between Babygirl and He (as, in codified shorthand, they referred to him): how, initially, the pair resisted each other most strenuously, even hysterically, Babygirl shrieking even through the gag stuffed in her mouth as He was netted in the bed with her, such a struggle, such acrobatics, He squeaking in animal panic edged with indignant rage, biting, clawing, fighting as if for His very life, and Babygirl, despite her flaccid muscles and her seemingly indolent ways, putting up a fight as if for *her* very life! And this went on for hours, for an entire night, and the night following, and the night following that. And there was never anything so remarkable on Burlingame Way, the attractive residential street where Mr. X made his home.

20.

He did not want this, no certainly he did not want this, resisting with all the strength of his furry little being, as, with gloved hands, Mr. X forced him *there*—poor Babygirl spread-eagled and helpless bleeding from a thousand welts and lacerations made by his claws and teeth and why was he being forced snout-first, and then head-first, then his shoulders, his sleek muscular length, why *there*—in *there*—so he choked, near-suffocated, used his teeth to tear a way free for himself yet even as he did so Mr. X with hands trembling in excitement, as his companions, gathered round the bed, watched in awe pushed him in farther, and then *farther*—into the blood-hot pulsing toughly elastic tunnel between poor Babygirl's fatty thighs —and still *farther* until only the sleek-furry end of his rump and his trailing hind legs and, of course, the eight-inch pink tail were visible. His panicked gnawing of the fleshy walls that so tightly confined him released small geysers of blood that nearly drowned him, and the involuntary spasms of clenching of poor Babygirl's pelvic muscles nearly crushed him, thus how the struggle would have ended, if both he and Babygirl had not lost consciousness at the same instant, is problematic. Even Mr. X and his companions, virtually beside themselves in unholy arousal, were relieved that, for that night, the *agon* had ceased.

21.

As, at her martyrdom, at the stake in Rouen, as the flames licked mindlessly ever higher and higher to consume her, to turn her to ashes, Jeanne d'Arc is reported to have cried out "Jesu! Jesu! Jesu!" in a voice of rapture.

22.

And who would clean up the mess. And who, with a migraine, sanitary pad soaked between her chafed thighs, she's fearful of seeing her swollen jaw, blackened eye in any mirrored surface weeping quietly to herself, padding gingerly about in her bedroom slippers, mock-Japanese quilted housecoat. The only consolation is at least there's a TV in most of the rooms so, even when the vacuum is roaring, she isn't alone: there's Reverend Tim, there's Brother Jessie, there's Sweet Alabam' MacGowan. A consolation at least. For, not only did Babygirl suffer such insult and ignominy at the hands of the very man who, of all the world, was most responsible for her emotional well-being, not only was she groggy in the aftermath of only dimly remembered physical trauma, running the risk, as she sensed, of infection, sterility, and a recrudescence of her old female maladies—not only this but she was obliged to clean up the mess next morning, who else. Laundering the sheets, blood-stained sheets are no joke. On her hands and knees trying (with minimal success) to remove the stains from the carpet. Vacuum the carpet. And the dirt bag is full and there's a problem putting in a new dirt bag, there always is. Faint-headed, wracked several times with white-hot bolts of pain so she had to sit, catch her breath. And the pad between her legs soaked hard in blackish blood like blood-sausage. And the steel wool disintegrating in her fingers as gamely she tries to scour the casserole dish clean, dissolves in tears, Oh! where has love gone! so one evening he surprises her, in that melancholy repose, the children are in on it too, what's today but Babygirl's birthday and she'd tormented herself thinking no one would remember but as they sweep into the restaurant, the Gondola that's one of the few good Italian restaurants in the city where you can order pizza too, the staff is waiting, Happy Birthday! balloons, half-chiding there's a chorus, Did you think we'd forgotten? and Babygirl orders a sloe gin fizz which goes straight to her head and she giggles and suppresses a tiny belch patting her fingers to her mouth, later her husband is scolding one of the boys but *she's* going to steer clear of the conflict, goes to the powder room, checks her makeup in the rose-lit flattering mirrors seeing yes, thank God the bruise under her left eye is fading, then she takes care to affix squares of toilet paper to the toilet seat to prevent picking up an infectious disease, since AIDS Babygirl is even more methodical, then she's sitting on the toilet her mind for a moment blissful and empty until, turning her head, just happening to turn her head, though probably she sensed its presence, she sees, not six inches away, on the slightly grimy sill of a frosted-glass window, the red-blinking eyes of a large rodent, oh dear God is it a rat, these eyes fixed upon *hers*, her heart gives a violent kick and nearly *stops*. Poor Babygirl's screams penetrate every wall of the building.

Afterword:
Reflections on
the Grotesque

What is the "grotesque"—and what is "horror"—in art? And why do these seemingly repellent states of mind possess, for some, an abiding attraction?

I take as the most profound mystery of our human experience the fact that, though we each exist subjectively, and know the world only through the prism of self, this "subjectivity" is inaccessible, thus unreal, and mysterious, to others. And the obverse—all *others* are, in the deepest sense, *strangers*.

The arts of the grotesque are so various as to resist definition. Here we have the plenitude of the imagination itself. From the Anglo-Saxon saga of Grendel's monster-mother, in *Beowulf*, to impish-ugly gargoyles carved on cathedral walls; from terrifyingly matter-of-fact scenes of carnage in the *Iliad*, to the hallucinatory vividness of the "remarkable piece of apparatus" of Franz Kafka's "In the Penal Colony"; from the comic-nightmare images of Hieronymus Bosch to the strategic artfulness of twentieth-century film—Werner Herzog's 1979 remake of the 1922 classic of the German silent screen, F. W. Murnau's *Nosferatu the Vampyr*, to give but one example. The "grotesque" is a sensibility that accommodates the genius of Goya and the kitsch-Surrealism of Dali; the crude visceral power of H. P. Lovecraft and the baroque elegance of Isak

Dinesen; the fatalistic simplicity of Grimm's fairy tales and the complexity of vision of which, for instance, William Faulkner's "A Rose for Emily" is a supreme example—the grotesque image as historical commentary.

The protracted onstage torture of Shakespeare's Gloucester in *King Lear* is the very height of the theatrical grotesque, but so is, in less graphic terms, the fate of Samuel Beckett's hapless heroes and heroines—the female mouth of *Mouth*, for instance. From Nikolay Gogol's "The Nose" to Paul Bowles's "A Distant Episode," from images of demonic flesh of Max Klinger, Edvard Munch, Gustav Klimt and Egon Schiele to Francis Bacon, Eric Fischl, Robert Gober; from Jeremias Gotthelf ("The Black Spider," 1842) to postmodern fantasists Angela Carter, Thomas Ligotti, Clive Barker, Lisa Tuttle and mainstream best-sellers Stephen King, Peter Straub, Anne Rice—we recognize the bold strokes of the grotesque, however widely styles vary. (Is a ghost story inevitably of the genre of the grotesque?—no. Victorian ghost stories, on the whole, are too "nice"—too ladylike, whatever the sex of the writer. Much of Henry James's ghostly fiction, like that of his contemporaries Edith Wharton and Gertrude Atherton, though elegantly written, is too genteel to qualify.) The grotesque is the hideous animal-men of H.G. Wells's *The Island of Dr. Moreau*, or the taboo-images of the most inspired filmmaker of the grotesque of our time, David Cronenberg (*The Fly, The Brood, Dead Ringers, Naked Lunch*)—that is, the grotesque always possesses a blunt *physicality* that no amount of epistemological exegesis can exorcise. One might define it, in fact, as the very antithesis of "nice."

It was in 1840 that Edgar Allan Poe, our greatest, and most beleaguered, artist of the grotesque published *Tales of the Grotesque and Arabesque*, containing works that would become classics—"The Fall of the House of Usher," "The Tell-Tale Heart," "The Pit and the Pendulum," "The Mask of the Red Death," "The Cask of Amontillado." At this time there existed a rich, diverse literature to which the architectural term "Gothic" had been applied. Poe was well aware of this literature: Horace Walpole's *The Castle of Otranto: A Gothic Tale* (1764), Richard Cumberland's *The Poisoner of Montremos*

(1791), Ann Radcliffe's masterpiece *Mysteries of Udolpho* (1794) and *The Italian* (1797), M. G. Lewis's *The Monk* (1796), Mary Shelley's *Frankenstein* (1818), C. R. Maturin's *Melmoth the Wanderer* (1820); the uncanny fables of E.T.A. Hoffmann, of which "The Sand-Man" (1817) is most Poe-like; and the tales of Poe's fellow Americans Washington Irving (whose affable prose style masks the grotesqueries of "Rip Van Winkle," "The Legend of Sleepy Hollow") and Nathaniel Hawthorne. And there was Charles Brockden Brown's *Wieland* (1798), our premier American-Gothic novel. In turn, Poe's influence upon the literature of the grotesque—and the mystery-detective genre—has been so universal as to be incalculable. Who has *not* been influenced by Poe?—however obliquely, indirectly; however the influence, absorbed in adolescence or even in childhood, would seem to be far behind us.

This predilection for art that promises we will be frightened by it, shaken by it, at times repulsed by it seems to be as deeply imprinted in the human psyche as the counter-impulse toward daylight, rationality, scientific skepticism, truth and the "real." (Leaving aside for the moment whether rationality is in fact in contact with the "real.") Are Aubrey Beardsley's sly-sinister hermaphrodite figures less "real" than the commissioned portraits of James McNeill Whistler? A sensibility that would find intolerable the lurid excesses of Sheridan Le Fanu's *Carmilla* (1871) or Bram Stoker's *Dracula* (1897) might respond with much feeling to vampire tales cast in a more "literary" mode, like Henry James's *The Turn of the Screw*, and such Symbolist-"realist" works by Thomas Mann as *Death in Venice*, "Mario the Magician," "Tristan" (". . . while the child, Anton Kloterjahn, a magnificent specimen of a baby, seized on his place in life with prodigious energy and ruthlessness, a low, unobservable fever seemed to waste the young mother daily."). Of all monstrous creatures it has been the vampire that by tradition both attracts and repels, for vampires have nearly always been portrayed as aesthetically (that is, erotically) appealing. (Peter Quint is the hinge, red-haired, wearing no hat, "very erect," upon which James's *The Turn of the Screw* turns—unless he is the screw itself.) And this is the forbidden truth, the unspeakable taboo—that evil is not always repellent but frequently attractive; that it has the power to make of us not simply victims, as nature and accident do, but active accomplices.

Children are particularly susceptible to images of the grotesque, for children are learning to monitor what is "real" and what is "not real"; what is benign, and what not. The mental experiences of very young children, afterward layered over by time and forgotten, must be a kaleidoscope of sensations, impressions, events, "images" linked with "meanings"—how to make sense of this blooming, buzzing universe? The earliest and most horrific image of my childhood, as deeply embedded in my consciousness as any "real" event (and I lived on a small farm, where the slaughtering of chickens must have been frequent) sprang at me out of a seemingly benign children's book, Lewis Carroll's *Alice's Adventures Through the Looking-Glass*. In the concluding chapter of this generally disturbing book Alice is being crowned Queen at a banquet that begins with promise then rapidly degenerates into anarchy:

> "Take care of yourself!" screamed the White Queen, seizing Alice's hair with both hands. "Something's going to happen!"
>
> And then . . . all sorts of things happened in a moment. The candles all grew up to the ceiling . . . As to the bottles, they each took a pair of plates, which they hastily fitted as wings, and so, with forks for legs, went fluttering about in all directions . . .
>
> At this moment Alice heard a hoarse laugh at her side, and turned to see what was the matter with the White Queen, but, instead of the Queen, there was the leg of mutton sitting in a chair. "Here I am!" cried a voice from the soup tureen, and Alice turned again, just in time to see the Queen's broad, good-natured face grinning at her for a moment over the edge of the tureen, before she disappeared into the soup.
>
> There was not a moment to be lost. Already several of the guests were lying down in the dishes, and the soup ladle was walking up toward Alice's chair . . .

Alice escapes the nightmare prospect of being eaten by waking from her dream as, in her *Wonderland* adventure, she woke from that dream. But what solace, if the memory retains the unspeakable, and the unspeakable can't be reduced to a dream?

Mankind's place in the food chain—is *this* the unspeakable knowledge, the ultimate taboo, that generates the art of the grotesque?—or all art, culture, civilization?

In a more technical sense, art that presents "horror" in aesthetic terms is related to Expressionism and Surrealism in its elevation of interior (and perhaps repressed) states of the soul to exterior status. Even if we were not now, in this Age of Deconstruction, psychologically and anthropologically capable of deciphering seemingly opaque documents, whether fairy tales, legends, works of art or putatively objective histories and scientific reports, we should sense immediately, in the presence of the grotesque, that it is both "real" and "unreal" simultaneously, as states of mind are real enough—emotions, moods, shifting obsessions, beliefs—though immeasurable. The subjectivity that is the essence of the human is also the mystery that divides us irrevocably from one another.

One criterion for horror fiction is that we are compelled to read it swiftly, with a rising sense of dread, and so total a suspension of ordinary skepticism, we inhabit the material without question and virtually as its protagonist; we can see no way out except to go forward. Like fairy tales, the art of the grotesque and horror renders us children again, evoking something primal in the soul. The outward aspects of horror are variable, multiple, infinite—the inner, inaccessible. What the vision is we might guess, but, inhabiting a brightly populated, sociable, intensely engaging outer world, in which we are defined to one another as social beings with names, professions, roles, public identities, and in which, most of the time, we believe ourselves *at home*—isn't it wisest not to?

Joyce Carol Oates
April 1993

ACKNOWLEDGMENTS

"Haunted" first published in *The Architecture of Fear* (Arbor House, 1987) and reprinted in *The Year's Best Fantasy* (St. Martin's Press, 1988).

"The Doll" first published in *Epoch* and reprinted in *The Arbor House Treasury of Horror and the Supernatural* (1981).

"The Bingo Master" first published in *Dark Forces* (Viking, 1980).

"The White Cat" first published in *A Matter of Crime* (Harcourt Brace, 1987).

"The Model" first published in *Ellery Queen's Mystery Magazine*, October 1992, and reprinted in *The Best Mystery and Suspense Stories 1993*.

"Extenuating Circumstances" first published in *Sisters in Crime 5* (Berkley Books, 1992).

"Don't You Trust Me?" first published in *Glamour*, August 1992.

"The Guilty Party" first published in *Glamour*, July 1991.

"The Premonition" first published in *Playboy*, December 1992.

"Phase Change" first published in *Visions*, 1993.

"Poor Bibi" (under the title "Poor Thing") first published in *Tikkun*, May/June 1992.

"Thanksgiving" first published in *Omni*, December 1993.

"The Radio Astronomer" first published in *Antaeus*, Spring 1993.

"Accursed Inhabitants of the House of Bly" first published in *Antioch Review*, Winter 1992.

"Martyrdom" first published in *Metahorror* (Dell, 1992) and reprinted in *The Year's Best Fantasy and Horror 1993*.

To all these editors, acknowledgments and thanks are due.